BRASADA

Brasada ground-reined the dun within the shadows of a *bosquecillo* of white oaks and silver-leaved oaks. A flickering flame rose beside a bed of ashes and in the uncertain light Brasada saw the headless body of a man.

The moon rose higher. It revealed a severed head resting on a rock with the gray beard touching the ground. The moonlight reflected from the glazed eyes that stared intently at the Mountain.

"Jubal Conn," murmured Brasada. "It seems that I'm a little late for our meeting."

BLOOD JUSTICE

Jim Murdock stared at the rifleman. "Barney Kessler."

Barney let down the rifle hammer to half cock. "Jim Murdock!"

Jim smiled thinly. "Now take that gun outa my gut."

"Come on, Barney!" yelled a man from across the street. "Bring the hombre with you!"

"You got to come along, Jim," said Barney.

"What for?" Jim knew well enough why they were going to the hill.

"You seen us take them men from the calabozo. We don't want no witnesses...."

GORDON D. SHIRREFFS

BRASADA/ BLOOD JUSTICE

LEISURE BOOKS   **NEW YORK CITY**

A LEISURE BOOK®

March 1993

Published by

Dorchester Publishing Co., Inc.
276 Fifth Avenue
New York, NY 10001

GORDON D. SHIRREFFS

BRASADA

CHAPTER ONE

BRASADA RODE northward toward the Arizona border. On either hand were desolate mountains half buried in the parched earth and heat shimmering in the burning sunlight. He seemed alone for he had seen no other living creatures for many miles. An Apache is not seen unless he wants to be seen. It was Apache country, sun-cursed and as waterless as the moon.

The mountains on either side of Brasada lay half in Sonora and half in Arizona Territory with the higher elevations north of the border. In that empty country the border was not clearly defined except where the Mountain towered eight thousand feet above steeply inclined slopes and a labyrinth of desolate canyons that lay across the unmarked border line like a carelessly flung net of stone left there by a colossus. Once a man was within that network of canyons and with no way to orient himself he could unknowingly pass back and forth across the border until at last he might stumble out of the tangle half dead from heat and thirst—*if* he stumbled out at all—and not know whether he was in Arizona or Sonora. The whole land was an area of deception and sudden death.

Brasada knew the way north, guided by the great monolith of the Mountain that rose towering from the sun-baked talus slopes and seemed to sway gently back and forth in the heat-shimmering atmosphere like the warning finger of a wilderness prophet of biblical times. There was an eerie and even threatening quality about the Mountain that repelled a man and yet at the same time seemed to draw him toward it against his will.

In the late afternoon something hazy, almost on the verge of invisibility writhed slowly and sinuously upward from the canyon at the southern base of the Mountain. There wâs nothing friendly about that smoke. No one lived there. No Chiricahua would advertise his presence with a careless campfire.

A lone *zopilote,* the great land buzzard of Sonora, seemed to materialize out of the thin air to drift high over the smoke, resting his black, white-tipped wings on the wind. The only movements in that landscape of hell were the slow upward writhing of the lazy smoke and the dark silhouette of the *zopilote* rising and falling high above the source of the smoke like a scrap of charred paper.

The pre-moon darkness came when Brasada had reached the mouth of the canyon. He dismounted and laced rawhide boots on the dun and then led him on to the north. The only sounds in the darkness were the soft husking of the dun's rawhide boots on the graveled ground and the slapping of thorned branches against the leather-clad legs of Brasada.

Brasada looked up at the Mountain towering high above the canyon. In the deceptive darkness of the lower levels and the dim half-light of the upper reaches the Mountain almost seemed to lean threateningly toward him, an optical illusion, but realistic appearing at the time. "Get back, *bastardo,*" murmured Brasada. The Mountain did not get back.

The first traces of pale light from the rising gibbous moon tinted the eastern sky. It seemed to bring with it the mingled aura of resinous woodsmoke and burnt flesh.

Brasada ground-reined the dun within the shadows of a *bosquecillo* of white oaks and silver-leaved oaks. He overlooked a *tinaja* on the lower ground—a natural rock tank encircled by tip-tilted boulders that usually, but not always, held a shallow pool of gamey-tasting rainwater throughout the summer months.

The wind fanned across a bed of ashes to reveal here and there a malevolent ember eye that winked open and then as quickly closed itself. A flickering flame rose beside the bed of ashes and in the uncertain light Brasada saw the headless body of a man. The light came from his burning left sleeve.

The moon rose higher. It revealed a severed head resting on a rock with the gray beard touching the ground. The moonlight reflected from the glazed eyes that stared intently at the Mountain.

"Jubal Conn," murmured Brasada. "It seems I'm a little late for our meeting."

The wind ruffled the beard of the old man.

CHAPTER TWO

BRASADA CATFOOTED through the shadows until he could drag the headless body into the boulder-shielded area next to the *tinaja*. He went back for the head. "Hello, Jubal," he murmured. "Please don't get up for me." He picked up the head by its thick tangled mat of dirty gray hair and carried it to the body.

Brasada squatted and thumb-snapped a lucifer into flame. He whistled softly as he examined the head. A half-inch black-rimmed hole showed above the right ear where the bullet had entered the skull. When the slug had exited it had taken the left ear and a large piece of skull with it.

Brasada walked to the dying fire. He picked up a mutilated bullet. The head of it was splayed raggedly outward but the bottom of it was concave and ring-shaped where it had once fitted tightly into a fifty-caliber cartridge case.

Brasada thoroughly searched the body. He pried off the run-down heels of the boots and slit open the thin soles. He searched the shirt, trousers, and the long-john drawers and found nothing. He looked out toward the dying fire. Whoever had killed the old man had probably taken anything of value—and one thing in particular.

A rock detached itself high on the moonlit slope and came bounding and clattering down toward the *tinaja*. It struck not far from the fire. The hissing, rattling sound of displaced rock fragments and dry soil died away.

Brasada stepped out into the moonlight and looked up at the *bosquecillo*. The wind murmured the leaves. "You can come out now!" Brasada called. The canyon echoed his call.

Nothing moved. The wind died out.

Brasada grinned, white-toothed like a hunting wolf in the moonlight. He walked toward his Winchester.

"That's far enough!" a harsh voice called from the *bosquecillo*. "Raise your hands! Don't make a move!"

Brasada turned and slowly raised his hands. The wide brim of his sombrero shadowed his nose and eyes.

A spur jingled softly. A tall lean man came down the slope from the *bosquecillo*. The moonlight shone dully on the metal of his repeating rifle. There was a grayness about the man; the hair at the sides of his narrow skull below the rim of his hat was gray; his eyes were gray and so was his moustache. Most of all, thought Brasada, a winter-gray coldness seemed to emanate from the man. The moonlight shone on the deputy sheriff's badge pinned to his vest.

The deputy walked to Brasada's Winchester. He sniffed at the muzzle and the breech. He walked behind Brasada and plucked his Colt from the holster. The cylinder whirred stridently as it was spun to check the loads. The butt of the rifle tapped Brasada hard above the kidneys. "Who killed the old man?" asked the deputy.

"He was dead when I got here. You knew that," replied Brasada.

"Who are you?"

"I am called Brasada."

"I want your full name."

Brasada shrugged. "That's it—Brasada."

The deputy walked around in front of Brasada. "You speak English well," he said. "What are you? A breed of some sort?"

"American-born," replied Brasada, "but I am also a citizen of Mexico—an *emigrado,* if you prefer."

"You're all spics to me."

A rock broke loose on the heights and plummeted down to the talus slope where it rebounded, shattering into fragments that struck further down like canister shot.

"The Mountain is noisy tonight," commented Brasada.

"Monte Ruidoso—Noisy Mountain," translated the deputy. "The spics have a knack for such names."

"I have another name for it," said Brasada.

"Such as?"

"It looks like a giant turd set up on end."

The deputy suddenly flipped back the brim of Brasada's sombrero. The immediate effect was startling, almost uncanny, as though one had opened the lens of a magic lantern focused on the lean, saturnine face of the man named Brasada. A pair of eyes as gray and as cold-looking as icy winter rain looked unblinkingly into the eyes of the deputy.

Somewhere high on the mountain slope a coyote howled.

"Why did you take the body and the head of the old man out of sight?" demanded the deputy.

Brasada shrugged. "I wasn't sure that whoever had killed the old man might not still be up there watching me."

"And you knew all the time *I* was watching you, eh?"

Brasada nodded.

"What were you looking for on the body?"

Brasada shrugged. "Anything of value."

The deputy laughed. "On Jubal Conn? You knew the old man?"

"Years back."

"Why did you come here? To meet him?"

Brasada shook his head. "That was coincidence. I came for water."

The deputy studied Brasada with cold eyes. "Maybe you don't know the killing history around that mountain. Twelve men have been killed like Jubal was, in the past three years. He makes it a baker's dozen."

"So, the Mountain is still at it," commented Brasada.

"That's spic superstition," said the deputy. He tilted his head to one side. "Maybe you ain't a spic but you act, dress, and think like one."

"I find no dishonor in that," quietly said Brasada.

"Maybe it was Apache work?" suggested the deputy.

"Hardly. No Apache can shoot like that, and few white men can either."

"You know a helluva lot without evidence to back it up," said the deputy. "Show me, mister."

Brasada led the way up the slope beyond the waterhole. He pointed out a shallow brush-sheltered hole where three pairs of depressions showed in the soft drift soil. "Elbows, knees, and toes," explained Brasada. He looked about. "No empty brass. Probably picked up for reloading." He walked down the slope a little way and picked up a scrap of whitish banknote paper stained with grease. "Paper-patched bullet," he added. He looked down the long slope toward the *tinaja* and the dying fire. "A seven hundred-yard downhill shot with the afternoon sun in his eyes and he made a dead center head on the old man's *cabeza*." He held out the mutilated bullet. "Fifty-caliber slug. Explosive Express bullet. Goes in fifty caliber and comes out about four times as big as it went in. Murderous stuff."

The deputy nodded. "Very good. But why?"

Brasada looked up the slope at him. "The Soledad Silver," he calmly replied. "Legend has it that thirty tons of native silver was mined from that damned haunted mass of rock up there over one hundred and twenty-five years ago, molded into ingots, stamped with the mark of Charles III, King of Spain, and the cross of the padres, and hidden somewhere around there—God only knows where."

The deputy nodded. "Go on," he suggested.

"The padres knew they were going to be expelled from the New World, by edict of Charles, on twenty-four hours' notice, and they knew beforehand they would not be allowed to take anything with them other than the clothing on their backs, a Bible, a breviary, and a missal."

"And they supposedly placed a lasting curse on the treasure so that no man might find it and live to tell about it," added the deputy. "Which brings us up to date. Someone, perhaps *more* than one person, has taken it on himself to murder by long-range rifle fire anyone, at least in the past three years, who learns something of the possible location of the silver, or gets near the cache, whether he knows it or not, then severs the head, in a number of cases, to place it on a rock where it can stare at the Mountain until the coyotes dine on it."

"Macabre," murmured Brasada. "A man obsessed."

The deputy nodded. He looked up at the dreamlike Mountain. "Strange," he said quietly. "Old Jubal Conn had prospected around that Mountain for over twenty years. Even the Apaches let him alone."

"They thought he was Mind-Gone-Far, and so protected by the Gods."

The deputy looked down toward the *tinaja*. "Which means he knew something; something, perhaps he

had not known until recently. In short—whoever
killed him, must have known Old Jubal had learned
that certain something."

"Fine deduction," agreed Brasada.

"Which brings us right back to you."

Brasada felt for the makings.

The deputy full-cocked his rifle. "Why did you
really come here tonight?"

Brasada shaped a cigarette. "Put up the Winchester," he suggested.

The deputy studied him. "You're a cool one, or a
fool," he said.

Brasada placed the cigarette between his lips.
"We're being watched right now by someone up that
slope of the Mountain."

The deputy looked up the seemingly deserted
slope. "Bullshit," he said.

Brasada bent his head and lighted the cigarette.
"Now you're playing the fool. Let us walk quietly
together, like old *compañeros,* down to the *tinaja,*
and for God's sake—act unconcerned!" He started
walking down the slope toward the *tinaja.*

"I'm not through with you yet!" called out the
deputy.

A coyote howled far up the slope. His cry was
echoed by another, much closer to the *tinaja.* Then it
was eerily quiet again.

Brasada grinned as he heard the deputy scuffling
down the slope. Brasada placed the thumb and first
finger of his right hand between his teeth and whistled sharply. A moment later the dun appeared from
beyond the *bosquecillo* and trotted down toward
Brasada. Brasada led him to the water.

"Wait," ordered the deputy. He searched through
the saddlebags. Bottles clinked together.

"Have a drink," invited Brasada. The deputy lifted
the flap of a serape that was held under the cantle
straps.

"No white man would wear a thing like this," he said.

Brasada smiled. "Mexicans do," he said.

The deputy let Brasada lead the dun to the water. He studied Brasada. "I'll ask you once more," he said. "Why did you come here tonight?"

Brasada turned and he was not smiling. "And now I ask *you*—just what authority do you have to ask me that?"

"Why, damn you! I'm deputy sheriff of this county!"

Brasada looked surprised. He glanced about. "Are you? Is this Arizona or Sonora? If this is Arizona, I'll answer your questions. If it is Sonora, I will not answer them. It's as simple as that."

The deputy looked down at his rifle. "Maybe this is my authority, mister." He looked up at Brasada. "Just what is your game, Brasada?"

Brasada shrugged. "I turn an honest peso whenever and wherever I can."

"Shall I tell you how?"

Brasada politely bowed his head. "Please do."

The deputy eyed the silver-banded sombrero, the cross-chest bandoleer, the figured leather gunbelt and holster, and then finally the lean brown face with its gray eyes and short black pointed beard. "Gunfighter, mercenary, paid revolutionary, and bounty hunter."

"You left out scalp hunter," suggested Brasada.

"Thanks for reminding me."

"*Por nada*," murmured Brasada.

Their eyes seemed to cross blades, like knife fighters testing each other for possible weaknesses before settling down to the serious business of gutting each other.

"If you plan to stay around," suggested the deputy, "don't make an enemy of me, Brasada."

"I have not made an enemy that I did not have when I first saw you," responded Brasada.

"Is that the way it is to be?"

Brasada shrugged.

"It doesn't really matter one way or another to you, does it?"

Brasada shook his head.

A coyote broke the stillness and the tension with a sharp barking cry that died off into a long-drawn howling. Brasada slowly turned his head. A second coyote howled and then a third gave voice, each at a different point of the compass.

"You're in good company tonight, Brasada," suggested the deputy. "Your four-legged kin are out in force to greet you."

Brasada was still looking up the slope. "Those aren't coyotes, mister."

The deputy was vastly amused. "No?"

Brasada turned. "Those are Apaches. Chiricahuas. The bloodthirstiest of the lot. But, don't worry, they won't come down here now—not for twenty-four hours at least. Not while Old Jubal's spirit is hovering around here in the guise of Bú, the Owl, waiting for vengeance on his murderer. Now, if you just happen to hear an owl around here, mister, you'll know who it is. . . ."

The deputy looked up at the slopes, dreaming empty in the moonlight and at the great towering mass of the Mountain. He didn't want to get to hell out of the open and into the shelter of the *bosquecillo*, not with the man named Brasada watching him with cynically amused eyes, but neither could he discipline himself to stand there as Brasada did, knowing that he was right now being watched from the heights by Chiricahuas.

"Go back to Sonora, Brasada," warned the deputy.

Brasada shook his head. "Not yet," he said.

"I've warned you."

"I've heard you," countered Brasada.

The deputy started up the slope toward the trees.

"I never did get your name, mister!" called out Brasada.

The deputy turned and looked down at Brasada. "Manton," he replied. He started up the slope again.

"I'll remember that name," called out Brasada.

Manton turned when in the shelter of the tree shadows. He looked down at Brasada. Brasada was laughing, or so it seemed, for not a sound came from his bearded lips.

Somewhere beyond the *bosquecillo* an owl hooted.

In a little while the soft sound of hoofbeats came from the far side of the *bosquecillo*.

Brasada walked to the dun and withdrew a bottle of Jerez brandy from a saddlebag. He pulled out the cork with his even white teeth and then drank deeply. He wiped his mouth with the back of a hand and looked sideways up the slope toward the *bosquecillo*. "*Cabrón*," he murmured. He drank again and then drove the cork tightly into the mouth of the bottle.

Somewhere in the moonlit foothills a coyote barked and then howled, just once. . . .

CHAPTER THREE

BRASADA DRAGGED the headless corpse to a narrow cleft in the rocky soil and dumped it in. He went back for the head. "Jubal, old friend," he murmured, "so you came back once too often and the Mountain got you at last." He picked up the head by its thick mat of hair and carried it to the cleft. Something fell from the hair and landed on the chest of the corpse. Brasada fitted the head into place and closed his hand over the object that had fallen from its hiding place in the hair. It felt like thick paper or thin parchment in a roll half an inch in diameter and about three inches long and it felt blood greasy to the touch.

Brasada stood up and looked down into the grave. "Back together again, eh, Jubal?" he said drily. "Through eternity. By Jesus, old man, when the trump of resurrection sounds, you'll rise in one piece again—or so we're led to believe." He kicked in loose rock and rocky soil until the body was covered.

Something cracked with a sharp splitting sound high above the talus slopes of the Mountain. Brasada leaped sideways and hit the ground, rolling over and over until he was within the shelter of the rocks about the *tinaja*.

A keg-sized rock struck the hard earth right where Brasada had just been standing. It shattered into dozens of flinty pieces that pattered hard against the ground. One shard struck Brasada on the left cheekbone like the impact of a striking diamondback.

It was quiet again. Brasada slowly raised a hand and felt the blood running from the face wound. He looked up at the Mountain. Nothing moved. He looked at his blood-tipped fingers. An uneasy feeling coursed through his mind.

High on the rocky slope above the *tinaja* with the sheer wall of the peak as a backdrop a man lay death-still, hardly daring to breathe. He had closed his one good eye and cold sweat ran down his face and sides. *Mother of God*, he thought. He would not look at the silently moving figures that passed within fifty feet of him as he lay there wetting his trousers. He did not know from where the Chiricahuas had appeared. It had seemed to him that they had materialized out of the rocks themselves, moving as silently as phantoms up the slopes, out of sight of the lone man down at the *tinaja*, to pass almost within spitting distance of Ignacio One-Eye.

Ignacio at last had the courage to open his one eye. The Chiricahuas were gone. He wiped the cold and greasy sweat from his forehead. He picked up his battered field glasses, stolen from the gear of a murdered *rurale*, and adjusted them to study the man who was down at the *tinaja*. The man's bearded face was often in shadow from the great brim of the sombrero. He moved like a hunting cat, or a Yaqui. The last thought was very disquieting to Ignacio One-Eye. He had seen the bearded stranger bury the old man Jubal Conn. "In *two* pieces," Ignacio had breathed to himself. It was the Mountain again. Ignacio was sure of that.

Brasada submerged one of his large canteens in

the gamey *tinaja* water. He listened to it blubber and slobber as it filled. The dun whinnied. Brasada looked quickly at him. The dun slanted its ears toward the moonlit slope above the *tinaja*. Brasada looked upward. Someone had moved up there. He caught the faintest reflection of moonlight from the barrel of a gun.

Brasada sat back out of sight of the heights and thumb-snapped a match into light to look at the roll he had found. It was banknote paper, similar to that which he had found near where the rifleman had fired to kill Jubal. The paper was bloodstained. It was lettered with signs and symbols. Brasada shrugged. He looked out at the grave of Jubal Conn. "Was this bit of paper the price of your life, old man?" he softly asked.

He led the dun up past the *bosquecillo* and along a draw, out of sight of anyone on the slopes above the *tinaja*. A quarter of a mile from the *tinaja* he found a pile of horse manure. He raked his fingers through it testing it for heat, content, and moisture. He cast about until he found the place where the horse had been picketed on softer ground. He studied the hoof-prints. There was a dark patch on the earth where the horse had voided. A mare, because it had urinated behind its legs. It had been oat-fed, therefore likely the horse of a white man rather than a Chiricahua. The manure pile was perhaps six or seven hours old. Brasada looked toward the Mountain. A man could walk hidden from the place where the mare had been picketed to get into position to overlook the *tinaja*.

Brasada looked across the dreaming landscape. The moonlight shone on a lonely bell tower, seemingly rising from the great rocky flow of a landslide that had long ago broken loose from the great mass of the Mountain. He could just make out other walls beyond the tower. There were no lights. No one lived there. No one had lived there for several decades. It was Soledad, or Solitary, and no one could have named it more fittingly.

Brasada led the dun on toward the distant hills to the east of Soledad. In a little while the soft sound of the rawhide-booted hoofs was gone.

Ignacio One-Eye looked down at the now deserted *tinaja*. He knew he would have to go down there. The bearded stranger had likely thoroughly searched the headless body. Still, he might have missed something.

Nothing moved. It was deathly quiet—it was *too* quiet for the nerves of Ignacio One-Eye.

Ignacio mentally girded his loins. He took one step down the slope.

An owl hooted somberly from the shadowed depths of the *bosquecillo*.

The sound of Ignacio's booted feet striking the hardness of the rocky ground beyond the *tinaja* echoed and died away. In a little while the sound of hurried hoofbeats came from where he had vanished from sight. The hoofbeats died away.

Time did not seem to move.

A lean grayish-yellow shape came cautiously down the slope from beyond the *bosquecillo*. The coyote padded to the *tinaja* and drank a little. It raised its dripping jaws from the water and the moonlight turned the drops into a chain of quicksilver. Soundlessly the coyote padded to the grave of Jubal Conn. It looked about once more with the moonlight shining on its eyes. Then it began to dig industriously through the loose rock and earth. In a little while three more coyotes came out of the thickening shadows and began to dig alongside the first coyote.

CHAPTER FOUR

It was Celedon Vega, the tinhorn monte dealer of La Placita, dozing behind his worn dealing cloth spread on the ground in front of a sun-warmed adobe wall, who was the first citizen of La Placita to see the coming of Brasada. Seeing Brasada that day was an experience Celedon Vega was never to forget and in the light of certain forthcoming events he never tired of the telling of it.

No one had ever managed to improve on Celedon's description of the man called Brasada as Celedon had seen him that bright and windy morning. "It was the low rolling thunder of the horse's hoofs on the plank bridge that first aroused me," Celedon would begin. "I glanced up sleepily to see the tall horseman riding up the very center of the street. He rode a fine horse of a lively light brown color, the hue of which is often called *tostado*, or toasted color. The horse was a *bayo coyote* dun and such a horse has a dark line running down its backbone, and rare indeed is such a horse marked by dark lines on the shoulders so that the effect is of a cross, or *cruz* mark. It is often said that such a marked horse has been chosen by God.

"But, if the dun horse had indeed been chosen by God, such was not the case with his rider. His face was lean and brown and he wore moustache and beard in the Sonoran style. His clothing and gear was well worn and of good but common material and it was evident that he had ridden very far in many days.

"He did not look at me as he passed by, but his shadow and that of the *cruz*-marked horse fell across me and in spite of the good warmth of the morning sun, I seemed to feel the coldness of my own grave enveloping me before my time. I pressed my back against the wall, averted my eyes and thrust out my right hand so. . . ." Here Celedon would always close his right hand into a fist and then he would spring out the first and little fingers in the symbol of horns. He would then punch out the hand in a short and sharp gesture well known to his listeners—it was the symbolic protection against a *brujo*, a male witch.

For a moment or two Celedon would not continue his tale until he had his listeners sitting on the very edges of their bar stools in anticipation. (Celedon was a veritable master teller of tales.) "It was then that the rider turned to look directly at me as though he had felt something, and, before God, *I knew he had seen me make the gesture as though he had eyes in the back of his head!*" Again Celedon's hushed voice would fade away and he would look about the circle of dark faces watching him intently, to gain the fullest dramatic effect before he gave the punch line—"Mother of God, my friends, when I looked into those eyes of his, the color of icy winter rain, *it seemed as though I was looking into my own grave. . . ."*

Brasada rode through the side streets of La Placita past eroded adobes and sagging *jacales* patched with flattened tin cans. Women watched the stranger from within the shadows of their doorways and men spoke to each other out of the sides of their mouths after the stranger had passed. The dogs that came barking toward Brasada suddenly stopped their noise when they saw the lean brown face beneath the great brim of the sombrero and slunk away baring their teeth. Half-naked *ninos* and *ninas* played in the dusty street, paying no attention to Brasada while their older sisters and brothers ran toward him with outstretched hands, but then stopped, as the dogs had done when they had seen his cold gray eyes, for to the children the Devil himself had such gray gringo eyes.

Brasada turned into the main street and reined in the dun beside the largest building in town and the only one that boasted two stories. Brasada dismounted and tethered the dun and then looked across his saddle to the west, toward the Mountain. In the clear morning air it seemed but a short distance from La Placita but with the coming of the day's heat the disturbed atmosphere would make the Mountain appear to move and change shape and retreat farther to the west. But now, in the bright light of the morning the Mountain seemed to be very close indeed and it dominated the great shallow valley that lay west of La Placita, the rolling foothills and the *poblado* of La Placita itself, as it did everything else for hundreds of square miles—the empty Soledad foothills to the southeast, the tangled crisscross of baking waterless canyons due south and to the southwest, and the motionless sandy waves of the great desert that was due west, dry frozen in great waterless rifts and hollows that seemed to wash up against and break into motionless foam against the barren western slopes.

Brasada felt for the makings. La Placita wasn't much different from other *poblados* in that part of the Territory, and those south over the border in Northern Sonora—isolated, utterly provincial, and old, long old before their time, with little to look back upon and less to look forward to.

Two riders, a man and a woman, entered the main
street from the Soledad Road. The sun glinted from
the twin rows of little brass bell buttons that rode the
magnificent swell of bosom of the woman beneath
the taut uniform-blue serge of the semimilitary style
of feminine jacket called a basque. A too-small forage cap was tilted rakishly to one side of the woman's
glorious mass of titian-red hair and the sun shone on
the polished brass crossed sabers pinned on the forward slanted crown of the forage cap. She rode side-
saddle, with her full blue riding skirt cascading down
to just above a pair of small highly polished boots
armed with dainty silvered spurs. She rode proudly,
head up, looking neither to right nor to left, knowing
that all eyes were on her and accepting it as though
it were her due.

"*Madre de Dios*," breathed Brasada.

"You can say that again, stranger," a nasal voice
put in from behind Brasada.

"I was talking to myself," said Brasada over his
shoulder.

"A bad habit. Gives a man away," said nasal voice.
"Man who maybe spends too much time by himself
in the desert and mountains."

Brasada placed his cigarette in his mouth. He
cupped his hands about the flame of the lucifer to
light his cigarette but his gray eyes looked across his
hands to the man who rode beside the redhead. He
was flat of face and his nose was askew, and he was
handsome enough in an empty sort of way. He gave
look for look to any man who thoughtfully eyed the
woman, and it was always the other man whose eyes
gave way, until the man glanced at Brasada. The
horseman's eyes were a curious yellow-brown color
and in keeping with the rest of his features there was
a flatness about his curious eyes. He and the woman
dismounted in front of the large two-storied building.

Brasada turned to look into a gaunt triangular face seamed like very old well-tanned leather that had long ago lost its natural oil—a sort of leather mask through which peered two watered-down blue eyes from under the brim of a faded and stained campaign hat which still sported a frayed yellow cavalry cord.

"Who is she?" asked Brasada.

"Mrs. Major O'Neil. Can you spare me the makings?"

Brasada handed him the makings. He looked just in time to see the woman looking boldly and speculatively at him with eyes of an incredible emerald green.

"They's only one thing a man can rightly think about when she looks at him like that," observed nasal voice.

"You've got a dirty mouth," said Brasada. *"But, you're right."*

"I got a dirty mind too and I *know* I'm right."

The man and the woman went into the building together and some of the tinsel glory of the morning seemed to vanish along with her, and perhaps some of the inert menace with him.

"I'm Barney Gadkin," volunteered nasal voice.

"She must have married old Major Peter O'Neil," said Brasada.

"The same. You know him?"

"Long ago," replied Brasada, "and a long way from here."

"She married him about a year or so ago. She sort of took over the reins out to his Soledad Rancho."

"She's young for him," mused Brasada.

"Yeh. Well, the old man is still out there, but maybe more in mind than in body. Sits out in the sun while she ramrods the rancho. He just sits there lookin' at that Gawd-damned mountain with his old army telescope when the sun is right. Lookin', lookin', always lookin'—for God knows what."

Brasada turned to look at the man. Gadkin wore a faded army issue shirt accompanied by a miasma of ancient sweat, blue issue trousers with the two half-inch yellow stripes of a corporal-trumpeter along the seams.

"Maybe he's looking for the 'shadow writing'?" suggested Brasada.

The blue eyes became veiled. "Who the hell are you, anyway?"

"Men call me Brasada."

Barney nodded as though he understood, which he certainly did not. He looked at the fine dun horse and at the sheathed Winchester, then up into the lean bearded face and the cold gray eyes, then down at the Sonoran-style clothing and the Chihuahua boots and spurs. Last of all he eyed the low-slung, tied-down, cutaway holster from which protruded the well-worn ivory butt of a Colt, and *that* he liked even less than the rest of the view. "Never saw you around here before," he said.

"We were talking about the old major," reminded Brasada.

"Yeh. I was trumpeter for him back in the old Third Cavalry. Odd sort of a bird. Kept much to himself. Some said he was always mournin' a long-lost love. Others said he was always thinking about the Soledad Hills. Anyway, he came out here after retirement, bought the ranch, and finally married her —God help him!"

"You seem to know a lot about him."

Gadkin shrugged. "Not much more than most people around here. I came out here all the way from New Mexico when my hitch was up to work for the old man. Things was all right until one day he come back from Tucson with *her*, blushing like a bride."

"*Him*, or *her*?" drily asked Brasada.

Barney laughed. "Yeh—old fool. I get it!" He

looked at the Mountain. "Well, anyway I didn't last long out there when she took over—her and that flat-faced sonofabitch, Mick Dallas, that was with her. He's her 'foreman.' Some foreman! He's a hired gun, is all."

"Why did she marry the old man, Barney?"

Barney tried to look vague. "Well, that pension ain't enough to keep her in them sheer silk stockings she fancies and them black lace drawers she always wears. Man, what I seen out there. . . . And the powder and perfume, like a really high-class Kansas City whore."

Brasada grinned knowingly. "Some of that hot French stuff, eh?"

"Yaaaah . . . makes a gelding think he's a real stud. Well, anyway, it ain't the ranch that keeps her out there."

"That leaves the 'shadow writing,'" suggested Brasada.

Barney looked away from Brasada. "You see that man walking down the center of the street? Ask *him* about the 'shadow writing.' That's Luke Harkness— The Hermit of Soledad, as some call him. Knows more about the Mountain than about anybody, maybe exceptin' the old major."

A huge broad-shouldered man was walking down the center of the street leading a dusty burro with empty kyacks on its back. The man wore no hat and the sun shone on his thatch of gray hair and on his great beard. He carried a rifle in his left hand. The buttstock of the rifle was missing, shattered just behind the tang.

"He's still alive after five years on the Mountain," added Barney.

"So?" asked Brasada.

"Which means he ain't been lookin' for what you think he's been lookin'. If he had been, like some others I could name, he'd of been shot dead long ago, and his head left on a rock to look at the Mountain."

"So, you believe in that fairy tale too?" asked Brasada.

"Fairy tale!" exploded Barney. "Twelve men dead on that damned Mountain in the past three years and nobody knows the killer and *you* call it a fairy tale!"

"Make it thirteen," said Brasada.

Barney looked quickly at Brasada. "Another one?" he asked.

Brasada nodded. "Jubal Conn. You knew him?"

Barney paled. He passed a shaking hand across his watery eyes. He nodded. "How'd he die?" he asked.

"Explosive bullet through the head; fired at about seven hundred yards."

"And the head?" asked Barney.

"Cut off and placed on a rock to look at the Mountain."

"Jesus," said Barney softly.

Harkness had tethered his burro to a hitching rail in front of Tatum's Gun Shop and had gone inside carrying his rifle.

"Getting back to the major," suddenly said Brasada. "Maybe he doesn't know the 'shadow writing' at all."

"By God! You'd better believe it!" cried Barney. He stopped short and looked into Brasada's eyes, suddenly realizing the trap into which he had fallen. "Well, all right," he added. "I think he does know it, but the secretive old bastard is too smart to write down *what* he knows! They used to say back in the Old Third that he had a map of the Soledad area, but no one ever got to see it. That is, no one except Cass Weed. He's the sheriff here now. Used to be in the Third too. Long before the war he was stationed at Soledad when the old Mounted Rifles were there. Him, and O'Neil. They was just lieutenants then."

"You say Cass Weed saw it?" asked Brasada.

Barney had clammed up again. Brasada took a bottle of Jerez from a saddlebag, drank a little, and handed the bottle to Barney. Barney drank mechanically, but well.

"Cass Weed?" prompted Brasada.

Barney drank again. He wiped his mouth with the back of a hand. "That was long ago," he said. "Him and the major got drunk one night and O'Neil showed Weed the map. Next day Weed remembered seeing the map, but he couldn't remember one detail of it. O'Neil never showed it to him again."

"And Weed came here after he retired too?"

Barney looked at the two-storied building. "Yep. Built that building there. Opened up a general store and a saloon in there. He run for sheriff and made it—that was three years ago. He still wears the star, but it's Manton, his deppity that does the law and order bit in this county—all alone, too." Barney drank again. He looked at the Mountain. "Funny thing, O'Neil and Weed served together in the Mexican War and the Civil War, and out on the Plains together, and they retired about the same time, O'Neil ahead of Weed, and they both end up here. Loco, hey?"

Brasada shrugged. He took the bottle and drank a little. "Maybe they value their old friendship."

Barney grinned. "They ain't talked together socially since O'Neil showed Weed that map years past."

Brasada handed Barney the bottle. "Drink up," he urged.

Barney drank up. He drank a lot.

"Maybe the old man still has the map," suggested Brasada.

Barney shook his head. "I never saw it when I worked out there."

"But you looked for it?"

The watery blue eyes looked suspiciously at Brasada. "No," lied Barney. "But if there was a map, that redheaded harpy of a wife of his and that flat-

·faced sonofabitch that's always with her would'a maybe got it out of the old man."

"God help the old man," murmured Brasada.

"Anyways, she can't argue him, or sweet-talk him out'a what he knows—he ain't that simple. Now me, I worked for the old man before she showed up and I never would'a harmed the old man to get any information out'a him. I got *some* loyalty to my old commanding officer!"

"You're all heart, Barney," murmured Brasada. He watched the bottle. tilt upward again and gurgle musically.

Barney lowered the bottle. "Onct he gave me a tip, by accident, but I was too stupid to figger it out at the time."

"So you went to the Mountain?"

Barney nodded. "But that ol' Mountain ain't ever goin' to give up no treasure."

"Bullshit! The old padres took it out of there, didn't they?"

"And they put it right back again, didn't they?" challenged Barney.

"Who's to say the silver can't be found again?"

"The Mountain," replied Barney in a low voice, as though the great mass of rock shining in the sunlight miles away could overhear him.

Brasada laughed.

"Go on, damn you! Laugh!" cried Barney. "A jackass can laugh like that and he ain't got any more sense than you have! But, then you ain't seen what I seen up there on that mountain, and maybe you ain't had nothing happen to you up there like it done to me. Dried-out skeletons without skulls—and the skulls lying a long ways from the bodies with bullet holes clean through them." He looked at Brasada. "Well, they never found anything, and I didn't find anything, and you ain't never goin' to find anything, mister, whoever you really are. . . ."

Brasada shrugged. "I've got other things on my mind."

Harkness came out of the gunshop and walked to the general store.

"Such as?" asked Barney.

"There's reward money out for the killer, or killers of those twelve men up there," replied Brasada.

"Thousands," replied Barney. "It's been piling up for three years and no one has tapped any of it yet —not even Manton."

"Then maybe that's the real treasure to be had from the Mountain," suggested Brasada.

Barney looked at him. "Go on up there, Brasada. Things will sometimes happen to you like they was perfectly natural and you won't ever be able to explain it—*if you live to think back on it*. And if you do live through it, like I done, them things begin to work on your mind, and you ain't ever goin' to be the same again—not ever. . . ." Barney looked past Brasada toward the Mountain. Brasada leaned a little sideways to look into the man's eyes and he seemed to see, deep within them, something like a festering, purulent abscess of deadly fear; a look of such sheer horror that it even touched and abraded the rawhide-tough mind of Brasada with its contagion.

"Keep the bottle," invited Brasada.

Barney nodded without looking at Brasada. "*Gracias*," he murmured.

"*Por nada*," countered Brasada.

Brasada walked toward the gun shop. Once he turned and looked back at Barney. The man was still standing there, looking at the Mountain, with the half-empty bottle dangling from his left hand.

CHAPTER FIVE

THERE WAS a light van wagon standing in front of Tatum's Gun Shop. One of the rear doors was open and Brasada glanced inside the van. Rifles and shotguns were neatly racked inside it and shelved cartridge boxes and boxes of reloading gear stood next to gunpowder canisters. Brasada looked back at the side of the van as he stepped up onto the boardwalk. A neatly lettered sign on the side of the van read E. Keesey, Guns and Gun Supplies. Brasada opened the gun shop door. A bell tinkled overhead.

A bald-headed man stood behind a counter looking down at Harkness's rifle. He looked up at Brasada. "Help you?" he asked.

"Take your time," said Brasada pleasantly.

A dark bearded man was placing boxes of cartridges on a shelf. "Two dozen boxes Blue Whistlers, 12-gauge, number Four shot," he said over his shoulder to the gunsmith. "Dozen boxes .45/70, one dozen 500-grain bullets, one dozen 405-grain bullets. Anything else?"

"You got a Greener 12-gauge double-barrel shotgun, Keesey?" asked Tatum.

"Not with me. I'll bring it next trip."

Tatum nodded. He took a used buttstock and fitted it into place on the rifle left there by Harkness.

"Nice antique," observed Brasada as he shaped a cigarette. "I didn't know there was any buffalo hunting going on around here."

Tatum grinned. "There ain't," he said.

"Sharps Big Fifty, eh?" asked Brasada as he lighted up. "What is it—a .50/90?"

Tatum shook his head. "It was originally. I rechambered it to .50/140. Takes a longer cartridge case."

Brasada whistled. "I didn't know anyone made up Sharps cartridges as big as that," he said.

The bearded man came from behind the counter. "Winchester makes them only on special order," he explained. "They load the cases with the 473-grain bullet. U.M.C. makes only the cartridge case. They don't load them. That's a helluva good rifle, mister. Used two of them Big Fifties myself in the old days —buffalo hunting, that was. Pair of fine .50/90's. Got a lot of prime hides with them."

Tatum was replacing the stock screws. "Them were the days, Keesey," he said sadly.

"Uses a paper-patched bullet, doesn't it?" asked Brasada.

Tatum nodded. "The 700-grain bullet—biggest there is." He pulled out the hinge pin of the breechblock and took out the breechblock. He handed the rifle to Brasada. "Take a look," he invited. "You can see the longer chamber. The 700-grain bullet is 15/16ths of an inch long." Brasada looked down the bore. He whistled softly. "Mirror bright," he said in appreciation. "Is that the solid bullet, the 700-grain?"

"Solid or Express," put in Keesey. "Express has a hole drilled in the head of the bullet for a .22-caliber blank. Blank explodes on impact. Goes in about .50 caliber and comes out about four or five times as big. Messy killing wound, mister."

Tatum took the Sharps and placed the extractor

against the face of the breechblock in the slot provided for it. He slid the block up into the breech and replaced the hinge pin. He closed the breechblock and let the hammer down from halfcock to rest against the firing pin base.

"You don't see many of them around the border country anymore," observed Brasada.

"The old major out to the Soledad Rancho has a .50-caliber Sharps," volunteered Tatum. "But it ain't a Big Fifty. It's an issue Civil War New Model 1863. His was originally issued to Berdan's First United States Sharpshooters during the war."

"So?" asked Brasada. "Maybe he was a Sharpshooter?"

Tatum shook his head. "Third United States Cavalry that used to be the old Mounted Rifles. They carried the shorter New Model 1863 carbine—that is, the troopers did. The old man was a captain in them days."

Keesey lighted a cigar. "The old man's rifle was issued to some of the finest riflemen this country, and maybe the world, has ever seen. Hunters they were, from Maine, Michigan, upstate New York, Vermont, and Pennsylvania where there were still many large wilderness areas. Man *had* to be good to get past Colonel Berdan's qualifications—had to put ten consecutive shots into a ten-inch circle at two hundred yards. At Kelly's Ford in 1863 two Sharpshooters from different companies both aimed at and hit the same running Rebel at seven hundred yards. I know—I was there."

"Anyway," put in Tatum, "it was the old man's wife who bought the Sharps rifle from me for the old man. She thought it was like the one he used in the war. I didn't tell her different."

Keesey grinned. "The redheaded bosomy doxie?"

"Yep," agreed Tatum, "but so far she's ahead—she ain't paid me for it yet and she won't give it back."

He looked at Brasada. "Can I help you now, mister?"

"Two boxes of .44/40 cartridges," replied Brasada.

Tatum nodded. He placed the boxes on the counter. "Passing through?" he asked. Brasada nodded as he paid for the cartridges.

"Haven't I seen you somewhere before?" asked Keesey. "Sonora, maybe? I travel down that way every now and then."

"I've been there," said Brasada.

"There was a sergeant of *rurales* down there," persisted Keesey. "An *emigrado*. The *paisanos* were deathly afraid of him. They called him Sargento Diablo."

"Sounds romantic," said Brasada drily.

The doorbell tinkled and Luke Harkness towered through the doorway. "Your rifle is ready, Harkness," said Tatum.

"How's the prospecting, Harkness?" asked Keesey.

"I'll take two cans of blasting powder, a coil of fuse, and a bar of lead, Mister Tatum," said Harkness.

"Apaches never seem to bother you on the Mountain," observed Keesey.

"How much do I owe you?" asked Harkness of Tatum.

"Beats the hell out of me how you can live around Soledad and the Apaches never bother you, Harkness," persisted Keesey.

"That'll be eighteen dollars even," said Tatum. He looked at Keesey. "Maybe the Apaches don't bother Harkness because he don't bother them. You ever think of that?"

Keesey looked at the rifle. "Fine rifle," he said. "Used two of them myself. 50/95's they were. Killed many a prime buffalo hide with 'em."

Harkness slowly turned. "A senseless and murderous slaughter, sir. A great blot of reeking blood that has forever stained the Great Plains and the memory of living man."

"Hear, hear," jeered Keesey. "Maybe you did some of that senseless and murderous slaughtering yourself."

Harkness turned abruptly away from Keesey. He reached into a pocket and placed a handful of small chunks of what looked like pure silver on the counter. Tatum weighed the silver on a small scale. "I figure I owe you about twenty dollars change," he said over his shoulder.

Brasada glanced quickly at the giant. Tatum was rooking him. Harkness took his change, his rifle, and his purchases and walked out of the gun shop.

"You were treading on dangerous ground there, Keesey," warned Tatum.

Keesey grinned. "I was only trying to get a rise out of him."

Tatum shook his head. "You know how he feels about useless killing."

"So his killing is useful?" demanded Keesey. "Come off it!"

"They say he kills only to eat," said Tatum.

"That's what he says! Maybe he's the one who's been doing all the killing on that mountain."

Tatum looked quickly toward the door. "For God's sake!" he snapped. "Be careful what you say!"

Keesey looked at Brasada. "What do you think?" he asked.

"About him being the killer?" asked Brasada. "It's a little too obvious, isn't it?"

Keesey shrugged. "I never thought of it like that." He looked at the bits of silver. "Still, he always pays his way with pure silver. Where does he get it? Maybe he's found the Soledad Silver."

Tatum grinned. "I never asked him," he said. "And, I ain't about to."

"Not with the profit you make out of him," said Keesey.

"Besides," countered Tatum. "The Soledad Silver is supposed to be in ingots—thirty tons of it."

"Did it ever occur to you," sweetly asked Keesey, "that maybe he takes an ingot and melts it down, then cuts it up and bashes it around to make it *look* like chunks of pure native silver?"

"You ever see pure silver like this out of the ground, mister?" asked Tatum of Brasada.

Brasada pocketed his cartridges. "Not around here," he said. "It's possible though." He walked to the door. "Good day," he said back over his shoulder. He closed the door behind him.

"Now who the hell was he?" asked Keesey. "You ever see him before, Tatum?"

"No."

"You think he's a spic?"

"He didn't talk English like one."

"Look at the clothes he was wearing."

Tatum shrugged. "Clowns wear funny clothes to make people laugh but that don't mean they have to be happy themselves."

"Now what the hell is that supposed to mean?"

Tatum grinned. "You figure it out."

Keesey walked to the window and looked through it at Brasada across the street. "I know I seen him before."

"He didn't think so."

"He said he had been in Sonora, didn't he?"

"So have I," Tatum said drily.

"There's something familiar about that man. Something strange, Tatum," ruminated Keesey.

Tatum looked at him. "I don't often give advice, Keesey, but you've got a bad habit of poking into other people's lives and business. So, take my advice, and keep your nose out of his business."

"Well maybe you're right. I don't mean any harm.

I suppose I spend so much time alone riding in that damned van out there, and camping by myself in the loneliest parts of this lonely country, I get interested in other people." Keesey looked out through the window again. "Still," he added thoughtfully, "I'm sure I saw him down in Sonora. There's a sergeant of *Rurales* down there—the best manhunter in the business—who is always sent out on the most difficult cases—the ones with the highest amount of reward money, by the way, and always they read Dead or Alive. This man, the one they call Sargento Diablo, *always* gets his man, they say. Some say he acts as arresting agent, judge, jury, and then executioner, to save the State of Sonora the time and money of a trial."

Tatum looked up at the salesman. "Sounds almost like Manton," he said quickly. "How does this Sargento Diablo, as you call him, prove he got his man?"

Keesey came closer to the counter. "They say he brings back the head in a sack," he said in a hushed voice.

"Best proof in the world," said Tatum. He spat into a spittoon and wiped his mouth. "Do you really believe that man out there is this Sargento Diablo?"

Keesey did not reply for a moment, and then he looked directly at the gunsmith. "Did you see those eyes of his?" he quietly asked.

CHAPTER SIX

"Brasada," said Manton from behind Brasada. "Sheriff Weed wants to talk with you about Jubal Conn."

"He's dead," said Brasada over his shoulder as he unstrapped a saddlebag.

"That's exactly why he wants to talk with you."

Brasada turned. "Where do I find him?"

Manton pointed to the two-story building. "There," he said.

"His office is in there?"

"So's his saloon, the Union Forever," put in Barney. "He's more likely to be in the saloon than his office."

Manton looked at the drifter. "Barney," he said quietly, "I've warned you about that kind of talk."

"I'll be along," said Brasada.

Manton nodded. "You aim to stay around long?" he asked.

"Not in La Placita."

"I meant—in general."

Brasada shrugged. "¿Quien sabe?" he asked.

Manton looked thoughtfully up and down the street. "This is a nice place," he said quietly, almost as though to himself. "Most people like it here."

"Each to his own," commented Brasada.

"We don't have too much trouble around here," added Manton.

"Except little things like having peaceable old Jubal Conn getting his head half blown off and then suffering the final indignity of having his head cut off and placed on a rock to look at the Mountain with eyes that could no longer see anything. Like maybe twelve other men getting murdered about the same way in the past three years and no one finding out who killed them."

Manton studied Brasada. "You're quite the humorist." He turned on a heel and walked a little way. He turned. "I won't come again to ask you to see the sheriff," he warned. He walked on, a tall lean gray lath of a man who looked to Brasada like a very disciple of legalized man-killer.

"*You* are *loco*," precisely commented Barney Gadkin.

"*You* are *drunk*," precisely countered Brasada.

"Each to his own," parroted Barney. "*That* was *Manton.*"

"So he told me," said Brasada.

Barney rolled his eyes upwards. "Sweet Jesus," he murmured.

"You don't miss much that's going on around here, do you?"

"What else I got to do?" asked Barney.

"You've got me there," drily admitted Brasada.

Luke Harkness came out of the general store and walked to his burro, trailing his Sharps rifle and carrying a sack of supplies over a shoulder. He loaded the burro and untethered it, to lead it down the street toward the bridge that spanned the dry watercourse.

"He's loco," commented Barney.

"Why?" asked Brasada.

"He always walks instead of rides. He never wears a hat—in *this* country."

"That makes him loco?" asked Brasada.

"He talks to animals," added Barney.

"So do I."

"And trees and flowers," continued Barney.

"You've got me again," admitted Brasada.

A dog began to bark near the river.

"Watch this," suggested Barney.

A racketing chorus of barking dogs began to echo from the close-in hills. Harkness led the burro onto the bridge. A huge dog suddenly appeared from within a dusty *bosquecillo* of willows and cottonwoods. He loped, rather than ran, to meet Harkness.

"Jesus!" snapped Brasada. He reached for his Winchester.

"Wait," advised Barney.

Harkness reached down and gently patted the animal's lean and flat skull. Together they turned down the Soledad Road beyond the bridge, with the burro trotting along behind them.

"You think that's a wolf?" asked Barney.

Brasada looked quickly at him. "Don't you?" he asked.

Barney shrugged. "*Quien sabe?* I don't think anyone around here has ever gotten close enough to *it* to find out *what* it is. I'll tell you something else—no man, not even an Apache, can get anywhere near Harkness when that animal is around him."

The chorus of barking died away as Harkness and his animals disappeared around a bend in the road.

Brasada felt in a saddlebag and drew out a bottle of Jerez.

"I don't think any man in history has ever had his way with wild animals," said Barney.

Brasada drank a little and handed the bottle to Barney. "There was one—once," he said quietly.

"Who?" asked Barney.

"Saint Francis of Assisi," replied Brasada.

"Oh—*him*," said Barney. He drank deeply. He

lowered the bottle. "Don't look now," he suggested,
"but look casual like at that spic across the street—
the one tightening his saddle cinch. He's been watching you."

Brasada nodded. "I know. You know him?"

Barney reached into Brasada's shirt pocket and
withdrew the makings. He hiccupped. He began to
shape a cigarette. "Name of Ramon Sanchez."

"A local?" asked Brasada.

Barney ran his tongue along the edge of the cigarette paper. "Sort of," he said. He grinned. He twisted
the end of the quirly together and placed the cigarette between his lips. "He's a spic from Sonora.
Passes back and forth across the border. You know
—if it gets too hot in Sonora he heads for Arizona
until things cool off, and vice versa. Hangs out in the
Soledad Hills with a thievin' bunch that used to be
big time until a few years past. Now they're down to
petty larceny, a little horse thievin' and suchlike."

"I noticed he vanished when Manton showed up
and then came back again when Manton went away,"
observed Brasada.

"You're very bright," admitted Barney. He lighted
the cigarette.

"Maybe he's got his eye on my dun," suggested
Brasada. He ran a hand on the dun's shoulders. "A
cruz-marked dun is a rarity, especially to a spic."

"Yeh, but there ain't no luck in stealin' such a
horse." Barney shifted a little. "Look up at the second-floor porch of the big building," he suggested.
Brasada looked up out of the sides of his eyes. Manton was standing on the porch with his hands resting
on the railing and he was looking directly at Brasada.
The sun glinted from his deputy badge. When Brasada looked away he noticed that Ramon Sanchez
had again vanished.

"You're playin' with fire, Brasada," warned Barney.

Brasada nodded. "Keep an eye on the dun, in case

Ramon comes back," he said. He walked toward the big building.

"Brasada!" called out Barney.

Brasada turned and looked at the drunk.

"They say the gang Ramon rides with is run by a woman," said Barney. He grinned.

"What's that got to do with me?"

Barney shrugged. "I just thought you might be interested, is all." He watched Brasada walk on. He grinned again.

CHAPTER SEVEN

BRASADA WALKED into the Union Forever. A bald-headed bartender was serving two trail-dusty men who stood at the end of the bar. Mrs. Major O'Neil and Mick Dallas sat in a leather-upholstered booth at the rear of the saloon next to a door that was labeled Family Entrance. Brasada could not help but smile at the sign over the two of them in the booth.

A hulk of a man sat at a table near a doorway over which was another sign—Office. Cassius Weed must have been handsome and imposing in the blue and brass of his army uniform but now his big body had swelled into unhealthy fat and his florid face was marked by strong drink. A fine network of red and purple capillaries patterned his cheeks and his Roman nose was now swollen and spongy looking. A silver sheriff's star was pinned to his coat. He looked up at Brasada as Brasada stopped beside the table. "Well?" he asked.

"I am Brasada," said Brasada.

"My deputy Manton tells me that old Jubal Conn has been murdered and he found you at the scene of the crime."

Brasada nodded. "He's right, sheriff. He also knows I did not kill the old man."

Weed reached for a bottle and filled a glass. "Maybe you know a lot more than what you told him," suggested Weed.

Brasada shook his head.

"What were you doing at the *tinaja?*" asked Weed.

"I came there for water," replied Brasada. "That was after moonrise. The old man was killed some time in the late afternoon."

"You're sure about that?"

Brasada nodded. "Maybe about the time Manton was there."

It was very quiet in the saloon. The bartender flicked his eyes toward Brasada looking over the head of the sheriff. He shook his head. The two trail-dusty men slanted their eyes toward Brasada. Mick Dallas studied Brasada with his curious flat brown eyes. The woman was the only one who did not look at Brasada.

Brasada turned his head a little. Manton stood just within the batwing doors looking at Brasada.

Weed drained his glass. "Just what do you mean by that?" he asked.

"Nothing," replied Brasada. "I was just fixing the time element."

Weed looked up at him. "Are you a spic?" he bluntly asked.

"I am an *emigrado*. I hold dual citizenship in the United States and Mexico."

"Very convenient," said Weed. "Where were you born?" .

"In Texas."

"*Where*, in Texas?"

Brasada smiled a little. "My name will tell you that—in the Brasada country."

"What's your business here?"

The woman looked up just as Brasada replied. "Prospecting," said Brasada.

"Where?" asked Weed.

"The Soledad Hills," replied Brasada.

"Waste of time," said Weed. "There's no color there."

"There was," said Brasada.

Weed waved a hand. "Perhaps thirty years ago."

"The only color left around those hills is lead—in the shape of a bullet fired into your skull," put in Manton. He walked to the bar and leaned back against it, folding his arms and watching Brasada.

"And blood red," added Weed. "It's a dangerous place, Brasada." He looked down into his glass as though into a crystal ball to foresee the future, which was not a far-fetched idea, thought Brasada, considering Weed's drinking habit. "I was stationed in Soledad before the war, with the old Mounted Rifles. The padres had been gone for almost ninety years at that time, but men were still working some of the mines." He looked toward Mrs. Major O'Neil. "Pete O'Neil was a brother officer of mine in those days. He had a great deal of interest in the history of the area, especially that of the old padres."

"And he still does," put in Manton.

"When the war came," reminisced the sheriff, almost as though he had forgotten anyone else was in the saloon, "the Mounted Rifles were ordered east. The Chiricahuas moved in on Soledad while the dust of our departure was still settling on the road through the hills. There were no survivors."

"The Massacre of Soledad," said Brasada.

Weed looked up. "You've heard about that, eh?" He filled his glass. "Men tried to rebuild Soledad after the war. Fortune, however, no longer smiled upon the place. The Chiricahuas controlled the area beyond the range of a trooper's carbine. Landslides cascaded down the side of the Mountain and in time buried the old mines and half of the town. Men began to say that the padres had put a lasting curse on the place. The town is said to be haunted. No one goes there anymore."

"Except those who hunt the Soledad Silver," said Brasada.

"A legend, no more," said Manton.

Weed looked at his deputy. "There is truth behind that legend, Manton. I *know*." Manton glanced at the whiskey bottle on the table and then looked up at Brasada. Weed flushed a little, but he would not shut his loose mouth. "The Soledad Silver still lies hidden somewhere on that mountain. Perhaps in a place a man might very well see from the streets of La Placita when the sun strikes the peak at a certain angle, but unless a man knows how to interpret that which he might see, *he will not know he is looking at the lost cache of the Soledad Silver.*"

"Have a drink, Cass," urged Manton.

Weed waved a fat hand. "Think of it!" he husked. "*Thirty tons of pure native silver!* The hoard of Croesus or the gift of Midas!"

"Are you through with me, sir?" asked Brasada.

Weed was startled. "What was our business, sir?" he asked with the exaggerated politeness of the truly drunk.

"Jubal Conn," replied Brasada.

"Oh, yes! Well, I believe that you had nothing to do with his death." He closed his eyes for a moment and then opened them. "But you did know the old man, eh, Brasada?"

Brasada nodded. "Years ago."

Weed opened his eyes. "Maybe you planned to meet him there at the *tinaja?*"

Brasada shook his head. "Coincidence, sir." He knew well enough that no one in the saloon believed him.

"Perhaps he meant to tell you something, eh, Brasada?" persisted the sheriff.

"We'll never know, will we, sheriff?" asked Brasada.

He looked up at Manton. "Jubal Conn is now just another unsolved murder on the Mountain—the thirteenth, to be exact."

Weed looked at Manton. Manton nodded. There was no expression on his face. "One thing you should know, Brasada," said Manton, "if you intend to try for some of the reward money offered for those unsolved murders, is that four of the twelve men killed up there before the murder of Jubal Conn were bounty hunters. It's a dangerous business."

"Like hunting for the Soledad Silver," suggested Brasada.

"I would not like to choose between the two of them in that respect," murmured Weed.

Brasada smiled. "Maybe I'll find out," he said. He walked toward the door.

"Keep us informed, Brasada!" called out Manton.

Brasada looked back at the deputy. It was the first time he had seen Manton smiling—that is, the face smiled, but the eyes did not.

Brasada pushed through the batwings. He walked down the street to a small store that dealt in Mexican-style food supplies and liquor and had a sack filled with food and another with straw-padded bottles of Jerez. As he left the store he saw Mrs. Major O'Neil and Mick Dallas leave the saloon and walk toward their horses. Dallas gave the woman a hand up into her saddle. She turned and looked at Brasada.

"You," said Dallas, as Brasada drew abreast of the woman.

Brasada stopped. "Are you speaking to me?" he asked pleasantly.

The woman looked down at him with those incredible emerald eyes of hers. "I overheard you say in the saloon that you planned to prospect in the Soledad Hills," she said.

"That is correct," said Brasada.

She studied him. "Who are you? Where do you come from?"

"The name is Brasada," he replied. "The name and the place of my origin are the same."

She nodded. "I also heard that in the saloon."

He smiled. "You overhear a great deal," he said.

"You have no other name?" she asked.

"None," explained Brasada. "I was a foundling, lady. *Vaqueros* found me in the Brasada country of Texas. My little nose was running and my diaper had been filled twice and was crawling with big red ants. But I wasn't crying, ma'am, not me! Not Brasada! I was being suckled by a coyote bitch at the time, you understand. Turns out she was to be the only mother I was ever to know. God bless her soul! But, the *vaqueros* shot her and brought me to their *estancia*. They made a cradle for me out of an old brandy keg and lined it with her pelt, so's I wouldn't get lonely for her. They were the toughest *vaqueros* in all the Brasada country, and that's saying something, lady! They fed me on bull meat and mare's milk so that I would learn to know the mystic lore of cows and horses. They were father, mother, sister and brother to me. And all they ever called me was Brasada. I got used to it, ma'am."

"Why, you . . . ," said Mick Dallas.

She cut Mick Dallas short with a wave of her gloved hand.

Brasada smiled. "Can I go now, lady?" he asked. He nodded pleasantly and walked carefully around Mick Dallas. Barney Gadkin was watching them from a nearby doorway. Brasada placed his sack of supplies over his cantle roll.

"You ought to get taught some manners about speaking to a lady," said Mick Dallas from behind Brasada.

Brasada carefully placed the sack of bottles on the sidewalk. "And it seems as though you're going to volunteer to do it?" asked Brasada pleasantly as he straightened up.

Brasada's answer was a hard hand that gripped his left shoulder at the same time that his Colt was plucked from its holster. He was roughly spun about. Dallas never had a chance to start his lesson. A piston-like left fist caught him in his lean belly just above the ornate gun belt buckle. He bent forward involuntarily to meet an upcoming right uppercut that connected solidly under his chin. His head snapped back and he sat down hard on his flat horse-man's butt in a fresh pile of manure that had been strategically dropped there by Brasada's dun.

"Jeeeesus!" cried Barney Gadkin in delight.

Mick Dallas clawed for his Colt. A right bootheel connected solidly with his jaw and snapped his head backward so that he fell flat on his back.

"Stand back, you!" the woman snapped.

Brasada looked up into the twin muzzles of a double-barreled derringer she held in her little gloved hand. "Get up, Mick!" she ordered. Mick tried to get up. "Get up, damn you!" she snapped. Mick got slowly to his feet, wiping the blood from his mouth with the back of a hand but his flat eyes were fixed on Brasada. He dropped his bloody hand to the butt of his Colt.

"Wait," warned Brasada in a curiously soft voice.

Mick Dallas looked at the slim-bladed knife held by its tip in Brasada's right hand. He looked up into Brasada's gray eyes and he did not close his hand about the butt of his Colt.

"Pick up my Colt and hand it to me," ordered Brasada. "Butt first."

Mick Dallas didn't want to do it; God Almighty how he hated to humble himself in front of the bearded stranger from Sonora, but he saw the hint of sudden death in those cold gray eyes. He backed slowly to the Colt and picked it up, keeping his eyes on Brasada. He walked slowly to Brasada and handed him the Colt, butt foremost. Brasada took the proffered Colt and stepped back. He did the border shift, the knife passing from right to left hand and the Colt from left to right. He sheathed the Colt and held the knife down at his left side. He glanced up at the woman. "Put away the stingy gun," he suggested.

Mrs. Major O'Neil put away the gun. "The Soledad Hills are part of my husband's property," she said to Brasada. "Do you know that?"

Brasada shook his head. "The Soledad Hills *and* Soledad may be on Sonoran soil," he corrected her. "Until an international surveying team definitely locates the exact border line, Mrs. O'Neil, it is questionable on which side of the border they are."

"The original Spanish land grant included them as part of the Soledad Rancho," she countered. "At least the old town."

"Since that time," he said, "the land became Mexican, and then part of the United States through the Gadsden Purchase, and the rights to it may be in some doubt."

"Listen to the saloon lawyer," sneered Dallas.

Brasada smiled at him. "You haven't quite learned to keep your nose out of my affairs," he said.

"Keep off that land," warned the woman.

Brasada looked up at her. "I can always ask permission from the major," he suggested.

She narrowed her eyes. "You know my husband?" she asked.

Brasada nodded. "Long ago, ma'am. And before he took on a young wife to warm his aged bones."

"Jeeeesus," chortled Barney.

"Come on, Mick," said the woman.

Dallas mounted his roan. He and the woman looked down at Brasada. "Listen, you spic, or whatever you are," she warned. "Keep out of the Soledad

Hills and especially away from Soledad. Is that clear?"

Brasada nodded. He tipped his sombrero to her.

"I'll remember you, Brasada," warned Dallas.

Brasada smiled. "It's always nice to be remembered," he said pleasantly.

They rode together down the middle of the street toward the bridge. "He made a complete ass out of you," she said to Mick Dallas. Dallas looked back at Brasada. "He'll never get another chance," he said. "See that he doesn't," she warned.

Brasada put away his knife. He began to shape a cigarette. He looked up and saw the lean face of Manton watching him from the second-floor porch of the big building. The dun impatiently stamped a hoof. Brasada picked up the sack of brandy bottles. The necks of the bottles clinked musically. Barney coughed from the background. "You don't miss much," said Brasada over his shoulder.

"Are you really going to Soledad?" asked Barney.

Brasada lighted the cigarette and handed the makings to Barney.

"If you are," said Barney, "your head ain't working too well." He began to shape a cigarette. He looked after the woman and Dallas. "That was Mick Dallas, you loco fool," he said.

Brasada mounted the dun. "I promised you a drink or two for watching the dun," he reminded Barney.

Barney lighted the cigarette. "Is it the Soledad Silver you're looking for, or are you after the reward money for the killer of those men who died on that damned mountain?"

"Maybe both," suggested Brasada. He flipped a silver adobe dollar to Barney. "Buy a bottle on me, Barney."

Barney caught the coin. He nodded. "I don't get it," he said. He looked at the Mountain. "Why?" he added.

"The best way to find out who is killing those men who hunt for the Soledad Silver is to go look for the Soledad Silver. So, maybe I'll find the killer, and maybe I'll find the silver, and maybe I'll find both."

"All you'll find up there is an unmarked grave," warned Barney. "You got a Bible, or a crucifix or anything like that?"

"No, and no religion to speak of either." Brasada touched the dun with his spurs.

"Well, you'd better, by God, get one if you intend to stay around Soledad very long!" yelled Barney.

Ramon Sanchez listened from a side street. The strange bearded man did not look at him as he rode past toward the bridge. Ramon rode through the side street until he reached the dry cornfields beyond the town. He sank the steel into his sorrel and rode across country toward the hazy Soledad Hills below the great Mountain.

Celedon Vega looked up from his monte blanket upon which he was cheating himself at solitaire to while away the time between customers when the shadow of Brasada and his *cruz*-marked dun horse fell across the blanket and Celedon himself. Swiftly Celedon raked together the greasy cards and then shuffled them. Slowly, ever so slowly, he turned over the top card. "Mother of God," husked Celedon as he looked at the ace of spades. He looked up toward the broad, sweat-darkened back of the bearded stranger who called himself simply Brasada and suddenly the bright sunlight felt cold against his body.

CHAPTER EIGHT

THE BROODING woman looked up from the dying campfire. Hard-pounding hoofs echoed flatly from the close-in hills. Ramon Sanchez crashed through the brush and drew up his lathered sorrel in a hoof-pawing rear within a few feet of the woman. "The bearded one is riding to Soledad this night," he reported.

She did not look up at him. "How close is he?" she asked.

"A half a mile, no more, Consuelo."

She spat into the dying fire and stood up. "Did you not think he would see your dust? You goat with horns! Do I have to do the thinking for all four of us?"

Ramon swung down from his horse. "What difference does it make if he does see my dust?" he angrily retorted. "There are four of us and he is only one man!"

She looked sideways at him. "I ought to know," she pointedly said. "Three gutless men and a woman."

He glanced up at the darkening ridge above the draw in which they stood. Two sombreros could be

seen close together outlined against the lighter color
of the dusky sky. "Take care," he warned the woman.
"Sometimes of late, you go too far."

She looked casually at him. "Shit," she said lazily.
"Now, get up on that ridge with those other two he-
goats. Tell them to take off those God-damned hats!
A blind man would know they were up there!"

Ramon started up the slope accompanied by the
clashing of his great spurs.

"And take off those God-damned spurs!" she called
out. "Do you think the bearded one is deaf, *cabrón?*"

Ramon cursed with beautiful feeling, but under his
breath as he sat down and unbuckled his spurs. He
then walked up the ridge and sat down behind the
other two men. Ignacio One-Eye looked down at
Ramon. "She is in a foul mood, Ramon," he said.

"The bitch! Lately she is *always* in a foul mood!"
he snapped. "Look at her, the *bruja!* Some day I'll
grab her by those big *chichonas* of hers and heave
her as far as I can into the crucifixion brush!"

"She'd have her *saca tripas* blade hilt deep in your
belly before you laid a hand on her," warned Ignacio.

"Take off your hats," said Ramon.

Fat Pamfilo looked stupidly at him. "Why? This is
not a church," he said.

"Stupid!" snapped Ramon. "Your sombreros show
up on the skyline. The bearded one rides to Soledad
this night. He's up the road about half a mile."

"You're sure it is him?" asked Ignacio.

Ramon nodded. "He fits your description of the
bearded man at the *tinaja* where the old man was
killed. Besides, I heard him say he was going to Soledad. Also, he rides a *cruz*-marked *bayo coyote* dun
horse, as you described."

"Such a horse gives the rider good fortune," gloomily said Pamfilo.

"But he is not a Catholic," reasoned Ramon. "I
heard him say he has no religion. Therefore it is

logical to assume that he is not protected by the *cruz*-marked dun horse. I recall I had a cousin once, he that was an Abeyta, who was a confirmed atheist, and *he* rode such a horse. Well, one time in the Sierra del Pinitos . . . ."

"Shut your *bocas*, you cackling geese!" called the woman.

"Bitch," breathed Ramon.

They watched her smother the fire by kicking sand over it. "She'll want us to follow him to Soledad—after dark," said Pamfilo.

"She can follow him there herself!" snapped Ramon. "I wouldn't go within a mile of that place during broad daylight, much less after dark, for all the treasure hidden on that mountain."

Ignacio looked quickly at him. "*She* does not fear that place. If we let her go alone to kill the bearded one and she finds on him what he might have found on the body of the old one murdered at the *tinaja* last night do you think she'll bring it back to us like a good little *muchacha?*"

They heard the faint ringing of hoofs on the road.

"Why not kill him now?" asked Pamfilo.

Ignacio shook his melon of a head. "The range is too far and the light is too bad. If he is warned, we'll never catch him."

In a little while the ringing sound of the hoofs died away.

"Well?" called up the woman.

Ignacio One-Eye looked down at her. He wanted to follow the bearded stranger, but not to Soledad.

"Was that him?" she demanded. "Are you struck dumb, you one-eyed goat?"

Ignacio rolled his one good eye upward. "God give me strength," he pleaded.

"She's your cousin," reminded Ramon. He spat to one side.

"Twice removed," said Ignacio, "and I'm not even

sure of that." He glanced sideways at his two companions. "I can tell her it was not him," he speculated.

"You think she'll believe that?" jeered Ramon.

"You one-eyed bastard!" she called up. "Was that him?"

Ignacio shrugged. He looked down at her. "Yes," he replied.

"Then send that fatass Pamfilo down for the horses!" she ordered.

Pamfilo buckled on his spurs. "She means then to go to Soledad this night," he said.

Ramon thoughtfully picked his beak of a nose. "After all," he quietly suggested, "there are three of us, and *we* are *men*. Would it not be better to wait until tomorrow and wait to see what the bearded one does? Perhaps he will leave Soledad. Thus it would be a simple matter to ambush him elsewhere, thus avoiding Soledad altogether. Now I . . ."

Pamfilo stood up and put on his hat. "I agree," he said. He looked down at his two companions. "Who will tell her this?" he asked. There was no answer. Pamfilo waddled down the hill to round up the horses.

"What do you think he found on the old man at the *tinaja?*" asked Ramon as he began to shape a cigarette.

"Which *part* of the old man?" gloomily asked Ignacio.

They both looked quickly over their shoulders at the great dark mass of the Mountain, as though it was listening to them.

"You should have killed him at the *tinaja,*" accused Ramon.

"With Chiricahuas within a hundred yards of where I was hidden and Manton prowling around somewhere in the shadows?" demanded Ignacio. "Would you have done it?"

Ramon lighted his cigarette. "She would have made you go down there if she had been with you."

"Put out that light, you long-eared jackass!" she called.

Ramon quickly snubbed out the match. "She would have made you go down there if the devil himself had been down there."

Ignacio looked toward the darkening Soledad Hills. "Maybe he *was* down there," he said quietly. "There is something strangely familiar about that bearded one. I do not like it."

Ramon grinned. "Can you be sure he is not the devil?"

Ignacio stood up. "One can never be sure of anything around that mountain," he said. He started down the slope. Ramon placed his unlighted cigarette behind an ear and followed him.

Pamfilo led up the horses. The woman mounted. "Who is this bearded stranger?" she asked Ramon.

"I didn't hear him mentioned by name while I was near him," he replied.

"Can we be sure he found anything of value on the body of the old man?" asked Ignacio.

"Do I have to go over that again?" she demanded. "The old man Jubal was on to something, I tell you! I think the old major at the Soledad Rancho told him something. That was why he risked his ass at the *tinaja*."

"But the old man was around the Mountain for many years," reasoned Ramon. "He never found anything in all that time and no one ever bothered him."

"Ass!" she snapped. "Do I have to explain everything as though you were children? He never knew anything about the Soledad Silver all the years he was not harmed. Then he goes to the *tinaja*, where he has been many times before, and gets a bullet through his skull and his head cut off. Why? Because

he knew something, I tell you!" She touched her
horse with her spurs. "And why has the bearded one
gone to Soledad, of all places? Because he now
knows what the old man knew!"

"She has something there," agreed Pamfilo.

She looked back as she rode off. "What is it you
fear now?" she called back. "*One* man? Mother of
God!" She was still laughing as she vanished into the
deep shadows.

"She may be right, all the same," cautiously said
Ramon.

"*And*, after all, he *is* only one man," agreed Pamfilo.

Ignacio was uncertain. He looked at the Mountain.
"There is something about that bearded one that
bothers me, *amigos*. Something about him should be
remembered by me, but I cannot do it."

"He's a stranger," said Ramon. "No more."

"Meanwhile, *she* rides on to Soledad," reminded
Pamfilo.

"Maybe she's bluffing," suggested Ramon.

Ignacio gloomily shook his head. "She *never* bluffs,
that one." He looked again at the dark towering
mass of the Mountain with its rock helmet of a peak.
"God help us all," he said softly. "Soledad. . . ." He
crossed himself for the first time in many years.

They rode into the darkness. The sound of the
hoofs died away. In a little while a coyote cried
from the darkened ridge. A moment later one of his
mates echoed his cry from the opposite hill. Then
faintly a third coyote called, this time from the direction of the Soledad Hills. No one, except perhaps
such a man as Brasada, would have recognized the
crying as those of human rather than animal voices,
so diabolically clever was the mimicking.

CHAPTER NINE

THE MOON was rising but the Soledad Hills at the base of the Mountain were still in darkness. Brasada did not move as the moonlight crept across the valley and lighted the upper part of the Mountain and the tops of the hills. Then the moonlight touched the bell tower of the ancient church of Soledad. In a little while the upper parts of the larger buildings that had not been buried by landslides were slowly lighted by the moon and it seemed to Brasada that the darkness was really an ebbing tide and that the ruins were those of some ancient, long-forgotten civilization emerging from the depths.

There was no one there. *"The only color left around Soledad is lead—in the shape of a bullet fired into your skull,"* Manton had said. *"And blood red,"* Weed had added. *"It's a dangerous place, Brasada."*

Brasada watched the moonlight as it grew, lighting the half-buried *poblado*. It was almost like a dream landscape.

"Men tried to rebuild Soledad after the war," Weed had reminisced. *"Fortune, however, no longer smiled upon the place. The Chiricahuas controlled the area beyond the range of a trooper's carbine. Landslides*

cascaded down the side of the Mountain and in time buried the old mines and half of the town. Men began to say that the padres had put a lasting curse on the place. The town is said to be haunted. No one goes there anymore."

The air was absolutely still.

"All you'll find up there is an unmarked grave," Barney had warned Brasada.

Brasada could see the Campo Santo, the old burial ground behind the ancient church, now deeply undercut by the dry wash that ran in flash floods during the heavy rains. Some rotting coffins protruded from the bank, like the snags of rotting teeth in the mouth of a skull.

"When the war came," Weed had said, "the Mounted Rifles were ordered east. The Chiricahuas moved in on Soledad while the dust of our departure was still settling on the road through the hills. There were no survivors."

The bell in the moonlit church tower rang faintly, just once, and the echo quickly died out against the side of the Mountain. There was no wind.

Brasada led the rawhide-booted dun down to the wash and across it. He led it into the shadows of a thick *bosquecillo* of willows and cottonwoods that lined the bank of the dry wash.

Beyond the *bosquecillo*, and between it and the church, should be the everflowing spring that had made Soledad famous at the time of the padres. Brasada eye-scouted the half-buried plaza from the sheltered shadows. The church had been built there because of the ever-flowing spring. The story was that the padres, half dead from thirst, harried by the Chiricahuas, and lost along the base of the Mountain had taken refuge in the waterless hills. During the night a great rock had fallen from the Mountain and had struck the hard earth not far from where the weary padres lay sleeping. The sound of bubbling

water had awakened them at dawn and in the bright
sunlight that came like a benediction they had seen
the miracle of the spring that had been brought forth
from the sterile ground by the rock that had struck
it like the staff of Moses.

"So, naturally, they had to build a church there,"
said Brasada. He grinned. Still, the spring had never
stopped flowing since that time.

He led the dun to the water that welled up from
some hidden source deep below the church into a
chest-deep pool whose bottom had been neatly covered with stones and gravel and whose rim was
neatly flagged. Thick untended shrubbery, planted
by the padres, was still nourished by the overflow of
water and surrounded the pool. Brasada let the dun
drink. He withdrew his Winchester from its scabbard
and levered a round into the chamber, letting the
hammer down to half cock.

He walked to the front of the church and looked
out across that half of the plaza which had not been
buried by the foot of the great landslide. Empty
streets ended against the landslide. Decaying houses
stared back at Brasada with empty windows that
looked like eyesockets in a bleached skull.

Nothing moved. The shade trees in what was left
of the plaza stood absolutely motionless. There was
nothing there, and yet Brasada found himself looking quickly back and forth, almost as though there
was someone, or *something*, watching him from the
shadows—something that moved quickly back out
of sight a fraction of a second before he looked toward
it.

Brasada eased into the church through the opening
between the sagging double doors. Moonlight
streamed into the nave from small windows set high
in the southern wall of the church. Dust rose thinly
about his silent footfalls as he walked toward the
sanctuary. Here and there along the walls and in the

paved floor of the nave holes had been gouged by treasure seekers. The moonlight sent a ray through a window to rest it on the stolid Indian-carved visage of a crudely shaped and painted saint, or *bulto,* that stood in a dusty niche. Brasada tipped his sombrero. "Did they forget and leave you behind, my friend?" he quietly asked. He looked about curiously. The spicy odor of recently burned wax was strong.

Even the sanctuary had been desecrated by the treasure seekers. Where the altar had once stood was nothing but a chest-deep hole. Something squeaked in terror and scuttled for cover in the darkness when he pushed open the door into the sacristy and stepped down into the musty room. He snapped a match into flame and looked about. Plaster peeled from the walls. A pile of dried grass lay thickly against one wall. He opened the door at the rear of the sacristy and looked out across the rubble of the collapsed mortuary and the Campo Santo to the moonlit slopes beyond the dry watercourse.

He closed the rear door and walked out into the sanctuary and through the nave to the baptistry at the front of the church. He walked into the baptistry past the moldering baptismal fount and up the narrow winding stairway built into the immensely thick walls. Something struck at his face in the darkness and drew blood. He swept the squeaking bat hard against the stone wall and heard the little lifeless body fall down the stairway.

Brasada lighted a match. The trapdoor to the belfry was half ajar and even as he looked he saw the last of the bats flying through the gap in the trapdoor opening. He pushed up the trapdoor and stood up in the belfry beside the big single bell that still hung from its wooden crossbar, still held there by wide strips of rawhide that had set as hard as iron to hold the heavy bell in place for over one hundred and twenty-five years.

He looked out across the plaza and watched the bats wavering in an uneven line of flight toward the shade trees that lined the sides of the plaza. Then they too were gone, and the plaza was as empty and as lifeless as it had been when he got there.

Brasada looked under the thick rim of the bell to see the heavy clapper still hanging there. He touched it with a finger. It would take a helluva breeze to start that clapper banging against the side of the bell and there had been no wind at all when he had heard the bell ring. Yet he had distinctly heard it ring.

The dun whinnied softly.

Brasada dropped through the trapdoor opening and landed lightly on the stone steps. He made his way down to the baptistry and through the front of the nave to the church door. He rounded the side of the church and catfooted through the shrubbery to the dun. He led the dun around to the back of the sacristy and swiftly stripped it of saddle and gear. He carried the saddle and gear into the sacristy and quickly placed his two good Opata woven blankets on the pile of grass, then molded his saddlebags and cantle roll on the grass to look like the shape of a sleeping figure. He drew the blankets across the gear and raised his head to listen. The dun whinnied again.

Brasada opened the narrow door at the side of the sacristy that gave access to the narrow, twisting stairway which led up to the pulpit. He went silently up the stairs and stood up in the pulpit, perhaps six feet above the floor of the nave.

Minute after minute ticked past.

A stone clicked against the low steps at the front of the church.

Brasada stood back in the darkness of the narrow doorway at the back of the pulpit and looked sideways toward the front of the nave. One of the double doors creaked.

Three men seemed to materialize out of the shadowed darkness at the front of the nave. They passed silently from one shaft of moonlight to the other with their faces shadowed under the brims of their great sombreros. The moonlight shone on the naked blades they held in their hands. So intent were they on stealth, they looked only toward the sanctuary and not up at the shadowed pulpit and the man standing in the doorway.

Brasada stood just within the door at the bottom of the pulpit stairs. Moonlight leaked into the sacristy from a crack in the south wall. A shadowy figure moved toward the improvised bed on the floor. The moonlight reflected from a knife blade as it was raised high and plunged downward. The knifer dropped down on one knee to add killing weight to the knife thrust. Two more shadowy figures closed in on the bed.

The heavy barrel of the Winchester struck with killing force against the nape of the neck of the rearmost man. He went down without a sound. The second man quickly turned. The butt of the rifle caught him in the privates and as his body bent forward involuntarily from the agony of the low blow the rifle barrel caught him across the back of the head to dump him unconscious across the body of the dead man.

The knifer whirled and drew back his arm for a cast. The Winchester exploded at hip level and the 200-grain bullet smashed into the man's gut just as the knife was cast. Brasada neatly parried the thrown knife with the barrel of the rifle. The knife clattered against the wall and the dead man fell across Brasada's bed. Brasada hooked a boot toe under the body and rolled it from the bed. "Bleed somewhere else, *cabrón*," he said.

Gunsmoke rifted in the room and wavered toward the open door into the sanctuary. Brasada lighted a candle and stuck it in its own wax on the narrow mantel over the beehive fireplace in a corner. He leaned his rifle against the wall and shaped a cigarette. He lighted the cigarette from the candle.

The unconscious man moved a little. He opened one sick eye.

Brasada looked down at him with his back to the candlelight and his lean face shadowed by the great sombrero brim. "Do not try to reach the knife, *cabrón*," he warned. "Sit up!"

Ignacio One-Eye sat up and felt his melon head. "Mother of God," he murmured.

"I could have smashed it in," reminded Brasada.

Ignacio looked uneasily at the shadowed face. "Why didn't you?" he asked. He didn't really *want* to know.

"I want to ask you a few questions."

"I meant no harm," said Ignacio.

The sombreroed head shook back and forth. "You and your *compañeros* had naked blades in your hands. You came to kill." Brasada drew in on the cigarette and the glowing of the tip faintly lighted his face. Ignacio had a sudden queasy feeling in his rounded belly and an urgent desire to relieve his full bladder.

Brasada studied the caricature of a face worn by the Mexican. It was broad and dark, like well-oiled and very old leather. The skin was deeply pocked and a furrowed knife scar started where the bridge of the fist-flattened nose met the upper part of the empty left eyesocket. The knife in its course had taken the eyeball with it and then had curved under the cheekbone to vanish into the shaggy moustache that drooped on either side of the froglike mouth.

"Ignacio One-Eye," said Brasada quietly.

The one eye was fearfully startled. It peered anxiously up at the face of Brasada trying to penetrate the shadow of the sombrero brim. "I do not have the honor," said Ignacio with his best manners.

"Why did you come here to kill?" asked Brasada.

Ignacio smiled weakly. "Who meant to kill?"

There was no answer from Brasada. A cold bead of sweat worked its way from under Ignacio's thatch of dusty hair and wandered down the furrow of the scar like a tiny seed pearl to vanish into the dusty thicket of the moustache.

Brasada smiled. "But, you are still alive, *cabrón*," he murmured. "For a time at least. Now, get up!"

Ignacio stood up. He swallowed a little.

"Who sent you here?" asked Brasada. He reached for his rifle.

"No one," replied Ignacio. He smiled beautifully. "I thank you for sparing my life, señor. You could have killed me as easily as you did the others. Such swift and efficient killing! It is an honor to know you, Señor . . . ?" He stared at the shadowed face trying desperately to link the quiet voice to someone he had known in his serried past and he was quite sure that he would be not at all happy at the reunion.

The rifle butt swung forward swiftly and tapped Ignacio hard over the privates and the Mexican felt his guts go loose. "No one sent us," he husked. "We saw you and the fine *cruz*-marked horse. We saw the good guns and the well-filled saddlebags. Times have been hard of late in the *bandido* business. I . . . ," Ignacio's voice died away. Sweat broke out on his face. "I think I know you now. . . . *Yes, I know you now!*"

Brasada slowly turned his head and raised it a little so that the candlelight touched his face.

"Mother of God!" cried Ignacio. "*Sargento Diablo!*"

Brasada smiled coldly. "So, you remember me, eh, *cabrón?*"

"It is impossible! I am sure I saw you killed by bandits at Imuris three years ago!"

"I am here, *cabrón.*"

"Is it possibly a miracle? Strange things happen here at Soledad."

"Touch me," suggested Brasada.

Ignacio reached out a hand and then quickly withdrew it. "No," he said softly, "for if I touch something, it is indeed proof that you are alive, *but if I do not . . .*" He looked away from Brasada. "I *knew* this place was haunted but she would not listen to me."

"Who is *she?*" asked Brasada.

"He talks about me," the quiet and hard feminine voice said from the rear doorway of the sacristy behind Brasada. "Do not turn too quickly, mister. That stupid one there thinks you are not flesh and blood. My knife can easily prove the issue."

Brasada slowly turned his head to look at the woman who stood in the doorway.

CHAPTER TEN

SHE WAS young but she had seen much of the seamy side of border life. Her face was broad and her cheekbones were high and her mouth was wide and full, but there was no feminine softness about it. Her hair was long and jet black and tied carelessly at the nape of her neck. Her eyes were as dark as her hair, large and dark, and there was no softness within them. She wore a low-cut *camisola* stained with old sweat, with a low neck that showed the deep V between her full breasts and the brown of her nipples showed through the thin worn material of the *camisola*. She wore a dusty *charro* jacket and soft leather trousers thrust into small boots. A pearl-handled pistol was holstered at her right side with the butt forward for a reverse draw and she held a slim-bladed throwing knife flat in her right hand extended toward Brasada.

Brasada politely bowed his head. "My house is your house," he murmured.

"A gentleman," said Ignacio. He glanced at Brasada. "Sargento Diablo," he warned the woman.

"He is mistaken in that," said Brasada. "I am Brasada."

"You seem proud of that," she said drily. She

glanced down at the two stiffening bodies. "You kill well," she complimented him.

"A marvel of scientific killing," agreed Ignacio.

She looked at him. "Shut your mouth, toad," she ordered. "You and those two stiffs there made a mess of this."

"It was you that sent them to kill me?" asked Brasada.

She shrugged. "Perhaps. As it was, they feared Soledad more than they did you."

"*That* was a mistake," he said. "Now, put down the knife."

She studied him, watching his eyes for warning of what might come to happen.

"Now!" he ordered.

She moved like a cat turning in midair. The knife flashed with accuracy toward Brasada's throat. He bent his head to one side and slapped the barrel of the Winchester hard across Ignacio's rounded belly to drive the wind from him. The woman dropped her hand to her pistol. Brasada kicked her low in the belly and as she bent to fall forward he caught at her to keep her from hitting her face against the flagged floor. His hand closed instead on the side of the jacket collar and the neck of the *camisola* and as she fell both jacket and *camisola* ripped completely down the side so that her upper body was stripped naked as she hit the floor leaving him holding jacket and *camisola*.

She rolled quickly over and over on the dirty floor and then rose to her knees, with her fine solid breasts, brown-budded, swinging fully with the motion of her body, and for a fraction of a second he almost forgot the business at hand. She reached for the knife. He kicked out at her and drove her flat on her back. She came to her feet like a bouncing ball and raked his face with her fingernails. Brasada straightened her out with a left jab and then followed through with a right cross that drove her into the doorway and flat on her back on the stones of the sanctuary where she lay still with a thin worm of blood wriggling from the side of her mouth.

Brasada wiped the blood from his face with the back of a hand. "Don't move again," he curtly warned Ignacio.

"I have no place to go," gasped Ignacio. "Is she dead?" It was almost a hopeful question.

He gripped her heels and dragged her into the sacristy. Her full breasts rose and fell with her erratic breathing. "*Ay de mi*," breathed Brasada in appreciation.

"Take her now, if you like," eagerly suggested Ignacio. "Otherwise, she fights, and it is hardly worth the effort."

"I wonder?" murmured Brasada. He looked curiously at Ignacio. "Have you added pimping to your many other felonies, Ignacio One-Eye?"

Ignacio was horrified. "She may be my cousin, twice removed!" he cried in outraged dignity.

"She is a murderous bitch," said Brasada flatly.

Ignacio nodded. "Worse than that at times."

Brasada picked up his rifle. "Why have you come to Soledad?" he asked.

Ignacio suddenly became brave. "Do you ask me as Sargento Diablo of the *rurales* or as a private citizen of the United States?"

"Either way," said Brasada. "*If* you still think I am a *rurale*."

"You have no authority here as a *rurale*. Therefore, I do not have to reply to your question. I . . ." Ignacio stopped short as the butt of the Winchester tapped him over the privates.

"Who really knows if this is Sonora or Arizona?" asked Brasada thoughtfully, as though to himself. He looked at Ignacio. "There are many charges against you in Sonora, *cabrón*. Horse thieving, petty larceny, rustling, possibly murder, and of course, a little pimping on the side." He looked at the woman.

"I never pimped in my life!" cried Ignacio.

The woman coughed. She raised her head and looked at Brasada.

"Well, anyway, *that* brought her around," said Brasada drily.

"This is not Sonora," primly insisted Ignacio. "Therefore, as I have said, you have no authority here."

Brasada looked down at the rifle. "No matter," he said quietly. "I can easily 'naturalize' you into becoming a good citizen of the United States, and you can even have a plot of good old American soil all to yourself—say six feet long and deep and three feet wide. . . ."

She sat up slowly and braced her hands back on the floor, thrusting forward those magnificent sweat-dewed *chichonas*. "You hit like a kicking mule," she said. Blood leaked from the sides of her mouth.

He touched his bleeding face. "You do pretty well yourself."

"You have food?" she asked.

He nodded. "Enough."

She studied him. "And the price?"

"All you have to do is ask. I am not a hard man. The price is up to you."

She stood up. "You horny ones are all alike," she accused. She picked up her ruined *camisola*. "Damn you! It's the only one I have."

"Then don't wear it when you plan to kill someone," he suggested.

She drew it carelessly about her upper body and knotted it. She looked sideways at Ignacio. "Did that ugly one-eyed toad talk too much?" she asked.

"Not yet," said Brasada.

"She knew this place is haunted," moaned Ignacio. "Evil always comes to those who come here looking for the treasure of the padres." He stopped suddenly. He glanced at her. "I have tried to tell her that, but she would not listen. But, she is always hungry, or thirsty, or crying for pesos or clothing, and so on and so on. . . ."

"A real woman," sympathized Brasada.

She wiped the blood from her mouth and eyed him over her hand. "You're right about that anyway," she agreed.

Ignacio glanced toward the doorway. "You do not have enough food for us, Brasada. Therefore, I suggest we leave now while there is still moonlight by which to see the way from these accursed hills."

It was very quiet in the room. The candlelight glittered on the staring eyes of Ramon who lay stiffening on the floor.

Ignacio turned and looked into the cold eyes of Brasada. "Mother of God," he muttered. He swiftly crossed himself. His one eye flicked down at the rifle and once again he began to calculate the odds on him getting as far as the sanctuary before a soft lead .44/40 slug would catch him between the shoulder-blades. "You can have the woman," he offered.

"She is not yours to give," countered Brasada.

Ignacio resignedly sat down on the steps that led up to the pulpit. "What is it you plan to do here in Soledad, my good friend? Hunting? There is little game. Prospecting? There is little color."

"Prospecting here will be better pay than that of a sergeant of *Rurales*," replied Brasada.

A faint ray of hope sparked into life within Ignacio's breast, but he knew well enough he was not yet out of the net. "I can help you, Brasada. As you probably know from my past, few men in Sonora and Arizona know the lore of prospecting better than Ignacio One-Eye. I recall one time, perhaps twenty years ago, when I was prospecting near Baroyeca. They all laughed, those witless ones. 'Look at him!'

they would jeer. Well, I . . ." His voice died away.

The woman laughed.

Brasada studied Ignacio. The Mexican was right. Few men in Arizona or Sonora knew the lore of prospecting better than did Ignacio One-Eye, except that he did not mean prospecting, but rather the lore and legend of lost mines, probably including the Soledad Silver. In short, he was a remarkably unsuccessful treasure hunter.

Sweat greased Ignacio's dark face. He swallowed a little. Life or death was probably in the next cast of the dice.

"All right," said Brasada at last. "I can use you a little. But, if you doublecross me, Ignacio . . ." His voice died away. Ignacio had looked startled down at the front of his trousers and then he fled at great speed through the door that led to the Campo Santo.

"God, how he fears you," said the woman. "He has wet both his legs with relief."

"Do you come along with the deal?" he asked.

She shrugged. "Why not? I am more of a man than he is."

"I hope not," he said suggestively.

She walked to him and withdrew the makings from his shirt pocket. He caught the full animal scent of her, compounded of stale sweat, cheap perfume, and an indefinite something else that drew him to her and repelled him at the same time. She expertly shaped a cigarette and placed it between his lips, then fashioned one swiftly for herself. He held the candle to light her cigarette and his.

"Can you cook?" he asked.

"Get rid of that carrion," she said casually, jerking a thumb at the two dead men.

Brasada dragged Ramon out by the heels and laid him neatly beside the mortuary. He returned for Pamfilo. She was inspecting the contents of his saddlebags. He dragged Pamfilo out to his companion.

"Together, in death, as in life," he drily quoted.

The three of them ate, squatting on their heels about the dying fire in the fireplace. Ignacio mopped his plate with a piece of tortilla. He belched politely. Brasada handed him the makings. Ignacio shaped a cigarette and lighted it. He sat on the pulpit steps and looked curiously at Brasada.

"What is it you see, Ignacio One-Eye?" asked Brasada.

"I am not sure. The youth is gone from your face."

"I am five years older than the last time I chased you from Sonora into Arizona."

"It is more than that. Why have you really come back, my old friend?"

"To find the lost silver of the padres," said Brasada.

The cigarette fell from Ignacio's suddenly opened mouth. The woman stopped eating her beans. A little trickling of chile juice ran from the corners of her mouth.

Brasada filled three cups with brandy. "Your surprised act is very good," he complimented them. He grinned. "You knew why I had come here all along." He handed them their brandy. "I recall, some years back, Ignacio, that few men knew more about the Soledad Silver than you did."

"It is true," agreed Ignacio.

"A madness," put in the woman.

Brasada looked at her. "Still, *you* are here," he said. He looked at Ignacio. "But you never got close to it, eh?"

"Why do you say so?" asked Ignacio.

"Because you are still alive."

Ignacio looked quickly about and then crossed himself. "It is even dangerous to talk about the lost silver ingots while one is in Soledad."

"The Soledad Silver?" innocently asked Brasada.

"Careful!" hissed Ignacio.

The woman laughed. "Superstitious shit," she jeered.

Ignacio leaned forward toward Brasada. "One is always being watched if he hunts for the silver, therefore, when I did hunt for it, I hunted only on the darkest of nights."

"Which is why you never found it," said the woman.

"Before the good God," continued Ignacio, ignoring the laughing woman. "To even *talk* about hunting for the silver is dangerous. The Mountain *listens*, Brasada! The Mountain *knows!* To hunt for the treasure in the daylight or moonlight is to invite a bullet into the skull! Look from the front door of this very church, Brasada! Almost within the range of the eye in any direction twelve men have died in such a way in the past few years."

"And another such a one died last night," added Brasada.

The Mexican and the woman looked at each other past Brasada.

"I, myself, have been fired upon while on the slopes of the Mountain not far from the *tinaja* where the old man was murdered yesterday. I was up there one sunny day. I saw nothing. I heard nothing. Then the big bullet came whining through the still hot air, and, far up the slopes, where a gecko lizard would not risk his life by crawling about, I saw the deadly white puff of smoke from the rifle!" related Ignacio.

"And you were not hit?" asked Brasada.

"Am I not here in good health? Only by God's grace was I saved. At the instant the shot was fired a rattlesnake struck my leg and the fangs caught in my thick legging." Ignacio picked up his dusty sombrero and thrust a finger into a neat black-rimmed hole in the side of the sombrero. He turned the hat to show where the bullet had exited. "The slug passed through

my hair. An inch or two lower and I would not be
here to tell about it."

"What happened to the bullet?" asked Brasada.

Ignacio looked curiously at him. "It struck a rock
and seemed to explode."

"Can you remember the place where you were
fired upon?" asked Brasada.

The one eye became veiled. "I am not sure."

"You have no idea who fired upon you?"

"Who knows? The killer has never been seen. He
might have been seen by some, but they never lived
to tell about it."

"Maybe he was only trying to scare you off," suggested Brasada.

"No! He meant to kill me! As I said, it was only
by God's grace that I was saved by the snake."

"God thinks so highly of you," murmured the
woman.

"I am here, am I not?" angrily demanded Ignacio.

"But not by *God's* grace!" insisted the woman.
"How would you know if God had intervened to
save you?"

"I was born with a caul on my head," proudly explained Ignacio.

"You were born with shit on your head!"

"One does not joke about such matters," fiercely
warned Ignacio.

Somewhere beyond the Campo Santo and the dry
watercourse a rifle cracked like a splitting board. The
slug smashed through the thin dried wood of the
partially open rear door and struck the brandy bottle, smashing it into needle-like shards. The deflected
bullet struck the wall with explosive force and then
dropped to strike Ignacio between the shoulder-
blades.

Brasada swept the candle from the mantelpiece. He
snatched up his rifle with one hand and shoved the

woman back into the corner between the fireplace
and the wall away from the doorway.

Brasada's faint footfalls echoed in the sanctuary.

The pungent brandy odor hung in the sacristy.

"Mother of God!" moaned Ignacio.

"Shut up, *cabrón*," she hissed.

Brasada catfooted up the bell tower stairs. He
thrust himself through the trapdoor and lay flat on
the dusty warped flooring. Slowly, very slowly, he
raised his hatless head.

The rifle cracked redly from beyond the watercourse.

Brasada ducked.

The bullet struck the bell and shattered itself with
a sharp report. The bell rang loudly, echoing from
the moonlighted hills.

Brasada slowly picked a lead shard from his cheek.
He looked up at the leaden splotch against the pati-
naed bronze of the bell. "*Bastardo*," he breathed.

It was quiet again in Soledad. Brasada slid down
through the trapdoor and eased down the stairway.
He slid between the double doors and rounded the
shadowed side of the church to step behind a buttress
and look toward the naked hills. Nothing moved.

Brasada walked back into the church.

"It was a warning," moaned Ignacio.

The woman was watching Brasada. "He is right,
you know," she said.

"He fired at my shadow on the wall, thinking it
was me," said Brasada. "He meant to kill."

She shook her head. "If he had meant to kill he
would have waited for a better chance."

Ignacio looked sadly at the shattered brandy bottle.

"There are more bottles," said Brasada. He looked
at the woman. She stood beside the fireplace looking
at Brasada like a hungry cat.

"One had great foresight," murmured Ignacio,
glancing at Brasada's supplies.

"Get the horses from the *bosquecillo*," she ordered Ignacio.

He looked warily at the woman.

"Take good care," advised Brasada. "There might not be a God-sent rattlesnake in the *bosquecillo*."

Ignacio padded into the nave and was gone.

Brasada took the woman by a wrist and drew her close. She did not resist. He slid his other arm about her slim waist and drew her close and hard against his body. Her full breasts pressed hard against him. He kissed her. She worked her mouth sensuously against his. He tasted the blood and brandy on her wide mouth. He let her go and looked down into her face. She tilted her head to one side and laughed. "Sargento Diablo," she said, almost as though to herself.

In a little while they heard the soft thud of hoofs behind the sacristy and then Ignacio came in, humming softly to himself. He threw two blankets on the pile of dried grass and reached for a brandy bottle.

Brasada shaped two cigarettes. He placed one in the mouth of the woman and lighted it, and then lighted his own. He looked into her eyes.

"You have enough bedding?" he asked.

She shrugged. "One thin wornout thing," she replied. She looked at his finely woven Opata blankets.

"You can use mine if you like," he offered.

"Alone?" she asked speculatively.

Ignacio drank a little and then began to spread out the blankets.

"In the sanctuary, you," she said to Ignacio.

He looked up at her in horror. "That would be desecration," he protested.

"You're right about that," she agreed. "*Vamonos!*"

"Take a bottle with you," suggested Brasada.

He looked from one to the other of them and then picked up his blankets and the brandy bottle. He vanished into the sanctuary and they listened to his footfalls in the darkened nave.

"He'll sleep in the baptistry," said Brasada.

She grinned. "So, maybe he can start life anew tomorrow."

The fire was almost out. She blew out the candle and picked up a brandy bottle, pulling the cork out with her strong white teeth. He took the bottle from her after she drank and then drank himself. The moonlight still slanted in through the one small window high in the wall. The woman quickly undressed and lay down on the bed. Brasada drank again. He looked out through the partly ajar rear door. The moonlight glittered on the staring eyes of the two dead men lying near the ruined mortuary. He walked back to the bed and looked down at her. "How are you called?" he asked.

"Consuelo," she replied. She laughed softly.

From somewhere high on the slopes of the Mountain came the hoarse coughing cry of a hunting puma.

CHAPTER ELEVEN

BRASADA SQUATTED on his heels in the hot sunlight with his Winchester leaning against a tombstone beside him. The tombstone was between him and the dry watercourse and the place on the hillside beyond where the rifleman had fired from the night before. Brasada idly tossed up and down the heavy .50-caliber slug that had been fired into the sacristy the night before.

Ignacio clambered out of the old grave he had emptied of drifted earth and the rotting pieces of an old casket. "It would have been just as easy to have left them for the *zopilotes*," he grumbled as he wiped the sweat from his forehead.

Brasada looked up at the cloudless sky. Three *zopilotes* swung in lazy circles high overhead. "Drop them in," he said. "They're beginning to swell and smell." He looked at the slug in his hand. It had been partially deflected by striking the brandy bottle, and from the sharp sound of the report as it had hit the wall he knew it had been an Express bullet fitted with a .22 blank at the tip of the bullet.

Ignacio dragged Ramon to the grave and rolled him in. He glanced curiously sideways at Brasada as he went back for Pamfilo.

"Fifty-caliber explosive," mused Brasada. He looked across the dry watercourse and up the long heat-shimmering slope to the first line of the hills to about where he had seen the flash of the rifle fire. "Five hundred yards at least," he added.

Ignacio rolled fat Pamfilo into the grave on top of Ramon. He began to spade in the dirt.

"If he had meant to kill you he would have waited for a better chance," Consuelo had said.

"You searched the bodies of course?" asked Brasada.

Ignacio nodded. "Of course. A few pesos, no more. As I told you—times have been hard of late in the *bandido* business."

"But you believe there will be better times hunting for the Silver of Soledad?"

Ignacio looked quickly about. "The Mountain may be listening," he warned.

Brasada studied the caricature of a face worn by Ignacio. "You believe that, Ignacio One-Eye?"

"I know it," simply replied the Mexican. He rudely shaped the earth over the grave and then took off his hat. Brasada was caught by surprise. He stood up. Ignacio spoke out of the side of his mouth. "One never knows when God is watching. It is always wise to act as though He is."

"But how does that account for the fact that you came here last night to kill me?"

Ignacio looked quickly at Brasada. "Had I known who you were such a thought would have never entered my mind."

"One can take that two ways," suggested Brasada.

They walked together toward the door to the sacristy. "There will be a full moon tonight," said Ignacio.

Brasada nodded. "You're willing then to show the place where you were fired upon?"

Ignacio shrugged. "Why not? I learned nothing up

there." He looked sideways at Brasada. "Sometimes, my companion, I think you are more interested in the Killer of the Mountain than you are in the treasure."

"What about the woman?" asked Brasada. "Do we let her in on this treasure-hunting business?"

"She knows the Mountain as well, or maybe better, than any man I know, including myself." He looked sideways. "Perhaps even *you*, Brasada."

"But, can she be trusted?" asked Brasada.

"Not as much as me," replied Ignacio.

They looked at each other and grinned.

"Where is she now?" asked Brasada.

"She bathes. In a country where water is more valuable than gold or silver, she *bathes* in it. Mother of God! Such cleanliness!"

"Cleanliness is next to godliness, it is said," quoted Brasada.

The one eye studied Brasada. "With *her?*" asked Ignacio.

"Take your rifle up into the bell tower and keep watch," said Brasada.

"Will you show me what you found at the *tinaja?*" asked Ignacio.

Brasada nodded. "When I find out where she hid it," he replied. He walked around the side of the church.

"Well, I'll be Gawd-damned!" said Ignacio in good old Anglo-Saxon.

Doves cooed softly from the shady *bosquecillo* beyond the pool and the church. A sicklebill echoed a mockingbird beyond the *bosquecillo* in the hot shade of a canyon. Water splashed in the pool as the woman bathed.

Consuelo stood chest deep in the clear water in the shade of the trees that overhung the side of the pool but a shaft of dusty sunlight came through an opening in the leafy ceiling and shone on the wet brown back of the woman turning it into a soft golden hue. Her thick black hair was unbound and had been swung forward over one golden shoulder. The woman was softly singing as though deeply pleased with herself.

Brasada squatted beside her heaped-up clothing and shaped a cigarette as he listened to her pleasing voice. She turned slowly and looked searchingly at him and then waded toward him with the clear water parting from each side of her full breasts. Fine silt swirled upward from the graveled bottom of the pool and clouded the water. He reached out and placed the cigarette between her full lips and then lighted it for her. She rested her back against the side of the pool and stretched her arms out on either side of her on the rim of the pool.

She looked up at the towering Mountain with its afternoon veil of heated air shimmering up from the baking rock slopes.

"You won't find silver up there," she prophesied. "Only hot lead."

"One pays a price," said Brasada philosophically as he lighted a cigarette for himself.

"Where is the one-eyed toad?" she asked without interest.

"Up in the bell tower standing guard," he replied. He laughed. "Watching us with his one eye is more like it."

"The thought of the treasure is the only thing that will get him to go with you tonight up on the Mountain."

"You know all about that, eh? You listened?"

She shook her head. "One does not have to listen to figure that out."

"You've been up there with him?"

"I was raised a Catholic. I do not believe in suicide."

Brasada nodded. He watched the silt slowly settling

to the bottom of the pool to form a velvety brown
carpet over the neat stones and gravel that paved the
bottom of it. "What did you do with the thin roll of
paper you took from under the buttplate of my rifle
before dawn this morning?" he suddenly asked.

"I don't know what you're talking about," she said
easily.

The razor edge of the knife rested firmly against
her smooth brown throat. "It is hidden behind the
bulto in the nave," she said. He withdrew the knife
and gave her a hand from the pool. He watched her
in appreciation as she began to dry her hair. The
dappled sunlight brought out the rich golden brown
of her skin and the highlights from her jet-black hair.
She began to comb her hair with long and vigorous
strokes, shaking her head now and then as she did so.

"Where are your people?" he asked.

She looked down at him. "Where are yours?" she
countered.

"I never knew them," he replied.

"Then we're two of a kind, except that I *think* I
knew my mother."

Brasada grinned. "I was too young when they
killed mine," he said.

She looked quickly at him. "Mine was killed too,"
she said, "but I remember her well—that is, if she
was my mother."

"So?" he asked.

"Mexican soldiers raided a Chiricahua *rancheria*
not far from here about ten years ago," she said.
"They took me from my dying mother, if it *was* my
mother. She was pure blood Chiricahua. She was the
only mother I ever knew. She insisted to the soldiers
that my father had been a Mexican. They spared me.
I was the only one taken alive from that place of
blood."

He studied her. "I think she was your mother," he
said. "Perhaps she was right, Consuelo."

"Shit!" she snapped. "I would rather have been one or the other—a spic or pure Chiricahua rather than a 'breed.' Do you know what *that* means?"

He stood up. "Look closely at me," he suggested.

She studied him. "I don't know. The eyes. . . ."

"It was Comanche country then—the Brasada."

She picked up her trousers and stepped into them. "But no man dared call you 'breed' to your face." He handed her the *camisola* and watched those fine breasts become shrouded. She looked up into his face. "You know what happened to me when I was fourteen years of age?" She sat down and tugged on her small boots. "That was seven years ago." She stood up and swung her gunbelt about her slim waist with practised ease and then settled it. "I stayed then with the head man of the village. They called him 'alcalde.'" She spat to one side. "One night he came drunk to my room and had me there, a virgin, while his drunken wife laughed at the look on my face. After that, he had me regularly when his wife was too drunk to respond." She took her pearl-handled pistol from the holster and spun the cylinder to check the loads.

"You're good with the knife," he said. "Can you use that as well?"

"Try me," she suggested.

He took a silver adobe dollar from his shirt pocket and instantly flipped it high into the air with a spinning motion. The coin flashed in the sunlight beyond the tops of the trees and for a second it seemed to hang in the air. The pistol cracked flatly. The sharp report broke the drowsy stillness of Soledad. The dollar seemed to shoot upward with its own power and then it dropped swiftly to splash into the pool. The shot echo racketed through the empty hills and then died away.

Concentric rings of waves lapped against the sides of the pool. The coin lay on the silted bottom of the pool, shining brightly with reflected sunlight.

"You ruined a good dollar," said Brasada drily.

She dropped flat on her belly and thrust a stick under the water to draw the coin toward her. "Not for me," she said over her shoulder. She hooked the coin out of the water with the tip of the stick through the bullet hole. "I told you I had been broken in when I was fourteen. When the *alcalde* died I was fair game for every horny stud in the village. I stole a knife and a pistol and when I was out herding the goats I practised every day. After that, no man ever took me unless I let him do so. You understand?"

Brasada nodded. He watched her hip and rump action in appreciation as she walked toward the rear of the church. He shaped another cigarette and walked around to the front of the church. He softly walked inside into the shadowed nave and walked to the candle-scented *bulto*. His fingers closed on the roll of paper she had removed from under the butt-plate of his rifle when she thought he had been asleep, sated with sex and full of brandy. He grinned to himself.

He walked into the baptistry. Ignacio's brandy bottle stood in the baptismal fount. Brasada drank a little. He went up the narrow staircase. The bats had evidently abandoned it, at least until after the intruders left the church.

Ignacio was looking out across the half-buried town. "Nothing," he said over his shoulder.

Brasada handed him the bottle. "What did you expect?" he asked.

Brasada unrolled the paper and rolled it back the other way to flatten it out. He placed it on the wide coping of the belfry opening that faced toward the Mountain. He studied the markings on the paper. "Can you read it?" he asked Ignacio.

"Who can read bloodstains?" asked Ignacio gloomily.

"There are still marks and lines on it," said Brasada. "See? Here is what looks like a bell and here a cross."

"A big help," grunted Ignacio. A drop of nervous sweat dropped from his forehead. "Perhaps we can soak the blood from the paper," he suggested.

"No, it would soak out the marks as well. These lines look like the bottom and part of the sides of an equilateral triangle, but the top is covered by the blood and dirt."

Ignacio held the paper up toward the sun. "There is something marked at the top," he said. "It looks like a few wavy lines, but what it is I cannot tell."

"What does the bell mean?"

Ignacio shrugged. "Usually a church, but it can have other meanings, depending on other marks. The cross is the same—it may mean 'A Christian has passed this way,' which is a big help."

"Or it can mean 'Riches of the Church are buried here,'" added Brasada. He grinned. "*That* is also a big help."

"So," said Ignacio, "the symbols then must indicate Soledad, for there is no other church in this area, outside the one church in La Placita."

"And the Baptists didn't hide any silver around here," said Brasada, "at least from the looks of their church in La Placita."

"A Greek cross with a circle around it means that there is treasure close by," mused Ignacio, "but this cross has no circle around it and it seems to lean. There is another kind of cross, but I cannot think of the name of it."

"Saint Andrews," said Brasada.

Ignacio nodded. "Which means one is on the line of treasure."

"This is not such a cross. What about the wavy lines?"

"*Quien sabe?* Who can tell *what* they are? Perhaps

the symbol of the snake whose head points in the direction to be followed, but I see no heads on these snakes—if they *are* snakes."

Brasada shook his head. He looked across the heat-shimmering slope of the Mountain. "Wavy lines may mean water," he said.

"These do not look the same," said Ignacio.

"Jubal Conn was at the *tinaja* water hole. That is where he was killed because he knew too much. One of the lines of the sides of the triangle, if it *is* a closed triangle, extends from the wavy lines up the slope."

"To about where I was fired upon," added Ignacio quietly.

They looked at each other.

Brasada rolled up the paper. "The woman does not want to go with us—she claims there is no silver up there, but only hot lead."

"She knows too much," said Ignacio darkly. He looked up at the Mountain. "It is said that she was born somewhere on that mountain, spawn of the Chiricahuas. It is also said that anyone born on that mountain must some day return there to learn their fate."

Brasada grinned. "That should be easy enough. A bullet through the skull easily settles that issue."

"That is not what I mean. If she *is* pure Chiricahua, she knows that she must return to the Mountain some day."

"She's too border-wise for that," said Brasada. "No, Ignacio One-Eye, she will never return to the Mountain for that reason."

Brasada listened to the Mexican's heavy footfall on the stone stairway. He felt within a shirt pocket and withdrew the scrap of paper he had found on the slope below the position from where the killer had fired upon Jubal Conn. He took out a small round leather case and turned a strong magnifying lens out of it. He examined the paper scrap and then the paper map. As closely as he could tell, they were exactly the same.

CHAPTER TWELVE

THE LOWER slopes of the Mountain above the *tinaja* were still in pre-moon darkness but the peak itself was lighted by the rising moon. There was no wind. The quietness was almost overpowering.

"Look!" said the woman.

The whitish rounded object lay in their path as they left the *bosquecillo* and walked down toward the *tinaja*. The two bullet holes showed darkly on the sides of the flesh-stripped skull. The odor of decomposition hung about the *tinaja* area. It was particularly heavy in the area of Jubal Conn's coyote-opened grave.

Ignacio took the lead once they were beyond the *tinaja*. "There," he indicated, pointing up the darkened slope to where a rock dike thrust itself up against the loose flow of earth and rock like a ship's prow breasting waves.

They stopped in the deep shadow of the dike. "Where did the shot come from?" asked Brasada of Ignacio.

Ignacio pointed. "There," he said, "at the base of that line of dark belted material that lies across the base of the sheer rock wall."

"A trained mountain goat couldn't find a place to fire from up there," jeered Consuelo.

"At least six hundred yards or more," mused Brasada. "Why did you come here, Ignacio?"

Ignacio pointed wordlessly to where an arrow thirty feet long had been neatly chiseled into the rock. The dike itself slanted upward and the line of the arrow followed the upward slant of the dike so that the tip or point of the arrow indicated a course further upward across the talus slope.

Brasada traced the line of the arrow with a finger and stopped where the feathers should have been chiseled. He looked up the slope. An arrow without heft should indicate that the seeker of treasure should then go on to the next symbol.

"See?" crowed Ignacio. "It means the treasure is up there!"

"Or water," added Brasada.

"Do you know of any water up there?" demanded Ignacio. "A bird flying over there must carry his own canteen."

Consuelo hooked a small boot toe under a thin flat slab of rock that lay at the foot of the dike. She flipped it over. Plainly to be seen on the surface of the slab were the chiseled feathers of the arrow. "What does this mean?" she asked. Brasada had a feeling she already knew the answer. "You tell us," he suggested. She looked down the slope. "It means the treasure, or the water, is *not* up there," she replied.

Ignacio pointed up the slope in the direction indicated by the course of the arrow. "I had started up in that direction when the shot was fired at me," he explained.

"You can continue your interrupted journey now," suggested Brasada.

"The moonlight begins to light the slope," protested Ignacio.

Brasada smiled. "I'll cover you," he promised.

"*That's* a big help!" jeered Ignacio. "Why not let

me cover *you* while *you* go up there?"

Brasada smiled sweetly. "Because *I* have the *rifle*."

Ignacio wasted no time, hurrying to get ahead of the growing moonlight. In a little while his head bobbed up near a huge truncated boulder that thrust itself up boldly from amongst its lesser fellows.

Brasada was watching the upper slopes. Nothing moved. It was as lifeless as a lunar landscape.

"Something has excited the toad's dull brain," said Consuelo.

They followed Ignacio's course through the broken boulders. They were twenty feet from Ignacio when the stillness was sharply broken by a splitting sound high on the rock wall overlooking the slopes. Brasada threw an upward glance over his left shoulder. He handed the Winchester to the woman and dug in his feet driving hard to get footage on the loose rock of the slope. He extended his arms and caught Ignacio around his middle to drive him backward down the slope.

The huge detached rock slab struck the slope above the truncated boulder and then rebounded as though made of some elastic material. The slab rose into the air and dropped with uncanny accuracy right where Ignacio had been standing. Shards of razor-sharp rock flew through the air and rattled angrily on the slope. One of them struck Brasada on the nape of the neck and drew blood. The woman grunted in pain. Pieces of the broken slab rumbled down the steep lower slope followed by the rattling, hissing sound of displaced gravel and bits of broken rock. The echoes bounded and rebounded from the sheer wall of rock and then died away in the distance.

Brasada got to his feet. He plucked the shard of rock from his neck. "Bastard must be saving cartridges," he muttered.

Ignacio sat up and braced himself on his hands. Cold sweat ran down his face. "It is the Mountain! It is fighting back! It does not want to lose the treasure of silver again!"

"Bullshit!" snapped Brasada.

"But the rock fell right where I had been standing!"

Brasada reached down and gripped the Mexican by the front of the jacket and shirt close up under the throat. He drew him to his feet and thrust his bearded face and cold eyes close to that of Ignacio One-Eye. "Was it the Mountain that shot at you the first time you were here? The Mountain is *always* dropping such rocks!"

"But it was aimed at me! What if it had hit me?"

Consuelo rubbed a rock-bruised shoulder. "Beautiful flowers would have sprouted here after the spring rains. You're so full of crap, you toad, you'd make the finest of manure."

Brasada took the rifle from the hand of the woman. He looked up toward the place where the slab had become detached. Maybe Ignacio *was* right—it almost seemed as though it had been aimed with diabolical skill.

"Now you're thinking like him," accused the woman.

Brasada did not turn to look at her, but it was almost as though she had read his mind. He studied the moonlit, dreamlike heights that seemed to be ancient battlements, turreted towers, and thick keeps massively buttressed. "Home of the Thunder Gods," he murmured, almost as though to himself.

"It's true," said the woman.

"You really believe it then?" he asked.

"I can believe *anything* about the Mountain," she said simply.

He looked back at her. At that moment it seemed as though she really was pure quill Chiricahua.

Ignacio pointed at the boulder. "Look," he invited. There was another arrow chiseled into the rock and this one did not have heft and it did not seem as though such feathers had ever been chiseled at the end of the shaft. "If you are right, Brasada," he said, "we must return the way we came."

"Loco," said Brasada. He looked down the long slope toward the dim environs of the *tinaja* and the faint whitish shape of the skull of Jubal Conn. "But where?" he added.

"Crap!" put in the woman. "The arrows have nothing to do with that stinking treasure. They are Chiricahua. They simply mean that a Chiricahua is protected from evil spirits while on this part of the Mountain."

"How did you know that?" asked Brasada quietly.

"My mother was Chiricahua, and a *diyi.* You know what that is?"

"Medicine woman," replied Brasada.

She looked at him quickly. "You know much," she said.

Brasada waved a casual hand. "Get on with it," he said.

She shrugged. "These arrows were not chiseled here by the old padres. There was no need for them to do so. Why? The treasure is not here, Brasada."

"Go on," urged Brasada.

"And, if it ever was, it was hidden here well over a hundred years ago. So, for all those years, bits and pieces, great chunks and slabs such as almost landed on the toad there, have fallen from the Mountain onto the slope every day. So, Brasada, how deeply does your treasure now lie buried?"

Ignacio cursed softly under his breath. "The moonlight comes," he said. He reached inside his jacket and withdrew a misshapen dirty-looking lump of wax from which protruded four long candlewicks.

"God help us," the woman murmured.

Brasada eyed the evil-looking lump with distaste. "What is *that?*" he asked.

"It is a treasure-finding candle," explained Ignacio. "I got this candle from a very old man in Vado Hondo who told me that it is greased with the fat of a criminal who was hung for murdering his own mother and then buried in unsanctified ground. The old man was starving and too old to use it himself, therefore he sold it to me, swearing on the bones of his sainted mother (she that was a Salazar of good family) that it was infallible for finding buried treasure at night, providing that it was properly used."

"And that there was treasure there," drily added Consuelo.

"Go on," said Brasada, with a straight face.

"One lights each wick," explained Ignacio seriously, "then each of us grasps a wick and we walk in the direction where we suspect there is buried treasure. The wick that burns the longest indicates the direction in which we must proceed. Thus, by trial and error, we eventually find the treasure."

"There are four wicks and but three of us," said Consuelo.

"So I will hold two of the wicks," brightly said Ignacio.

"The moonlight is bright on the slopes," continued Consuelo. "We can be seen for a mile out there."

"We'll wait until the moon is gone!" cried Ignacio.

"So we can light ourselves with the wicks," said Consuelo. She shook her head. "What a lovely target."

Brasada grinned. "I can't believe it," he said.

Consuelo nodded. "Look at that stupid expression of his. *He* believes in *it*."

"We can go without her!" cried Ignacio. "Each of us has two hands, eh, Brasada?"

Brasada's shoulders shook as he turned away.

"You can go alone," said Consuelo.

"I can only hold two wicks!" snapped Ignacio.

"Then use your tail, *cabrón*," she said.

Ignacio looked at Brasada. "I swear by the bones of my sainted mother that this is true."

"You bastard," said Consuelo. "You once told me you never knew your mother."

"That was my father, you sacrilegious bitch!"

"He that was a priest?" she asked cynically.

Brasada picked up his rifle. "Come on," he ordered. He walked down the slope. The woman followed him. They reached the bottom of the slope with Ignacio puffing and muttering behind them.

Brasada turned to look up at the Mountain. His eyes narrowed. "Before God," breathed Ignacio. "Who is it?"

The man-figure came slowly and noiselessly down the slope on an angle from where the dark line of belted rock material appeared on the sheer rock wall.

"Apache!" cried Ignacio. "*Shoot*, Brasada!"

"Wait," put in the woman.

The man-figure came steadily on down the slope. As he came closer Brasada could see that he was an old man, a *very* old man, clad in thin worn buckskin. His figure was thin and emaciated. As he neared the waiting trio his face could be seen, an intricately worked masterpiece of lines and wrinkles imposed and superimposed on the aged skin. The eyes looked straight ahead out of that spiderweb of a face. He came closer and Brasada then saw the painted decorations on the thin faded buckskin shirt the old man wore. There were mystic symbols of the sun, moon, stars, thunder and lightning, water beetle, spider, and many other cryptic symbols. He was a *diyi*.

"Shoot!" said Ignacio. He grabbed for the rifle. The butt instantaneously came up and slapped him a little across the side of his melon-shaped head.

"No," said the woman. "Let him come on. I knew him as a child." She looked enigmatically at Brasada. "He is the grandfather of my mother."

"How you got around," murmured Brasada.

"He can't harm you and the toad," she said. "See? He is blind."

The ancient Chiricahua stopped and seemingly looked at them with his eyes. They were the color of cloudy milk. The head tilted backward as though the old medicine man was testing the night with senses other than his sightless eyes. But still, at least to Brasada, it seemed as though the ancient one *could see them*. The frightened words of Barney Gadkin came thronging through Brasada's mind: *Things will sometimes happen to you like they was perfectly natural and you won't ever be able to explain it—if you live to think back on it. And, if you do live through it like I done, them things begin to work on your mind, and you ain't ever goin' to be the same again—not ever. . . .*

The cracked voice of the old man broke the quietness. "Go back," he warned in Spanish. "The Mountain is not for such as you. This is a holy place."

"Where did you come from, old one?" asked Brasada.

The old man turned and pointed upward toward the sheer rock wall and the line of dark belted material. "There," he replied.

"No man can climb up there," said Brasada.

There was no response from the old Chiricahua.

Brasada raised his rifle. "I want to know," he insisted.

The woman held up a hand to Brasada. "Wait," she said.

It was very quiet now. There was a depth to the stillness as though it had been placed layer upon layer through the ages of time and not to be broken by man.

She spoke to him in the soft and slurring tongue of the Chiricahuas.

"Listen to her!" hissed Ignacio. "Before God! I always suspected she was the pure quill!"

The old man turned again and pointed toward the peak. He spoke in a low and insistent tone.

She looked back at Brasada. "He insists that you should go back while you can."

"Ask him why."

"It is said, with good authority," said Ignacio from behind Brasada, "that the only way one can find the Soledad Silver is to make a pact with the Devil."

Brasada nodded. "By selling him your soul." He watched the woman talking to the ancient man. "You should be willing enough to do that," he quietly added.

"*That* I do not have to do," said Ignacio happily. "For I have made a pact with *you*, my good friend. Together we will find the treasure, eh?"

Perhaps it was the moonlight, or the spell of the Mountain, but whatever it was, it seemed to Brasada as though the woman had subtly changed from the tough border type she was, clad in men's clothing, into something entirely different. He watched her broad face with its high cheekbones and dark eyes and the brown skin of her and the words of Ignacio rooted themselves in his mind. *Before God, I always suspected she was the pure quill!*

"So, then our souls will be saved," prattled on Ignacio, "because neither of us will then make a pact with the Devil."

Brasada turned slowly. "*Whose* soul will be saved?" he asked. Ignacio looked into the bearded mask that Brasada wore for a face and into those eyes of gray, like icy winter rain, and for an infinitesimal fraction of a fleeting second he almost thought he *knew* something. A weak warm trickling ran down his left leg and he ran into the shadows of the draw before he would unman himself in front of the bearded gray-eyed man who was now silently laughing at him in the moonlight.

Brasada turned. "Are you talking over old times?" he called out. "Get done with it, woman!"

She turned. "He says that white men must not hunt over the Mountain for treasures. They belong to the Gods."

"Shit!" snapped Brasada.

"Those are his words, not mine," she added.

"And you believe him?"

She shrugged. "The Mountain is not like other places. To *them* it is a church, Brasada."

"And you?" he asked.

"I am a baptized Christian," she replied.

"But the old ways have not died out within you, eh?"

"The silver is owned by the Mountain and the Mountain is the home of the Thunder Gods. The silver must not be taken from the Mountain. The Gods will prevent it," she warned.

He walked toward them accompanied by a soft silvery chiming of his spurs. "The padres took the silver," he jeered. "Where were his Gods then?"

"The padres took the silver," agreed the old man, speaking in good Spanish, "but they put it back, Brasada."

"You know my name?" demanded Brasada.

The old man nodded.

"The woman told you, eh?"

"I did *not* tell him," she said.

The old man looked up at the Mountain. "The silver is back where it belongs, and no living man will ever find it again."

"Wrong," said Brasada flatly.

The old man spoke again to the woman in slurring Chiricahua. She nodded. He walked down the slope picking his way with absolute surety, and again an eerie feeling came over Brasada.

The *diyi* stopped. He slowly turned and looked up at the two of them standing there in the bright moonlight. Ignacio shambled from the shadows, buttoning his trousers. The old man spoke clearly, almost with the voice of a far younger man, or so it seemed to Brasada. The *diyi* turned again and walked down into the shadows.

"What did he say?" asked Brasada.

She looked away from him. "I didn't understand him."

He gripped her by the arm and drew her close, thrusting his bearded face close to hers and holding her with his gray eyes. For the first time since she had met him fear weakened her bowels.

"Tell me," he demanded.

She closed her eyes to get away from his. "He said that unless we left the Mountain and never came back again to hunt for the silver, that two of us would never leave the Mountain."

"Mother of God," breathed Ignacio. He crossed himself.

"And you believe him?" asked Brasada of the woman.

"He has the power to forecast the future," she replied.

He pushed her back and turned to look into the deep shadows where the old man had vanished.

"He never lies," quietly added Consuelo.

"Shit," said Brasada.

"We should have killed him," grumbled Ignacio.

She looked quickly at Ignacio. "You shit in human form!" she snapped. "Would *you* have done it?"

Ignacio looked away.

Brasada looked up at the silent, grinning peak. He knew they were being watched right then.

They walked quietly to the horses and rode from the draw. The echoing of the hoof taps died away. Nothing moved on the Mountain as the moon drifted farther and farther westerly across the great sea of tumbled sand.

CHAPTER THIRTEEN

IGNACIO REFILLED his tin cup with brandy. The firelight glittered from his one eye. "There is only one living man who knows the meaning of that paper," he said. "The old major at the Soledad Rancho." He drank a little brandy. "The old one who has the redheaded *zopilote* for a wife. God's blood! Such a body! To know such a one in the feathers, eh, Brasada?"

"You were talking about the map," reminded Brasada.

But Ignacio's fertile imagination had taken the bit in its mouth and was not to be stopped. "Why did the redheaded one marry such a weak old man? She that devours men as a starving pig devours corn, and then casts aside their empty useless husks. They say she is an eater of men . . . and more men. . . ."

"Jesus God," breathed Consuelo. "Now the toad philosophizes."

"There was a better map once," continued Ignacio, "not this grubby little piece of bloodstained paper. The old major made it here in Soledad in the old days before the big American war."

Brasada nodded. "Cass Weed saw it once when he

was in his cups and he claims he forgot what he saw."

"Bullshit!" snapped Ignacio. "No man, drunk or sober, could have forgotten such a map!"

"He has a point there," agreed Consuelo.

Brasada lighted a cigar. "So, you think the old man still has that map, eh, Ignacio?"

"I give you a riddle," countered Ignacio. "There is no longer such a map, but it still exists."

"My God," breathed Consuelo. "Now we get riddles!"

"I'll explain," said Ignacio confidently.

"You'll have to," said Brasada.

Ignacio got to his feet. He walked to the rear door of the sacristy and eased it open to look out into the darkness.

"Watch out for a bullet in your melon head," warned Consuelo.

Ignacio closed the door and vanished into the sanctuary. They heard his soft footfalls in the echoing nave.

"There is no one there," said the woman.

"Just bats," added Brasada.

She spat in : the fire. "Including Ignacio."

"There *was* a map," said Ignacio from the sacristy doorway. "But no longer. Now it exists only in the mind of the old major."

"And the old major is also the only one who may know the secret message of the 'shadow writing,'" added Brasada.

It was very quiet. A faggot snapped in the fireplace.

"All right," admitted Ignacio after a time. His one eye studied Brasada seemingly with a new light. "But I did not know you knew of the 'shadow writing,' Brasada."

"Of it," agreed Brasada, "but not how to read it." He looked up at Ignacio. "But, you agree, the old man knows how to read it?"

"Before God," breathed Ignacio. "*He knows how to read it.*"

Brasada stood up and picked up his rifle.

"Where do you go?" asked Ignacio.

"To see the old major," replied Brasada.

"You're mad," accused the woman. "She'll never let you get near him."

"Stay here," warned Brasada. "Don't try looking for the treasure without me. Wait until I return."

"*If* you return," said Ignacio gloomily.

Brasada saddled the dun in the darkness. A cold wind felt its way through the darkness of the hills. The dawn was not far off.

"You know the old major has sent other men into the hills and to the Mountain to look for the treasure with information he gave them," said the woman from behind Brasada.

"Only of Jubal Conn," said Brasada.

"You know then that he gave the little map to Jubal Conn?"

Brasada nodded. He slid his rifle into the saddle scabbard.

"How did you know?" she quietly asked.

"Jubal sent a message to me in Sonora and told me about it," replied Brasada. "He wanted me to come and hunt for the treasure with him and to hell with the old major. I got here a little too late."

"He handed Jubal Conn a death sentence," said the woman.

He looked at her. "And you knew all along that Jubal had the map, eh? Who was watching me and Manton at the *tinaja?*"

"The toad."

"He could have killed me for the paper."

"He didn't have the guts to try."

He studied her shadowed face. "And you?" he asked.

She smiled a little. "*I* wasn't there."

He mounted the dun and reached down to hand her the little roll of paper. "Hide this," he advised her.

"You trust me with it?"

He shrugged. "You can't read it," he said.

"You're sure about that?"

He touched the dun with his heels. "I'm not sure about anything around the Mountain," he replied.

"Let me go with you, Brasada!" she called after him.

He looked back at her. "I work alone."

"She can kill if she has to," she warned him.

"So can I," called back Brasada.

In a little while the soft sound of the hoofbeats died away.

Ignacio spoke from the darkness behind her. "She'll never let him get near the old man," he prophesied.

"That was why I wanted to go along," she said.

"To protect him against a bullet in the head or from the woman?"

She walked into the sacristy. "Let me see the map," he suggested from behind her. She turned and looked at him. He shrugged. "Who can read it anyway?" he asked. He reached for the brandy bottle.

CHAPTER FOURTEEN

THE WOMAN came out of the ranch house and walked toward her saddled mare, slapping a quirt alongside her split skirt riding habit. Mick Dallas gave her a hand up into the saddle. He mounted his horse and the two of them rode off together.

The sun was warming Brasada's back as he lay in the tall grass of a scrub tree *bosquecillo* that wigged a low ridge overlooking the Soledad Rancho. Nothing moved at the *estancia* except the spinning blades of a windmill.

The old man came out of the house carrying a folding chair and a black-cased telescope. He walked down a grassy slope to a low knoll. He set up the chair and the telescope and threw back the cape of his old blue army overcoat. He lighted a cigar and sat down. He applied his eye to the telescope and began to study the sunlit heights above distant Soledad.

Brasada looked down at the scrawny birdlike neck of the old soldier. "Can you really read the 'shadow writing,' Major O'Neil?" he asked.

O'Neil calmly raised his head from the telescope but he did not turn. "So, it's really ye, Brasada?" he quietly asked. "She said ye had been seen in La Placita. How long has it been?"

"Over three years."

"A long time."

"Not so long," said Brasada.

"For *ye*, but not for *me*, Brasada. Were ye not afraid to come here to the *estancia?*"

"Of you?" asked Brasada.

"Ye have no need to fear me, Brasada."

"You are the only one here," said Brasada.

"Ye made sure all the others were gone?"

"And I've been through all the buildings to make absolutely sure, major."

Brasada walked around the old man and bent to peer through the telescope. The excellent German lens brought out the sharp striations and features of the sunlit peak. "You didn't answer my question," he said over his shoulder. "Men have killed and will kill again for the information you have, major."

"Maybe," agreed the old man. "But if *I* am killed, Brasada, no man will ever know the 'shadow writing.' "

Brasada shaped a cigarette. "But the map," he said. "Maybe that still exists, eh?"

"There are some who believe so," cautiously agreed O'Neil.

"But only you know the truth, eh, major?"

The old man nodded, almost complacently.

"And the young wife of your dotage is also waiting," suggested Brasada.

"She and that human wolf Mick Dallas. But I no longer fear them, Brasada. Fear is only for the young. I had more than my fill of it as a soldier."

Brasada lighted the cigarette. He looked at the sunlit peak. "There is a certain time of the day, perhaps also at a certain time of the year, when the sun strikes that peak and the heights below it, overlooking Soledad, and at that time the sun is at the right angle to shadow and bring out the symbols carved there many years ago by the old padres so that they might find their way back to the cache of the Soledad Silver. It is also said that only the old padres knew how to read and interpret such symbols. So, unless the padres gave this information to someone so that he might read the 'shadow writing' the cache of the silver will never be found."

Brasada turned to look down at the old soldier. "And every day," he quietly continued, "in the late summer and fall of every year since you came here to the Soledad Rancho, when the sun strikes that peak and the heights below it at a certain angle, you come out here to study the peak and the heights through your telescope as though it were the naked body of a beautiful and wanton woman."

"Yer simile is very poorly chosen," murmured O'Neil.

"But can you really read the 'shadow writing'?"

"Do ye believe in it?" countered the old man.

Brasada shrugged.

"Ye're lying!" accused the old man.

"Few men have the courage to say that to my face," warned Brasada.

"I have, and I will," insisted O'Neil. "I do not fear ye, as other men fear ye, Brasada. It is too late in my life for me to fear anything or anyone."

Brasada looked down at him. "You're sure about that, old man?" he softly asked.

"Why have ye come back to the Mountain?" asked the old man.

"Perhaps to help an old friend."

"Ye? Helping a friend? Is that all? Do ye speak of Jubal Conn then?"

Brasada suddenly looked across the head of Major O'Neil. The ridge was as it had been before with the scrub trees and wigged grass moving gently in the morning wind. "What did you give Jubal Conn?" he asked.

"Nothing. I hardly knew the old drifter."

"Now it is you who are lying." Brasada looked down at O'Neil. "Old Jubal is dead. Shot through the skull with an Express bullet from seven hundred yards range. His head was severed from his body and placed upon a rock at the *tinaja* so that he might look at the Mountain whose secret it would never learn."

"Ye talk like a drunken poet," jeered the old man.

"But whoever killed him did not find on his body that which you gave Jubal Conn."

"I wish I knew what ye were talking about!"

"You know," insisted Brasada. "You gambled with *his* life, not *yours*, by sending him out with that damned map. You weren't sure about that map, so you experimented by letting Jubal have it, to see what might happen. Well, now you know."

The wind died away and the windmill blades whirled slowly to a halt. The scrub trees and grasses on the ridge stood still. Nothing moved. It was very quiet.

"How many other poor fools have gone up on that mountain with information from you, old man?" asked Brasada. "How many of them ever came back to tell you what they learned?"

The old man looked up at the bearded face. "Did ye really come back to help old Jubal Conn, Brasada, or did ye come back to get the Soledad Silver for yerself?"

"Why do you ask?"

"Because I know ye of old. Ye are not the man to take unnecessary risks, Brasada."

Brasada smiled. "Most of my life has been a risk, major."

"But a calculated risk—*always*," countered the old man.

Brasada looked up at the Mountain. "You could be right," he admitted.

O'Neil placed a thin hand on the wrist of Brasada. "Take me with ye," he quietly pleaded.

Brasada looked down into the drawn face in which the bones of the skull were already asserting themselves in preparation for the death of the old man. Only the Irish blue eyes seemed alive in that skull of a face. "There are two reasons I won't, major," he said. "The first is that you could not live a day on that mountain. The second reason is your wife. Do you really think she'd let me take you from here with the knowledge you have of the Soledad Silver?"

"Ye'll never find the treasure without me," warned O'Neil.

Brasada laughed. "Old man," he taunted, "how many more years have you left to sit out here in the sun staring at that mountain just to keep alive? You know well enough that is the only reason she lets you live, because she believes, like many other fools, that you can really read the 'shadow writing.' "

"Damn ye!" snapped O'Neil. "Look through the telescope! If I show ye enough to prove to ye that I can read the 'shadow writing'—that I can really do that—*something that no other living man can do*, will ye then believe me?"

Brasada bent to the telescope.

"Sight on the very tip of the peak," instructed O'Neil. "Lower yer line of sight about five hundred feet. See there? The faint straight line that slants down about thirty degrees?"

"Just a split in the rock," said Brasada.

"Ye idiot! Look more closely! Do ye see any *other* line in that living rock that is as straight as that is and is at such an angle?"

"No," admitted Brasada.

"But ye also note how cleverly the natural lines of the rock blend with it, so that unless the sun strikes it at such an angle as we have now, it cannot be told from the rest of the rock lines?"

Brasada nodded.

"For the love av God, man! Study it! Stare at it with no other thought in yer mind, as I have studied it all these years, and know that it is not natural, but man-made, although how in the name of all that is holy those old padres got up there in the first place to mark such a line, *no man will ever know. . . .*"

Brasada studied the line. He could see now why it had taken so many years for the old Irishman to locate the line. If O'Neil had not told him the line was there, and man-made, he might never have seen it. He narrowed his eyes. He thought he saw something else, but the major had not yet mentioned it.

"Now look lower and to the right, at the base of the peak, above the talus slope, where the sheer wall is rounded—see there a line of dark belted material?" continued the major.

A tense feeling grew through Brasada. It was the same line of dark belted material he had seen the night before, sharp in the bright moonlight.

"What do ye see cut into the living rock, Brasada?"

Brasada stared. "Jesusss . . . ," he said softly. "What does it mean?"

"Ye'll take me with ye then? Up there?"

"You know I can't do that," replied Brasada.

Something cold and hard pressed at the nape of his neck. He heard the crisp double clicking of a pistol hammer being cocked. "Tis a double-barreled derringer," softly said the old man. "Forty-one caliber, it is, Brasada. Don't ye turn on me! The slightest pressure on this hair trigger will serve to blow off the top of yer head!"

A trickle of icy sweat worked down Brasada's sides from his armpits. The merciless old bastard had him cold.

"Ye know too much to leave here alive, Brasada," warned O'Neil.

It was very quiet in the windless air.

The flat crack of a distant rifle broke the deadly stillness. A sound like a stick being whipped into thick mud came from behind Brasada as he instinctively turned sideways. The derringer exploded and the slug skinned past Brasada's neck and the flame seared the skin. Something warm and wet struck the side of his face as he went to earth. The mingled shot echoes died away against the low hills.

Brasada looked up at the old man. His stomach almost revolted at the sight. The head had been driven sideways by the savage impact of the explosive rifle bullet that had slammed clean through the skull exiting on the left side leaving a hole into which a lemon could have fitted with ease. Blood and brain matter dripped down on Brasada's trousers. He rolled over once and lay flat with the major and his chair between him and the distant killer.

Nothing moved. A faint wisp of gunsmoke drifted upward from the *bosquecillo* on the ridge.

Brasada crayfished along the hard ground and rolled quickly into a hollow. He bellied along it to the shelter of the side of the house and sprinted for his dun. He mounted and wheeled the dun, ripping the Winchester from his scabbard as the dun let itself out in a free swinging stride up the long grassy slope.

The *bosquecillo* was empty of life. The fresh acrid smell of burnt powder hung in the quiet grove. Faint footprints crushed the dried grasses. Brasada picked up a scrap of grease-stained paper bullet patch. He walked down the slope and in a draw he found hoof-marks. A faint wraith of dust hung in the quiet air to the west—toward Soledad.

Brasada walked back to the *bosquecillo* and looked down toward the old man. The major sat slumped sideways in his chair, a distant tiny figure in an old coat of army blue. Brasada narrowed his eyes. In his imagination he saw a handsome blue-eyed Irishman, brave in brass and blue, riding to fight against Mexico. He saw him walking the plaza of Soledad looking up at the grim peak of the Mountain, even then probing for its secret. He saw him riding from Soledad into the battle smoke of half a dozen hard-fought battles of the Civil War. He saw him on the Great Plains, following the trail of Kiowa or Comanche. Now all that was left was a frail rag doll with a great hole in its skull and perhaps the secret of a great fortune in silver ingots gone forever.

A shadow drifted over the sunlit-yellowed grasses. Brasada looked up. A lone *zopilote* hung high overhead drifting with his outstretched wings resting on the rising wind, silhouetted like an ebony crucifix against the clear blue sky. Brasada raised his Winchester. The rifle cracked flatly and the echo tumbled over the rolling land to rebound from the Soledad Hills. The *zopilote* was flung upward by the impact of the .44/40 bullet and then it fell swiftly, end over end to strike the hard ground fifty feet from the old man.

Brasada ejected the smoking brass hull. It tinkled on the ground. He shaped a cigarette and lighted it, looking down the long sunlit slope over the flare of the match as he cupped it about the tip of the cigarette. He did not take his eyes from the old man as he slid the rifle into the saddle scabbard. He mounted the dun and touched him with his heels. In a little while a second wraith of dust drifted on the rising wind in the direction of Soledad.

CHAPTER FIFTEEN

A BLUEBOTTLE fly buzzed drunkenly over a drying pool of beer slops on the mahogany bar of the Union Forever. The sound was very clear in the quiet of the saloon.

Cass Weed carefully began to pour himself a drink. Manton's eyes followed the action from bottle to glass and then to the flushed face of the sheriff.

"It was the man Brasada who murdered my husband," insisted the Widow O'Neil.

"It was Brasada all right," added Mick Dallas.

The bartender was busy polishing glasses and not missing a word. There wasn't much else to do. The morning regulars had not shown up that day, chiefly Barney Gadkin.

Weed was puzzled. "But from what you told me, neither of you were at the ranch house when the major was killed, therefore how can you be sure that it was Brasada who murdered him?"

"One of my *vaqueros* saw him from a distance," confidently explained the widow.

"But the man Brasada is a stranger around here," said Weed patiently. "Was this *vaquero* of yours close enough to recognize Brasada?"

"Yes," replied the widow.

"And he described him to you, is that it?" asked Weed.

"That is correct," replied the woman.

"But you had only seen him once, here in La Placita, was it not?"

She nodded. "I'll never forget that face of his and those icy-looking eyes."

"And the *vaquero* was close enough to see those icy-looking eyes?" drily asked Manton.

She looked at him but he did not look away from the ice in *her* eyes. "It seems to me, Mister Manton," she said, "that you should be out tracking down the man named Brasada, with your well-known skill, rather than standing there and badgering the widow of the murdered man."

Weed looked into his glass. "He has had time to get back across the border," he mused.

"No!" she snapped. "He is near Soledad."

He looked at her. "You're quite sure about that?" he asked. "Why would he go to Soledad, knowing that he would be suspected of the murder of the major?"

She smiled a little. "Why, indeed?" she countered.

"And, even so, if he has gone to Soledad," added Weed, "he might *still* be in Sonora. We have no authority there, if that is the case, Mrs. O'Neil."

She looked at Manton. "It never stopped your deputy before," she said.

Weed refilled his glass. "Madam," he warned, "do not attempt to take the law into your own hands. That is all for now." He watched her and Mick Dallas leave the saloon.

"She'll be heading for Soledad," said Manton. "Maybe I'd better get on out there in case things get out of hand."

Weed shrugged. "It still may be part of Sonora, Manton."

Manton looked down at him. "It never stopped me before," he said. "She was right there."

Weed nodded. "Maybe you had better get out there. I don't want Brasada killed before I can question him."

"About the murder?" asked Manton quietly.

Weed did not look at him. "I want him brought back alive," he said.

"Sometimes I don't have a choice," said Manton.

Weed looked up at him and studied the lean triangular face with its perpetual look of gray coldness about it. "Maybe I'd better ride along," he suggested.

"I can handle it alone," said Manton.

Weed shook his head. "I want Brasada alive," he repeated.

"How long do you think you'll last out there?" asked Manton.

Weed got to his feet. He was a little unsteady. "I'll make it," he promised. He walked into the saloon office.

The bartender shook his head. "You shouldn't ought to let him go, Manton," he said.

Manton shrugged. "You heard what he said. I'll go get the horses." He walked out of the saloon.

Weed came out of the office buckling his gunbelt about his fat waist. "You take over, Baldy," he said.

"You sure you know what you're doing, Boss?" asked Baldy.

Weed put on his hat. He nodded. "Manton is too quick in his judgments; too quick with the gun. Brasada is probably innocent. Baldy, I can't risk letting Manton kill him before I know whether or not he is guilty." He walked heavily from the saloon.

Baldy poured himself a drink from Weed's private stock. He turned and looked into the mirror. "And he can't risk the chance that Brasada might know something he learned from the old major before he killed him—*if* he killed him." He downed the liquor.

The bluebottle fly buzzed sluggishly toward the bat-wings. Baldy watched him go. "Heading for the blood, you drunken bastard?" he asked. He mopped up the bar and then laughed at his own macabre joke.

Barney Gadkin stood behind the dusty window of Tatum's Gun Shop. He had watched Mrs. Major O'Neil and Mick Dallas leave town and ride toward the Soledad Road. Now he saw Manton and Weed riding the same way.

"You know damned well where they're going," said Tatum from behind Barney. He popped the cork on another bottle.

"And they can damned well go there," said Barney.

"You were the only one around here who was friendly with Brasada," added Tatum. He handed the bottle to Barney. "He's a friend of yours, ain't he?"

Barney shrugged. "I ain't got any real friends. Come to think of it, neither has Brasada."

"Well, anyways, you owe it to him to find him and tell him they're after him. They might kill him or something."

Barney laughed. "Brasada?" He shook his head.

"But he knows something about the Soledad Silver," persisted Tatum. "The old major must of told him."

"We don't know that."

"And he killed the old man once he knew the secret."

"We don't know that either," wearily said Barney. He drank a little.

"All right then! Let's get to the truth! The old man once told you something about the Soledad Silver. You told me that yourself. Thirty tons of silver, Barney! Think of it!"

"I've thought aplenty about it, Tatum."

"And you know the Mountain, Barney. You've been up there. You must have learned plenty up there."

"Yeh," said Barney drily. He turned and looked at Tatum. "If Brasada ever gets the idea I'm following him around up there I'll never leave that mountain alive, Will."

"You don't have to let him see you."

"Brasada?" asked Barney. He slowly shook his head. "Besides, there are other *things* beside Brasada up there."

Tatum grinned. "Like Mick Dallas and that red-headed bitch? And Cass Weed and Manton? What have you got to fear from them, Barney?" Tatum came closer to Barney. "Look, you go and warn Brasada. He'll be eternally indebted to you. Maybe he'll tell you all he knows about the Soledad Silver."

Barney studied the excited gunsmith. "I could swear you wasn't born yesterday," he murmured. "What's in all this for you, Will?"

"Just a fair share of the silver, Barney. Look, I'll give you guns and cartridges, a horse and some grub. And, best of all, all the booze you can drink."

"You want me to go up on that damned mountain to track down Brasada while I'm full of booze?"

"You can go easy on the drinking," suggested Tatum.

Barney laughed. "You got a great sense of humor, Tatum."

"Then you won't go?"

Barney looked through the dusty window toward the distant mountain, now somewhat vague and indistinct through the shimmering heat veils of the early afternoon.

"Barney?" asked Tatum.

Barney turned slowly. "Yes," he said quietly. "I'll go."

Tatum walked quickly behind his counter and took a Colt .44 from a rack. He quickly loaded it and then loaded a Winchester '73. "These guns are well used, but they work fine," he said quickly. "Better than the new ones, if the facts be known." He looked sideways at Barney. "What made you change your mind?"

Barney drank a little and then lowered the bottle. "For over a year I been standing around La Placita, wanting to go back up on the damned Mountain, and knowing all the time what might be waiting for me, and anyone like me who looks for the Soledad Silver. But, I got to go back, seems like. I . . . got . . . to . . . go . . . back. . ."

"You sound funny," said Tatum. "You sure you're all right? Why do you have to go back?"

Barney looked directly into the gunsmith's eyes. "Maybe it's the curse, Will. Maybe I know more about the Soledad Silver than I think I do. Maybe there's someone up there who knows about that. I just got to go back, is all."

Later, as Celedon Vega looked up from his monte blanket, he saw Barney Gadkin riding slowly toward the Soledad Road. In all the time Celedon Vega had sat there in the past months he had never seen so many travelers in one afternoon on the Soledad Road. He shuffled and cut his deck. He turned over the top card. "Sweet Jesus," he said softly. It was the ace of spades. He swiftly snatched up his blanket and headed for the nearest cantina.

CHAPTER SIXTEEN

"CAN YOU SEE IT NOW?" asked Brasada.

Ignacio stood in front of Brasada in the belfry of the church with Brasada's field glasses held to his eyes. "The sun is not at the right angle," he said.

The woman stood with her back to Brasada watching the ring of sunlit hills to the east, beyond the dry watercourse. "Nothing moves," she reported.

"Before God!" exploded Ignacio.

"You see it now?" asked Brasada. "It slants .downward about fifteen degrees."

"He can't count beyond ten," said the woman over her shoulder. "He has only ten fingers."

"Father Christ!" exclaimed Ignacio. "I see it at last!"

"Just think what he could do with two eyes," said the woman.

"What do you think it is?" asked Brasada.

Ignacio traced a design in the thin dust that lay on the wide coping of the belfry opening so— ⟜🗝 : "It is a key" he explained. "Let me see the map, amigo."

Brasada spread out the bloodstained piece of paper. "A bell, or what looks like a bell, perhaps part of a

gourd, which means water," said Ignacio. "A Latin
or Christian cross, and a broken triangle."

"Perhaps a continuous triangle," said Brasada. "The
bloodstains cover much of the top of the triangle."

"Sainted Backsides!" cried Ignacio in frustration.
A drop of sweat fell from the tip of his nose and
splashed on the paper.

"He'll wash all of it away," warned the woman.

"Water will not remove those stains," said Ignacio.

"Alcohol might," she said drily. "Your blood is
mostly alcohol by now."

"Listen to her!" jeered Ignacio. He looked at the
paper. "Then there are the faint wavy lines at the top
of the triangle."

"Snakes?" asked Consuelo.

"Water, more likely," said Brasada, "which brings
us right back to the *tinaja*."

"But the key, if it *is* a key, is at the other end of
the triangle," mused Ignacio.

"Which means one thing," put in Consuelo over
her shoulder.

"What?" asked Ignacio, turning to look at her.

"Your map is useless," she replied. She wasn't smiling, as though it was a joke.

"She means it," said Ignacio to Brasada.

"She is only a woman," said Brasada.

Ignacio nodded. He leaned from the belfry opening
and spat fully into the air as hard as he could. He
closely watched the falling spittle. He looked back at
Brasada. "It bounced to the left," he reported. "Thus,
I think, the symbols are in reverse, so the key must
indicate the *tinaja*."

Brasada looked at the woman. She shrugged. "He
means it," she said. "We might as well try it," she
added, "for someone is coming here from the hills."

Brasada picked up the field glasses. He focused
them on the two horsemen. He saw the shape and
movement of breasts on the smaller of the two riders.

"There is dust rising from the canyon to the southeast," reported Ignacio.

"Get down below and get the horses," ordered Brasada.

Ignacio fitted himself down through the trapdoor opening and was gone. The woman looked at Brasada. "You don't seem much concerned," she said.

He shrugged. "Why should I be?"

"They're looking for you," she said.

"So?"

She let herself down within the trapdoor opening and looked up at him. "That's what you wanted, isn't it?" she asked.

He raised the glasses again.

"The trap is baited," the woman added. "They come like flies to a honeypot."

When he looked down again she was gone.

A sharp splitting cracking sound came from the side of the Mountain. Brasada dropped to the floor of the belfry. Slowly he raised his head as he heard the thundering sound of the broken rock rolling down the steep talus slopes. Masses of rock struck with stunning force against the upper parts of the buildings that still stood above the earth and rock of earlier landslides. Gravel and loose rock hissed and rattled down the slope to move the bottom of the slope a little nearer to the side of the plaza on which the church fronted, and much closer to the old church itself. The echoes of the fall died away. Dust from the fall drifted away on the wind.

Brasada went below. Ignacio was leading the horses through the echoing nave toward the front of the church. Brasada walked into the sacristy. "Quiet," hissed the woman. "Listen!"

A thirsty horse whinnied from the shadows of the *bosquecillo.*

CHAPTER SEVENTEEN

"WHY DO WE WAIT HERE?" impatiently asked Ignacio. "The sun will soon be gone and the moonrise will make it dangerous to hunt on the slopes. Now we have the afternoon shadows. I . . . ." His voice died away. A horse had whinnied beyond the *tinaja* in the shadows of the *bosquecillo*.

"Keep that melon head of yours down," warned Consuelo lazily.

Brasada raised his head a little and looked down toward the *tinaja*. Nothing moved except the leaves of the white oaks and silver oaks of the *bosquecillo*.

"One man," said Consuelo, "with a thirsty horse."

Barney Gadkin came out of the shadows of the *bosquecillo* leading his horse. He staggered a little as he walked.

"He is very tired," observed Ignacio. "See how he staggers with weariness."

"He's drunk," said Brasada drily.

"You know him?" asked Consuelo.

"Barney Gadkin," replied Brasada. He watched the drunken man. "God alone knows what brought him back to the Mountain."

Barney let the horse trot to the water. He sat down

on a rock and raised his bottle. He looked up at the Mountain. "Up your ass, Mountain!" he yelled. The Mountain did not even bother to echo the insult.

Barney got up. He walked further down the slope and much closer to the Mountain. He threw back his head and yelled again. "Brasada!"

"Brasada . . . Brasada . . . Brasada! . . ." echoed the Mountain.

"You lookin' for him too, Mountain?" called out Barney.

"Mother of God," breathed Ignacio. "He plays with sudden death!"

"I know you're around here, Brasada!" yelled Barney.

The woman reached over for Brasada's Winchester.

"No," said Brasada.

"An easy downhill shot," she said.

Brasada shook his head.

She shrugged. "No matter. The Mountain will take care of him." Brasada looked sideways at her. There was no expression on her face.

"After everyone within two miles knows we're around here," grumbled Ignacio.

"If you shoot," said Brasada, "everyone within five miles will know we're around here."

Consuelo shrugged. "Everyone knows we're around here anyway." She slanted her great dark eyes at Brasada.

"Shut up," warned Brasada.

The dying sunlight sent a shaft of light through the tree tops and softly illuminated the bullet-shattered skull of Jubal Conn. The wind died away. It was very quiet.

Barney sat down and looked moodily at the skull. He raised the bottle to his lips and emptied it. He hurled it crashing against the rocks.

"He hasn't got long," prophesied the woman.

Barney staggered to the horse and withdrew a fresh

bottle from a saddlebag. He staggered back to his rock and sat down. He pulled out the cork and drank deeply.

High on the Mountain a rock detached itself and dropped far below to crash onto the slope with a sound like the report of a large bored rifle. Barney shot to his feet. He dropped his bottle and whirled toward the Mountain, clawing clumsily for his holstered pistol. He got it out of the holster all right and thumb-cocked it in the proper fashion and then he saw the rock bounding toward him with terrific momentum. He turned to run and dropped the pistol. The Colt, beautifully balanced in the hand, had a nasty habit of dropping on the heel of the butt. The ground was rock hard and the pistol was second-hand and had been well used, as Tatum had said. The sear was worn and it slipped on the impact of the butt. The Colt exploded. The soft .44/40 caliber bullet struck Barney behind the tip of his chin and clove upward through his mouth and the upper palate to drive with smashing force into his brain. He dropped as though poleaxed. The echo of the rock fall and the pistol shot racketed away together. Barney lay flat on his back, staring at the Mountain while dark blood dripped from his hairy ears onto the light-colored ground and formed black circles.

"Mother of God," breathed Ignacio.

Brasada looked at the woman. He almost expected to hear her say, "I told you so."

"Let's get away from here," pleaded Ignacio. "Look! The great shadows are forming on the mountainside. In a little while the sun will be gone. There is yet time to get to the arrow markings, Brasada. We can start from there."

"Those marks are Chiricahua," said the woman.

"Protection from evil spirits," jeered Ignacio.

"She might be right," said Brasada.

"You're getting as loco as she is," accused Ignacio.

"But if they are not," continued Brasada, "they point upward, which means, if we reverse all symbols and meanings, that the arrows indicate the area of the *tinaja*."

"Where we are now," added the woman.

"There may be other markings *above* the arrows," said Ignacio.

Brasada looked sideways at him. "Then go and look," he suggested.

Ignacio lost some of his bravado. "I can't go alone," he said.

Brasada drew his Colt and half-cocked it. "Git!" he said.

Ignacio got to his feet and looked down at the strange bearded face of Brasada. "Perhaps I was only jesting," he said.

"No," said Brasada. "Get up there!"

"You have the map," reminded Ignacio.

"You've memorized it by now."

It was very quiet. Ignacio slanted his one eye downward to look at the sprawled body of Barney Gadkin and beyond him the bullet-riven skull of Jubal Conn.

Brasada full-cocked the Colt.

Ignacio placed one slow foot ahead of the other as he walked from the rocky slope down toward the foot of the talus. Brasada let down the hammer of his Colt and sheathed it. Two minutes ticked past. Ignacio was out of sight in the rock jumble below Brasada and the woman. Brasada suddenly raised his head. He reached for his Winchester and quietly levered a round of .44/40 into the chamber. He raised the rear sight.

"He's out in the open now," said the woman.

Brasada nodded. He raised the rifle.

Ignacio looked up toward Brasada.

"Drop!" barked Brasada over his shoulder.

Ignacio hit the talus slope.

A flash of gunfire sparked on the slope beyond the *tinaja* and near the edge of the *bosquecillo*. The crack and echo of the big-bore rifle was instantaneously echoed by Brasada's Winchester. The echoes rolled and tumbled over each other and died away against the Mountain. A wraith of gunsmoke drifted up near the *bosquecillo*.

The woman raised her head. Brasada was gone. Only the smoke from his rifle hung in the quiet air. She bellied to the edge of the rocks. "Lie still," she softly called down to Ignacio, "or he'll get you with the next shot."

Nothing could be seen moving but the drifting gunsmoke.

Brasada worked his way bellyflat through the *bosquecillo* with his Winchester cradled in his bent arms. The acrid stink of burnt gunpowder drifted among the trees.

The faint sound of hoofbeats came from the gathering darkness. Brasada ran from the *bosquecillo* and dropped into a draw. He sprinted up it and then climbed up the side of it to look across the darkened open area. Something moved. He threw up his rifle for a snap shot but it was no use. There was nothing at which to sight.

Brasada stood there in the last of the light cursing softly beneath his breath. He had been so damned close.

Manton raised his head. He shoved forward his rifle and full-cocked it. "It's him," he said over his shoulder. "Brasada." Cass Weed crawled heavily up the darkened slope with his shallow breathing coming and going in a rasping, husking sound. "Wait, damn you!" he ordered. Manton slowly turned his narrow head. "Why?" he asked. He knew why.

Weed dropped flat, fighting for life-giving air into his lungs. "We don't know if he killed the old man.

He's innocent until proven guilty."

Manton turned his head. Brasada had vanished into the darkness. Manton let the hammer of his rifle down to half cock. "Bullshit," he said over his shoulder. "You don't give a tinker's dam if he's innocent or not. You think he *knows* something about the Soledad Silver. Well, maybe he does, but he's also a suspect in the O'Neil killing. He won't surrender to me, Weed, and I'll be God-damned if I'll give him a chance to shoot back at me!"

"Well, he's gone now," said Weed, with some satisfaction.

"I had him cold," said Manton.

"There's no reward posted for him yet," reminded Weed.

Manton turned and there was almost a satanic expression on his lean triangular face. "His head can keep until that time," he said.

Weed narrowed his eyes. "What the hell kind of a man are you anyway?"

Manton slid the rifle forward until the muzzle almost touched Weed's forehead. He full-cocked the rifle. A bead of sweat worked down Weed's fat flushed face. "Never once, in the years I've worked for you, Weed," reminded Manton, "have you ever questioned my methods, or the possibility that some of the men that I brought in dead, killed while resisting arrest, might have been innocent."

"I'm not the judge and jury," hoarsely argued Weed.

Manton nodded. "Why should you be, when I acted as unofficial executioner?"

"You got all the reward money, didn't you? I never claimed a cent of it."

"Why should you?" sneered Manton. "You sat on your fat ass in La Placita listening to your cash registers jingle while I was out on the Mountain or in the desert, risking my ass every minute I was out here!

Actually I'm the sheriff! Me, Manton! Not you, you tub of guts!"

"You could have quit," said Weed.

Manton shook his head. "It's all I know how to do and I'm good at it, Weed. Maybe the best in the business."

"Except for Brasada," corrected Weed. "I think I know who he is now, Manton. You'll never get him."

"I had him once!"

"He let you," said Weed. "And you know it."

Manton looked down at the rifle. "Well, it doesn't matter, because he and I will settle that issue tonight."

"You damned fool!" husked Weed. "Forget about killing Brasada to prove you're the best manhunter in the business. Don't you believe in the Soledad Silver? Brasada may know the key to it. Kill him and we'll never know."

Manton stood up and let the rifle hammer down to half cock. He looked down at the older man. "Maybe I figured on getting the secret out of him before he dies, old man," he said quietly. "Did you ever think of that?" He turned on a heel and walked away.

"You'll get nothing out of him," warned Weed. "You'll have to kill him first."

Manton turned. He smiled, except for his eyes. "I'll hold that thought," he said.

"Wait for me, Manton!" pleaded Weed. "I don't know this area! Wait for me!"

"Keep up if you can," said Manton coldly. He walked on.

Weed got to his feet. His breathing was shallow and irregular and he felt dizzy. He started down the slope in the direction where Manton had gone into the shadows. There was still some afterlight left when Weed stopped for breath. He could hardly go on. He leaned on his rifle, fighting for breath and then he realized he was standing out in the open. There was still enough light to silhouette his big body for a rifle shot.

"Manton?" called Weed.

It was very quiet except for the wind which was starting to blow down the slopes as it always did with the coming of the darkness.

"Manton?" husked Weed. He suddenly felt unutterably lonely. All the stories about that area crowded into his mind. He seemed to see in the distance obscenely moving figures of the night world, gibbering at him. He passed a fat hand across his perspiring face.

The rifle cracked flatly to the right of Weed. He thought he felt the passage of the bullet. He forced himself to run. The rifle cracked again. Weed plunged down the treacherous slope. Then he lost control and no longer could he hold himself back. He dropped his rifle. He awkwardly hurdled a dark place on the slope thinking it was a deep hole and when he landed his balance was gone. He careened wildly and then gained his balance again. He saw the looming trees of the *bosquecillo* but he could not stop his headlong flight. He stumbled and then smashed full tilt, face first, against a tree. He staggered backward holding his smashed nose and lips. He fell on his back and his head struck a rock half buried in the soil. He lay there, almost unconscious, trying to get up off his back because the blood from his nose and mouth was running down his throat. He beat feebly on the ground with his fat hands. "Manton!" he blubbered thickly through a spray of blood.

There was no answer from the clinging shadows of the *bosquecillo*.

Weed fought his losing battle alone. In a little while only his head moved back and forth and then his heart stopped. His head tilted sideways. Blood ran from his mouth and darkened the dried leaves. In a little while that stopped too.

Manton ejected the spent rifle cartridge as he looked down at the body of the sheriff. There was no expression on his face. He knelt and withdrew Weed's wallet. He emptied it. He worked Weed's diamond ring off and put it into a vest pocket. He stood up and vanished silently into the shadows.

Brasada catfooted through the *bosquecillo*. He looked down at Weed's smashed and bloodstained face.

"Manton could not have saved him," the woman said from the shadows.

Brasada shook his head. "It was likely his heart," he said.

"You know he could not have saved him," the woman said.

Brasada looked at her. "He panicked him," he said. "He let him run to his death." He looked down at the dead man. "But he could have prevented him from doing that. Still, one might say he died by his own hand."

She shook her head. "It was the Mountain," she insisted.

He laughed at her.

"It is true," she said simply. "The Mountain makes men die by their own weaknesses. Greed killed Major O'Neil and Jubal Conn—greed for the Soledad Silver. Liquor killed Barney Gadkin. This one was killed by fear."

"You make it sound scientific," he said. "Did the Mountain fire the rifle shots that killed Major O'Neil and Jubal Conn? Did the Mountain make a drunkard out of Barney Gadkin? Did the Mountain . . . ?" Brasada's voice died away. He looked down at Weed.

"Go on," she suggested. "I'll tell you. The rifleman is only the agent that kills. Barney Gadkin turned to drink because of what he had seen on the Mountain. This one? Was he not frightened by the Mountain and ran to his own death?"

He looked away from her. "Where is Ignacio?"

She shrugged. "About where you left him," she replied.

"Why did you follow me?"

"There are men prowling out there in the darkness who would kill you on sight."

He shook his head. "Not while they think I have the secret of the Soledad Silver."

She studied his bearded face and those strange gray eyes. "And when they learn that secret?" she asked.

He had no answer for that one. "*Vamonos,*" he ordered.

They vanished silently into the shadows.

Minutes ticked past. A gaunt yellowish-gray shape moved furtively down the dark slope. The lean triangular mask of a face poked into the edge of the *bosquecillo.* The narrow nose took in its fill of the fresh blood scent that had brought it out of the darkness. The coyote padded silently toward the stiffening body of Cassius Weed.

CHAPTER EIGHTEEN

THEY HAD reached the horses in the darkness before the coming of the moon. Brasada took a bottle of Jerez from one of his saddlebags. He drank deeply and handed the bottle to the woman. She shook her head and gave the bottle to Ignacio.

Brasada looked to the east. The faintest touch of light showed beyond the mountains. "We can't find anything in the dark," he said. "And in an hour those slopes will be lighted by the moon as though it was daylight. An ant could not cross them without being seen."

"There is no silver up there anyway," said Consuelo.

"Just how much do you really know?" asked Brasada.

"She talks shit, Brasada," said Ignacio. "The silver is up there."

"So is the rifleman," said Consuelo.

Brasada held up his rifle. "We could bait him again. I won't miss the rifleman this time if I get another chance at him."

"A good point, well put," agreed Ignacio. He suddenly realized who would be the bait. "Mother of God! Not *me* again!"

"Drink some more courage, toad," the woman suggested. "Brandy is the drink for heroes."

Ignacio raised the bottle and then as quickly lowered it without drinking in a magnificent display of discipline for him. He corked the bottle and gave it to Brasada. "But we may have the key to the treasure," he persisted.

"Then go and use it," suggested Brasada. "We will wait here."

"*Vaya con Dios*, cousin," added Consuelo.

Ignacio glanced fearfully at the Mountain. "But, if I go up there and find the treasure by myself, then it will be mine alone, eh?"

Consuelo shrugged. "Spend it in good health," she said drily.

Brasada leaned back against the dun and watched the desperate struggle going on between greed and fear portrayed on the face of Ignacio.

"Then it will all be mine," added Ignacio. "*That* is the law."

Consuelo looked at her fingernails. "Two men have already died this day because of that accursed treasure, cousin," she reminded Ignacio.

"Crap!" cried Ignacio. "It is plain that one died because of drink and the other because of fear."

Brasada took the reins of the dun and led him off into the darkness toward Soledad.

"What's the matter with him?" asked Ignacio of the woman.

Consuelo shrugged. "I'm not sure," she replied.

"Is it that he is afraid to go up on the Mountain for the treasure?"

"Brasada?" She laughed softly and shook her dark head. "Not him, I think. It is not fear, cousin. But still, it is true that the old Chiricahua said that only one of the three of us would leave the Mountain."

"Do you think he is fool enough to believe that?"

"He may have Indian blood," she said quietly.

"Brasada? It is to laugh!"

Consuelo picked up the reins of her mount. "Comanche," she added. She looked back at Ignacio. "Do you know what that means?"

"I don't want to think about it! Look! If the old Chiricahua was right, perhaps Brasada would be one that would not leave the Mountain. That leaves the two of us. We therefore seek and find the treasure and gamble on the fifty-fifty chance that one of us would survive. Is it not worth the risk, cousin? Think of it! Thirty tons of pure silver!"

"You think of it," she said. "I don't want any part of it."

His one eye was puzzled. "Then why have you helped him?" he asked. "Why did you come with us today?"

"You are too stupid to understand," she replied.

He studied her. "Perhaps you *are* Chiricahua," he said softly. "Before God! That's it! You would stand in our way to prevent us from finding the treasure!"

She led her horse a little way and then turned to look at him. "Haven't you figured it out yet? Brasada is not really seeking the Soledad Silver, you toad that stands like a man."

"Then what *is* he seeking?" demanded Ignacio. "For, before God, cousin, *that man seeks something!*" He was talking to himself, for she was already gone into the darkness.

For a moment or two Ignacio stood there, waggling his melon of a head and casting about with his one eye and then the goad of fear prodded him and became too much for him—that and the darkness and the lingering silence. He snatched up the reins of his horse and began to run after the others until he remembered what Brasada had said about Cassius Weed: "*He panicked and ran himself to death. He drowned in his own damned blood.*" Ignacio forced himself to walk on, swiftly of course, but with dignity. He would not look up at the Mountain whose very tip was faintly lighted by the rising moon.

Manton moved through the darkness toward where he and Weed had left their horses. He slapped Weed's horse on the rump with the butt of his Winchester and watched it gallop off into the darkness.

Mick Dallas raised his head and then his rifle.

"Wait, damn you!" snapped the woman. "That's Manton!"

Dallas turned to look at her. "I know," he said. "Maybe we ought to get him out of the way."

"And have the whole county down on us by tomorrow?"

He lowered the rifle. "Well, what idea do *you* have to get him out of the way?"

"Let Brasada do it," she said. "Get the horses."

Dallas carelessly stood up. He started after the horses. A rifle cracked flatly from the darkness and the bullet fanned past Mick's head. He hit the ground cursing and lay still.

The woman bellied to Mick. "It came from the slopes beyond the *tinaja*," she whispered. "How in God's name did he see you?"

Dallas wiped the cold sweat from his face. "God damn," he whispered. "That was close. If the light had been better. . . ."

"Brasada?" she asked.

He shrugged. "Listen," he said.

The sound of hoofbeats came from the darkness.

"Manton?" she said.

Dallas shrugged. "It might just be the sonofabitch who shoots at anyone who looks for the Soledad Silver," he whispered.

"You believe that fairy tale?" she demanded.

He looked at her in the darkness. "You're God-damned right I do!"

She began to laugh, pounding her clenched gloved

fists on the hard ground. "I've heard everything now!" she said.

Mick Dallas stared at her. A slow burn began inside of him. Mick could stand a lot if he had to but he couldn't stand having a woman, *any* woman, laugh at him.

She looked at him, and realized what she had done. "We're losing time lying here," she said.

Mick Dallas never took his eyes from her and he did not speak. She sat up. "Brasada will be long gone," she said.

She stood up and brushed off her gloved hands.

He looked up at her. "I hope to God you get a bullet through your head," he said coldly.

"To prove you're right?" she asked.

He shook his head. "To shut up that big mouth of yours," he replied. "Go on! Get on your horse! See what might happen!"

"All right," she agreed. "You lie there like a kid in bed afraid of the dark and *I'll* go find Brasada."

He watched her walk off into the darkness. In a little while he heard the sound of her horse's hooves. He sat up and looked toward the Mountain.

It was very quiet in the pre-moon darkness. Nothing moved and the wind was still. In a little while Mick Dallas crawled through the darkness to get his horse.

CHAPTER NINETEEN

THE MOON was rising above the far eastern end of the valley but the lower levels of Soledad were still in shadows, shielded from the moonlight by the Soledad Hills. Only the bell tower of the church was touched by the growing moonlight, that and the higher parts of the landslide slope that more than half buried the *poblado*.

"There is no one here," hissed Ignacio into the ear of Brasada.

Brasada did not move. He held up a hand for silence. He looked at the woman. She pointed up beyond the shadowed limits of the *poblado* toward the moonlit upper slopes.

"Some of her Chiricahua relatives," sneered Ignacio.

The woman shook her head. "They won't come near Soledad at any time, even for the water," she said.

Brasada looked at the high slope. "Who?" he asked, almost as though to himself.

Ignacio raised his rifle. "Let us go up there and find out," he suggested. There wasn't much enthusiasm in his voice.

"You'll get an explosive bullet through your melon head, toad," she warned.

"Lead the horses to the rear of the church," said Brasada to Ignacio. "While there is still darkness there."

The dun whinnied softly, thrusting forward its ears toward the landslide area.

"A horse speaks with its ears," said the woman. "*He* knows, Brasada."

Ignacio was grumbling to himself as he went to get the horses. He gathered the reins together. Ignacio's roan whinnied sharply. The sound echoed clearly. There was a spark of fire on the slope right where the shadows made a sharp line of demarcation at the edge of the moonlight. Consuelo's sorrel threw up its head. The savage impact of the explosive bullet threw its head sideways, striking Ignacio in the face. He cursed as the sorrel went down. Ignacio's roan galloped off into the darkness. The shot echo died away along the side of the Mountain and it was again very quiet.

"Up there," said the woman. She pointed to where a large dike of rock seemed to breast itself against the great flood of broken talus, forming a shadowed hollow on the low side. Brasada nodded. A faint wisp of smoke had drifted up into the moonlight.

"Shoot!" hissed Ignacio from the ground.

"He's not there now," said Brasada over his shoulder. He shook his head in grudging respect for the unknown rifleman's marksmanship. "Six hundred yards, downhill, in uncertain light," he murmured.

The woman nodded. "He might have centered that bullet in the toad's melon of a head if my poor sorrel had not thrown up its head at that exact instant. That was a good horse too. Damn the luck!"

Manton had been under the flight of the bullet. As the bellowing discharge of the gun report died away along the side of the Mountain he tethered his horse in a roofless ruin on the outskirts of Soledad and

ripped his Winchester from its saddle sheath. He came
out of the doorway like a hunting cat and vanished
into a shadowed street that led toward the *placita*.

"It looks like I was right all the time," said Mick
Dallas from behind Mrs. Major O'Neil as the shot
echo died away. She turned on him furiously.

"Damn you! Don't sneak up on me that way!" she
snapped.

He grinned. "Getting nervous?"

She turned away from him. "They're over there,
near the church," she said. "Keep your voice down."

"Who's with him?" he asked.

She shrugged. "A spic and some kind of breed
woman. I saw them moving around."

"You should have taken a shot at them," he said.

"And warn Brasada?" she asked. "What's the matter? Are you afraid of him? That's it! You *are* afraid
of him. He could have killed you easily enough that
day in La Placita."

"He was lucky!"

She laughed softly as she turned away from him.
Slowly he raised his rifle and aimed the brass-shod
butt at the base of her shapely neck. Slowly he lowered it. It wasn't quite the time.

They walked slowly through a shadowed street. A
horse whinnied softly. Mick Dallas catfooted toward
a ruin. He walked inside. "It's Manton's horse," he
softly called back to her. "He's after Brasada all right.
I should have done it my way. I had Manton cold
back there. We could have blamed it on Brasada or
those spics with him. No, you had to let him go and
now we've got him in our way."

She looked up at the Mountain. "If that's Manton's
horse," she said thoughtfully, "and Brasada and his
spics are over at the church, who fired that shot?"

He came quietly to the doorway. "And you were
the one that said that the killer who shoots from that

damned mountain is nothing but a fairy tale?" His voice cracked a little.

There was no answer from the woman. Mick Dallas wet his dry lips and slowly passed the back of a hand across them. He slanted his eyes up toward the place from where the shot had been fired. The woman looked white-faced over her shoulder up into the taut face of Mick Dallas. She saw something there she had never seen before—fear, fear of the unknown.

Brasada stood back in the deep shadows of the *bosquecillo,* scanning the moonlit slopes with his field glasses. It was almost as bright as daylight up there. Nothing moved.

"You'll never find him," the woman said from behind Brasada.

"He's only a man," said Brasada.

She looked quickly toward the plaza. "Look!" she said.

By the time Brasada lowered the glasses the plaza was empty as it had been before. "Did you see who it was?" he asked.

"One man—Manton," she quietly replied.

Brasada nodded. He looked at her. "I'm going up on the slopes," he said.

"You're wasting your time."

"We can't be sure of anything with *him* up there."

"Manton?"

He shook his head. "The rifleman."

She looked past him and suddenly pointed. Brasada whirled and raised his glasses. A tall bareheaded man moved from one rock formation to another and then he was gone as quickly as he had appeared. "Harkness," she said. He looked back at her.

"You've seen him around here before?"

She nodded. "He stays somewhere around here. I don't know where."

He nodded. "Do the Chiricahuas know where he stays?"

She shrugged. "If they do, they've never bothered him. He probably gets his water here at the pool."

Brasada looked over the ruins and the tumbled landslide slope. "I'm going up there to take a look," he said.

"I told you you'd waste your time. You'll never find your phantom rifleman and the silver isn't up there."

He cased the field glasses and picked up his rifle. "All the same," he said, "I've got to go up there."

"I'll go with you then."

He shook his head. "I work alone," he said.

She watched him pass silently through the *bosque-cillo* and in a little while he was gone from her sight. She walked through the *bosquecillo* and slid down into the dry wash. She walked through the wash, out of sight of anyone in the town or on the moonlit heights until she could reach the rear of the church without being seen. She walked into the sacristy.

Ignacio was drinking from a brandy bottle. He lowered the bottle and looked sideways at her. There was fear and greed seemingly mingled in his one eye and the look on his dark sweating face. "Has he gone?" he asked.

The woman nodded. She looked sideways at the bottle. "Don't befuddle your simple brain with that poison," she warned him. "Manton is somewhere here in the town. You know him. He shoots first and asks questions later. He's still got warrants out for the both of us. If he has his way he'll reap a nice crop of them tonight."

Ignacio looked wistfully at the bottle. "I was just getting up my courage," he murmured.

"With *that*? It'll only betray you in the end, toad."

He nodded. He eyed her. "There are others here in town as well—the redheaded *zopilote* and Mick Dallas. I was up in the belfry and saw them amongst the

ruins." He grinned. "Manton was just in the next
street to them."

"Where have they gone?" she asked.

He shrugged. "*¿Quien sabe?*" he asked.

She fashioned a cigarette and lighted it. "Luke Harkness is somewhere up there," she said around the cigarette. She threw the match into the littered fireplace.

"Was it him who shot at me?"

She shook her head. "It is not Harkness who kills
on the Mountain." She laughed drily. "He's probably
the only one who doesn't."

"And the other one?" Ignacio asked fearfully.

She shrugged. "*¿Quien sabe?* He's up there all right.
Brasada has gone after him. The fool thinks he can
find him."

"There is a madness in Brasada," murmured Ignacio. He looked at her. "Does he really seek the Soledad Silver?"

She looked at the end of her cigarette as though to
find the answer there. "I don't know."

The one eye glittered under its shaggy eyebrow as
Ignacio watched the woman. "Would you tell him
where it was if you knew?" he softly asked.

She looked at him, but she did not speak, and a
great truth dawned in the slow mind of Ignacio One-
Eye. He slowly lowered the bottle to the floor as she
walked past him to the door that led into the sanctuary. She knew, he thought. Mother of the Devil!—
she knew!

He listened to her faintest of footfalls in the nave.
Ignacio wiped his mouth. He drank again. He
checked the loads in his pistol and loosened his knife
in its sheath. Still, he was afraid of her. She was fast-
er and more deadly with knife and pistol than he
would ever be. Yet he knew she'd never willingly tell
him about the silver. Brasada yes, but her own cousin, twice removed, would not get the truth freely
from her.

Ignacio drank a little more. His courage was fortified now and he did not fear her. He padded softly
through the sanctuary and the echoing nave with the
fine dust of over a century rising up to drift into the
slanted rays of the moonlight that shone into the nave
from the tiny windows high up under the eaves of
the church.

Ignacio peered into the shadowed baptistry. "Consuelo?" he softly called out. There was no answer. A
mouse squeaked and ran between his legs into the
nave. Ignacio soft-footed to the base of the narrow
stairway built into the thick walls that led up to the
belfry. A faint line of light showed through the partially opened trapdoor. Ignacio wet his lips. He wished
now for the bottle, but, as she had so well pointed
out, "it will only betray you in the end, toad."

Ignacio padded up the dusty stairway. He placed
his one eye to the crack in the trapdoor and slewed
it about trying to locate her. Gently he slid a hand
over the edge of the door. The hard boot heel
pressed down on the back of his hand and twisted.
"Mother of God!" he yelled.

She was on her knees as she pushed back the trapdoor and pushed her face close to his. "Shut your
boca," she hissed. "Come up here." He dutifully
obeyed her, sucking at the back of his hand, and his
one eye seemed to fill with venom as he looked at
her back. She was peering through a crack in the side
of the belfry, below the coping, looking toward the
Mountain. She held her cocked rifle in one hand. Ignacio slid his hand down to his pistol, shook his head,
then reached for his knife. Finally he crawled to her.
"What is it?" he asked.

"Look," she said.

Ignacio peered through the crack with his one eye.
The redheaded woman and Mick Dallas were standing just within the shadowed mouth of a narrow
street looking toward the front of the church. Even

as Ignacio looked at them they faded back out of sight. "They'll be coming here soon," said Consuelo.

Ignacio nodded. He turned to look at her. "Where is the silver?" he asked.

She looked down at his right hand. Ignacio's razor-edged knife was pointed at her belly. "Not here," she calmly replied. She studied his one eye. "If you shoot me, toad," she warned him, "you'll never know, nor will anyone else."

Ignacio's knife hand shook a little. "Then you do know," he said softly. She nodded. "Where is it?" he demanded.

The woman yawned. "If I tell you, toad, you'll probably die on the way to find it."

"But you will tell me?" he demanded hoarsely.

She shrugged. "Why not? If you want to die, I won't stand in the way."

He passed his free hand across his mouth. "Where?" he asked.

She stood up on the shadowed side of the belfry and with the bell between her and whoever might sight at her from the Mountain. "You can see it from here," she told Ignacio.

"Mother of God!" he husked. "Where?"

She laughed. "All I will tell you is that you can see it from here. Look here, over the edge of the belfry."

"You do not lie?"

She shook her head. She watched him sweat.

Ignacio slowly stood up. The rifle cracked flatly. Ignacio dropped flat as the bullet struck the bell inches from where his head had been. The explosive impact of the bullet made the old bell ring hollowly and the echo of the bell chased that of the rifle report until both of them died away against the mountainside.

"Before God," breathed Ignacio. He pointed the knife at the face of the woman. "You knew he'd shoot!"

"You stood up, ass," she replied. "Put away that knife before I take it away from you. Now go and find your silver."

He wiped the sweat from his face and started down the trapdoor. He looked back at her once. She was laughing, but silently, as Brasada laughed, and a cold and eerie feeling coursed through him but the fear was washed away in a roaring freshet of greed that flushed through his mind. He plunged recklessly down the stairs and into the baptistry. He pushed his way through the gap in the sagging double doors at the front of the church and stood there in the bright moonlight, looking frantically first one way and then another. He started to run, changed his mind, then ran the other way. He rounded the corner of the church. He looked up at the belfry. "Where? Where?" he yelled. He could not see her.

Ignacio looked toward the shadowed *bosquecillo*. He ran that way. He glanced once up at the Mountain but it seemed empty. He plunged into the *bosquecillo* and ran through it. Thirst began to grip at his dry throat. He turned and ran back through the *bosquecillo* with his breath coming short and erratic. The moonlight shone down through the treetops about the pool. He ran toward it and dropped to his knees to drink.

Mick Dallas came swiftly and silently out of the shadows behind Ignacio. He reversed his rifle and raised it. Ignacio bent his head down toward the water and at that exact instant the brass-shod butt of the rifle hit him hard and truly right at the nape of the neck. Ignacio fell silently forward and splashed into the pool and he did not come up again.

The moonlight shone down on the ever-widening circles that lapped against the flagged side of the pool but Mick Dallas was gone into the shadows from where he had appeared.

CHAPTER TWENTY

BRASADA RAISED his head from behind a rock ledge and looked down on moonlit Soledad. He could see someone moving about in the church belfry. He raised his rifle and looked up the slope. A rifle flashed and cracked. Brasada fired toward the flash just as the bell was struck by the explosive bullet. Brasada dropped and crawled along behind the rock ledge, half expecting a bullet in return for his. He reached the end of the ledge and saw something out of the corner of his eye. He turned and raised his rifle.

Harkness was running silently down the long rocky slope with his Sharps rifle at the trail. Brasada aimed at the big man and then lowered the rifle. He watched Harkness pass behind a rock formation that was situated in front of a sheer rock wall. Brasada catfooted toward the rock formation with his rifle held at low port ready to fire.

He paused in the shadowed shelter of a boulder. Someone was calling out down in Soledad. "Where? Where?" the voice wailed. Brasada grinned wryly as he looked toward the place where Harkness had seemingly vanished into solid rock. "Where, indeed?" he whispered.

Brasada padded forward. It was very quiet. He rounded the rock formation and stopped short. There was nothing to be seen except sheer rock towering upward and lighted clearly by the bright moon.

Something made Brasada turn his head. The wolf dog had seemingly appeared from nowhere. His ears were laid back and his tail was stiffly outthrust. His black lips were drawn tightly back from his long white fangs. The moonlight glistened on his eyes. Brasada did not move. He did not want to risk a shot and give away his position. Very slowly he leaned his rifle against a rock.

The wolf dog launched his charge. Brasada dropped his left hand to the haft of his knife and raised his right hand to the brim of his sombrero. He swung the heavy hat downward and sideways, turning his body a little, to cup the inside of the hat neatly over the head of the jaws. He heard the sharp snap of the closing jaws as he drove the knife home into the throat of the dog. Hard scrabbling hind claws ripped at Brasada's legs for a few seconds and then the dog dropped heavily to the ground. He coughed hard, spraying bright droplets of blood on Brasada's legs and then his head dropped.

Brasada stepped backward. He leaned forward and wiped the bloody blade on the pelt of the dead dog. Again something warned him. He turned quickly to look into the calm blue eyes of Luke Harkness. Brasada lowered his gaze and looked into the one black eye of the Sharps rifle muzzle pointed directly at him.

"You kill professionally, Brasada," said Harkness.

"It was him or me, Harkness," said Brasada.

"Can you kill me with the knife before the bullet strikes you?"

"Try me," coldly suggested Brasada.

The blue eyes studied Brasada. "You've very sure of yourself."

Brasada nodded. "Always," he said.

"And now you think you have found the madman who kills so often on this mountain."

Brasada looked down at the heavy, big-bore rifle. "It looks like it," he admitted.

"Drop the knife, Brasada," ordered the giant.

Brasada slowly shook his head.

Harkness levered down the breechblock. The ejector clicked crisply but no heavy cartridge struck the hard ground. "I have not fired this rifle in almost two years," said Harkness.

Brasada sheathed the knife. He felt for the makings. "I know," he said. "You don't kill, or so the story goes."

"Only for food," said Harkness, "and now I do not do that." He eyed Brasada. "And you, Brasada, why do you kill?"

Brasada lighted up. "Why, my giant friend, for the same reason you used to kill—to eat, but indirectly. How do you know my name?"

"I've heard it mentioned a few times. On the Mountain."

"You were that close to me and I didn't know it?"

"A number of times," admitted Harkness.

Brasada blew a smoke ring and watched it lift and waver in the still air. "What's your game anyway, Harkness?"

"Follow me, Brasada," suggested Harkness. He turned and walked toward the sheer rock wall and it seemed to Brasada that the man had walked right into the living rock. Brasada walked toward the wall with an eerie feeling crawling through his body. "In here," said Harkness. Brasada put out a hand. He touched solid rock. He stepped sideways and looked into a

man-wide passageway in the rock. He looked back. It
was almost impossible to know that the passageway
was there unless one was almost touching the side of
it. Brasada walked ahead and looked to his left into
what certainly must have been at one time the entrance to a mine. He walked in a little way and
came face to face again with what seemed like solid
rock until he realized it was a false wall. He rounded
it and walked into what had been the main drift of
the mine itself.

Harkness stood with his back toward Brasada, lighting a candle lantern. Another candle guttered and
flared in the cool draft blowing through the mine. A
bunk bed stood to one side. A rough fireplace was
piled high with ashes. Wooden shelves had been
rested on hardwood pegs driven into holes bored into
the mine wall. The shelves held food supplies and
many books. In a wall niche stood a stolid-faced
wooden carved *bulto,* almost the exact twin of the
one Brasada had seen in the nave of the ancient
church of Soledad. A candle in a red glass guttered
feebly, lighting the high planes of the crudely carved
face of the *bulto.*

The candlelight reflected from a massive cross of
silver that hung over the fireplace. Brasada whistled
softly.

"You are standing in the entrance to the great silver
mine of Soledad, Brasada," explained Harkness as he
turned. If he had expected to see excitement, greed,
or any emotion on the bearded face of Brasada he
was disappointed. "I have lived here the past four
years," he added.

Brasada slanted his gray eyes toward the darkness
of the inner drift.

Harkness took the lantern. "Would you like to see
the mine where thirty tons of pure native silver was
taken from the Mountain and cast into ingots by the
old padres?" he asked. He did not wait for an an-

swer. He walked into the darkness followed by Brasada.

The wavering lantern light alternately played
against the glistening walls of the drift or plunged
them into shadowed darkness. The light played across
a deep wall niche, fully the height of a man, and on a
bony face that stared back at Brasada with hollow
sightless eyes from beneath a dusty cowl. The ancient robe draped itself into the hollows of the skeleton beneath it and the bony toes peeped from beneath the ragged hem of the robe.

"He was here long before our time," explained
Harkness. He looked at Brasada. "The Church of the
Immaculate Conception in Rome has the open ceme-
tery of the Capuchin Fathers, which has displayed
the bones of over four thousand Religious who died
in the service of the Church between 1528 and 1870.
Some of them are as you see this one, still wearing
the robe of his order."

"I have seen such cemeteries in Mexico," said Brasada. He patted the robed skeleton on the head.
"How did he get here?"

Harkness seemed to look beyond Brasada, as
though into the past. "I found him here, as you see
him, left by the old padres when the mine was
closed."

"A *patron*, eh?" asked Brasada. "The ghostly guardian of the mine. How did he die, Harkness?"

Harkness did not look at Brasada. "I don't know,"
he replied.

"Was he left here to die of hunger, Harkness, perhaps because he had violated a rule of the order?"
persisted Brasada. "Have you heard his spectral voice
in the dark hours of the night crying out for food?"

Harkness held out the lantern to Brasada. "Would
you like to see the mine?" he quietly asked.

"How long has it been since you wore such a
robe?" asked Brasada.

The blue eyes did not blink. "Ten years," replied Harkness.

"You were sent here by your order to find the Soledad Silver?"

Harkness shook his head. "I broke my vows and came here alone, for my own purpose."

"After joining the order to learn all you could about the treasure from the present-day padres and after researching the archives of the order, perhaps in both Spain and Mexico, until you were sure you could find the silver?"

There was no answer from Harkness. His silence gave Brasada the answer. He took the lantern from Harkness and walked cautiously up the drift. Then he stopped short, more by instinct than by intelligence. The faint sound of rushing water came to him. He lowered the lantern and looked down at the floor. A yawning black hole was right at his boot toes. He took out the mutilated bullet he had found in the sacristy the night he had been fired upon. He dropped it. The faint sound of a splash came from far below.

Brasada walked back to Harkness. He held up the lantern to look at the calm face of the giant. "But," he said drily, "you never kill."

"It proves conclusively that there is someone, or something watching over you," quietly said Harkness.

Brasada nodded. "You could have asked me," he said drily. They walked together into the living quarters. Brasada looked at the massive silver cross.

"I made that," said Harkness. There was a touch of pride in his tone.

"From silver out of the mine?"

Harkness looked at Brasada. "Why do you ask that?"

"Where is the Soledad Silver?" asked Brasada.

"Do not try to find it, Brasada."

"You believe in the curse then?"

Harkness nodded. "I *know*," he said simply. "I came here with that one purpose in mind. It took me a year to find the mine and know that it was exhausted except for a handful of silver here and there —enough to grubstake me, Brasada. In time I began to realize what I had done. There was no going back to my vows. I stayed on."

"To find the Soledad Silver or to act as guardian for it?"

"Neither," replied Harkness. He looked at the stolid-faced *bulto* and then at the massive silver cross. "I took it on myself to act as caretaker of the church in Soledad."

Brasada nodded. "I thought it seemed to be in too good repair," he said. He looked at the *bulto*. "His twin is still there in the church. Someone had burned a candle before the one in the nave not too long ago. The pool, too, seems to be too clean and well maintained for having been abandoned for so many years." He looked at Harkness. "Someday the old Mountain out there will slide itself completely over the church and the pool. What will you do then?"

"Not in my lifetime," replied Harkness. "God wills it so."

Brasada shrugged as he began to shape a cigarette. "Each to his own," he commented. "You won't tell me where the silver is?"

Harkness shook his head.

"But you do know?"

Harkness nodded.

It was very quiet in the room as Brasada lighted his cigarette. "And the one who kills with the rifle? He's never bothered you?"

"The dog always knew when he was on the Mountain. I never took any risks, Brasada. But after awhile it seemed as though he was not really interested in me. Perhaps he knew I did not want the silver for myself. He seems only to kill those who are looking for it."

Brasada lighted the cigarette. "Who is he?" he asked.

"He is a sick man," replied Harkness.

"You have a quaint way of putting it," observed Brasada.

"Would you spare his life if you found him?"

"Sure," agreed Brasada.

"Can I believe you, Brasada?"

Brasada looked at the cross and then at the *bulto*. He quickly crossed himself. "There—you see?" he asked.

Harkness studied Brasada for a moment. "I am not absolutely sure," he said. "But for three years I have been fitting pieces of the puzzle into place until only two men seem qualified to fit the picture. Both of them are often in La Placita. Both of them are often around the Soledad Hills and the Mountain. Both of them are masters of the rifle. Both of them are most accomplished hunters of men, perhaps as good as you are in your profession, Brasada. Both of them are in a position to know who is looking for the Soledad Silver. Neither of them quite know where it is, but they believe they must be quite close to it."

"Maybe they do know where it is," suggested Brasada.

"That is also possible, but I do not think so."

Brasada studied the big man. "Manton?" he asked.

Harkness nodded.

"And the other?"

"I am less sure of him," replied Harkness. "You spoke to him in La Placita one day."

"I was only there a few hours."

"But you spoke with him. *Think!*"

Brasada shaped another cigarette. "Tatum?" he asked.

Harkness shook his head. "Tatum hasn't the guts to

come up here on the Mountain."

Brasada narrowed his eyes. He lighted his cigarette. He looked at Harkness's big Sharps rifle. Something someone had said came back to him—"That's a helluva good rifle, mister. Used two of them Big Fifties myself in the old days—buffalo hunting, that was. Pair of fine .50/90's. Got a lot of prime hides with them." Brasada looked at Harkness. "You've seen him on the Mountain?" he asked.

"Only at a great distance. He moves like a phantom."

Brasada nodded. Something else he had heard drifted into his mind—"Solid or Express. Express has a hole drilled in the head of the bullet for a .22-caliber blank. Blank explodes on impact. Goes in about .50 caliber and comes out about four or five times that big. Messy killing wound, mister."

"Before God," murmured Brasada. "*Keesey!*"

Harkness nodded. "That is my suspicion."

"The sonofabitch moves around this country selling his guns and ammunition," said Brasada. "He knows just who is going after the Soledad Silver and instead of selling his goods in Tucson or in Sonora, he comes to the Mountain, *and* he must be a master rifleman."

"Sharpshooter with The First United States Sharpshooters," added Harkness, "during the Civil War and later a hunter of buffalo. Either one of those would qualify him as one of the finest riflemen the world has ever seen. In addition, Brasada, he is diabolically clever. But, remember, Manton has most of those qualifications as well. Is it possible that it might be him?"

"Not a chance," said Manton from the mine entrance.

Brasada looked past Harkness into the lean triangular face of the deputy. "That at least pins it on Keesey," he said drily.

Manton looked about. "Very cosy," he commented. "I often wondered where you holed up, Harkness."

"How did you know where to find us?" asked Harkness.

Manton smiled. "You left your dead dog on your doorstep. Raise your hands, gentlemen. Turn around." Brasada felt Manton pluck his Colt and knife from their sheaths. "Where's the Soledad Silver, Harkness?" asked Manton.

"I thought you came after me, Manton," said Brasada over his shoulder.

"I did, but I don't mind adding thirty tons of silver to your reward money, spic."

"Dead or alive?" said Brasada.

"You can figure it out. I don't want you talking, and I don't want the trouble of trying to get you back to La Placita. They say you're a dangerous man, Brasada."

"I have my admirers," murmured Brasada.

"How do you want it?" asked Manton. "Belly or head? It wouldn't look nice shooting you in the back. Appearances count for so much these days."

"If I show you the silver," said Harkness, "will you free Brasada, Manton?"

"There's a good possibility, Harkness."

"He's lying, Harkness," warned Brasada.

"I know," said the big man.

"Show me the silver and find out," suggested Manton. He reached for the lantern. "It must be up the tunnel, eh?"

Harkness nodded.

"Beats me why you never got it out of here," murmured Manton. "You could have lived like a king in Denver or Chicago, New York even. Well, each to his own, I say. Lead the way, Harkness."

Harkness turned. He struck out with an arm thewed like an oak tree and staggered the deputy. The lantern clattered to the floor and went out, leaving only the guttering candle in front of the *bulto* to light the room. Brasada made his move. He darted for his rifle. Manton fired at Brasada from the hip as Harkness struck at him again. The big man went staggering against the wall. Manton whirled.

Brasada swung about and ran up the drift in almost complete darkness. He heard the thudding of Manton's boots on the floor of the tunnel. Brasada passed the dim shrouded figure of the old *patron*. He counted his steps and risked a long jump. His feet struck solid rock.

Manton yelled. Metal struck the side of the pit. There was a resounding splash far below and then it was quiet again except for the faint subterranean sound of rushing water.

Brasada went down on his belly and crawled until his hands were over the pit. He stood up, wiped the cold sweat from his face, and risked another jump in the darkness. His feet struck solid rock.

Harkness lay on his back with his arms outflung. His clear blue eyes stared at the massive cross hanging on the wall. Brasada closed the lids. "Rest in peace," he murmured. "At long last," he added.

Brasada shaped and lighted a cigarette. He checked through Harkness's supplies. There were half a dozen cans of Kepauno Giant Blasting Powder and several coils of fuse. He found a cigar box filled with loaded .50/140 cartridges with the 700-grain bullet and he marveled at the heft and size of them. He picked up Harkness's fine Sharps rifle—it was the one thing he could not leave with the dead man's effects. He tucked the cigar box of cartridges under an arm and walked outside.

The moonlight was clear on the wide slopes. Nothing moved. He looked far down the slopes toward the church. A woman and a man moved into the shadows of the church even as he watched.

Brasada catfooted down the slope trailing the two

rifles. Now and again he would look back toward the Mountain. There was nothing to be seen except the Mountain—that, and the full moon sailing in an absolutely cloudless sky.

CHAPTER TWENTY-ONE

THE Soledad Silver must be right within his grasp.
The thought was in the mind of Brasada as he catfooted through the *bosquecillo*. He stopped within the
deep shadows and looked up at the Mountain. If it
was Keesey who was up there, he must be as Harkness said he was—a man who moved like a phantom.
There were no signs of life on the moonlit slopes
above the landslide area.

Brasada looked down at the massive silver crucifix
in his hand. It was almost worth a small fortune in itself. With Weed and Manton dead, even if Brasada
captured Keesey, it wouldn't be very wise to take him
into La Placita. There would be too many questions
asked; questions that Brasada would have to answer,
to the best of his knowledge, and he knew well
enough that he would hardly be believed if he told
of the deaths that had occurred on the Mountain that
moonlit night.

He turned the crucifix over. Shallow letters had
been struck into the soft metal. "Carlos III," he read.
He looked up the slopes toward where Harkness lay
buried forever. Had the man been lying when he said
he had made the crucifix himself? Then the light

struck Brasada. Of course he had made the crucifix!
He had hammered it out of solid silver ingots!

Brasada buried the crucifix and Sharps rifle under
leaves at the far end of the *bosquecillo* and then
padded back through the shadows to look toward
the church. It was very quiet. It seemed almost the
same as it had been the first night he had been there.

Something moved in the belfry. Brasada looked up.
It was the woman. He could see her back and then
she was gone. He moved as silently as wind-driven
smoke to the shelter of the trees and shrubbery
around the flagged pool. Someone lay face downward
at the bottom of the pool with clawed hands dug in
between some of the bottom stones. A bullet punc-
tured sombrero floated at the far end of the pool.
There was no mistaking the melon-shaped head of
Ignacio One-Eye. "Two of us will not leave the Mountain," the woman had said.

He eased himself through the partly ajar rear door
of the sacristy. He looked suspiciously about. It seemed
as though someone had just been there. He walked
softly into the sanctuary and looked toward the
front of the church. Dimly he saw the woman coming
from the baptistry. He walked forward to meet her.

"Brasada," the cold voice said from the pulpit behind Brasada. At the same time the woman walked
into one of the rays of moonlight that streamed down
into the nave from the small windows set high up
close under the eaves. Brasada saw the red hair and
the fine bosom of the woman. "You took your time,"
she said.

Brasada looked back over his shoulder. Mick Dallas dropped lightly to the floor of the nave, but he
kept his rifle pointed at Brasada. When Brasada turned
he saw the pistol in the hands of the woman. He
dropped his rifle to the floor and raised his hands.
Dallas neatly plucked Brasada's knife and Colt from
their sheaths.

The rifle butt hit him behind the ear, just enough to half stun him. He went down on one knee. The boot heel caught him on the back of the head and drove him to the floor. The rifle butt was rammed down onto his back above his kidneys.

"Come on, big man!" challenged Dallas. "Get up! Get up! There's more for you, *bien parecido!*"

"Do you want to kill him now, you idiot?" snapped the woman. "I didn't come all the way here to this Godforsaken hole just to see you get cheap revenge! You can have him later—*after* he talks."

"*Gracias,*" murmured Brasada.

"*Por nada,*" she said sweetly. "Get up."

He looked into the eyes of Mick Dallas. By contrast, the eyes of Harkness's wolf dog had seemed almost humane.

"What did you learn from my husband?" she asked.

He smiled. "How much he loved you, ma'am."

"You're wasting time," snarled Mick Dallas. "I'll make him talk."

She tilted her head to one side. "Where is the breed woman?"

Brasada shrugged. "I truly don't know," he said.

"What was going on up there on the Mountain?"

Brasada shrugged again. "A murder and an execution," he said.

"Who?" she demanded.

"Luke Harkness," replied Brasada. "*And* Manton . . . ."

"What the hell are you talking about?" she demanded.

"Manton murdered Harkness," said Brasada evenly.

She narrowed her eyes. "And you killed Manton for it?"

Brasada shook his head. "He died accidentally." He smiled. "With a little help from me and the Mountain."

"Where did all this take place?" she asked.

"In the great Soledad Mine," replied Brasada. He held up a hand. "The Soledad Silver is no longer there, ma'am. It was mined from there—but the silver was never cached there."

"Where is it then?"

Brasada shook his head. "Before God, I do not know."

She tapped a little booted toe on the paving. "Once more, my dramatic friend—what did my husband tell you?"

"A lot of misinformation," he replied. He shook his head sadly. "All those years he dreamt of the silver, believing all the time that the 'shadow writing' was the key. And the men he sent up here with that misinformation, to die by violence—sent to their executions by that mad old man."

She looked past Brasada. "All right, Mick," she said.

The rifle butt tapped Brasada over the kidneys. "We begin here," Mick said professionally.

"And end there too," said Consuelo from the front of the church. She walked catlike toward them. "If you shoot him, mister, the woman dies at the same time." She did not have a gun in her hand.

Mick Dallas stared at her. "You think that would stop me?" he asked.

"You bastard," said Mrs. Major O'Neil.

"Always the lady," murmured Brasada.

"Drop the rifle, mister," ordered Consuelo.

Mick Dallas went along with the gag. He dropped the rifle.

"And the pistol," added Consuelo.

Dallas slowly tilted his head to one side. "Are you loco, breed?" he asked. "If I touch that pistol butt you'll be dead in two seconds flat."

It was very quiet now. No one moved.

Dallas made his play. In one swift action he dropped his right hand to the butt of his Colt, drawing it and cocking it in a fluid, lightning-fast motion.

He thrust it forward to fire, never taking his eyes
from Consuelo. That was how he died with a bullet
in his chest and a look of utter disbelief in his flat
yellow-brown eyes. His pistol struck the floor and exploded, driving a bullet into the ceiling. The close-
bound explosions of the two pistols half deafened the
living. Powder smoke rifted in the still air. Bits and
pieces of ancient plaster pattered down on Mick Dallas to form an impromptu shroud.

Mrs. Major O'Neil dropped her pistol. Consuelo
flipped open the loading gate of her pistol, ejected
the smoking empty brass hull, and then fed a fresh
round into the chamber. She snapped shut the loading
gate and slid the pistol into her holster. She walked
gracefully toward Brasada and the woman. She looked
sideways at the whitefaced redhead. "Do you want to
kill her or should I?" she asked matter-of-factly.

Brasada shook his head. He picked up his knife and
pistol and sheathed them. He rubbed the place at the
back of his head where Dallas had struck him with
the rifle.

"So Harkness is dead," said Consuelo.

Brasada nodded. "And so is Manton."

"And Ignacio," added Consuelo. She looked down at
Dallas. "The Mountain's blood hunger has been well
fed tonight. Is it sated, Brasada?"

Brasada shook his head. He picked up his rifle.
"There is one left," he said.

"Forget him," said Consuelo. "I said you would be
wasting your time. You'll never find your phantom rifleman and the silver isn't up there."

Brasada shaped and lighted a cigarette. He placed
it in the mouth of the woman and then made one for
himself. "What about this one?" he asked, jerking his
head toward Mrs. Major O'Neil.

"You know my answer," said Consuelo.

Brasada looked at the woman. Fear was etched onto her beautiful face. "Git," he said.

"Where?" she asked.

He shrugged. "You've got a horse. You've got a ranch. Go there, and mourn your dead husband."

"I can't go out there," she said. "That madman is somewhere out there."

"You're safe from him," said Brasada. "You know nothing about the Soledad Silver." He grinned. "And you never will."

She looked at the two of them. There were no expressions on their faces. She knew the woman was a breed, possibly pure quill, but she had never noticed such a strain in Brasada. It was the eyes that had deluded her, but now she thought she knew.

"Maybe she'd make good bait," suggested Consuelo.

"Not for him," said Brasada.

They waited. In a little while Mrs. Major O'Neil walked slowly toward the door. She turned. "You're sending me to my death!" she shrilled. Her strident voice echoed through the nave. There was no reply. The two of them stood there like the carved wooden *bulto* in his niche. In a little while she left the church and they heard the hard and hurried pattering of her boots on the ancient pavement and then that died away and the quietness flowed back again into Soledad.

Consuelo reached up behind the *bulto* and withdrew a full bottle of brandy. She pulled the cork with her strong white teeth and handed him the bottle. They drank together for a little while.

"Do you still mean to go up there?" she asked.

He nodded.

"The moonlight will soon be gone."

"There is still time. Just what is your real game?" he asked.

"Perhaps I love you, Brasada. Perhaps I want to save you from the Mountain."

He shook his head. "You love no man. You might, for a little while, but it never lasts."

"And you, Brasada. Do you love me? Can you love anyone?"

He reached for the bottle and drank a little.

"The old *diyi* said of the three of us, that two of us would never leave the Mountain. Ignacio won't, Brasada."

"And he never saw the silver," said Brasada sadly.

"Perhaps he did," she said.

"Brasada!" came the faint yell from the slopes above the town. "*Brasada . . . Brasada . . . Brasada . . .*" repeated the Mountain.

The woman was startled. "He has a voice," she said.

Brasada shrugged. "Why not?" he asked.

"You can't kill him."

"I'm going to try."

"He'll kill you first!"

Brasada shook his head. "He's too damned sure of himself, otherwise he would not have called me by name. He knows I am the only one left to kill."

"What about me?" she asked.

He lighted a cigarette and placed it between her lips. "A very curious thing," he said quietly. "He's never shot at you. But I have thought for some time you are the only living person who really knows the cache of the Soledad Silver."

She looked away from him. He lighted his own cigarette. "I knew that when you said those rock symbols on the Mountain were Chiricahua rather than made by the old padres. I have yet to see a Chiricahua who had the skill, tools, and patience to chisel such clean, neat arrows in hard rock. And the map, I think you knew how to read it all the time."

She raised her head to listen as the man on the slopes called again. "*Brasada . . . Brasada . . . Brasada. . . .*" She looked at Brasada. "The water was really the key. The map was useless. It referred to the original cache of the silver. Some time in the past five years the silver was moved, but I never knew where."

"The water meant the *tinaja?*"

She shook her head. "Originally it did. There was a triangle, with the cache in the center of it. One point of the triangle was the *tinaja,* another the church, and the third was the old mine. The original hiding place of the silver was buried by landslides a few years ago."

"You said the water was the key."

She nodded. "But not from the map, Brasada. If I show you the silver cache will you leave the Mountain?"

"Brasada . . . !" came the cry.

"When I get him," said Brasada.

"Follow me, then," she said quietly.

She led the way through the shadowed shrubbery to the edge of the pool, shielded from the view of anyone on the slopes. She pointed to where Ignacio lay on the bottom of the pool with his stiffening clawed hands dug into the paving. His last spasmodic clutchings had disturbed the loose layer of silt, small rounded stones, and gravel that covered the original paving. "Look closely," she said to Brasada.

He narrowed his eyes. The uncovered paving blocks were exactly the shape of silver ingots he had seen in Mexico, stamped with the mark of the padres and the name of Carlos III, King of Spain. "Before God," he murmured. "How long have you known this?"

"Since the day I bathed there."

"How long has it been there?"

She shrugged. "I came alone here as a child to bathe in this pool. In those days the bottom was softer, a layer of gravel and stones on top of clay—there was no paving then."

Brasada looked up the slope to where Harkness lay dead in the great Soledad Mine. "It *was* Harkness then," he said softly. "Mother of God! Thirty tons of it!"

She shook her head. "Hardly, but a fortune, none-theless."

"Why didn't you tell me about this before?"

"Because it is accursed!" she cried. "You've seen yourself what happens to anyone who seeks it! Jubal Conn and those before him! The old major, Barney Gadkin, Cassius Weed, Luke Harkness, Manton, Ignacio, and Mick Dallas!"

"The roll of the dead," said Brasada drily. "I admit Jubal Conn was killed, possibly by Keesey, if that *is* Keesey up there now. You yourself might have killed the old major, to keep him from telling me what he knew. Barney Gadkin accidentally shot himself. Cass Weed was drowning in his own blood when his heart gave out. Manton killed Harkness and Manton drowned in the Soledad Mine. Ignacio One-Eye either fell into the pool or Brother Dallas knocked him into it. And finally, it was *you* who killed Dallas."

"They were killed because of the curse! And you will be too—by that madman up there!"

"So, he's part of the curse too?"

"He is only one of the instruments of the Mountain."

Brasada was silently laughing.

She came close to him and looked up into his bearded face. "Touch that damned silver and you'll die, Brasada; accidentally or otherwise, but it will be on purpose. It does not matter how you will die, Brasada, *but you will die. . . .*"

He looked toward the Mountain. "According to your theory that madman up there is only the instrument of the Mountain. Therefore, if I get *him*, the Mountain loses the game and I get the Soledad Silver."

She shook her head firmly.

"He's only a man," said Brasada. He unbuckled his gunbelt and dropped it. He sat down and pulled off his boots. "Take my rifle," he told her. "Watch the slope."

Brasada let himself down into the pool. He waded

to Ignacio and hooked a hand under the Mexican's gunbelt. He towed him back to the side of the pool. Ignacio's stiffened clawed hands seemed to dig at the bottom of the pool as though in death he would get what he had not been able to get in life.

Brasada got out of the pool and lifted Ignacio to his shoulders. The rifle cracked on the slopes and was instantly echoed by that of Consuelo. Ignacio's body jerked on Brasada's shoulders. Brasada dumped him on the ground in the shelter of the shrubbery. He pulled on his boots and buckled on his gunbelt. "Sonofabitch *can* shoot," he grudgingly admitted.

"I saw nothing but the rifle flash," she said.

"He won't be there now," said Brasada.

She looked down at Ignacio. "Do you plan a Christian burial too?" she asked.

"He was polluting the pool. Good water is scarce enough in this country." Brasada took his rifle from her hands. "We can get through the *bosquecillo* to a deep draw at the farther end of it, and from there along behind the ruins to the foot of the slope, without being seen by him—I hope." He studied her. "That is, if you have the guts to come with me to help kill him," he added.

He turned on a heel and walked away from her.

She looked toward the Mountain and then after Brasada. She crossed herself for the first time in many years and followed Brasada.

Brasada was waiting for her at the edge of the *bosquecillo*. He held a Sharps rifle in his right hand and with his left hand he extended his Winchester '73 toward her. "I figure I can do better with this Big Fifty," he told her.

She shook her head. "It doesn't matter, Brasada."

He laughed as he led the way from the *bosquecillo* into the shadowed draw that led up behind the ruins on the north side of Soledad.

CHAPTER TWENTY-TWO

BRASADA LOWERED the breechblock of the Big Fifty and slid a long cartridge into the chamber. He closed the breech and looked sideways at the woman. "You want to act as bait?" he asked with a crooked grin.

"Not the way he can shoot," she replied.

They lay on the rocky earth on the side slope behind the half-buried ruins and below the Soledad Mine. Consuelo looked down on the moonlit town. "Look," she said. "It is the redheaded *zopilote*, Brasada."

The woman was standing between two buildings looking up the slope toward the Mountain.

"She should have left when she had the chance," said Consuelo. She looked down at the Winchester. "Shall I give her a little help in making up her mind?"

"You'd more likely put a bullet through her," he said.

Consuelo smiled. "Maybe that's what I had in mind."

He looked sideways at her. "If she needs killing," he said, "your Mountain will take care of it."

She had no comment to make on that.

Something cracked high on the side of the Mountain. Brasada instinctively ducked. The detached rock struck loose rock at the base of the sheer wall. The hissing, rattling rush of displaced rock echoed from the Mountain as it poured down the slope and moved the talus slope at the side of the ruins just a little closer to what remained of the plaza, and closer to the church.

The woman watched the rock sliding down to the ruins. "How many more of those will it take to bury Soledad forever?" she asked, almost as though to herself.

Brasada shrugged. "A few hundred more," he replied, "or one big one. That would be all."

"And the church will be gone too?" she asked.

He nodded. "And the pool with its expensive bottom paving."

"The water is far more valuable than the silver," she said.

He shrugged. "Who will come here to use it?"

"Only fools and animals," she replied.

A coyote howled from somewhere above the Soledad Mine. The woman looked up quickly.

Brasada grinned. "One of your relatives, or *mine*?" he asked.

A rifle cracked higher up the slope and the bullet exploded on a rock not a yard from Brasada's head. Shards of lead and bits of rock stung the side of Brasada's face. He rolled over and lay flat.

"Soon it will be dark and he can move in closer," warned the woman.

"He can't see any better in the dark than I can," said Brasada.

"Maybe he doesn't have to," she suggested.

"Don't start that again!" he snapped.

"You've never even seen him, by day or by night," she persisted.

The rifle blasted on the slope, closer this time, and the bullet shattered itself against a rock a foot above their heads. The woman winced. "Are you all right?"

asked Brasada. She nodded. "Maybe you'd better get out of here," he suggested. "I can handle him alone."

She looked at him. "You're doing a fine job," she said drily.

He peered between two rocks, half expecting a bullet in the face. "How good is your timing?" he asked.

"Perfect," she said modestly.

"I'm going down the slope to the ruins. Shoot at him now and then to show we're still here, but for God's sake, be careful! When I am in the ruins, show yourself, and then drop flat. By that time, I may see him and get a shot at him."

"You'll only get a bullet in that hard head of yours."

There was no answer from Brasada. He bellywormed down the rock-cluttered slope, half expecting a bullet, but nothing happened. It was very quiet again. He crawled through the shadows until he lay flat against the side of a house whose front half was buried under rock and earth. He crawled in through a doorway and stood up within the room. One of the side windows had a view up the slope to about where Brasada calculated the rifleman had his position. Brasada catfooted to the window. He slid the long rifle through the window and rested it on the rock and earth that had mounded beyond the window. He fullcocked the big outside hammer and then looked up the slope.

The moonlight was bright on the southern side of the rock formations but shadows mantled the northern sides. A mouse could not have found concealment on the moonlit sides, but the shadowed sides could easily have concealed a man on a horse.

He looked sideways up and out of the window to where the woman was concealed. Just as he looked she popped up out of cover and Brasada quickly turned his head to look back up the slope, while at the same time he drew back on the rear trigger, hearing the faint click of the front trigger as it was set.

Something moved. Brasada raised the rifle. The rifle up the slope blasted flame and smoke just as Brasada fired and the explosive bullet struck with savage impact at the side of the window, inches from Brasada's head. He dropped to the floor with the smoking rifle in his hands, half deafened from the explosion of the bullet that had struck the wall.

The echoes died away. Brasada slowly raised his ringing head. Someone was laughing. The sound almost sent a chill through Brasada. He looked through the window. A rift of smoke was wavering along the slopes above a shadowed area. Something instinctively made him drop his head as the rifle flashed and smoke billowed fifty yards down the slope and closer to the ruin and the bullet whipped right over Brasada's head to smash into the opposite wall. Shards of musty yeso plaster pattered to the floor. The shot echo died. Nothing moved except the silent smoke drifting along the slopes.

Brasada sat with his back against the wall. He half-cocked the Sharps and lowered the breechblock. The long brass hull was ejected. It tinkled on the floor. Brasada rubbed his ringing ear and then slid a cartridge into the smoking breech. He snapped up the breechblock.

"He never even looked at me," the woman said from the shadows about the rear doorway. "He knew where you were all the time."

Brasada nodded. "Don't give me a lecture," he requested.

She came into the room and took the makings from his shirt pocket. She shaped a cigarette and placed it in his mouth and then made one for herself. She lighted both cigarettes. She squatted in front of him. They smoked quietly in the dimness.

He looked at her. "You think I'm licked?" he asked.

She inspected her cigarette. "*You?* The Great Brasada?"

"I should have known better than to ask," he said.

"He was laughing at you, Brasada."

"I heard," said Brasada. He stood up and walked to a window. He placed his back against the wall and looked over his left shoulder and a second later he snapped his head back to the front as the rifle cracked flatly and the bullet whipped through the window to strike the opposite wall and explode.

Brasada crawled to the rear doorway. He stood up in the shadows and eased toward the end of the building. He held out the barrel of the rifle. The bullet slapped into it and the shock of the impact tingled Brasada's hands. He withdrew the rifle and looked at it. He rubbed at the leaden splotch on the polished barrel. "Bastard," he murmured.

"A cannon cannot get him," the woman said.

"You're a big help," he said.

"Why not leave Soledad now? If you must, you can come back for the silver. He can't stay up there all the time."

"He seems able to."

A rock cracked loose high above the slope and fell heavily far below to start a miniature landslide. In a little while the displaced rock and earth pushed against the part of the ruin that had not been covered. Brasada raised his head. He looked up the slope toward the rock wall.

"Brasada!" cried the voice. "*Brasada . . . Brasada . . . Brasada . . .*" echoed the Mountain.

"Is it really Keesey?" asked Consuelo.

He shrugged. "Follow me," he said. He led the way to the east, past the rear of the ruin and down a deep draw. He turned left at the end of the draw and started up toward the Soledad Mine.

"Brasada!" yelled the voice. It had moved.

"You're being paged," she said.

Brasada nodded. "I'll answer him in a little while," he promised, "in a way he won't expect."

Brasada led the way to the mine, out of sight of the rifleman. He stepped behind the false wall and walked into the mine. The guttering candle still lighted the stolid face of the *bulto* and played its fitful light over the composed face of Harkness.

"Mother of God!" the woman cried.

Brasada found a sack and began to pack it with the heavy cans of blasting powder. He shoved a coil of fuse inside his shirt.

"Where is Manton?" she asked.

Brasada turned, heaving the heavy sack up onto his shoulders. "Having a midnight swim," he replied. He grinned. He walked outside and stood behind a huge boulder. "Can you handle the Big Fifty?" he asked.

"I hope I can do better than you did with it."

He nodded. "Keep him busy. Fire a round, then move, fire another and move again, but don't try to hit him, because if you try, he'll be sure to get you. Just shoot in his general direction."

"Where are you going, Brasada?"

He looked up the long slopes to the base of the sheer rock wall. "Up there," he said.

"Why?" she asked. She already knew why.

He did not answer as he slid down into a shadowed draw and vanished from her sight.

She shrugged. She walked to a place where she could see the last position of the rifleman without being seen. She fired in the general direction and jumped back out of sight. The reaction was instantaneous. The bullet hit the face of a boulder and exploded. "*Bastardo,*" she murmured as she reloaded.

"Brasada!" yelled the voice. "Is that the best you can do? Quit while you're ahead, Brasada!" The voice came from still another position.

Brasada was breathing hard and the sweat was running down his face and his sides. He placed the sack on the ground and lay down beside it. He heard a rifle crack, echoed immediately by another, and the double echoes chased each other along the side of the Mountain.

Brasada picked up the sack and bent low, driving his aching legs up the steep slope. Once he slipped and came down hard on one knee. Loose rock slithered down behind him and rattled far down the slope.

The rifle duet kept on while Brasada worked his way higher and higher until at last he dropped flat behind a rock ledge. His chest heaved and his breath came harshly and erratically.

He raised his head and bellied to the ledge. He looked over it. As he did so he saw the rifle flash almost directly below him, perhaps two hundred yards away, but all he could see of the rifleman was a shadowed movement. Red flame sparked and white smoke billowed out as Consuelo fired up the long slope. Brasada grinned. She'd have a sore shoulder in the morning.

He crawled up to the higher end of the ledge and looked along the slope. Even as he looked a loose shard of rock fell from the scaling wall to drop not fifty feet from him and to slide lower down. He studied the base of the wall. There was one place he could put his charge, but to reach it, he would have to walk fifty yards in the open clearly lighted by the moon.

Brasada went back to the powder sack. He looked up at the moon. There wasn't much time left. He risked a cigarette and sat there with the sweat running down his face and his lungs seemingly afire.

He snubbed out the cigarette and picked up the sack. Now and again he had heard the shooting going on. If she ran out of cartridges the game might very well be up for Brasada.

He stepped out into the open and looked downward. The moonlight was still on the facade of the old church but now the pool was in the shadow of the

church. He thought he saw someone walking near
the church, but he wasn't sure.

Brasada worked his way slowly along the base of
the sheer rock wall. Now and then a displaced stone
or piece of rock would slide down, down, and down
with a rattling rush of loose gravel and soil.

It was very quiet now. Brasada froze tight against
the rock wall. He had the eerie feeling that he was being watched. One shot from below could hit the sack
of powder cans and lift Brasada swiftly to heaven if
the rock wall didn't first fall in on him from the blasting concussion.

The woman was not shooting. There was now no
going back for Brasada. He reached the hollow place
at the foot of the wall.

"Brasada!" yelled the voice. "*Brasada . . . Brasada
. . . Brasada . . .*" echoed the Mountain, seemingly
right above Brasada's head, so much that he involuntarily jerked his head to look upward toward the
source of the voice.

He opened the sack and took out a powder can. He
stowed it deeply in the crevice, lying on his belly, hoping to God the decomposing rock would not fall in on
him. Can after can was stowed neatly and tightly at
the rear of the crevice. He inserted his fuse and paid it
out over his shoulder and his back. He crawfished
backward and began to pack rock about the cans and
over the fuse, inching backward until his long legs
were out in the moonlight.

"I see you, Brasada!" yelled the voice.

"Christ's blood," cursed Brasada. A rock fell and
hit between his legs just below the crotch. "Another
inch or two and I'd be a gelding," he muttered.

He finished packing in the rock and lay flat against
the base of the cliff looking down the long slope. The
woman fired and her shot was echoed by the rifleman.

He worked his way back along the base of the rock
wall, paying out the kinky fuse. Fifty yards from the

powder cache he ran out of fuse. He lay flat, resting
his head against the rock. The fuse was far too short
for his safety. He eyed the slopes ahead of him. There
was a chance he could make his break down that way
once he lighted the fuse, but he would be clearly seen
in the open, leaping like an antelope down the slope,
fair game for an explosive bullet.

He regained his breath and felt for his matches. He
looked once more down the slopes, struck a match,
held it to the tip of the fuse, saw it catch fire, and
then leaped to his feet to plunge transversely down
the steep slope toward the area above the Soledad
Mine.

He was halfway down the slope when the shot
came. He felt his right boot heel get smashed completely off by the bullet and he was spun around by
the impact and as he did so he looked upward to see
the snake of fire racing along the base of the rock
wall. As he fell bellyflat and slid downward he heard
the dull, reverberating boom of the explosion.

A thunderous crashing sound filled the air as the
face of the rock wall fell like a descending theater cur-
tain and was followed by a roaring, grating, grinding
cacophony of sound as though the very earth had
split. The ground shook beneath Brasada's feet as he
plunged recklessly downward.

He saw the woman running down the slope beyond
the mine, trailing his Winchester. Rocks that had been
blown high into the air began to land with solid impact all about him and the displaced air of the explosion struck him on the back and drove him downward at ever increasing speed although by some miracle he managed to keep his feet.

He passed the mine and looked sideways. He
thought he saw a man running desperately across the
slope fifty feet ahead of the great mass of rock that
was inexorably sliding down toward the ruins of
Soledad.

Consuelo looked back at him and pointed down toward the church. A woman had run from a side street into what little remained of the plaza in front of the church. Her face was stark white in the remaining moonlight as she looked back over her shoulder at the vast moving mass of rock. She ran into the church and closed the doors behind her. The mass of earth and rock poured down into the last of the plaza and struck the front of the church. The bell tower swayed. The bell clanged discordantly as it fell. Somewhere within the darkened nave the woman must be screaming for the last time.

Brasada looked over his shoulder as the side of the landslide lapped over beyond Soledad and poured against the Soledad Mine to bury it forever. The rock and earth mass had covered the church, the Campo Santo, and the dry wash and had even begun to rise up the slope of the Soledad Hills because of the inexorable pressure from behind and below and then the hills held their own and the landslide was stopped. Gradually the echoes died away. Only the dust pall moved over Soledad as though to cover it with its shroud, for now Soledad with its treasure and its phantoms was buried forever.

CHAPTER TWENTY-THREE

BRASADA TOOK the last brandy bottle from a saddle-bag. He handed the bottle to the woman, but all the while he was looking at the great slanted mass of rock and earth that now covered Soledad and its many secrets. The moonlight was about gone. A faint cool wind crept timidly from the hills and wafted back the dust pall, neatly tidying up the air. Now and then there was a faint rumbling sound as the slide settled itself comfortably for a long rest.

"You see?" asked the woman. "The Mountain took back its own."

"Bullshit," he said. "Anyway it's the first time in my manhunting career I had to drop a mountain on a man to get rid of him." He looked toward the buried church. "*And* a few tons of pure native silver," he drily added.

"The Mountain took it back," she insisted.

An owl hooted from what remained of the *bosque-cillo*.

The woman looked hurriedly over her shoulder with fear on her face.

"You're still Chiricahua, lady," accused Brasada. "Did you think that was the voice of Mick Dallas speaking through Bú, the Owl? If it is, I'd get the hell out of here and stand not on the order of my going."

"You killed men too," she accused.

"Who *me?*" he innocently asked. "Only Ramon and Pamfilo, and that was too long ago for owl voices to be talking about it."

"But what about all the others?" she asked.

He shrugged and held out his hands, palms upwards. "Did *I* kill anyone else?"

"There was the man on the Mountain," she said.

He smiled. "According to you, it was the Mountain that killed him."

She looked up in his lean, saturnine face. "Who are you, Brasada?" she asked. "*Who are you?*" She looked into his ice-gray eyes and a cold and uneasy feeling worked deep within her bowels. She knew then a fear she had never known before in her entire life. Lucifer had been a fallen angel, she reasoned, but in the Great Plan, he too had served a purpose. "Mother of the Devil," she murmured as she turned away from those icy eyes.

"Think what you will," he said in an amused tone. "Where will you go now?"

"With you?" she asked.

He shook his head. "It is a long way, and the way is hard."

"You can't stay here in Arizona. Not now."

He shrugged. "The story of my life. But you can't stay here either. Go to Sonora for awhile at least."

She looked up at the Mountain. "There is only one place for me to go," she said quietly, almost as though she was talking to herself.

"Your true people—the Chiricahuas?"

She nodded. "Come with me," she suggested.

He shook his head. "Whatever purpose brought us together is no longer necessary."

For the first time that evening and night a coyote called from the shadows beyond buried Soledad.

The woman looked toward the sound. "The old man is very old, Brasada. He is the grandfather of my mother. She too was a *diyi*. He has not long to live. Someone must learn his medicine before he dies."

"You?" he asked.

"There is nothing for me anywhere else," she replied.

"Goodbye, then," he said.

He watched her walk silently toward the shadows. He drank some brandy and then lowered the bottle. The coyote cried for a little while and then he suddenly stopped and Brasada knew then that the woman was gone from his life forever.

He dug the leaves away from the silver crucifix and mounted the dun. He rode up the newly formed slopes below the buried site of the Soledad Mine. He sat the dun there for a little while, hefting the great cross. Once he looked up at the Mountain. It was again, as it had always been, towering high above the shadowed slopes, majestic and implacable—repelling all men and yet at the same time drawing them to it against their wills.

He tore his gaze from the Mountain and stood up in his stirrups. He hurled the heavy cross with all his strength up the slope to about where Luke Harkness lay entombed forever. He sat down and touched the dun with his spurs to ride swiftly down the long dangerous slopes and he did not look back.

CHAPTER TWENTY-FOUR

THE ASTRINGENT smell of woodsmoke came drifting on the night wind to Brasada. He reined in the dun and swung down from the saddle. He withdrew his Winchester from its scabbard and levered a round into the chamber. He hobbled through the *bosque* toward the stream. Now and then he saw the flare of firelight against the overhanging leaves near the stream bank.

He stopped behind a tree and looked down the sloped bank to a clearing where a fire was burning down into a bed of coals. A lamp stood on a small folding table. A man sat with his back toward Brasada working at something on the table. A horse whinnied from the shadows beyond the stream and was joined by another one.

The man slowly turned. "Come on down, mister," he invited in English. A dark beard mantled the upper part of his chest.

Brasada held the rifle at hip level. He looked at the light van wagon that stood in the shadows. The firelight flared up and Brasada saw the lettering on the side of the vehicle—E. Keesey, Guns and Gun Supplies.

The man waved a hand, beckoning Brasada to him. "Come on down," he repeated. "Got coffee in the pot and liquor in the bottle. This water makes the best coffee in Sonora."

Brasada narrowed his eyes. The table held reloading gear and the firelight shone on the fat brass bodies of big cartridges. A lead ladle rested in the embers of the fire.

"Doing a little reloading," explained Keesey. He narrowed his eyes. "Ain't I seen you somewhere before?"

Brasada took a step or two down the slope. "That's what you said the last time I saw you," he said.

Keesey studied him. "Yes! I recall! In La Placita! In Tatum's gun shop about a week or so ago."

Brasada nodded.

"You aiming to camp here tonight?" asked Keesey. "Plenty of room! I sleep in the van myself, but the ground ain't too hard." He smiled.

Brasada glanced about. There was no gun of any sort near the man.

"You're the *rurale?* Ain't you?" asked Keesey.

Brasada came hobbling down to the fire.

"You hurt yourself?" asked Keesey solicitously.

Brasada shook his head. "Lost a heel last night over near Soledad," he replied.

"So? Well, don't worry. I got an extra heel in the van. Set down and have a drink. Pull off that boot, mister, and I'll show you I'm as good a cobbler as I am a reloader!"

Brasada sat down on a rock and looked at the smiling face of Keesey. Mechanically he pulled off the boot and handed it to the man. Keesey eyed it professionally. "You broke it off neat and clean anyway," he said.

Brasada nodded. "I had a little help," he said.

Keesey bustled about the rear of the wagon. In a little while the tap, tap, tapping of his hammer echoed through the *bosque.* "You come this way often?" he asked over his shoulder.

"Now and then," replied Brasada. "It's the closest water to the border, outside of the old *tinaja* near Soledad."

"So they tell me! Never been there myself. Can't get the team and the wagon in there, but there ain't no business in there anyway, so I lose nothing. Camp here every time I come this way."

"Anyone ever bother you?" asked Brasada.

Keesey turned and studied Brasada. "Why, no," he said.

"Chiricahuas? Yaquis? *Bandidos?*"

Keesey shook his head.

Brasada looked at the wagon, then at the reloading gear. "You'd be a fine prize for any of them," he suggested.

Keesey turned with the boot in his hand. "No, they never bother me, mister," he explained. He smiled. "I shoot quite a bit on both sides of the border. Got quite a reputation. That reputation is a sort of insurance that no one bothers me." He walked to Brasada and handed him the boot. "Now, coffee or brandy?"

"Nothing," replied Brasada. He pulled on the boot. *"Gracias."*

"Por nada," replied Keesey. "Sure you don't want a drink?"

Brasada shook his head. "I've got to push on."

Keesey nodded. He smiled. "Sure, sure, I get it! No drinking on duty, eh?"

Brasada stood up. "Where do you go from here?" he asked.

"Oh, Caborca first. Then to Santa Ana and Magdalena. Maybe north again after that, or south to Hermosillo, depending on how good business is."

Brasada placed the thumb and first finger of his left hand in his mouth and whistled sharply for his dun. The dun trotted to the stream and began to drink.

"Fine horse there," remarked Keesey. "*Bayo coyote* dun eh? Plenty of bottom to them, and smart too. By God! He's *cruz*-marked too! You're a fortunate man, mister. They say a man who rides such a horse is protected by God. Any truth in that?" He smiled.

Brasada took out the makings. He handed them to Keesey. Keesey shook his head. "Never smoke. Interferes with my shooting."

Brasada nodded as he shaped a cigarette.

"You didn't answer my question," said Keesey. "About the rider of such a horse being protected by God."

Brasada looked at the horse and then at Keesey. "I'm beginning to believe it," he replied as he lighted up.

The dun trotted to Brasada. Brasada unhooked his canteens and began to fill them, but he did not take his eyes from Keesey. He hooked the dripping canteens to the saddle and then slid his rifle into the scabbard. He mounted the dun and looked down at the smiling man. "Sorry I can't take advantage of your hospitality," he said.

"Some other time," said Keesey expansively. "Duty first, eh?"

"Something like that," agreed Brasada.

They looked at each other for a moment. Then Brasada nodded. He touched the dun with his spurs and rode into the *bosque*. Once he looked back. Keesey was back at his reloading table at work again.

Beyond the *bosque* Brasada saw the first light of the rising moon. From a ridge he looked back, far back across the border to the peak of the Mountain, just faintly lighted by the moon. He shrugged and rode on into the pre-moon darkness.

The Mountain is still there with the great landslide at its eastern foot. There are no traces left of Soledad, and even the name and exact site of the old *poblado*

are no longer remembered in that border country.
The silver may still be there, although no one knows
exactly where it is. The clue would be the water, as it
was before the coming of Brasada. The spring had
never run dry since the time the Mountain had per-
formed the miracle of striking the barren earth with
a rock as Moses had struck the desert ground with his
staff to bring forth the clear gushing water. Perhaps
someday the spring may again work its way to the
surface. Some say it has already done so, and by so
doing, revealed to Brasada the cache of perhaps thirty
tons of pure native silver—when, and *if* he returned to
Soledad. *¿Quien sabe?*

GORDON D. SHIRREFFS

BLOOD JUSTICE

Chapter One

It was almost time for the first snow of the year. The first cold light of the dawn fingered the dark reaches of the eastern sky, but it was still dark in the valley of the Ute, while the river itself was a dull pewter ribbon against the shadows of the valley floor. The dawn wind had shifted and was driving up the valley, whipping the willows and thrashing the great limbs of the giant cottonwoods of the bottoms. Not a light showed in the sprawling town across the river. It was as though Ute Crossing were as dead as the Indian summer that had just fled to warmer climes. Beyond the sleeping town rose the low approaches to the tumbled, naked foothills, while beyond them, towering over the valley, dominating it while concealing the vast country westward, rose the grim saw-toothed mountains.

Jim Murdock shivered in the searching wind as he rode down the eastward slope of the valley floor toward the bridge that had long spanned the ford that had given the town its name. He hunched the collar of his sheepskin coat up under the brim of his faded stetson, and thrust a cold hand inside the coat to feel for the makings. It had been a long and lonely ride that dark night from the railhead to the east and he should have stayed the night there, but for some reason, unknown even to himself, he had wanted to get back to Ute Crossing as quickly as possible. To some of the people who lived there the name of Jim Murdock was still a bitter thing, almost an epithet, or so he had learned from his brother Ben's long, informative letters. But while there were a few who might remember him with warmer feelings, it was really the country that had brought him back.

He fashioned a quirly, protecting the loose tobacco from the boisterous wind with his broad back, then placed the cigarette between his lips. He snapped a match on a thumbnail and lighted the cigarette, the quick spurt of flame from the match revealing his gray eyes, the mahogany hue of his face, a product of too many border suns, the tiny sun wrinkles at the corners of his eyes, and the thin scar that traced a course from his left cheekbone down to the point of his hard jaw. Looking at Jim Murdock one would instinctively lower his voice and avoid looking for trouble, for here indeed was a lobo of a man.

He drew rein at the edge of the river and looked down at the swirling waters. He eyed the bridge, creaking in the strong liquid grip of the current, and then looked beyond the bridge toward the wide main street of Ute Crossing. It was almost as dark as the inside of a boot. He sat there for a few minutes, drawing in on the cigarette, and when he did so the flare of the burning tobacco made the hard planes of his face almost like a death mask. He would not look up at the gaunt saddle-backed ridge that rose just south of the town and bordered the tumbling waters of the Ute. Something kept him from looking up at that accursed hill that knobbed the near end of the ridge, and yet he knew that if he was made welcome in Ute Crossing and decided to live in that area, he would have to look at that damned hill many, many times in the long years to come.

The eastern sky was faintly lighted by the false dawn when Jim Murdock looked up at the hill, and the sight of the three great trees still standing there struck him like a blow across the face. They, at least, had not changed much in the seven years since he had left the valley of the Ute, saved by the grace of God and a fast buckskin horse. It was almost as though nature had placed those three trees there for some special purpose, for the rest of the hill and the gaunt ridge beyond it were as naked of growth as a suburb of hell itself.

He flipped the butt into the river and slowly rolled another smoke to drive the grinding hunger from his guts. From the looks of Ute Crossing he'd get no breakfast for quite some time. He lighted the fresh smoke and shoved back his hat. Crossing the Ute might be something like crossing the Styx, for there might never be a return. Many people had not forgotten Jim Murdock and his record in Ute Crossing, despite the fact that he had long been cleared of the charges that had sent him pounding through Wind Pass with a posse not too far behind him. There were still hard-eyed men who did not believe that Jim was innocent of the death of Curt Crowley, only son of Big Cass Crowley, the man who had run that part of the country as far back as most people could remember.

He looked up the dark street, and as he did so he saw a quick spurt of yellow light beyond the slab-sided double-decker building that served as the county seat as well as the calabozo. Maybe somebody was opening up early. Someone who could feed a man who had ridden almost thirty miles that night through the windy darkness.

He touched the sorrel with his heels and crossed the bridge to the far side. The horse's hoofs rang clearly on the hard-packed earth of the street. There was another flare-up of yellow light near the building, and for the first time Jim saw what looked like a group of men walking toward the entrance of the jail. He drew rein, narrowing his eyes. A cold feeling of hostility seemed to flow from that group of men, and yet none of them was looking toward the lone horseman near the bridge. They were intent on other business. A thudding noise came from the wide double door.

Jim dismounted and led the tired sorrel into an alleyway beside Slade's Livery Stable. He ground-reined the horse and walked to the dark mouth of the alleyway to look obliquely toward the jail. There wasn't a light on anywhere in the ugly yellow structure. A shift in the wind brought voices to him.

"Get a-goin', Barney," said one man.

"I'm doin' the best I can, Van," said the man at the door. Something snapped and one side of the door opened. "There! Slick as goose grease!"

The men crowded into the building. There were at least fifteen of them, sheepskin- or mackinaw-coated, hats pulled low, hard heels punching into the sagging wooden flooring, spurs chiming softly now and then. Three men stood outside the door, looking up and down the deserted street, Winchesters in hand.

A cold feeling flowed through Jim, turning his blood into what felt like icy red crystals, for there was something altogether too familiar about the scene spread out before him. It was almost as though part of his past were being played out. For an eerie moment the strange thought played through his mind that Ute Crossing was indeed a ghost town, haunted by the ghosts of the men who had broken into the jail one winter morning just before dawn and had hauled Jim Murdock from his cell while there was neither sight nor sound of the sheriff and his deputies.

He could hear them now within the building. A yellow rectangle of light showed where one of the windows was located on the east side of the building, and its bars cast a gridiron shadow on the dirty alleyway that bordered the structure. A cat scurried silently for cover from the revealing light. Something crashed hollowly within the jail, and a man shouted hoarsely. A door slammed.

They were making enough noise to awaken the whole

7

town, thought Jim. But the dark street remained empty, except for the three men who stood outside the jail with rifles in their hands, looking up and down the street and talking in low voices.

There was a clanging of metal against metal within the jail. Once more a man shouted, and then it was very quiet. The light winked out in the cell window.

Jim padded to the mouth of the alleyway. Through the dirty windows of the jail he saw occasional flashes of wavering light, as though a lantern was being carried through the echoing halls. He looked up and down the street. Not another light showed. Not a man moved. The bitter wind picked up dust and gravel and rattled it against windows and walls like a boy playing ticktacktoe on a Halloween night. A tattered newspaper rose from the street, glided upward, and then sailed off to vanish in the windy darkness.

There was a brief struggle at the jail door, and then a man's voice boomed out, "We've got 'em, boys! Jules, you get the horses! Get the three extra ones too, Webb! We can't expect our friends here to ride to the top of the hill!" He laughed loudly.

Jim wet his dry lips. Three men stood among the group. It was easy to spot them in the half-darkness for they did not wear hats. The wind blew the long dark hair of one of them down over his white face.

Two men hurried around the side of the jail and came back with some horses, followed by a third man with more horses. He held a rifle in his free hand.

Jim watched while the three hatless men were hoisted up into the saddles. They could not use their hands for they had been bound behind their backs. The lantern guttered on the jail steps. "Should we take the lantern along, Van?" called out a tall man.

"What for? We don't need any light for this job. Besides, it's almost dawn, Slim."

A boot heel drove against the lantern, smashing it against the side of the doorway, and it winked out. The smell of coal oil drifted across the wide street.

An intolerable crawling feeling came over Jim. Violence and blood were not strangers to him, for a man could hardly be raised in this country, or have spent as much time along the border as Jim had, without being accustomed to it, but there was something utterly alien about the activities across the street, as though these were not men of flesh and blood at all, but rather chimeras conjured up from the depths by some unseen sorcerer who chuckled evilly in the whining voice of the cold, bitter wind that scoured the valley of the Ute. The very evil of their actions and thoughts flowed outward from the group and enveloped Jim Murdock, and for a moment he was almost tempted to turn back, away from Ute Crossing, never to return, for he knew as sure as fate that the evil which had driven him from Ute Crossing was still extant.

There was enough light now to see more clearly. A horse nickered. Another danced sideways as his cursing owner, left foot thrust into stirrup, right hand gripping Winchester, hopped on his right foot trying to make the saddle. "Damn you, Spade!" he said to the skittish horse. "Stand still or we'll miss the hanging!"

What Jim had already realized was now fully proved by the man's statement. These *were* the preliminaries for a lynching; *a hanging at dawn*. The strange thought fled through his mind that such activity might indeed have become the sole occupation of the men of Ute Crossing and its environs. He had left to escape such a lynching, with himself as the victim, and had returned by some Devil's trick, to see another lynching. How many others had happened in his absence? His brother Ben had never written of such activities, but then Ben wouldn't. All he had ever written about was his teaching job, the future of Ute Crossing, the future of its young citizens entrusted to his care to learn to become good citizens. *Good citizens?* By the gods, it seemed to Jim as though lynchers were the only ultimate product of Ute Crossing's citizenry!

Horses were kneed aside to let the cursing man on foot mount his horse. "Stick with him, Lyss!" jeered one of the mounted men. "By God, he'll have his comeuppance when and *if* you straddle him. Hawww!"

There was a sudden movement from one of the bound, hatless men who had been brought from the jail. He raised a leg and slid agilely from the saddle, then ran like a spooked deer across the broad street, his chin outthrust and his eyes wide with fear and panic, expecting at any moment a soft-nosed slug between his shoulder blades. His booted feet slammed against the hard earth. For a moment it looked as though he'd make it from the street, although his chances of ever getting away were impossible.

Two horsemen broke loose from the group. One of them snatched his reata free and fashioned a loop as he rode toward the fleeing man, while the other raised his rifle.

"Christ's sake, Barney, don't shoot!" roared a man from the group. "We want him to swing!"

The fugitive veered, almost as though he expected a loop to drop about his shoulders. He raced toward the alleyway where Jim Murdock stood watching expressionlessly. For a moment he did not see Jim, and then his mouth squared, almost in agony. "For God's sake, mister! Stop them! We haven't done anything! We're innocent, I tell you!" There was a Mexican quality to his voice.

"Trip the bastard up!" yelled the man with the poised loop.

Jim stood aside, pressing back against the worn clapboard of the livery stable. All he had to do was thrust out a foot and the frightened man would drive his face cruelly against the flinty ground, but he could not bring himself to do it.

"Son of a bitch!" yelled the man with the rifle.

The man with the reata reached the alleyway first and threw a neat *peal*, catching the fugitive's feet in a figure-eight loop, as skillful an exhibition of roping as Jim had ever seen. Jim darted forward and dropped to a knee, catching the lassoed man across the chest with his left arm, saving his face from the hard-packed earth. The roper dropped from his saddle and came hand over hand down the rope as though he had roped a calf. "Who the hell are you?" he asked in a brittle voice of Jim.

Jim stood up and saw the man named Barney drop from his horse and plunge forward, stiff-legged, rifle at hip level, lever slamming down and up to load. The metallic sound grated like the creaking of the rusty gates of hell. Jim's .44 was holstered beneath his buttoned sheepskin, and he was twenty feet from his saddle-scabbarded Winchester. The rifleman stopped as Jim rose to his feet. The muzzle of his rifle touched one of the buttons of the sheepskin right over Jim's shrinking navel, and Jim found himself looking into pale gray eyes that were somehow disconcertingly familiar.

The roper coiled his reata and pulled the fugitive to his feet by twisting his free hand down under the man's collar, half choking him. He manhandled him toward the mouth of the alleyway. "Bring that bastard along, Barney," he said over his shoulder.

Jim wet his lips. He stared at the rifleman. "Barney Kessler," he said quietly.

Kessler stared back at Jim. "You know me?" he demanded.

"Ought to. We went to school together at the crossroads," said Jim dryly. "You've come a long way, Barney."

Barney's face looked even more ill-adjusted than it had in the old days. It had always seemed to Jim that Barney was really two different people, each one struggling to get the upper hand and neither ever succeeding, but managing to raise a pocket-sized edition of hell between them in the struggle.

Barney let down the rifle hammer to half cock. "By ginger," he said quietly. "Jim! Jim Murdock!"

Jim smiled thinly. "Now take that gun outa my gut, Barney, like a good boy. This coat is old and too thin to stop a .44/40 at this range."

Barney grounded the rifle. He smiled; then the smile vanished, then reappeared again, while his loose mouth worked a little. "You shouldn't ought to have done that, Jim," he said reproachfully.

"What?" asked Jim.

The smile came and fled. The eyes widened and narrowed. Barney Kessler's face had a way of looking like a picture coming into focus and then as rapidly slipping out of it, so one was never quite sure what he was seeing. "Been in the way," said Barney a little stupidly. The rich, fruity odor of spirits drifted to Jim.

"Come on, Barney!" yelled a man from across the street. "Bring that hombre with you!"

"You got to come along, Jim," said Barney.

"Where?"

"To the hill, of course."

"What for, Barney?" Jim knew well enough why they were going to the hill.

Barney jerked his head. "You're a witness," he said.

"To what?"

"You seen us take them men from the calabozo, didn' you, Jim?"

Jim nodded.

"We don't want no witnesses," repeated Barney.

The picture came clearly to Jim. They'd *invite* him along. He'd be under gun surveillance of course. He'd thus be considered one of the lynchers, unable to bear witness against them. He knew now why the streets of Ute Crossing were so empty, why no early riser's lights were showing.

"Get your hoss," said Barney. "Keep your hands away from that saddle gun."

Jim picked up the reins. He led the sorrel as Barney walked beside him toward the waiting group of men.

"Who is he?" called out a hard-voiced man.

11

"Jim Murdock," said Barney.

There was a moment's silence, and then a broad-shouldered, meaty-bellied man, kneed his horse toward them. "You're drunker than I thought you was," he said.

"You think I'm bullcrapping you, Lassen?" said Barney in an aggrieved tone. "I went to school with ol' Jim here and we was amigos in the old days, working for Cass Crowley, wasn't we?"

"I hope he didn't come back lookin' for his job with Cass," said another of the men. He laughed shortly. "He sure as hell made a long trip for nothing."

"Shut up, Jules," said Lassen. He peered at Jim. "By God! It's Murdock, all right!"

Jim looked up at the big man. "I see you haven't changed much, Lassen," he said quietly and coldly.

Lassen's eyes, hard as amber, studied Jim. "You always were loose with your lip, Murdock," he said.

"Let's get on with this, Van," said one of the men to Lassen. He looked nervously up and down the street. "We're making enough noise to wake the whole town."

Barney laughed. "Ain't no one going to come out and ask us what we're doing, Webb. You scairt?"

Webb flushed. "One of these days, Barney," he warned.

"You tough, Webb?" sneered Barney. "You wanta make something out of it?"

"Oh, my God," said another man. "The booze is making a fighting man outa Barney again."

Lassen slapped a hard hand down on his thigh. "You men think this is a damned church social? Shut up, I tell you! Maybe Webb is right at that! Look at the dawn!"

The eastern sky was strangely figured in dark and light grays, interwoven with a cold, pearly luminescence.

"Get up on that sorrel, Murdock," said Lassen.

Jim obediently mounted under the cold, hard eyes of the mob. Lassen jerked his head. Jim kneed the sorrel close beside the nearest of the prisoners, the one who had hopelessly tried to escape.

"All right, boys," said Van Lassen. "We all know the way, don't we!"

They clattered toward the eastern end of town where the ridge road ran at right angles to the main stem of Ute Crossing, a tight bunch of horsemen with the three prisoners, and Jim Murdock in the center of the group.

The man who had tried to escape looked at Jim. "*Gracias*," he said.

12

"*Por nada*," said Jim politely. He eyed the man. He was Mexican, all right. "You're a long way from home, amigo," he added quietly in his cowpen Spanish.

The dark eyes were sad. "This is a cold country and cold people. I might have expected something like this, amigo. A thousand Jesuses! I am not ready to die!"

"Cut out that spic talk!" snapped Barney Kessler. He slapped a hand on the breech of his rifle.

Jim reached inside his coat for the makings.

"Don't you pull no hideout gun on me!" roared Barney pugnaciously.

Jim withdrew the makings. He looked at Barney. "What kind of red-eye you been drinking, Barney?" he asked mildly. "You're almost talking like a real man."

Lassen laughed dryly.

Jim rolled a cigarette, lighted it, and placed it between the lips of the Mexican. He looked at the other two men. One of them was young, hardly out of his teens, maybe not even twenty yet, and his frightened blue eyes met Jim's with a sick look that almost repelled him. "Smoke?" said Jim.

The kid shook his head. His blond hair fell down over his forehead, and he impatiently threw it back with a toss of his head. The third man was older, plain of appearance, nondescript, looking ahead with no expression on his grizzled face. He looked to Jim like a man who had expected nothing better out of life than to die with a rope around his neck.

"Who's that?" said the man called Webb. He was still nervous.

Jim looked ahead. A slim man stood in the center of the street. His neat black hat was creased fore and aft. His dark coat was set off by a pure white shirt and string tie. His neat boots glistened with polish, and a badge of some sort shone on his coat lapel.

"By God," said Van Lassen. "It's Brady Short!"

Jim leaned forward in his saddle. He had not seen Brady Short for seven long years, and had often thought of him. Brady had been Jim's chief rival for the favor of Ann Whitcomb, only daughter of Judge Enos Whitcomb, chief legal light of that country. Ann had been head and shoulders the best-looking belle in Ute Crossing, if not in the whole valley of the Ute.

"You think he means to stop us, Van?" asked Webb.

Lassen turned in his saddle, and the look on his face seemed to lash Webb across the face like a quirt. "Ain't

13

nobody goin' to stop us, Webb," he said harshly. "Not even Brady Short!"

The riders drew to a halt as Brady Short raised a slim hand.

Chapter Two

"Do you men realize what you are doing?" asked Short.

"We got a pretty good idea," said Barney Kessler brightly.

"Don't give us none of your pretty lawyer talk, Brady," said the man named Lyss.

"I didn't plan to," said the lawyer. He touched the badge on his lapel. "As a deputy sheriff of this county, I advise you to return those men at once to the jail."

Barney guffawed. "Hell's fire, Brady!" he said. "Where'd you get that tin badge? In a box of taffy candy from Gamble's Drugstore?"

The lawyer flushed. "Certainly it's only an honorary title given to me by Sheriff Cullin, and if it doesn't mean anything to you, I then appeal to you as law-abiding citizens not to take the law into your own hands. Take those men back."

"After you've seen who we are?" asked Lassen.

"You didn't expect to get away with it, did you, Van?" asked Short.

"Was you planning to give us away, Mr. Short?" asked Lassen in return.

Lassen's implication was plain enough.

Short swallowed. He was scared, but he stood his ground. "That wasn't my point," he said.

"His point is that he'd make a lot of ground in his chasin' of the judge's position if he managed, single-handed, so to speak, to stop a mob," said a gray-haired man. He shifted in his saddle. "By God, Short, you get to hell outa our way or you'll never get no vote from me, and I been in your party since before you was born!"

Jim studied the lawyer. Brady hadn't lost any of his good looks. He was older than Jim by at least eight years, and the touch of gray at his temples and in his neat moustache had

14

added dignity to the clear freshness the "boy wonder" of the bar in that county had always had, coupled with a sharp, precise legal mind.

"Then you won't listen to me?" said the lawyer.

There was no answer. Hoofs thudded against the ground as though the horses too were anxious to get the business over with.

Lassen jerked his head. The lawyer walked toward his black horse, tethered to a hitching rack in front of the general store. As the group passed he mounted and rode behind them. Jim turned in his saddle. "Hello, Brady," he said.

Brady's dark eyes narrowed. "Jim Murdock!" he said. "What are you doing here?"

Jim shrugged. "Come home to roost," he said with a faint, bitter smile. "Find myself *invited* to this lynching. You follow me?"

Short nodded. "You picked a great time to come home," he said quietly.

"I have a habit of doing such things," said Jim.

"When this is over you must come and see us, Jim. Ann will be glad to see you, I'm sure."

Jim's eyes narrowed. "Ann Whitcomb?"

Brady smiled proudly. "Ann Short," he said. "Mrs. Brady Short, Jim."

Jim felt sick deep within his guts. He had known that Ann must be married by now. He had never asked Ben in his letters about her, for a man's stubborn pride is a hard thing to defeat, particularly in the case of women. It was logical enough she would have married Brady Short. Her father had been the best lawyer in that part of the country. She would have cottoned to one as good as Brady Short. It was in the cards, and the deck had not been stacked.

Jim turned again. He let his horse drift back toward Brady and no one stopped him. Their eyes were on the naked ridge and the ugly hill at the end of it, crowned with its three horrifying trees.

Brady held out a slim hand to meet the hard grasp of Jim's hand. "I did the best I could," he said. "You witnessed that."

"What did they do?" asked Jim.

Brady's eyes narrowed. "You don't know?"

"They never bothered to tell me," said Jim dryly.

"They murdered Cass Crowley," said the lawyer.

Jim stared at him. "Cass Crowley? Old Indestructible?"

"Yes. Cass had been negotiating to sell out his holdings.

There was supposed to be a lot of money at his place. Most of his men had been paid off. He was alone at the ranch house. He never had a chance, Jim. Three bullet holes in the back of his head. When Sheriff Cullin caught up with these three each of them had an empty chamber in his gun. Murray Cullin thinks each of them placed a bullet in Cass' head so that each of them would share the guilt. They're sharing the guilt all right."

"Cass Crowley," said Jim in wonderment. "He was like Warrior Peak around here." He looked back toward the saw-toothed mountains. The first light of the dawn was silvering the snow-capped tip of Warrior Peak, the great up-thrust finger of stone that had always seemed to admonish the valley of the Ute and the people who lived there. Nothing would ever destroy or bring down Warrior Peak.

The wind was sweeping along the river road, driving dust, papers and tumbleweeds ahead of it into the fence corners and against the trees that bordered the road in between it and the brawling Ute.

Van Lassen turned toward the faintly rutted, almost indistinguishable road that led vaguely up the side of the ridge. It was then that a buckboard was seen in the middle of the road. Its driver was standing up, reins in his left hand, right hand upraised, as Brady Short's hand had been raised back in town.

"It's 'Deacon' Hitchins," said Webb.

The group came to a halt, sitting their horses in the narrow road, hemmed in by the swaying bushes. Van Lassen rode forward. "You aimin' to stop us too, Deacon?" he said.

Jim stood up in his stirrups. It had been seven years since he had seen Alfred Hitchins, local businessman, city father, staunch pillar of the church, a man widely known for his sanctity and honesty, called "Deacon" with respect by one and all, although he had never served in such a capacity. It was Al Hitchins who had helped Ben Murdock get his education after he had been crippled, and who had damned well seen to it that Ben was installed as teacher in Ute Crossing Elementary School; despite the stigma of the name Murdock at that time.

The businessman dropped the reins. "Think of what you are doing, men," he said softly. His round face worked a little. "For the love of the God whom we all cherish and obey, do not do this thing."

Lassen touched the brim of his hat. "We're seeing that justice is done, Mr. Hitchins," he said, not without respect.

"This is not justice, Vanderbilt," said Hitchins quietly.

16

Alfred Hitchins was the only man Ute Crossing knew who could use Van Lassen's first name with impunity.

"You'd better get out of the way, sir," said Lassen.

"I have no way of stopping you. God give me the faith and the strength to do so. Think, men! Think of what you are doing! These men are God's lambs. It is not up to us to destroy them because we believe they have done wrong."

"Some lambs," said Barney Kessler. He looked about, expecting a laugh.

"Shut up, Barney," said Van Lassen shortly.

There was a long pause. The dawn light had almost tipped the eastern range far beyond the valley of the Ute. Slowly Al Hitchins drove his buckboard aside to an opening in the waving brush. The group jingled past up the slope of the hill, and not one of them looked at the man of God; no one except the kid looked at him. His face seemed to plead for help, but there was no help. Hitchins's eyes were moist. He raised a hand. "Jesus wept," he said. No one seemed to hear him except Jim Murdock.

Jim looked up at the three trees. They had a perpetual slant from the cruel battering winds that swept wildly up the valley of the Ute in the late fall, winter, and early spring. Maybe the wind should have felled them long ago, but for some reason they had resisted all efforts of the wind to do so. Battered and gnarled, twisted and ugly, they seemed to reek with an insensate evil. Jim looked away. One of them had almost borne his lifeless body, swinging stiff-legged in the constant wind, tongue protruding, seven long years ago. The sickness returned to his guts and his mind. There was nothing he could do for these three doomed men. Not a single blessed thing!

The horses were reined in. All dismounted except the three prisoners. The Mexican was stony-faced; only his great eyes were alive. The older man bowed his head and stared unseeingly at his saddle horn. Now and then his bottom lip quivered. The kid looked about him with unbelieving eyes. Once he looked quickly down at his trousers, and when he looked up again his face was deeply flushed. No one seemed to notice his embarrassment, but the wind, in its insensitivity to all human feeling, brought the odor of his embarrassment to the hard-faced men who stood there.

The roper stepped out into the open, coiled reata in his hand. He eyed the first of the trees, then smoothly cast the reata, uncoiling like a snake, up over a great limb, while the weight of the loop and honda brought the end down to his feet. Three times he made a perfect cast. He did not look

17

up at the three shivering prisoners as he quickly fashioned a hangman's noose at the end of each of the three reatas.

Barney Kessler swung up on his mare and picked up the first of the loops, widening it quickly, to drop it over the shoulders of the older man. He tightened and placed the knot in professional fashion under the man's left ear. The second loop went about the Mexican's slim neck. The kid bent his head, pressing his chin down against his thin chest to prevent the loop going about his neck. "Come on, kid," said Barney. "We ain't got all day."

The kid turned his head away, pressing down hard on his chin. Barney swung a big hand, catching the kid cruelly over the ear, so hard he must have broken an eardrum. The kid screamed in terror but did not raise his head. Barney drew back his hand once more.

"You hit that kid again, Barney," said Jim coldly, "and I'll break your dirty neck!"

Barney turned quickly. He had left his rifle leaning against one of the trees. There was pure hell in his pale, washed-out eyes. Then his eyes met those of Jim Murdock and his face seemed to slide, dissolve, go in and out of focus.

"He's right," said Webb.

"You keep outa this!" said Barney.

Webb turned a little and moved his rifle. "You heard me, you drunken son of a bitch," he said thinly.

The kid raised his head. "Go on," he said in a choked voice. "I ain't afraid."

Barney saw his out. He wanted no part of Webb and much less of Jim Murdock. "You ain't, kid?" he said in a kindly voice. He smiled benignly, almost like Alfred Hitchins.

"No!" said the kid desperately.

"Then how come you shit your drawers?" demanded Barney. He guffawed. He looked about at the others.

His cruelty struck even hard-faced Van Lassen. "Get on with it, Barney," he said. "Shoulda knowed better than to let you do anything around here."

"Aw, hell, Van," said Barney sheepishly. "I was only joshing."

"This ain't no time for joshing!" snapped Lassen.

But Barney Kessler, no man himself, had effectively stripped the last tatters of manhood from the kid. The boy was completely broken now, a sobbing, retching thing that made even Van Lassen look away.

The Mexican spat to one side. "*Cobarde!*" he said in a low voice to Barney. "Give me a knife, *bazofia*, and we will see the color of your guts! A month's pay they are yellow!"

18

Barney grinned loosely. "No bets," he said. "This is a serious occasion, spic! Besides, where would you get a month's pay? Shovelin' cinders in hell with the Devil ramroddin' you?"

Silence came, except for the whining of the wind and the snuffling of some of the horses.

Van Lassen looked up. "You men got anything to say?" he said, not unkindly.

The Mexican shrugged. "One day is as good as the next to die. It is not the thought of dying, hombres, that is painful, only the way of it." He bent his head and mouthed silent prayers.

"You?" said Lassen to the older man.

The man shook his head without raising it.

"Kid?" said Lassen.

"I got a sister," said the kid. His voice broke.

"He's got a sister," jeered Barney.

"Go on, kid," said Van Lassen.

"I got a sister," repeated the kid slowly. "Lives in Three Forks, over the mountains west of here. Name of Jessica. You'll tell her I died?"

Lassen nodded. He looked at Barney. Barney deftly tightened the nooses. Oh, he was good at *that,* thought Jim Murdock. The loose-mouthed polecat couldn't shoot, rope or ride, but he was good at anything like that.

There was a long pause, and then Lassen raised his hand. Three men, one of them Barney, of course, stepped behind the three horses. Barney grinned as he fingered his quirt. Lassen's hand was steady. All eyes were on it. Lassen dropped his hand with a sharp downward stroke. Three quirts struck the rumps of the three horses, and they buckjumped forward in sudden pain and fear. The Mexican's neck snapped cleanly. The older man raised his head, shrieked hoarsely, fought the rope for a moment, and then hung still. The kid fought like a tiger, kicking his legs upward as he fought the killing noose, thrashing and turning, until Barney ran forward and gripped his legs and pulled down on them.

There was a long silence as the three bodies swayed, twisting and turning in the wind, the tree limbs creaking beneath the unaccustomed weight. Although they should have been used to it by now, thought Jim. They had served this purpose before and might do it again. . . .

"Well," said Van Lassen. "There ain't no use in standin' around here freezin' our butts. Come on, boys! We'll drag Baldy outa his sack and get a few rounds of drinks. We earned it, I think."

Jim watched the men mount. Some of them took the riderless horses in tow as they started down the narrow, winding road. No one spoke to him. He was a dead issue now. He had participated in the merciless lynching just as much as most of them had, for he had stood there and had done nothing to save the three doomed men. It was then he noticed that Brady Short had not come up to the hill. Hoofs clattered on the hard earth, leather squeaked, a horse blew. In a few minutes they were all gone, leaving nothing behind but the acrid odor of fresh horse droppings and the cold, almost imperceptible odor of fresh death.

Jim rubbed his bristly jaws and looked up at the three men, and for the first time he realized he did not even know their names, nor had any of the others mentioned their names. The only thing Jim knew was that the kid had a sister named Jessica whom he had wanted to be notified about his death.

Jim slowly rolled a smoke and lighted it, looking up at the three dead men twisting in the wind, swinging stiffly back and forth in the gallows' dance. "Jessica," he said quietly. "How does a man tell a girl named Jessica her kid brother crapped in his drawers just before he was lynched for murder in Ute Crossing?"

There was no answer in the whining wind. It was getting colder and had an edge to its invisible teeth.

Jim felt in his pocket for his clasp knife and then shook his head. No use in him cutting them down, and besides he did not want to touch them, or have any part in their lynching, before or after. Dead men had relatives someplace, who might just come looking for the men who had lynched their kin.

He flipped his cigarette butt away and rolled another. The sun had peeked up above the eastern range, a cold, watery sun that would bring little heat, if any at all, to the valley of the Ute. The growing light had crept across the hills and worked its way down into the valley before Jim mounted his sorrel and rode him down the twisting road toward the river road.

There was a different feeling in the wind. A driving gust of it struck Jim's face like stinging, sharp-edged grit, and it wasn't until he reached the bottom of the slope that he realized that it wasn't grit at all, but the harsh reality of the first snowfall of the year.

20

Chapter Three

A knot of men sat their horses near the bridge as Jim Murdock rode into the teeth of the wind and the stinging snowflakes. It wasn't until he reached the first building at the southeastern corner of the main street and the river road that he realized the men were what was left of the posse, if one could call it a posse. More like a lynching bee, thought Jim. Some of them were there. Van Lassen, Barney, and the men named Webb, Slim, and Lyss. Brady Short stood to one side, holding the reins of his black, and beyond him Alfred Hitchins sat in his buckboard listening to the words of the tall, broad-shouldered man who sat his gray squarely in front of the hard-faced men who had just hanged three people. Jim recognized the tall man as Sheriff Murray Cullin, one of the best lawmen in the territory.

Cullin held a legal-looking paper in his left hand, the biting wind flapping it about. "I got clear to Benedict Junction late yesterday afternoon," said Cullin, "and sent a wire to the governor for a change of venue for those three men up on that hill there. The wires were down south of town and there was no time to waste. I took the freight train to Parthia and caught a fast passenger run to the capital. Caught the governor ten minutes before he was to leave for Washington and got the change of venue. Took the train back to Parthia, got a fast horse, the fastest horse I could get, and came over Wolf Pass in the dark, pushing that horse all the way, and got here twenty minutes too late! Well, you've had your way, men." He ripped up the paper and let the scraps drift from his big hand. They flew southward with the tiny flakes of snow. "You know what you've done. Brady Short and Mr. Hitchins did their duty as law-abiding citizens to stop you from this crime. You'd listen to no one, would you?"

"You sayin' they weren't guilty, Sheriff Cullin?" asked Slim.

The sheriff's face tightened and he tugged at his dragoon moustache. "Cass Crowley and I were raised together," he

21

said fiercely. "By God, he was like a brother to me! I could have killed those three men when I caught them and no one would have been the wiser, nor would they have cared. But I had the law to uphold. If I break it, then there is no restraint on men like you. The law would have dealt fairly with them, and there is no doubt in my mind that any jury would have found them guilty!"

"Then what's the beef about?" said Van Lassen. "We just saved the county a bill they can't afford right now. Ain't we citizens? Ain't we got rights? Well, we took those rights. We hung 'em, and you can do what you damned well like about it, Sheriff, but let me tell *you* something. You said there wasn't any doubt but what any jury would have found them guilty. Well, you bring us to trial and you won't find any jury that will find us guilty. Not here in Ute Crossing. Not in this county! Not in this whole damned state!"

Cullin shrugged. He knew these men. He also knew Van Lassen was right, and there wasn't anything Cullin could do about it now. He kneed his gray aside and watched the group ride toward the Grape Arbor, not the biggest but certainly the roughest saloon in Ute Crossing, if not in the county, if not in the whole damned state, as Van Lassen had just put it concerning juries.

"An eye for an eye," said Hitchins. " 'Vengeance is mine; I will repay, saith the Lord.' "

Cullin nodded. His eyes caught sight of Jim Murdock. "You," he said coldly.

"I didn't have any choice, Sheriff," said Jim. "They made me go along because I might be a witness against them—as though that mattered."

"I wasn't thinking of that, Murdock," said the lawman.

Jim rolled a cigarette. He looked at the tall man as he wet the edge with his tongue and folded over the paper. "I was cleared of those charges, Cullin," he said quietly.

"Not in my book you weren't, Murdock."

"Are you the sole judge of law around here?"

Cullin leaned forward in his saddle. "I keep two books," he said thinly. "One for those who have not been caught for committing crimes. One for those who have broken the law and gotten away with it."

"And no book for those who have been cleared?"

Cullin smiled without any light in his eyes. "I don't bother with them, mister," he said.

"So you still consider me guilty of killing Curt Crowley?"

There was no answer from the lawman. He turned his horse and rode toward the jail. It was answer enough for

Jim Murdock. He might have expected it from Murray Cullin.

Brady Short led his black toward Jim. "He doesn't mean that," he said.

"Thanks," said Jim dryly. "He sounded convincing enough to me."

Brady studied Jim. "You've changed," he said. "For a moment, when you first spoke to me, I didn't recognize you at all."

"I've been around a bit, Brady," said Jim.

"Where?"

Jim held out the makings to Brady. The lawyer shook his head. "Where, Jim?" he repeated.

"Along the border. Arizona. New Mexico. Texas. Mexico."

"You did all right for yourself?"

Jim smiled. "I worked most of the time," he said. "Made a small strike in the Guadalupes and have an Apache bullet scar on my left thigh to prove it."

"What kind of work, Jim?"

Jim rolled a cigarette. "Stock detective. Texas Rangers for a hitch. Scouted for the Army. You know the usual run of such things. It's been a long time, Brady."

The snow swirled high over the street. Alfred Hitchins had driven silently away, and his buckboard stood in front of the Ute Valley Mercantile Company. He was nowhere in sight.

Jim jerked a thumb over his shoulder, toward the hill and its grisly fruit. "What about them?" he said. "You surely don't want the kids, the future citizens of Ute Crossing, to see these products of justice, do you, Brady?"

"Murray Cullin will take care of it."

Jim drew in on his cigarette. "Who were they, Brady?"

"Drifters. Saddle tramps. Bums. No one really knows who they are or where they came from."

"Figures," said Jim.

"Where are you staying, Jim? With your brother?"

Jim shook his head. "Ben might not like my habits, Brady."

"You are welcome to stay with us. Ann and I have taken over the old Whitcomb place. The old judge passed away last year." The lawyer laughed. "You know how big that place is. We have help, of course. It's quite too much for Ann, you know."

"Any kids, Brady?"

The lawyer flushed. "Well, no. You see . . . I—Well, hang it all, Jim, it's a personal matter really, isn't it?"

"Sure, Brady. Clumsy of me to ask that way."

"You'll come, then?"

23

Jim shook his head. "Thanks just the same. I said Ben might not like my habits. I'm sure Ann and you wouldn't like them either."

"You'll come for dinner, then, sometime?"

"Be delighted," said Jim. He touched his sorrel with his heels and rode a few feet. He reined in and looked back at the lawyer. "The kid has a sister named Jessica," he said. "Lives in Three Forks. West of here, over the mountains."

Brady had a puzzled look on his handsome face. He nodded. He watched Jim ride toward the livery stable, shrugged, then mounted his horse and rode out on the river road, north of town, toward the big house that he called home.

Jim swung down in front of Slade's Livery Stable. Yellow light showed through a dusty, cracked window where Old Man Slade had had his office in the old days. Jim opened the door. An incredibly tall and incredibly thin man, all knobs and angles and no meat, turned quickly from a stove where he was brewing coffee. "Jesus God," he said. "Shut that damned door! We ain't open for business yet, mister."

"Meany Gillis," said Jim. "I thought you had withered away to all bones by now."

Meanwell Gillis eyed Jim with watery green eyes; then he grinned, revealing a gap-toothed mouth. "Jim," he said with genuine pleasure. He thrust out an incredibly thin hand. "Set and have some joe, amigo! Barney Kessler said you was in town."

"He ought to know," said Jim. "Let me put my sorrel up. He needs feed and rest."

"Sure thing, Jim. Lemme open the big door."

Jim went outside as Meany withdrew the bars and opened one of the front doors to let Jim in. Jim led the sorrel into a stall, unsaddled him, rubbed him down, and then gave him feed. He could hear Meany puttering around in the office, and the tantalizing smell of Arbuckle's best brew drifted out to him.

Jim peeled off his coat and hung it on a nail, then walked into the warm office. He twirled a chair and sat down in it, arms resting on the back, chin resting on his arms. "Where's Old Man Slade?" he said.

"Dead five years, Jim. I took over from Mrs. Slade."

"You always wanted this place, eh, Meany?"

The thin one grinned. "It ain't much, but I call it home." He served up the steaming brew in huge granite cups. He sat down in his desk chair and placed the cup on the littered desk. "Seems as though you picked one helluva time to come home, James."

"It's a habit of mine, Meany."

The man nodded. "Well, I never believed you was guilty. You can bet your bottom dollar on that, James."

"Why, Meany?" Jim sipped the coffee and felt it begin its good work.

Meany shrugged. "I been around horses all my life. You get to know 'em pretty well, I'd say. Dogs, too. They ain't too different from people, come to think of it."

"How about jackasses?"

Meany grinned. "Meaning you, James? You ain't no jackass, although there ain't nothing stupid about a good jackass. Bullheaded, maybe, but not stupid. Your father was no fool, and Ben certainly ain't."

Jim looked down at the dark circle of steaming coffee. "Seems like I cost my father his ranch supply business. No one wanted to do business with Jim Murdock's father."

"Well, you got to admit Cass Crowley was his best customer," said Meany.

Jim looked up. "And when Crowley stopped doing business with him so did every other rancher in this country."

Meany nodded. "It was like one of them boykits, or something like that, where nobody wants to do business with you."

"Boycott," said Jim. "From what I hear it was more like a quarantine. First it cost me my mother. She wasn't well, and sitting around watching my father worry and get old before her eyes didn't help much."

"Well, like you said, she wasn't well."

"There wasn't anything wrong with my father's health when I left here, Meany."

Meany sipped his coffee. He eyed Jim over the lip of the big cup. "Looks like your troubles cost you your pa and your ma and made a cripple outa your brother Ben."

"Meaning I should have stayed away, eh?"

Meany shook his head. "A man has a right to live his own life the way he wants to, James."

"What about those three men up on the hill, Meany?"

Meany looked away. "Well, what about them?" he echoed.

"Who were they?"

Meany shrugged. "They called them John Does or something like that."

"They had no names?"

"Oh, they gave names all right. No one believed them anyways."

"No one?"

Meany stood up and walked to the dirty window. "They

just wouldn't talk. The older hombre was called Gil. The Mex answered to the handle of Orlando. The young one only answered to the name of Kid."

"He has a sister named Jessica," said Jim.

Meany turned. "You know her?"

Jim shook his head. "He spoke about her at the last. He asked Van Lassen to get word to her."

Meany spat into the filthy garboon. "Yeh," he said.

"What do you mean?"

"You ought to know Van better'n that!"

"You mean he won't do it?"

Meany placed a thin hand on Jim's shoulder. "Didn't you know Van was ramroddin' for Cass Crowley when the old man was murdered?"

"There's a helluva lot I don't know," said Jim dryly.

"Cass Crowley was like God to Van Lassen. Maybe more. Ol' Cass was about the only rancher in the valley who could handle Van. By godfrey, he got work outa that man, too! Van seemed to appreciate the fact the old man gave him pretty much of a free rein up at the ranch. If it hadn't been for Crowley, Van would have had to leave this country."

Jim emptied his cup and held it out for Meany to fill it. "What beats me is that Murray Cullin walks outa here and lets those lynchers walk into the jail as sweet as you please. Where was the jailkeeper this morning? Where were Cullin's deputies?"

"They found old Mike Curry, the jailkeeper, out cold in one of the cells with a goose egg on his head. Harlan Meigs was deputy. Well, it seems as though some of the boys got him likkered up in the Ute House Bar last night. He got as far as the jail and passed out in the office. That answer your question?"

"Very neat," murmured Jim.

"Well, they did kill the old man," said Meany. "I don't cotton to lynchings, but they woulda been hung anyways, James."

Jim rolled a cigarette. *"It is not the thought of dying, hombres, that is painful, only the way of it,"* said Jim.

Meany smiled. "Say, that's pretty good! Who said that? One of them Greek philosophers, maybe?"

"Fellow by the name of Orlando," said Jim.

"Was he a philosopher?"

Jim lighted the cigarette and blew a smoke ring. He punched a lean forefinger through the ring. "You could call him that," he said.

The door swung open, letting in a blast of icy air and a

26

swirl of dry snowflakes. A short, potbellied man shook the snow from his hat. "I'll need the team, Meany," he said.

"You want the hearse too, Mr. Dakers?"

"Can't get it up that hill. I'll take the buckboard. I'll need some help. Can you get away?"

Meany shook his head.

"I can't get them down by myself and I can't lift them into the wagon. No one wants to go with me," said Dakers. He shook his head. "I don't know why."

"Maybe the whole town is ashamed of itself," said Jim.

Dakers eyed Jim. "I don't know you," he said.

"Jim Murdock."

Dakers's lips tightened into a straight line. "Oh," he said quietly.

"You've heard of me, then, Mr. Dakers?"

The undertaker nodded. "Some," he admitted.

"More likely a lot," said Jim. He flipped his cigarette into the garboon. "I'll go with you."

Dakers smiled. "That's very nice of you, Mr. Murdock."

"You might get into trouble with the leading citizens by associating with me, Mr. Dakers."

Dakers put on his hat. "My business is with the dead, not with the living. That's my rule, Mr. Murdock. I am a man of rules. I abide by them. Keeps a man disciplined and out of trouble. Follow a good set of rules, I say, and you'll keep out of trouble. Do you agree?"

Jim reached through the door that led into the stable and took his sheepskin from the nail. He shrugged into it and buttoned it. "We'll need something to cover the bodies," he said. "I'll get it." He walked into the stable where Meany was getting the team ready.

Dakers wet his thin lips, helped himself to a cup of coffee, and rubbed his plump jowls. "Jim Murdock," he said thoughtfully. He sipped the coffee. "Business might just pick up at that, after a poor fall season."

Jim led the team out through the front door in a swirling cloud of dry flakes. The wind cut through his thin sheepskin. He swung up into the seat and held out the reins to Dakers. The undertaker shook his head. Jim drove toward the river. There were lights on in some of the stores by this time. A number of horses stood hipshot at the racks, rumps against the biting wind, tails flying every which way. Here and there along the wide street stood men, hats pulled down over their eyebrows, shoulders hunched beneath their thick collars, hands thrust deep into side pockets, watching the buckboard rattling toward the river, and some of the men had eyes for Jim Murdock alone.

Jim halted the team at the crest of the hill and eyed the three stiff bodies swinging like grisly pendulums to and fro, twisting now and then as in some eerie sarabande, accompanied by the wild threnody of the wind and the undertone of the creaking tree limbs.

"Horrible," said Dakers.

Jim dropped to the ground. He took out his clasp knife and walked to the nearest tree.

"Those are fine ropes," said Dakers. "Can't you just untie them? They're worth a few dollars, Mr. Murdock."

Jim turned and looked at the man. Dakers flushed. "Well, there's not much profit in burying such people," he said.

"Did you get paid to bury them?"

Dakers nodded. "Mr. Hitchins stopped in this morning. Gave me a hundred dollars toward their burial. No profit, of course. I might just break even."

"I'll bet," said Jim dryly. He slashed the first rope, then whirled and caught the body of the man named Gil. He carried it to the buckboard and placed it inside. Next he cut down the Mexican and loaded him in beside Gil. For a moment he looked up at the set blue face of the kid, and then he cut him loose and carried him to the vehicle. He severed the taut nooses and threw the foul ropes into the brush.

The wind howled mournfully. It was likely the only sorrow that would be shown for these three unfortunates.

"The digging will be hard," said Dakers. "Business is always better in the early winter, but the ground is hard. Well, we do the best we can in all seasons, eh, Mr. Murdock?"

Jim climbed up into the seat and took the reins. "I wouldn't know," he said. He did not look back as he turned the team and drove down the hill, hearing Dakers's prattle, but not listening to it. Every time the wheels hit a bump or went into a rut he heard something else—the mute, heavy protestations of the bodies in the back.

Jim drove the buckboard up behind Dakers Funeral Parlor and carried the bodies inside for the undertaker, placing them on slabs. Dakers shut the door and took off his hat. "There's no need to hold them," he said. "There will be no one here to see them, poor fellows. Swiftly, swiftly. . . . Ashes to ashes; dust to dust, *et cetera, et cetera.* . . ."

Jim unbuttoned his coat and felt for the makings.

"No smoking in here, Mr. Murdock," said Dakers. "Respect for the dead, you know."

28

Jim rolled a cigarette and lighted it. He blew a reflective cloud of smoke. "I wonder who they really were," he said, more to himself than to Dakers.

"Their full names are not known."

Jim looked at the man. "Maybe we'd better try to find out," he said.

Dakers shrugged. He felt in his pocket and brought out a limp dollar bill which he extended to Jim. "Here," he said. "For services rendered."

Jim grinned. "Don't put a strain on yourself, Mr. Dakers. Like you said, there's no profit in burying men such as these."

The dollar bill vanished like a gopher into a hole. "If there is anything I can do for you, Mr. Murdock," said Dakers.

"There is."

"Say it, Mr. Murdock."

Jim looked at the bodies. "I'd like to search them."

Dakers frowned. "Why? This is most irregular."

Jim blew a smoke ring. "Someone has to find out who they really were. As far as I can see, no one wants to do that."

Dakers turned his hat around and around in his plump hands. "I can't let you do that. Sheriff Cullin might not like it."

"He doesn't have to know," said Jim.

"I abide by a simple set of rules, Mr. Murdock."

Jim shrugged. He held out a big hand. "I'll take that dollar, then, and two more, one for each body."

Dakers frowned. "Well, it *is* highly irregular, but go ahead." He smiled a rather oily smile. "Any valuables, of course, are to be entrusted to me."

Jim shook his head. "Any valuables go to the next of kin."

"Unknown," said Dakers.

Jim flipped his cigarette into the open front of the stove. "I'll have to ask Brady Short, Alfred Hitchins, or Sheriff Cullin the correct procedure for any valuables or possessions, Mr. Dakers."

Dakers flushed again. "As you please," he said. "Excuse me, Mr. Murdock." He walked into the front of the long building and shut the door behind him, leaving Jim with the dead.

Jim lighted a Rochester lamp that hung over the marble slabs. Swiftly he went through the pockets of the three corpses. He peeled back their clothing and looked for markings of any kind, but outside of manufacturers' labels in some of the cheap clothing there were no identifying marks.

29

Jim drew sheets over the bodies and covered the set blue faces. He heard the front door open and close. Swiftly he gathered up the items he had found and placed them in three different pockets, thus separating them according to the body from which he had removed them. He put out the lamp and left by the back door, coming through the alleyway in time to see Dakers talking to Sheriff Cullin on the front steps of the jail. Cullin nodded and walked with the little undertaker across the street through the swirling snow toward the funeral parlor.

Jim walked past the front of the funeral parlor as the two men walked into the back room where the bodies were. He went quickly to the livery stable and got his cantle roll, emptied his saddlebags of what he required, placed the items in a feed sack, told Meany that if anyone asked for him he'd gone out to see his brother Ben, then hurried through the rear alleyway to the back entrance of the Ute House. He registered for a second-floor corner room overlooking the central part of town and went upstairs.

He closed the door of his room and dropped his gear, then walked to the window, parting the heavy curtains with his forefinger in time to see Sheriff Cullin walk toward the livery stable. Jim grinned. He was unknown to the hotel clerk, so if anyone asked for him and did not ask to see the register, he had time enough to go through the items he had taken from the bodies before Murray Cullin tracked him down.

Chapter Four

Jim peeled off his sheepskin and scaled his hat at a hook. He unbuckled his gun belt and hung it over the back of a chair, then took out the silver-mounted, double-barreled derringer he had won in a poker game in El Paso and checked both chambers. He slid it into a pants pocket. He locked the door and then turned his attention to the three little piles of dead men's relics.

The man named Gil had a left a half-bitten plug of Winesap, a handful of change, a lead pencil with a broken point, a filthy bandanna, and a piece of paper, spotted, wrinkled and limp, with badly written words upon it.

Deer Sarah, [read Jim] I take pencil in hand to write you these few lines. I didn't get the job with Masterson like he said he would but there is a Mex I met at Maddows who is a nice fella, who says he and I can turn a trick or two together north of here. Well I don't know but I am out of scratch and need work so I can send for you my dear Sarah. I hocked my riffle and good saddel in Maddows to a Jew who seems like he is all right for scratch, to go with the Mex who is all right for a spic I tell you Sarah. I can't always have bad luck Sarah and you know no one to home will give me a job because of the old days which are long gone and won't never come back I tell you. I will mail this letter from Ute Crossing which the spic says is a good place for work. Ha ha Sarah any place is a good place of work for me. I say goodbye now and send you my best wishes, and be patent for I will soon have good work and scratch for both of us my dear Sarah.

Gil turned the pitiful letter over. There was no address. Who was Sarah? He shrugged and placed the letter in his wallet, and left the other items on the bed.

Orlando the Mexican had left a little more than Gil. A finely figured Mexican wallet with a badly faded picture of a woman and two little children seated in front of an adobe house with *ristras* of peppers hanging down like great bunches of fruit. He turned the picture over. He could just make out the faded words "Santa Fed . . ." There were a few Mexican bills in the wallet. A tobacco pouch and a few sweet Mexican cigarettes. A gilt button with the Mexican coat of arms of snake and eagle and the letter C embossed below them, likely from an army uniform. There was a worn leather box about the size of a medal box. Jim opened it. A beautiful, though worn, hunting-case watch was set in the faded green velvet. He opened the lid and looked at the dial. "American Horologe Company, Waltham, Mass.," he read. He worked a thumbnail under the back cover and snapped it open. A fine script had been engraved within. "To Teniente Teodoro . . . . For heroic services rendered at Colonia . . . ." read Jim. Part of the lettering had been scored through, making the names impossible to read. Jim closed the back cover and wound the watch. He pressed the repeater button and heard the expensive timepiece strike the nearest quarter hour. A helluva fine watch for a saddle bum to be carrying, but then it was likely stolen. The only other item left was a *barbiquejo* hat strap with coin-silver ornamentation.

The kid had left practically nothing. An empty bag of Ridgewood cigarette tobacco with a curious-looking bluish stone in it. A worn handkerchief. A box of matches, Round Dome Specials, with two matches still in it. A 'dobe dollar. A hardened half bar of Pears' soap. That was it, and the name of a sister—Jessica. . . .

Jim swiftly made his choices. He took the Mexican's picture, the gilt button, and the expensive watch. From the kid's possessions he took the curious-looking stone and nothing else. He could easily remember Round Dome Special matches and Pears' soap. The soap was common enough in that country; the type of matches was not.

Hard knuckles rapped on the door. "Murdock?" said a familiar voice. It was that of Murray Cullin. Jim walked softly to the garboon and placed the button and the watch in it. He slid the picture under the edge of the marble-topped dresser and the stone under the edge of the rug.

"Murdock? You in there?"

Jim picked up the lint-specked wad of Winesap and bit off a chew. He peeled off his vest and shirt and threw them on the bed, then walked to the door and opened it.

Cullin brushed past Jim and looked about. He saw the items on the bed. "What's this?" he said.

"Must be what you're looking for," said Jim. He worked his chew into pliability.

Cullin poked through the things with a spatulate finger. "You had no business taking these things," he said.

"Why? No one around here seemed interested in who those men were."

Cullin looked around the room, glancing at the worn walnut butt of the holstered Colt. "No one knew who they were," he said. "They wouldn't give their real names."

"John Does to you, eh, Cullin?"

Cullin turned slowly and studied Jim. "What's your game, Murdock?" he said coldly.

Jim leaned against the wall and shrugged. "Someone should notify the next of kin."

"Three killers? Is it worth it?"

"Cain had relatives," said Jim. "They must have been interested even in him."

"You've got a great sense of humor, Murdock. Maybe you've even read a book in your time."

"Some," admitted Jim.

Cullin poked through the items again. "Like your brother, eh?" he said.

"Maybe even you could learn something from him, Cullin."

Cullin turned again. "Put up your hands," he said.

Jim straightened up. As he did so he spat a juicy gob into the garboon. Cullin's practiced hands felt about Jim's hard body. "I didn't know you cared," murmured Jim.

Cullin took the derringer from Jim's pocket. "You could get into trouble with one of these stingy guns around here," said the lawman.

"Is there a local ordinance against it?"

"No." Cullin dropped it into Jim's pocket. He looked about the room again.

Jim walked over to the garboon and spat into it again.

"Filthy habit," said Cullin.

Jim wiped his mouth. "I wasn't brought up right," he said.

"That's a damned lie," said Cullin. "You came from fine stock, Murdock."

"As the twig is bent," said Jim.

Cullin looked about the room again. "What are your plans?" he said.

"Get a bath. Change these clothes. Get some breakfast."

"Damn it, Murdock! You know what I mean!"

Jim shifted his chew. "I don't know, and if I did know, I'd be damned if I'd tell you, Cullin."

The sheriff looked down at his big hands. "Sometimes it pains me to uphold the law. There are times when I'd enjoy breaking it myself."

"Any time. Any time," murmured Jim politely.

"You never avoid trouble, do you?"

Jim leaned against the wall again. "I didn't exactly want to go with those human wolves this morning, if that's what you mean."

"That's not what I meant."

Jim shrugged. "If you mean my coming back to Ute Crossing, then I say to you that I was cleared years ago of the charge of killing Curt Crowley. It went as high as the governor and he OK'd it, Cullin. Even in the face of Cass Crowley."

Cullin's eyes narrowed. "Just what do you mean by that?"

"You know as well as I do that the governor was just as afraid of Crowley's political power in this state as most officials are."

"Does that include me?"

"You've been sheriff for a long time, Cullin."

Cullin ground a balled fist into the palm of his other

33

hand. He walked to the bed and picked up the items there, dropping them indiscriminately into the side pockets of his coat.

"How will you know who owned those things?" said Jim. "In case anyone happens to ask for them."

Cullin walked to the door and turned. "I want no trouble from you in this county, Murdock. I have nothing but the greatest respect for Ben, like most people around Ute Crossing do, and I really believe Ben thinks he cleared you, but in my book you were never cleared. You walk quietly, mister. You walk *very* quietly." He opened the door and walked out.

Jim spat viciously into the garboon without thinking. He locked the door and then retrieved the watch and button. He wiped them off and pocketed them.

The snow was still falling when he finished his bath and dressed in fresh clothing. He placed his hat on his head and eyed himself in the gold-flecked, tarnished mirror. "You handsome dog, you," he said with a grin. "By God, you just walk quietly, mister, you just walk *very* quietly."

He ate well in the busy restaurant next door to the hotel, and was acutely conscious of the surreptitious glances he got from some of the other patrons. He bought half a dozen short sixes and stowed them away in his cigar case, lighting one of them at the counter before he strolled out into the open air and stood watching the falling snow beyond the wooden awning. The wide street was already an inch or more deep in snow, scored by hoof and wheel tracks. He'd have to go out and see Ben. He had mixed feelings about seeing Ben again. Ben had developed a penchant for preaching in his last letters, and Jim wasn't quite in the mood for sermonizing. "Settle down," Ben would say. "Get a nice wife. Get a steady job. Raise a family. Teach your kids the difference between right and wrong. Respect for the law."

Jim looked in the direction of the gallows hill. Nature was trying its best to hide the sight from the eyes of the people of Ute Crossing, but it could never erase the thought of what had been done there that very morning from the minds of every man, woman, and child in Ute Crossing. The ugly story would spread throughout the valley of the Ute and over the mountains with incredible speed, and the whole state would know about it before the start of the next week. This was Saturday morning. By Friday the story would have spread throughout all the neighboring states, with variations, embellishments, and changes to suit the taste and imagination of the teller.

He'd have to see Ben. Jim walked to the stable and got

a fresh horse from Meany. Ben lived three miles from town in a little place he had bought after he had sold the old Murdock place south of town. There had been too many memories, he had written, and being a cripple, he could no longer handle the place. All his life now was devoted to teaching. He'd be a good teacher, thought Jim, as he guided the gray from the stable and rode west along the main stem, sheepskin collar turned up high, cigar thrust out from taut jaw, eyes far away from Ute Crossing. For some odd reason he was thinking of a girl called Jessica.

If Jim Murdock's mind was far away as he rode out of Ute Crossing that morning, there were others that were quite conscious of his physical presence in the town. Four pairs of eyes peered through the dirty, streaked windows of Baldy Victor's Grape Arbor Saloon.

"I didn' like the way he talked to me this morning," said Barney Kessler. He hiccupped. "Him and me was amigos in the old days, all through school. I rode fence with him for Cass Crowley, too. Taught him all I know. Ridin', shootin', brandin' and roping. You seen the way he acted toward me."

Buck Grant, the man who had roped the Mexican Orlando and who had strung up the reatas to lynch the three prisoners, looked sideways at Barney. "*You* taught *him* ropin', Barney." He grinned loosely. "That's the best one I heard today."

Lyss Adams wiped his mouth and shifted his chew. "What'd Murdock have to show up today for, anyways? It was almost as though someone tipped him off to what was goin' to happen."

"You talk like a man with a hole in his head," said Baldy Victor as he wiped the bar. "Ain't no reason Jim Murdock would want to come back to witness a lynching. He come so goddamned close to one himself he wouldn't like to see another. He likely come back to see his brother."

Buck Grant turned from the window. "Yeh, but why, Baldy? Ben Murdock's been doin' a lot of talkin' around here. Drives like a madman into town in that buggy of his, lowers his wheelchair to the ground, then rolls that damned thing all over town. He wants to talk to them prisoners. He gets Murray Cullin all riled up. He sends a telegram to the governor. He tells the kids in his school them three hombres we strung up are innocent until proven guilty. That's the best I heard yet."

Van Lassen leaned his meaty belly against the bar and

curled a huge hand about his glass. "He was right about that, anyways."

"You mean we done wrong?" challenged Barney. "It was you who got the idea, Lassen."

"Shut up!" said Lassen. "I get tired of hearing you run off at the mouth."

They all lined the bar. Lyss shifted his chew and spat into the garboon. It rang with the wet impact. "All the same, what'd Murdock come back today for?" He looked at Lassen. "By God! You don't suppose he's a lawman, do you, Lass?"

Lassen's flat amber eyes studied Lyss. "So what if he is?"

"Well, we ain't got Cass Crowley around no more. Sure, we avenged him, like it says in the Bible, but he's gone now. Supposing Murdock is representing someone away up."

"Like God, maybe?" jeered Barney.

Lyss shook his head. "Like the governor, maybe?"

Buck Grant laughed. "The governor does what he's told in this state. He don't make no decisions."

Lassen looked down into his glass and then drained it. "There's another government, you know," he said quietly. "The federal Government." He did not look at the others.

It was very quiet in the saloon. Boot heels struck the wooden sidewalk outside. A dog barked. Baldy passed a moist hand over his shining skull.

"That's a lotta crap," said Barney boldly. "Ain't no jury in this state would prove us guilty, like I said this morning."

"*You* said this morning," mimicked Grant.

Lassen looked into the mirror behind the bar. "I don't like this," he said slowly. "Ben Murdock is a pain in the rump, always shootin' off his mouth about rights, justice, good citizenship, and all that crap, but Jim Murdock is a fightin' man. He always was and he always will be."

"Until someone cuts him down," said Barney loudly.

It was very quiet again. They all looked at each other.

Baldy Victor rubbed his jaw. "The drinks are on me," he said. He did not look at the four men as he said it.

Jim crossed the creaking bridge that spanned Warrior Creek. The swirling water was black against the newly fallen snow. To the south was the old Murdock place on the banks of Warrior Creek. The sight of the creek brought back many old memories to Jim. Ranching had been in his blood in those days, and until he had gotten into trouble for supposedly shooting Curt Crowley, he had practically run the Murdock ranch alone, for Ben, when he wasn't talking, always had his nose in a book and his thoughts on going to college. Well, he had finally achieved his hopes for an education—the hard way. Substituting a schoolroom for the open range and wheels for legs.

The low.bridge rails were capped with snow, and the flooring of the bridge was untouched as yet by wheel or hoof tracks. The black water looked icy cold to Jim, almost as though it would freeze solid at any time.

A wraith of smoke curled up from Ben's chimney and vanished in the snow. There were no other houses anywhere near the place, which likely suited Ben fine, for he wasn't much for company except in the schoolroom, or with men like Brady Short and Alfred Hitchins, who could match Ben's intellect and his thirst for knowledge.

Jim swung down from the gray and led him into the little barn where Ben kept his team. Jim eyed the two sleek mares Ben used to pull his buggy. He wondered if Ben still drove like Jehu. Ordinarily quiet and introspective, not given to sudden words or sudden movements, Ben seemed to change when he gripped the reins. One mare would have been aplenty to pull Ben's buggy, but Ben liked two. That team must have set him back a good piece of change, particularly on a schoolteacher's salary.

Jim walked around to the front of the house and rapped on the door.

"Who is it?" a familiar voice called out.

"It's Jim, Ben."

There was a moment's pause, and then a chain rattled behind the door and a key turned in the lock. The door swung open and Jim saw Ben seated in his wheelchair. For a moment Jim stared. Ben was only five years older than Jim, hardly thirty-three as yet, but he seemed to have aged immensely in the seven years since Jim had seen him. His hair was almost pure gray and his face was deeply lined. He held out a thin hand to Jim and gripped it tightly. "Why didn't you tell me you were coming home, Jim?" he said quietly.

"I wasn't sure I was coming, Ben."

Ben closed the door. He reached for the key in the lock, glanced uncertainly at Jim, then wheeled himself over beside the marble-topped table. A book lay open in the yellow light from an Argand lamp. "You might have let me know, Jim," said Ben.

Jim peeled off his coat and hung it and his hat on a hall tree. Ben's eyes flicked down to Jim's waist and saw the familiar bulge of holstered Colt beneath the dark coat. He narrowed his eyes.

37

Jim sat down and held out his cigar case to Ben. Ben shook his head. He watched Jim light up. "It didn't take you long to get into the swing of things," he said.

Jim looked through the wreathing smoke. "You heard about the lynching? I hardly had a choice, Ben."

Ben waved a hand. "I know that. You just seem to have the Devil's own luck."

Jim shrugged. "Seems as though no one will be called to account for it. Van Lassen practically defied Sheriff Cullin to do anything about it. Lassen said no jury in the state would convict them."

Ben drummed thin fingers on the table. "He's right," he said quietly. "Cass Crowley is here in death as he was here in life."

Jim inspected the end of his cigar. "There are no Crowleys left," he said.

"Cass Crowley had a host of friends," said Ben. "He was a hard man in many ways, but an honest man."

"Except in politics," said Jim.

Ben nodded. "That seemed to be an obsession with him. I never quite knew why. He had everything. Money, respect, position, and everything else most people want."

Jim leaned back in the chair. "Well, maybe Van Lassen was right when he said he'd save the taxpayers some money." He studied Ben as he spoke.

Ben flushed. "You talk like a fool!" he said hotly. "This is not justice! For hundreds of years we've struggled to have justice. Laws that punish and protect. Guilty or not, those three men had a right to the due process of law."

"To get hanged anyway," said Jim dryly.

"You've lost the point," said Ben coldly. He looked closely at Jim. "The very reason I fought to clear you is why I was fighting to help those three men, Jim. I was afraid something like this would happen. I *knew* it would happen!"

Jim relighted his cigar. "Why, Ben?"

Ben looked back at the door and then at the windows. "The evidence that was brought against those men did not satisfy me."

"It seemed to satisfy Brady Short, Alfred Hitchins, and Sheriff Cullin. Not to mention Meany Gillis and Mr. Dakers, the undertaker."

Ben leaned forward. "It was circumstantial evidence that was brought against you, Jim. Supposing I had not believed you were innocent?"

"I wouldn't be here now."

"Exactly."

38

"Then you think those men were innocent?"

"I do not."

"Then what's bothering you outside of the fact that the law was broken this morning?"

Ben looked again at the door.

"You want me to lock it again, Ben?" said Jim.

Ben quickly turned his head, and there was a faint trace of fear in his eyes. "No," he said.

"What's bothering you, Ben?"

Ben closed his eyes. "Make some coffee," he said.

Jim studied his brother. "You've been making trouble for yourself," he said. "You ought to know better than to stick your nose into every law case in this county. You've got no right to do that, Ben."

Ben opened his eyes. "It is the right of every good citizen."

"You're not in the classroom now, Ben."

Ben slammed his fists down on the arms of his chair. "You talk like a blind fool!" he said. "Go make that coffee before I lose my temper!"

Jim stood up and shrugged. The glass of the window just beyond his chair was suddenly shattered. Something smashed into the Argand lamp and hurled it from the table against the wall, splattering kerosene against the carpeting and the wallpaper. Ben grunted in savage pain as glass splinters lanced into his cheek. The report of a heavy rifle came echoing from somewhere across the creek.

Jim shoved his brother's wheelchair into a corner and dragged him from it. "Stay down!" he yelled. He dropped flat and bellied toward a window. The window shattered just over his head, and he winced as broken glass tinkled on the floor and struck his back and the back of his head.

Flames licked along the edge of the carpet and danced on the wooden floor, while a tiny runnel of flame worked its way along the soaked wallpaper. Jim snatched up a rug and beat out the flames. A cold wind poured into the room from the two shattered windows.

"Where's your rifle?" demanded Jim.

"I don't keep any guns," said Ben.

"That figures," said Jim dryly.

Minutes ticked past. There was no sound except the icy rushing of the snow-laden wind around the little house.

Chapter Five

Jim finished hanging rugs over the two shattered windows, nailing them to the frames, and then he walked warily outside to close the shutters. There was no sign of life in the shallow valley of the Warrior. The snow had lightened but there was still quite a bit of it, and the wind was much colder. Jim walked back inside the house and leaned his Winchester against the wall. Ben had lighted another lamp and was in the tiny kitchen making coffee. Jim dug the two slugs out of the wall. They were .44/40s, about as common a caliber as one could find in that part of the country, and throughout the West, for that matter, as they were interchangeable between rifle and pistol.

Ben rolled his chair back into the living room and placed the coffeepot on the table. "Cups in that cabinet there," he said. His face was white and taut.

Jim got the cups. "Why, Ben?" he asked.

Ben looked up. "They were after you," he said.

Jim filled the cups. "Why the double lock on the door?" he asked. "Why the look of fear in your eyes? You can't fool me, Ben. Who's been hurrahing you, and why?"

Ben measured sugar and cream into his cup. "I don't really know," he said. He looked up at Jim. "It was like the beating I got when I was fighting to clear you. I've never found out who did it."

"When did this start?"

"About the time I got interested in those three prisoners."

Jim sipped his coffee. "Seems odd," he said. "They were certainly guilty from what I've managed to learn. Were there any other suspects?"

"None."

"Maybe you should have kept your nose out of it, Ben." Jim smiled and raised a hand. "I know. Justice!"

"You're getting the idea," said Ben dryly. "I still say those shots were meant for you."

"He was a lousy shot, then," said Jim.

"Across the creek with the snow coming down? I think he did very well."

"That's because you're no rifleman, Ben. The range was hardly more than seventy-five yards, with the wind behind him and me silhouetted between the lamp and the window. I will admit I stood up just at the right time."

"All right, then! What do you think it was? Was it me or was it you they were after?"

Jim lighted a fresh cigar. "It was a warning for me," he said. He looked over the flame of the match. "You can bet your bottom dollar on that."

"What makes you so sure?"

Jim shrugged. "I didn't make myself too popular this morning. Besides, there's something else I intend to do."

"Such as?"

Jim took out the items he had taken from the bodies of the three lynched men. "Someone has to tell their people they died."

"That's not up to you."

"No one else seems much interested."

"They were tramps, Jim. Nobodies. Drifters. They saw a chance to kill Cass Crowley and they took it. They knew they'd never get away with just robbing Cass Crowley. They *had* to kill him."

Jim smiled. "Who's making up evidence now, Ben?"

Ben flushed. "All right! All right! It just doesn't make sense, your going away like this. How can you find their people, anyway? No one ever found out their real names or where they came from."

Jim eyed the little pile of possessions. "I'll try," he said.

"It might take a long time, and what profit is in it for you, Jim?"

"I've got the time," said Jim quietly. He looked at his brother. "It's my way of doing things, Ben. You've got your teaching and your interest in justice and citizenship. You cleared me, but it was me who damned near ended up on that hill with a rope around my neck in the cold light of dawn. It was me who stood up there this morning and saw those three wretches get strung up like pigs to be slaughtered."

Ben narrowed his eyes. "Go on," he said softly.

Jim looked at his brother. "The kid had a sister named Jessica," he said.

"So?"

"Someone has to tell her, Ben."

"I had hoped you'd stay here with me for awhile. Settle down. Get a nice wife. Get a steady job. Raise a family.

Teach your kids the difference between right and wrong. Respect for the law."

"Oh, God," murmured Jim. I knew it, he thought. I just knew it!

Ben's jaw tightened. "I've had my say," he said.

Jim stood up and drained his cup. "I've got a room at the Ute House," he said.

"I thought you'd stay with me, Jim," said Ben in a hurt tone.

"Later, Ben. I've got some plans."

"Sure! Sure! Gambling! Booze! Women! Is that it?"

Jim couldn't help it. "What else is there?" he said. He looked about the room. "I'll leave my rifle here and pick up a gun in town for you."

"I don't need any."

Jim shrugged. "As you will." He looked down at Ben. "These three men who were lynched. Tell me all you know about them, Ben."

Ben emptied his cup and refilled it. "They came from the south, maybe from New Mexico, about a month ago. One of them was a Mexican. They camped over on the Blue for a spell. Cullin later found traces of their camp there, and a sheepherder said they bought coffee from him. They told him they would be looking for jobs around Ute Crossing. Van Lassen was still working for Crowley then. It was him that found Crowley in his living room with three .44 slugs in the back of his head. The place had been ransacked. Lassen notified Cullin. Cullin formed three posses. One headed over Wind Pass. One headed west toward the Warrior Peak country. Cullin himself went back to the ranch with the third posse. It was Cullin alone who found the three killers hiding out near Brushy Creek. Cullin himself rounded them up. Murray Cullin has more solid guts than a brass monkey."

"So they were brought in to Ute Crossing."

Ben nodded. "There was a lot of talk going on in the saloons. Some of Crowley's riders and friends were ready to hang the three of them right then, but Murray Cullin isn't the man to be bluffed, and you can thank God for that. Brady Short suggested a change of venue, for everyone was clamoring for a trial, and you know what would have happened if a trial was held in this county."

"I have a good idea."

"One of my pupils heard the shooting over on the creek when Murray rounded up the three of them. It didn't last very long. They didn't seem to be desperate men to me."

Jim nodded. He could see the three of them as though

42

they now stood in front of him. "That's the whole story, then?"

Ben nodded. "Cullin kept a close guard over them. I suppose he was afraid of what would happen if he relaxed."

"Harlan Meigs sure relaxed last night," said Jim dryly. "The boys got him drunk as a hoot owl in the Ute House Bar last night. He was out cold in the office when the mob broke in. Old Mike Curry was laid out cold too. Maybe never had a chance to wake up."

Jim shrugged into his coat and put on his hat. "You sure you don't want a gun?"

Ben looked up. "That shot was for you, Jim. It was a warning. Why, I don't know."

"Maybe a lot of people still think I killed Curt Crowley."

Ben nodded.

"The only way they'll ever believe I'm innocent is when they find Curt's killer." Jim placed a hand on Ben's shoulder. "I'll be all right in time, Ben. Let me do what I want to do. Maybe then I'll come live with you and try to make something out of myself. After seven years I can't place myself in harness. Give me a little time, eh, Ben?"

Ben looked away. "You haven't changed much in some ways. You left here a wild, gun-flashing hellion. You don't seem wild now, and I don't know anything about your gunplay, but there is still much of the lobo in you. I had hoped for something better, Jim."

"The Mex border isn't exactly the place for peaceful pursuits, Ben. Besides, you've got a profession. You're a respected teacher. Me, I live the only way I know how. You talk about the law and justice, but all you really do is talk. No offense to you, Ben. There are some of us who have to do the dirty work, and being a lawman is accepting that kind of work. Murray Cullin will tell you the same thing."

"He still thinks you killed Curt Crowley."

"You proved I was miles away when Curt was killed."

"I proved that to the governor. I never convinced Cullin, or a lot of other people, for that matter. Curt Crowley was popular, Jim, and he was the son of Cass Crowley. Likely if it had been anyone else around here you would have been forgiven. Then, too, you were a hellion, as I said before." Ben looked up at his younger brother. "You know, kid," he added quietly, "if I could walk and ride again, I think I'd do the same thing you are doing."

"Change of heart?"

Ben shook his head. "There is a streak within us Murdocks that calls for justice, for doing things right. I don't know whether or not you will find the people of those three men, but in the search you will learn something. Something that you will never learn here."

"I'll see you before I go, Ben."

"I hope so, Jim."

They shook hands. Jim closed the door behind him and shivered in the biting wind. The snow had stopped and the sky was a steely gray, and the cold was a living thing.

He rode slowly back into town, cigar clenched in his even white teeth, his thoughts were miles away at times, but his eyes shifted constantly, studying each snow-covered mound, clump of trees, hump of rock, any place that just might afford enough cover for a rifleman. He knew that shooting had been a warning. Someone either wanted him to forget about finding the relatives of those three dead men, or wanted him to mind his own business if he stayed in Ute Crossing. He ran quickly through his mental file. He had hardly made any new friends, or renewed old acquaintances, since he had returned to Ute Crossing.

He spent several hours in making purchases for his search and knew, without doubt, that his activities had been observed. He placed his supplies in the livery stable and went back to his room. He wasn't in the room two minutes when he knew someone had been there in his absence. The room was as neat as when he had left, but someone had been up there.

Jim stood for a long time at the window, watching the slow approach of the winter dusk. At last he lighted the lamp and took out the cheap atlas he had bought in the general store. "Maddows," he said thoughtfully. He scanned the listing of towns in this state, as well as those that bordered it to the south, finding no such place as Maddows. The man named Gil had mentioned such a place. All Jim really knew was that Gil had been at such a place and that it was south of Ute Crossing. He located the Blue, a creek high in the rough mountains southwest of Ute Crossing. The three men had camped there for a month and had said they were moving north to Ute Crossing. Jim scanned the country in the area of the Blue, but there was no Maddows. The best he could do was to start southwest to the country of the Blue and work from there. Somehow he did not want to find Three Forks and the girl named Jessica until he had first found out about the man named Gil. He had almost canceled out the Mexican. He had no great desire to return to the border country at this time.

Someone rapped on the door. It was the lone bellhop of

44

the Ute House, with a message from Brady Short. It was imperative that Jim come and see him as quickly as possible. Jim put on hat and coat, put out the lamp, and hurried to the stable to get the gray. The wind had stopped and an icy hardness was settling over the country, unusually cold weather for that time of the year. The gray's hoofs rang on the iron-hard road as Jim rode north to where Judge Whitcomb had built his great house so many years past.

He saw the lights of the house long before he saw the house itself. Ann would be there. She had been nineteen when Jim had left Ute Crossing. An ash blonde with hazel eyes that could cut a man's heart to pieces like a Mexican *saca tripas*. It had almost been a foregone conclusion that Ann would marry Jim. The old judge hadn't been too happy about the matter. It wasn't Jim's family he had been concerned about. The Murdock name stood well in that country, and the judge had served with Sam Murdock in the volunteers during the war, down New Mexico way, and Sam Murdock had saved the judge's life at Glorieta. No, it had not been the family. Elizabeth Murdock had been a Hobbs, descendant of one of the pioneer fathers of the state. Ben had always ranked well among the young people of Ute Crossing. It had been Jim who had caused Jonas Whitcomb concern.

Now the Murdock family meant little. Elizabeth, never very strong, had died, and Sam Murdock had failed in his business and had passed on to his reward. Ben Murdock, a cripple, was still held in respect by Ute Crossing, but Jim had not gilded his own laurel wreath, if he had ever rated one. Sure, he was a fast gun, a good man with rope and branding iron, but the stigma of the brutal murder of Curt Crowley still hung about him like the dead albatross carried by the Ancient Mariner, no matter that Ben Murdock had cleared Jim's name.

He reined in the gray at the white picket fence and looked up at the familiar house with the wooden turrets, the gingerbread, the many tall windows with colored glass at the top, the wide verandas thick with crusted snow, and the swing swaying idly in the cold cat's paws of wind that crept now and then down the valley of the Ute. Jim remembered that swing. He wondered idly if it was the same one.

He led the gray into the huge barn and into a stall. There were at least a dozen other horses in the stalls. Brady Short had never been much of a rider, but he liked matched teams for his buggy, surrey, or buckboard. Jim wondered if Ann still rode as she had in the old days. The two of them had covered every mile of the valley of the Ute. Something

45

seemed to turn in his heart as he remembered those days.

He walked up to the house and twisted the doorbell key, listening to the strident echo within the house, and the sound of it took him back a full seven years, and for a moment he almost thought he had never been away.

He saw a woman come into the hallway, and at first he thought it might be the maid. *"We have help, of course,"* Brady had said. *"It's quite too much for Ann, you know."*

He narrowed his eyes. It was Ann who was coming to the door. The door swung open, and he swiftly took off his hat. "Ann," he said with a smile.

He wasn't sure if she had changed much. Her flowing ash-blonde hair was now atop her shapely head, set with an expensive but simple comb. Her figure was just as exquisite as it had ever been, set off by a dress that certainly had never been bought in Ute Crossing. She held out a hand and flashed that lovely smile of hers, and once again his thoughts back-leaped seven long years. "Jim," she said. "It's good to see you." She tilted her head to one side. "You've changed."

"You haven't, Ann," he said.

"Come in! Come in! We've so much to talk about." She led the way into the huge living room, lighted by a huge, polished Rochester hanging lamp, and at least half a dozen Argand table lamps. A fire crackled in the fireplace. She took his old sheepskin coat and faded stetson, Jim feeling somewhat ashamed of them the while, and placed them in the hall. He looked about the room. Hanging over the fireplace was the oil painting of Ann which almost looked as though it would come to life.

"Sit down, Jim," she said. "You may smoke if you like."

"Cigar?" he said with a sly grin.

She laughed. "I've gotten over that. Dad used to smoke them before he became bedridden and Brady, of course, is always receiving boxes of them from clients, friends, and admirers."

He glanced at her. She had slightly, ever so slightly, accented the word *admirers*. This time he managed to see through the facade of lovely memory and saw Ann Short as she really was, a twenty-six-year-old woman who still had her beauty, but with something a little glacial about it now. Jim lighted up a cigar from the humidor on a table and raised his eyebrows a little. Only in his plush days had he ever been able to afford a cigar like it.

"How is Ben?" she asked.

Jim shrugged. "Older looking. Perhaps you have not

noticed it. I've seen quite a few changes in people since I've returned."

"You've changed yourself. That scar, Jim. Isn't there anything you could have done to it?"

Jim passed the tips of his fingers down the disfiguring line. "There were no stitches taken in it," he said quietly. "It was a week before I reached a doctor. The man who did it meant to mark me for life if he did not kill me."

"And him, Jim? What happened to him?"

Jim dropped his hand. "I didn't have much choice," he said.

"You killed him?"

Jim nodded.

"Death seems to hover about you, Jim."

Jim eyed her. Her face was a little flushed. He looked toward a side table, set with glass decanter and wineglasses. The firelight danced against the ruby contents of the decanter. It looked like blood.

"Wine, Jim?" she said. "I have brandy too. Scotch. Rye. Bourbon. Gin."

"Sounds like the Ute House Bar," said Jim with a smile. "Scotch too?" He raised his eyebrows.

"Make your choice."

Jim blew a puff of smoke. "I'll have what you have been drinking," he said.

She flushed a little. "I don't quite know what you mean, Jim," she said quickly.

"It's getting to be a little obvious," he said.

"You never talked like that in the old days!"

He smiled. "I had no need to. I came to see Brady at his request, Ann. It was imperative. Those were Brady's words, not mine."

She walked to the side table. "Brady had to leave," she said over his shoulder. She filled two wineglasses.

Jim studied her shapely back. "Then I wouldn't have annoyed you," he said.

"You are not annoying me," she said. She turned, and the firelight brought her smooth ivory skin to warm life. "Besides, Brady told me to tell you what he had in mind."

"So?"

She placed the wineglass on the table beside Jim's chair. She did not move, looking down at him with those lovely eyes, gold-flecked, and for a moment he almost rose to take her in her arms. "Brady said I was to warn you, Jim," she said quietly.

47

"About what?"

"It's dangerous for you here in Ute Crossing."

Jim sipped the wine. It was excellent port. "Did Brady tell you why? Specifically, I mean."

She sat down across from him and sipped her wine in ladylike fashion, although the queer notion came to him that if he hadn't been there she'd have tossed off a glassful like a whiskey stud downing a shot of the friendly creature. "Brady said you had antagonized Van Lassen and some of Van's friends."

"I'm worried about that," he said.

"He also said Sheriff Cullin is keeping an eye on you."

"That would be nothing new for him, even after seven years. As he told me, I had never been cleared of the charge of killing Curt Crowley. Not in his book, as he stated it."

"He's a stickler, Brady says."

Ann emptied her glass and glanced surreptitiously at the decanter.

"I'll have another too," said Jim dryly.

She flushed again. She filled the glasses and sat down again, watching him with those great eyes of hers. A warmth, not entirely engendered by the port, crept through him.

"Why don't you leave Ute Crossing, Jim?" she asked.

"I haven't been here twenty-four hours," he said. He grinned. "I must admit they've been eventful hours. Too eventful. . . ."

"Where would you go if you left?" she asked.

He leaned back in his chair. "I think you know," he said. "Why are you asking me?"

She emptied half of the glass. "Some foolish notion of going to find the people of those three unfortunate men. Isn't that the idea?"

"Yes."

"What can you possibly gain by that?"

"Nothing," he said. He looked down into his glass and twirled it on its stem, watching the red port swirl high on the rim. "I wasn't thinking of gaining anything. Anything material, that is."

"Spiritual, then?"

"Perhaps."

"You have changed, then!" she said challengingly.

He looked into those eyes where a man could lose his soul. "So have you, Ann," he said.

She looked away. She knew what he meant.

Jim relighted his cigar. It was comfortable in the warm

room, sipping excellent wine, smoking a top-grade cigar, feeling the heat of the fire, but strangely enough the woman made him uneasy. He suddenly wanted to leave while he still had the old picture of her in his heart.

"Brady was so concerned about you," she said. Her voice slurred a little now and then. "He said there were too many people around here who still believed you had killed Curt Crowley. He said too that Ben had made enemies for clearing you."

"Ben is still here," said Jim quietly.

"Ben has powerful friends," she said. "My husband, for one. And Sheriff Cullin likes Ben, although he won't always admit it. Alfred Hitchins thinks there is no one like Ben."

"And I have no one."

"You have Brady," she said softly. "And me. . . ."

"I know that," he said. "I am leaving Ute Crossing, Ann. I *am* going to look for the people of those three men. This should make everyone satisfied, but it doesn't seem to be doing quite that. What difference does it make if I do find the people of those three men? I feel that I must do it. It's as simple as that." He emptied his glass and stood up. He had a feeling that the house was empty except for Ann and himself. The wine had warmed his blood and stirred his passion.

She studied him for a moment, almost languorously, like a purebred she-cat watching an alley tom, scornful of his breeding, but interested in his obvious masculinity. "There's no need to get angry or to leave," she murmured.

"I have Brady's message," he said coldly.

She passed a slim hand across her lovely column of a neck. "It's lonely here," she said. "Brady is gone much of the time. I have little in common with the women of Ute Crossing." She lifted her eyes and looked full into his, and he knew right then and there that she was practically asking for it. A half-drunken doxy in a bordello would hardly have done it any differently.

He glanced toward the door.

"We're all alone, Jim," she said.

He did not dare look at her.

"Brady won't be back for hours, perhaps not until tomorrow."

He felt the cold sweat break out on him. Damn her! He had never been a close friend of Brady Short, but he admired the man for his ability and honesty, his education and intelligence. He knew that all he had to do was turn the lamps low, or take her by the hand. The touch of her hand would loose the floodgates within him. He had never forgotten her in those damnable seven years, nor could he drive her from his mind now.

A log fell in the fireplace. The wind whispered coldly about the great house. It was now or never!

"Stay," she murmured.

He looked at her. A spark seemed to leap the gap between them. Use your head, he thought. Keep away from her. You'll never be able to live in the valley of the Ute if you start in with her where you left off so many years ago.

"Jim?"

He had changed. She had said so. Everyone had said so. Yes, he *had* changed. "Tell Brady I thank him for his warning and advice," he said, and it seemed to him as though his voice were far away, as though someone else were talking, not Jim Murdock.

"Is that all?"

"What more do you want?" he asked cruelly.

She got up slowly. "Your coat and hat are in the hall," she said icily. "Let yourself out, please."

He walked to the door and looked back at her, and the look in her eyes struck at him like a living thing of hate.

"I was planning to spend a few weeks in Denver," she said quietly. "I will likely leave in a week or so. Brady thinks I need some city life. Some shopping. A little gaiety."

"Very thoughtful of Brady," said Jim.

"I am going alone," she said. Her face flushed. "If you happen to be up that way, Jim, I'll be at the best hotel." The last words came with a rush. She turned and walked toward the side table.

He shrugged into his coat, placed his hat on his head, looked up the wide, carpeted staircase to the darkness of the second floor, and thought of the many rooms up there. Of her room, likely exquisitely feminine, a background for the lovely creature who slept there. He could almost smell the perfume of the room, the perfume of her shapely body. He opened the door and shut it quietly behind him. The stairs squeaked beneath his weight in the bitter cold.

He led the gray from the barn and stopped in the road. Swiftly and quietly he padded back to the house and up the wide stairs. He looked into the living room. She stood with her back to him, and this time she had the decanter to her lips, her throat gulping convulsively as she swilled the good port.

50

Jim Murdock returned to the horse and mounted it. He rode toward Ute Crossing, and he did not look back through the thick, cold darkness to that vast mausoleum of a house that harbored a corpse of love. A love that would never live again.

Chapter Six

Jim Murdock had crossed the hard-frozen Blue two days after leaving Ute Crossing. He had spent the first night in a sheepherder's abandoned shack, and the bitter, lingering cold had forced him to bring the sorrel within the shack as well, out of the freezing wind. The second night he had camped in the bottoms of an unnamed creek, with hardly an hour's uninterrupted sleep because of the cold and the distant howling of the wolves along the ridges. In those two days he had not seen another living thing, except for an occasional hawk drifting with motionless pinions against the cloudless sky like a scrap of charred paper.

He followed a faint trail down the southern slope of the foothills after leaving the Blue. The three men had camped there for a month, according to what he had learned, before heading northeast toward Ute Crossing. There was no use in looking for their campsite and the sheepherder who had told Sheriff Cullin about them. The sheepherder wouldn't be there now. The flocks would have been driven south into the lower country for the winter.

The sun came up but shed little heat over the cold world below it. It sparkled from the crusted snow and the frozen watercourses. Far down the slope, hidden in a dark fringe of trees, the sun sparkled and glinted from something else, surmounted by a hazy, drifting cloud. Smoke. Maybe a man could get a hot meal there.

Jim shifted stiffly in the saddle. Now and then he looked behind him. Always there was the feeling that someone was watching him. It was a reaction honed by his years on the border; a sixth sense that had saved his life more than once. But there was nothing behind him except the cold landscape and the glittering of the sun on the snow and

51

ice. He would be glad to get out into the more open country to the south.

The shifting wind trailed the smoke toward him, and he began to distinguish houses, the movements of people, the faint hum of life. It was a bigger town than he had suspected. He rode slowly up the main street and a sign caught his eye. Masterson's Freight Company. A wagonyard was beside it, with light and heavy freight wagons layered with snow. From a huge corral behind the building came the bawling of a mule. Steam rose from the corral and the sheds, mingling with the smoke from the chimneys.

Jim dismounted in front of a small restaurant. A boy plodded by. "What's the name of this place, son?" asked Jim.

"Meadows," said the urchin. "Useta be Masterson's Meadows, but people jus' call it Meadows now."

Jim flipped him a dime. "Is, there a hock shop here?"

The kid grinned. "You down on your luck, mister? You kin have the dime back if you are."

Jim grinned back. "No. The dime is yours."

The kid pointed up the street. "You see that buildin' down there? The one leanin' over a little like it's all tired out? That's the Jew's place. Sam buys and sells anything. Anything, I tell you!"

Jim ate in the restaurant and took the sorrel to the livery for a feed. It was almost noon when he crossed the street to the curiously leaning structure. While he had eaten he had put two and two together. Gil was a lousy speller. He had written Maddows instead of Meadows . . . *Masterson's* Meadows. He had mentioned not getting a job with a man named Masterson.

Jim opened the door and walked into a weird wonderland of a vast accumulation of anything and everything he could think of. Shelving ran from floor to ceiling, crammed with all kinds of odds and ends. Boxes cluttered the floor, filled to the brims with oddments. Wires had been strung from one side of the long building to the other, and from the wires hung pots and pans, whips, harness fittings, housewares of all kinds, including a row of elegant chamber pots. The bell stopped tinkling on its big coiled spring.

"You are wanting to buy or sell, maybe?" a soft voice asked.

A derby hat seemed to rise by itself from behind a rampart of dusty sacks of feed. A wizened face studied Jim with a pair of the softest brown eyes he had ever seen outside of a doe.

52

"I'm looking for Sam," said Jim.

"Speaking," said the little man.

Jim walked to the rampart and looked over to see an immense rolltop desk, the pigeonholes crammed with papers, the top inches deep in forms of one kind or another. A parrot hung in a cage over the desk. "The drinks are on you, stranger!" he squawked.

"That's the story of my life," said Jim with a smile.

"You are wanting to buy? To sell? Maybe you want to buy the business? A partner I couldn't use."

Jim shook his head. "I'm afraid I'd get lost in here, Sam."

"So? I've been lost in here for ten years. What can I do for you?"

Jim shoved back his hat and felt for the makings. He offered them to Sam, and the little man shook his head. "I got a cough," said Sam. "I came west from Pittsburg to get rid of it. I should smoke? Crazy I'd be!"

Jim rolled a cigarette and lighted it. "I'm looking for information on a man named Gil," he said.

"You're a lawman?"

Jim shook his head. "He hasn't done anything," he said. He half closed his eyes. "That isn't right either."

"You are talking riddles."

Jim blew a smoke ring. "A few days ago a man by that name was lynched in Ute Crossing with two other men."

"The men what killed Mr. Crowley," said the merchant.

Jim nodded. "I found a letter in his pocket written to a woman named Sarah, but there was no address. He mentioned being here in Meadows and that he had hocked his rifle and saddle to a Jewish merchant here."

There was no expression on Sam's face.

"Do you have the rifle and saddle?" asked Jim.

"I might have."

Jim studied the little man. "There's no trouble in this for you, Sam."

"How do I know?"

"Because I tell you so."

Sam eyed the hard gray eyes, the disfiguring scar, the outthrust jaw of the big man. "I believe you," he said. He walked around the desk and brought back a Sharps-Borchardt rifle which he placed on the rampart of sacks. He went back and hauled out a good-looking saddle which he just managed to lift to a place beside the rifle.

"Can I look at them?" asked Jim.

"Be my guest," said Sam. He sat down in his swivel chair and watched Jim.

The saddle was a rim-fire hull made by Pearson of El Paso. Gil had not exaggerated when he had said he had hocked his "good saddel" in Maddows.

"A hundred-dollar saddle on a forty-dollar horse," said Sam quietly.

Jim nodded. Gil had likely worked in Texas, for the rimfire or double-rigged hull was a favorite down that way. In this state the favorite was the Pueblo, made by either Gallup or Frazier, built more for rugged country and topping rough horses than for roping, where one had to be in and out of the saddle a lot. He had never heard Gil speak, so he couldn't tell if he had been a Lone Star stater.

The single-shot rifle was somewhat unusual, hardly the type to be carried as a saddle gun like the handy, quickfiring Winchester repeater. Jim checked the caliber. It was the government .45/70 with double-set trigger.

"A good rifle?" asked Sam.

Jim nodded.

"How much is it worth, maybe?"

Jim shrugged. "Fifteen dollars."

Sam paled a little. "I loaned him twenty-five on it. He didn't want to part with it, so I figured it was maybe worth something."

"You're all heart, Sam," said Jim.

"I know it," the little man said sadly.

"The drinks are on you, stranger!" squawked the parrot.

Jim examined the rifle. It was dented here and there, scratched quite a bit, but mechanically perfect. There were no identifying marks on it other than the maker's name and serial number.

There was a screwdriver lying on a table. Jim picked it up and removed the butt plate from the rifle. "Gil Drinkwater," he read. "Eighteen seventy-eight. Las Cruces."

"You're a clever fellow," said Sam. "In a hundred years I wouldn't have thought of that."

Jim replaced the butt plate. "Will you keep the saddle and rifle until I send for them?"

Sam shrugged. "Why not? Business is lousy. You wouldn't consider maybe buying me out?"

"Not today."

"The drinks are on you, stranger!" shrieked the parrot.

Sam stood up and watched Jim roll a cigarette. "You are maybe looking for the next of kin?"

Jim lighted up and then nodded.

"Why?"

Jim blew a smoke ring. "Someone has to do it," he said.

54

"He's got a wife, maybe? A family?"

"Someone named Sarah, Sam."

"A good Yiddish name."

"Did he come in here alone?" asked Jim.

"Yes."

"He was supposed to get a job with Masterson."

Sam nodded.

"Why didn't he get it?"

Sam rubbed his jaw. "About the dead I would not talk."

"Booze?"

Sam looked up. He nodded. "So drunk he was I didn't even want to take his goods, but he was desperate. You understand?"

"Yes."

Sam waved a hand. "He did not look like the kind of man who would kill an old man for money. Why, he didn't even have a gun when he left here, friend."

Jim looked up quickly from the rifle. "No belt gun?"

Sam shook his head. "I saw him ride from town with those two other fellows. A Mexican-looking fellow and a kid, a *boychik*. Someone said they were heading north to look for work. A strange trio, I thought. A drunkard, a sad-looking Mexican, and a scared-looking kid."

"You don't know anything about them?"

"No. We heard about the lynching last night. A mail carrier brought the news. A terrible thing for men to take justice into their own hands."

Jim nodded.

Sam leaned forward. "I'll keep the saddle and rifle for you. This woman. This Sarah. She has maybe no money?"

"Gil had written her that he would send for her when he had money and a job."

The sad doe eyes studied Jim. "Wait," said Sam. He vanished behind the desk. A door opened and closed. A few minutes later it opened and closed again. Sam reappeared. He handed Jim a wad of bills. "For the lady," he said.

Jim counted it. There were a hundred dollars in the wad. He whistled. "A lot of money, Sam. Maybe I'll take it and go off on a high lonesome."

The little man shrugged. "If you need a high lonesome, friend, more than Sarah needs the money, you go right ahead."

Jim grinned. "You're all right, Sam."

Sam shook his head. "It is you that is all right."

Jim walked to the door, followed by Sam. Jim turned and held out a hand.

The little man gripped it. "You will stop by on your way back, maybe? It was a pleasure doing business with you."

"The name is Murdock. Jim Murdock of Ute Crossing. I'll stop by, Sam, and let you know about Sarah. It might be a long time."

Sam smiled sadly. "What else do I have but time?"

Jim opened the door. The bell tinkled.

"The drinks are on you, stranger!" shrieked the parrot.

Sam shrugged. "He used to belong to a barkeeper. He ain't much company, but at least he talks to old Sam."

"Adios, Sam."

"Good-bye, Jim."

The bell tinkled as the door was closed behind Jim.

Jim crossed the border into New Mexico Territory at noon and camped that night in a ruined stone house in the valley of the San Juan. He reached Bernalillo four days later, put the sorrel into a freight car, and rattled down the valley of the Rio Grande to Socorro, where the railroad turned west. Then he crossed the old Jornado del Muerto in the bright winter sunlight, ninety waterless miles to San Diego Mountain, where he took the well-traveled road into Las Cruces. He took a room in the old Amador Hotel; its rooms still had marked over the doors the names of the girls —La Luz, Maria, Esperanza, Natalia, Dorotea, Muneca, and others, twenty-three in all—who had served the officers from Fort Selden to the north and Fort Fillmore to the south in the old days. Where were they now? thought Jim. La Luz, Maria, and the others. Perhaps respectable dowagers, happily married to the young men who had patiently waited for their future brides to earn their doweries in the big bedrooms of the Amador.

Three days of questioning brought no information about Sarah. He tried first with the name Gil Drinkwater, and found that most of the bartenders remembered Gil all too well. He had been cut off many times by every one of them. Sarah? They didn't know. The only lead he got was the fact that Gil had written infrequent letters to someone in Ysleta, a few miles southeast of El Paso. Jim knew the town well, having served for a time with the Frontier Battalion of the Texas Rangers, C Company, which had its headquarters in Ysleta, but he had never known anyone by the name of Sarah Drinkwater.

A cold drizzle was turning the streets of Las Cruces into pasty, gray-white mud when he headed toward the Amador after checking out his gear, for he meant to leave the next morning for El Paso and points south. Here and there he

56

caught glimpses of yellow light behind shuttered windows. He stopped in a doorway to light a cigar, his mind filled with thoughts, and as he raised his head and looked up he saw a man move swiftly into another deep doorway across the street. Jim winced as the match burned his fingertips. He lowered the cigar and held it behind him while he peered toward the dark doorway. There was no movement. Casually he thrust the cigar into his mouth and walked toward the next street, rounding the corner, then running as swiftly and as silently as possible to an alleyway. He darted into it, vaulted a low, crumbling adobe wall, cursing softly as his boots sank into the soft, odorous filth of someone's pigsty, then floundered across it to a gate set between two buildings. He walked swiftly toward the next street and stopped behind a sagging two-wheeled cart, peering between the rough slats so that his hat might not be silhouetted.

Boots thudded against the street, and a tall, broad-shouldered man passed the entrance of the alley. Jim padded to the mouth of the alley and looked up the narrow, twisting street. The man stood in front of a dimly lighted shop, also looking up the street. He turned as someone opened the shop door, letting a flood of yellow light into the wet street. His features were plain to be seen—a beak of a nose, a thick dragoon moustache, shaggy eyebrows that almost met over the deep-set eyes. "Lyss," said Jim to himself. There was no mistaking the man. Jim faded back into the darkness as Lyss walked toward the alley.

Jim unbuttoned his coat as an icy feeling poured through his body. He drew his Colt. A stream of cold water struck the back of his hat and flowed freely down his back. Boots squelched in the pasty mud of the street, and then the sound died away. This was no sheer coincidence, Jim thought. Lyss was looking for him, following him for some definite purpose. But why? It couldn't be a personal reason. Jim had not known the man in the old days, and he hadn't spoken to him when he had returned to Ute Crossing. But Lyss had seemed to be closer to Van Lassen than any of the other lynchers; about as close as any man could get to Lassen. Whatever Lyss had come to Las Cruces for prophesied no good to Jim Murdock.

Jim eased his way behind the cart. Boots squelched again, then stopped, then sounded again. Jim saw the wet back of Lyss's coat not two feet from him. Even as he looked, Lyss turned. Lyss opened his mouth. Jim's Colt barrel cracked alongside his head, but the heavy, wet brim of the hat saved the man from being coldcocked. Lyss staggered sideways, clawing for his Colt. He freed it. A knee came up into his groin. He grunted in agony. Once again the Colt barrel slapped at the side of his head, this time drawing blood from beneath the dark hair. Lyss swung wildly with his own Colt. The front sight traced a faint course down Jim's right cheek. Before the man could fire Jim kneed him again, and as his head came down in reflex the Colt barrel smashed across the base of his neck, driving his beak of a nose into the foul mud of the alleyway. He groaned once and lay still.

Jim padded to the mouth of the alley. No one was in sight. The shop lights were out. Jim wiped the blood from his face with the back of a hand and went back to Lyss. He rolled the man over, and wide, staring eyes looked up into his, but they did not see, nor would they ever see again.

Jim stood up, cursing softly. He had not meant to kill the man, but he knew as sure as fate that Lyss had meant to kill him. There was no time to stand there meditating about it. Perhaps Lyss had not come alone. Swiftly Jim ripped open Lyss's coat and took out his wallet. He took the bills from it, and the papers as well. He took the muddy Colt and thrust it into his coat pocket. He rolled the heavy body beneath the cart. If anyone found Lyss within the next day or so, they'd not be able to identify him, and if Jim could get clear of Las Cruces that night, it was possible he'd not be associated with the man's killing. Distasteful as his actions were, he knew he would have received the same treatment from Lyss.

Jim wiped the blood from his face again. He retreated the same way he had come. He had left word at the Amador that he would leave before dawn. There would be no one around to check what time he had left. He gathered his gear and left by the back way, walking to the stable where a hostler slept the deep sleep of the just. Jim tucked a bill into the man's shirt pocket and got the sorrel. He rode south on the El Paso road through the slanting rain. Ten miles from Las Cruces he dropped the empty wallet and the Colt into the well of an abandoned adobe. The bills he had placed in his own wallet. He ripped Lyss' papers to bits, letting the rain-laden wind scatter them through the muddy fields. He looked back through the darkness. A strange thought flitted through his mind. *Those who live by the sword . . .*

58

Chapter Seven

Ysleta dozed a little in the bright sunlight that had followed the two-day rainstorm that had swept across lower New Mexico and West Texas. The air was fresh and clear, with a few puffs of clouds in the blue sky. The crisp ringing of a sledge upon metal came from a blacksmith's shop, mingled with the insistent braying of a mule.

The tall Yanqui rode into town on a tired, mud-splashed sorrel. There were always such horsemen on the road, and what they did or where they went was of little moment to the people of Ysleta. There was never any serious trouble in Ysleta. There was a good enough reason. A company of level-eyed, quiet-spoken gentlemen known as Texas Rangers had their headquarters there.

Now and then these tall horsemen would look back over their shoulders as though expecting to see someone following them. This, too, was not unusual. It was better, senor, for a man to mind his own business, you understand, for if the stranger did not bother you, why bother the stranger?

This stranger was not one to be trifled with or stared at, for the thin scar on his left cheek and the hardness of his gray eyes were the stamp of his breed. He was better left to his master, likely El Diablo.

Jim Murdock found Sarah's little adobe easily. In such a town everyone knew everyone else. The adobe had a neat garden in front of it, and a cat dozed on a chair in the sun. Jim tethered the sorrel to the fence and opened the creaking gate. A woman opened the blue-painted door of the adobe as Jim walked toward the house. Jim took off his hat.

She narrowed her pale blue eyes. "You've come about Gil," she said quietly.

"Mrs. Drinkwater, ma'am?" asked Jim.

She was as plain as a fence post and as gaunt as a Joshua tree, with a rather long face, almost horselike in appearance, and the faint trace of a moustache showed on her lined upper lip. Her sparse hair was almost iron gray in color, drawn tightly back over her head. Her dress was black, with no adornment save a simple gold pin over her shallow breasts. All in all, hardly a woman a man would love, and yet the last lines of Gil's letter came back to Jim, almost as though imprinted on his mind. *"I say goodbye now and send you my best wishes, and be patent for I will soon have good work and scratch for both of us my dear Sarah."*

"Where is he?" she asked.

Jim hesitated. "My name is Jim Murdock," he said. "From up north. Ute Crossing."

There was no recognition in her pale eyes. "What is it you have to tell me?" she asked.

She didn't know. . . . She didn't know, but she expected the worst. . . .

"Please come in, Mr. Murdock," she said. "It was impolite of me to keep you standing here."

The living room was sparsely furnished but neat and clean. A large sewing basket stood on a chair beside a rather ancient Howe sewing machine. "You must excuse this mess," she said with a faint smile. "You must understand that this is my place of business as well as being my home." She sat down in a rocker, straight backed, thin, worn hands folded in her lap. A plain gold wedding band showed on her left hand.

"You didn't know he was at Ute Crossing, ma'am?" asked Jim.

"The last letter I had from him came from Albuquerque," she said. "He had had a promise of a job further north. A place called Maddows, I believe."

"Meadows," said Jim. "Masterson's Meadows."

She smiled that faint, mirthless smile. "I taught Gil how to read and write," she said. "I never could teach him how to spell and punctuate."

Jim wet his lips. He looked about. This was going to be worse than he had anticipated.

"You may smoke," she said.

"Thanks, ma'am." Jim rolled a cigarette and lighted it. He drew in the smoke gratefully.

"He's dead, isn't he?" she said. She nodded. "You wouldn't have come this long distance for any other reason."

Jim nodded. "You might never have found out," he said quietly. "I thought you should know."

"How did he die, Mr. Murdock?"

This was worse than admitting Gil was dead.

"You may tell me, Mr. Murdock. I will find out someday, in any case."

"He was taken from the Ute Crossing jail by an armed mob," said Jim. He could go no further.

"Shot?" she said softly, very softly.

He twisted the brim of his hat in his big hands. "He was hanged, ma'am," he said at last. He did not dare to look at her.

"Why?" she asked.

He managed to look at her. "He and two other men murdered Cass Crowley, a prominent rancher and a political power in the state. If it had been a lesser known person Gil might still be alive with a chance for his life. Believe me, Mrs. Drinkwater, there were men in Ute Crossing who did their best to save him and the others. The sheriff went all the way to the governor for a change of venue. It was while he was gone that the mob took justice into their own hands!"

There was a long silence. The thin hands worked a little. She was a lady, of good breeding, and she would not break down. The curious thought came into Jim's mind that she must have been a strange contrast to Gil and his rough ways. She had been educated.

"He was lynched, then?" she said suddenly in a clear voice. "My Gilbert was lynched?"

Dear God, thought Jim, *why did it have to be me that told her this news?*

"He meant to send for me," she said. "Somehow I knew he never would. That he would never come back."

Jim walked to the door and got rid of the suddenly tasteless cigarette. It was time to finish his business and leave her. There were others who had to be told. He wondered now if he could go through this experience two more times. He gently opened the thin hands and placed the badly written letter in them. "There was some money," he said.

She did not answer.

Jim took out his wallet. To the hundred Sam had given him he added the seventy-five dollars he had found in Lyss' wallet and added another hundred of his own. He placed the money on the side table beside the basket of sewing. "His saddle and rifle are up north," he said. "I can have them sent to you, if you like."

She shook her head. "Please accept them as compensation for your services."

"It's a fine saddle," he said.

"Yes. Gil wouldn't part with it for anything."

"No," lied Jim.

She looked up at Jim. "He had always been in trouble before we met in Amarillo," she said. "But those days were over. He only carried that rifle to shoot game when he needed it."

Jim studied her. "No belt gun? No six-shooter?"

She shook her head. "Gil never carried such a weapon. Not for many years."

"May I ask why?"

"Gil drank a lot. Years ago he accidentally killed his best friend in a drunken shooting match." She looked away. "Gil was a crack shot. When he was sober he'd win shooting matches with that rifle of his. He and his friend were shooting tin cups from each other's heads. Gil missed. He was exonerated, but he never carried a six-shooter again, and would only carry a single-shot rifle. It was a sort of taboo for him to have more than one cartridge. If he had stayed away from drink it would have been all right." She smiled. "I altered that."

"You stopped his drinking, then?" he asked.

She looked up. "Yes. They said I couldn't do it. He was a fine man when he wasn't drinking, Mr. Murdock." She narrowed her eyes. "Was he drinking up north?"

"No," lied Jim.

She stood up. "You want to leave," she said. "I don't blame you." She walked with him to the door. "How did Mr. Crowley die?"

"Shot through the back of the head. Three bullets. Forty-four caliber. Pistol bullets. They say each of the murderers had one empty shell in his six-gun when they were captured."

She placed a hand on his arm. "Then it was not Gil who was guilty," she said firmly. "He never carried such a weapon."

Gil Drinkwater had not been carrying a belt gun when he had been in Meadows. According to Sam, Gil didn't have any weapon at all, at least no gun of any kind. He could have picked up another, or borrowed one from the Mexican or the kid, who had been with him when Crowley was murdered.

"They did take care of his body?" she asked.

He nodded. "One of the leading citizens of the town paid for the burials," he said.

"Perhaps someday I will come and see his grave," she said.

"Perhaps you'd like to have his body brought down here," he said.

"No. He had no one who cared about him beyond me."

"I can't always have bad luck Sarah and you know no one

o home will give me a job because of the old days which are ong gone and won't never come back I tell you. . . ."

She looked up into his face. "Let him stay with the two nen with whom he died," she said. "They will have something in common, at least. They will be together. Good-bye, Ar. Murdock. It was kind and generous of you to let me now."

He walked to the gate without looking back and untied he sorrel. He mounted and rode swiftly away.

He was gone half an hour before she looked at the money or the first time, and she knew in her heart of hearts that Gil Drinkwater had never left her *that* much money.

It was Sergeant Les Gilson of C Company, Frontier Battalion, Texas Rangers, who gave Jim a possible tip-off on where the people of the man named Orlando might be ound. Gilson's strong, tobacco-stained fingers poked through Orlando's relics. "This button is from a Mex Army uniform," le said. He checked the inside of the watch as Jim had done. Looks like a presentation watch for some kind of service. Von by a Teniente Teodoro something or the other. At Colonia someplace or another. There are a lot of *colonias* n Mexico, Jim."

Jim turned over the faded picture. "San Fed . . ." he said. Gilson nodded. "Possibly San Fedro or San Federico."

"You know of such a place?"

Gilson pulled down a detailed roller map of the border ountry, and then one of the State of Chihuahua in northern Mexico. He studied it for a moment. "Let me see that watch gain," he said. He opened it and took a powerful magnifying glass from a drawer, studying the engraved script that had been scored through. "Eighteen seventy-two," he said at last.

Jim nodded. "Just as I suspected," he said. "The Mex nust have stolen it. He was too young to have earned such an award that many years ago as a *teniente* in the Mexican Army."

Gilson snapped shut the watch. "About 1872 there was a helluva big Apache raid down into Chihuahua. A small force of Mexican soldiers fought them to a standstill and defeated hem. There weren't many Apaches left alive after the fracas, and hardly enough soldiers left to bury the dead." He eyed the map. "The little *placita* where the Mexes held off the Apaches was abandoned by the people who had lived there because of the curse on it."

Jim rolled a cigarette and handed the makings to Gilson.

Gilson fashioned a smoke and lighted it. "By God!" he said "That place was called Colonia Federico!"

Jim took the cigarette from his mouth. "You're sure about that, Les?"

The ranger nodded. "It's down near Laguna de Haro There's nothing left down there now, Jim, except mounded graves and ruined dobes. I passed through that country some years ago on an undercover scout. You're wasting your time going down there."

Jim gathered together the relics of the man named Orlando "It's enough of a lead to warrant a little time down there."

Gilson shook his head. "Beats the hell out of me," he said "You were one helluva fine ranger, Jim, although I always did say you thought too much, too deep."

Jim grinned. "My mother used to say that about me." H gripped the sergeant's hand. "Much obliged, Les. I've found the kin of one of those poor men. I feel it is an obligation to find the others."

Les flipped his cigarette butt into a garboon. "Where'd you find the first of them?" he asked.

Jim looked Les full in the eyes. "It doesn't really matter does it, Les?"

Les shook his head. "I understand," he said.

The ranger watched Jim leave the headquarters building and lead the tired sorrel toward a livery stable. "Four hundred miles to tell the kin of a murdered man that he had died. Now he's riding south more than a hundred miles to do it again, *if* he can find the kin of the second murderer. I still think you think too much and too deep, Jim Murdock, but it's your life, and I know better than to tell you different."

Jim crossed the Rio Grande on a flatboat ferry to Zaragoz the day after he reached Ysleta, riding a chunky dapple gray he had traded the crippled sorrel for, plus twenty-five in cash. He had no desire to stay too long in Ysleta. There was extradition between New Mexico and Texas, of course, but none between those places and Mexico. They would have found the body of Lyss by now, and the law in Las Cruce and Dona Ana County might be more than passing inter ested in the man who had left the Hotel Amador in the dark of a rainy night to head south toward the border. He had registered under his own name, of course, for he had had no reason not to. If he had known he was being tailed by Lys he would have registered under an assumed name. The damage had been done, however. The dark streets of towns along the border and near the border quite frequently yielded

64

ead men staring at the cold dawn sky with eyes that did not ee, stripped of wallets and other valuables.

One thought ran constantly through his mind. Sam had said Gil Drinkwater had not carried a belt gun or rifle when he ad left Meadows. That in itself meant little, for it would ave been easy enough for Gil to pick up a six-gun. It was he deep sincerity of the woman Sarah, who had told him hat Gil would not carry a six-shooter, which stuck in his tubborn craw. Yet Cass Crowley had died with three .44 lugs in the back of his head, which also meant little, for the hooting could have been done by one of the killers with ither a rifle or a six-shooter. But the three killers had been ound armed with six-guns, *and an empty cartridge case in ach weapon!*

Now and then Jim would turn in his saddle and look back orth as he rode, as if it might help him to penetrate the ninor mystery of a man who would not carry a six-gun be- ause of a terrible accident in his past. *"Then it was not Gil ho was guilty,"* she had said firmly. *"He never carried such weapon."*

He took the stagecoach from Villa Palmito, after selling he gray for the fare, and arrived two days later in Chi- uahua at dusk. If he could find out Orlando's last name, e might possibly be able to trace the man. As it was, it ook him almost a week to get the information he wanted bout the siege of Colonia Federico by the Apaches, and the tout defense of the Mexican soldiers led by a Teniente eodoro Abeyta, who, severely wounded, had been forced to etire from the army. There was no mention of anyone alled Orlando, and no information about a place called an Federico in the State of Chihuahua.

He walked through the plaza his last night in Chihuahua City, ignoring the shrill-voiced boys pimping for their teen- ge sisters, listening instead to a deep-toned church bell vhich seemed to call to him. He lighted a cigar and walked lowly toward the church, watching the mantilla-clad heads f the women converging on the church. There was a small uilding beside the church, and an aged padre stood there, njoying the crispness of the night air.

"Good evening to you, father," said Jim.

"And to you, my son," said the old padre. "Can I be of help o you?"

"I am looking for a place called San Federico," said Jim.

"There are likely many San Federicos." The padre smiled. Have you no clue to locate it approximately?"

"None, except that it might be near a place called Laguna

de Haros. There was a place called Colonia Federico there some years ago, now abandoned."

The padre looked at him intently. "Yes, it comes to me now! The people there thought there was a curse upon the place. They moved, bag and baggage, as you Americans say, to another place, far to the west."

"But where, padre?"

The father held out his hands, palms upward, and shrugged his rounded shoulders. "Beyond the Sierra Vallecillos, it is said."

"Perhaps in the State of Sonora?"

"It is possible, my son." He eyed Jim. "Why do you ask?"

"There are possibly people there who would like to know of the death of a son, a father, a brother. I know nothing of the dead man except that his given name was Orlando and that someone he knew, possibly relatives, a wife and children, perhaps, lived in a place that could either be San Fedro or San Federico."

"You know only his given name? It is a very common one."

Jim shrugged. "Perhaps it is Orlando Abeyta. There is a possible connection between this man I knew and a Teniente Teodoro Abeyta."

"Ah," said the padre in a soft voice. "Abeyta! That is better. There was an Orlando Abeyta I once knew."

"Here in this city?"

The padre nodded. "Yes, but that was many years ago." He studied Jim. "How did this man die, senor?"

"Does it matter?"

"To me it does. You see, I was once the teacher of a young man named Orlando Abeyta."

The bell stopped ringing. It was very quiet in the dark street except for the low voices in the church.

"How did he die, senor?" repeated the padre. "Not badly I hope."

"He died like a man, padre. As he said at the last: '*It is not the thought of dying that is painful, only the way of it.*'" Jim looked steadily at the padre. "He was hanged for murder in the States, padre. You will tell no one?"

The padre's face was set and white, as though someone had struck him across it. "Hanged?" he said in a weak voice. "Orlando Abeyta hanged for murder? But this is impossible!"

"I swear it is true, padre."

"No, it cannot be. He was such a gentle lad. Brave in his own way. Not a hero like his elder brother, of course, but then Orlando had never wanted to be a soldier. Had he been

66

ronger in spirit he would have resisted all efforts to make
m a soldier, except for being a soldier of God. Tell me
out him, senor."

Jim quickly told his tragic story. "He was a brave man,"
e concluded.

"Why did you take this task upon yourself? What did this
an mean to you?" asked the padre.

Jim glanced at the church. "Perhaps it is a form of
enance. Perhaps an unspoken vow. I don't really know.
omething made me come."

"God moves in inscrutable ways, my son."

"You do not know if he was married and had a family?"

"He once told me he would never marry."

Jim took out the faded picture and lighted a match so that
e padre could see the woman and the two little children.
he padre shook his head. "I believe his elder brother was
arried. Yes! I remember now! She was a beautiful young
oman. Much younger than her husband. Somewhat older
an Orlando." The padre studied the picture again. "I
nnot tell. It is too faded. There is one thing I do know,
d that is that Orlando Abeyta was in love when he was
ry young, but that it was an unrequited love."

Jim replaced the picture in his wallet. "It is said that
eniente Abeyta was severely wounded at Colonia Federico
d was forced to retire because of his wounds. Perhaps, if
could find him, I could tell him of his brother's death."

"All those people moved west, my son, into the Sierra
allecillos. The Abeytas had lived near Laguna de Haros
r many generations. There are few people, if any, living
ere now."

Jim blew a reflective puff of smoke from his cigar. "Then
y best bet is to head west into the Sierra Vallecillos to
y and find the relatives of Orlando Abeyta."

"Do you know that country?"

"I've heard of it," said Jim dryly.

"It is almost impassable in places. Infested with outlaws,
ld animals, marauding Apaches and Yaquis."

"It is something I have to do, padre."

The padre nodded. "I will say prayers for the soul of
lando Abeyta," he said.

"He died a condemned man, padre. At least he was con-
mned by the people who hanged him."

"Do you believe he was guilty?"

"All the available evidence indicates that he was."

The padre shrugged. "It is impossible for me to believe

that he would murder a man. Continue on your quest, n
son. I will say prayers for you as well."

Jim smiled. "Likely I'll need them. Good night, padr
Thanks!"

The old man watched the tall Americano walk away, cig
at a jaunty angle, booted feet striking the street steadil
arms swinging by his sides. "Yes," said the padre softl
"You will need prayers, my son. Many prayers. Go wi
God!" He walked into the dimly lighted church. It would
well to begin right away.

The streets were dark except for an occasional lamp flarin
in the cold wind. It would be a cold, hard journey to the we
into the wild country of the Sierra Vallecillos, many are
of which were marked "impassable" or "unknown," the hon
of the wild ones, animals, white and red men, all as wild
the country.

He was within a block of his shabby hotel when somethin
seemed to warn him. He crossed to the other side of the da
street and worked his way toward the hotel. Two men stood
the corner in the biting wind, looking at the hotel, dark e
cept for faint lamplight in one or two windows and in t
little, dusty lobby where the clerk dozed in one of the ru
down chairs.

Jim watched the two men. One of them nodded his hea
He scraped a match against the nearest wall and lighted
cigarette, and in the dancing flare of the match flame Jim sa
a face he knew from Ute Crossing. It was the man nam
Slim. The match flickered out.

Jim stepped back into a deep doorway and eased his C
in its sheath. Once again an icy feeling surged through hi
as it had that wet night in Las Cruces when he had re
ognized Lyss. He was a long way from Las Cruces, whe
Lyss had likely been buried by now. He was a much long
distance from Ute Crossing. But it wasn't too far for me
from Ute Crossing to follow Jim clear down into Chihuahu

He had registered in the Amador Hotel in Cruces under h
own name, so they would know for sure he had been that f
south. He had left no written record of his presence in
Paso or in Ysleta, but Sarah Drinkwater and Sergeant L
Gilson had known he had been there, a week or more ag
It would have been logical enough for anyone following hi
to have crossed the Rio Grande into Zaragoza to ask a fe
questions. Perhaps someone there would remember the ta
Americano with the knife scar on his left cheek. They mig
have worked as far south as Villa Palmito and learned the
that he had taken the stagecoach to Chihuahua City. Th

68

might have arrived a few days behind him. They weren't just standing on that windy street corner speculating on where he was staying. They damned well knew!

He waited until he had a chance to slip back down the street. It took him only a few minutes to get to the run-down livery stable where he had left the coyote dun he had bought. Most of his gear was locked up in the storeroom of the stable. A handful of centavos was enough to send a hostler back to the hotel via the back way to get the rest of Jim's gear.

The wind shifted, blowing strongly from the northwest, as Jim left the city and rode through the darkness toward Gran Morelos.

Chapter Eight

"Colonia Federico," said the gray-haired Mexican. He shoved back his heavy felt steeplehat and looked at Jim Murdock. "Why would one want to come here, senor?"

Jim hooked a leg about the pommel of his saddle, rolled a cigarette, and passed the makings to the old man. His eyes were busy taking in the long-abandoned site of the *colonia*. One comes because one has a reason, Augustin," he said quietly. He lighted the cigarette and blew a puff of smoke that was taken away by the cold wind blowing from the north across the site of the old settlement.

"There is nothing here but ruin," said the old man. He deftly fashioned a cigarette, twisted the tip together, and accepted a light from Jim. *"Gracias,"* he said.

"Por nada," said Jim.

Augustin waved a brown, veinous old hand. "The bat and the owl, the lizard and the snake, live here. No humans will live here. It is an accursed place, senor."

"It is all in the mind, old man."

The sloe eyes of the Mexican studied Jim. "That is not so," he said quietly. "You yourself, perhaps, live under a curse?"

"Why do you ask?"

"Why would one come here? There is something in your eyes. Your voice. The way you say and do things. A man

69

who, perhaps, has a dog riding upon his back. A thing he must do? There are those under a curse who must wander on and on until the curse is lifted."

"And if it is not?"

Augustin shrugged. "Perhaps the senor knows that better than I do."

"Come, old man, let us see this place."

Augustin looked up at the sky. "It is almost dusk," he said. "There will be an early moon."

The Mexican shook his head. "There is no need to guide you, Senor Murdock. I will make the camp beyond this ridge. There is a water hole there. I will make the food."

Jim smiled. "One is not afraid?"

"Who? Me? I am not afraid, senor!"

Jim held his hands out, palms upward, smiled and shrugged. "I was but jesting, Augustin."

The old man smiled faintly. He tugged at his heavy gray moustache. "You have, perhaps, a cross? A Bible?"

Jim shook his head.

Augustin handed him a rosary. "Keep it in your hand," he said. "Senor, do not stay there after dark. . . ." He turned his mule and led the packmule up the ridge and was soon out of sight.

Jim hefted the rosary in his hand. He smiled and slipped it into his coat pocket.

The old man was right. Colonia Federico was now little more than a dusty name upon the empty landscape, soon to be completely forgotten. The home of the owl, the bat, the lizard, and the snake. There seemed to be little pattern in the humps of sand, gravel, and eroded adobe bricks that had once been houses, cantinas, shops, a small barracks and, of course, a church. Jim led the dun into the smoothly swept plaza, kept neat and tidy by the wind. By half closing his eyes he could visualize this little *placita* sleeping in the bright, hot suns of the summers, bowed beneath the bitter winter winds. Beyond the *placita* ruins he saw the vast, shallow bowl of the long-dry Laguna de Haros, which might fill up for a time during the heavy rains, or when the snow melted, although there would not be very many heavy snows.

Here it was that Teniente Teodoro Abeyta, with forty men, had held the *placita* against all the assaults of a combined force of Apaches and Yaquis, hundreds in number, it was said, who had been on their way south to strike at the gates of Parral, or perhaps even those of Durango itself. They had had no great interest in Colonia Federico save that they needed fresh meat, and there were many mules in those days

70

at the *colonia*, and the flesh of mules is sweet to an Apache or a Yaqui. Perhaps the alcalde could have dealt peacefully with the fierce warriors, the tigers of the mountains and deserts. It had been done before. The quixotic minds of the marauders might have let them take the mules and spare the inhabitants, as a sort of tribute to the fierceness and the power of the Apaches and their cousins the Yaquis. They might even have ignored the barefooted, shakoed infantrymen of Teniente Abeyta's company. This, too, had been done before. Likely the warriors were better armed than the little brown men whom they usually scorned.

But if the Apaches and the Yaquis were tigers of the mountains and deserts, there was also a tiger who had been sleeping in Colonia Federico. A man, an officer of the Mexican Army, whose blood was as proud and fierce as that of the warriors. A soldier whose fierce independence had caused his senior officer to practically bury him in Colonia Federico. His exile had done nothing to curb the spirit of Teodoro Abeyta.

No one knew to this day what had caused the spark to leap the gap from Mexican to Apache, but in the cold light of the early dawn, with the plaza filled with warriors, bands of white paint across their fierce noses and high cheekbones, the *n'deh b'keh,* the thick-soled, button-toed, thigh-length moccasins on their muscular legs, strong hands resting on rifle or lance, the spark had leaped. In the first few minutes of confused shooting Teniente Abeyta lost nine men, the Apaches six. The Apache and the Yaqui do not like hand-to-hand fighting. Their methods are those of the guerilla—the rifle shot from the mesquite, the ambush in the narrow pass, the killing of men before they have a chance to kill, then the leisurely knife and war-club work on the screaming wounded who see their deaths on the impassive brown faces of the warriors. Here, in the plaza, they had lost six good warriors. Perhaps if they had been fighting better troops, like those of the famous Indian-fighting Sixth Mexican Infantry, they might have taken their losses and retreated, for after all, they had killed more Mexicans than the Mexicans had killed warriors. But they did not retreat, and in the vicious infighting through the narrow streets of the *placita,* the Mexicans, led by Abeyta, drove the screaming warriors out to the naked land between the *placita* and the lagoon, which in those days was filled with water. Abeyta drove them out, but the price was high . . . too high, for he lost eight more men.

The blood madness came over Mexican and warrior. For two days they fought with the *heshke,* the "killing craze"

71

upon them all—the infantrymen behind their battered walls, the warriors working in close, using every scrap of cover to sharpshoot any head that appeared. Abeyta kept the frightened women and children behind the thick walls of the church. He armed every man and boy in the *placita*. He leavened the frightened civilians with his best fighting men. He was himself worth ten men.

When the warriors thought Abeyta was defeated, they charged into the plaza once more to meet Abeyta and the few men he had left. A blast of gunfire came from the church. The women and children, and the walking wounded caught the bucks in the flank with a hail of lead, and Abeyta then led his few soldiers into the melee of screaming bucks, firing a volley, then charging in with needle bayonets. Rifle butts smashed into the warriors, and when the rifles were shattered the Mexicans, masters of the knife, stayed to fight until the Apaches and Yaquis had enough. The warriors fled, although their numbers were still far greater than those of the enemy. Only a handful of the soldiers remained alive, and from beneath a heap of the contorted dead they dragged out the body of Teniente Teodoro Abeyta, riddled with wounds, more dead than alive.

The sun was dying in a welter of rose and gold in the west, and then swiftly it was gone, and as swiftly came the beginning of the night cold. In the quick rush of the darkness Jim Murdock saw the many mounded graves between the ruins of the *placita* and the empty *laguna*. He led the dun toward the graves, and as he walked the eeriness of the place suddenly came upon him. He turned and looked back, but there was nothing to see. Yet many men had died there in bloody violence, and a curse was upon this place.

There would be an early moon. Augustin would have made the camp and would have beans and tortillas ready. The old man had seemed glad to leave his granddaughter's comfortable casa in Gran Morelos to guide Jim to the west. It had been said of Augustin Galeras in the cantinas of Gran Morelos that he was *muy hombre,* still much of the man, despite his many years, and no one, senor, knew the country to the west better than he, unless perhaps it was the coyote or the eagle.

Jim sat down on a rock and smoked, listening to the wind sweeping across the desert to the north, hard at work tidying up the already immaculate and sterile neatness of Colonia Federico, or what had been Colonia Federico. With its phobia for neatness, the wind would in time sweep Colonia

72

Federico into its immense dustpan, and thence into the great dustbin of limbo, whence no human could ever return, even in memory. It made a big man feel damned insignificant. The desert and the mountains have a way of doing just that.

In the first faint light of the rising moon that silver-washed the low hills to the east, Jim walked about among the mounded graves. There were many of them, but most of them would be of people who had died before the great fight there. To one side, separated by a shallow ditch, he found a group of graves with a marker set among them, a yellowish-white stone set upon a rock base, cemented together. The new moon shone full upon the face of the rock and the inscription cut thereon, although wind and sharp-edged dust, rain, and snow had softened the words and partially erased some of them.

Jim shoved back his hat and studied the inscription, his lips moving silently until he got the gist of it, and then he read it aloud for the bat, the owl, the lizard, and the snake to hear, for there wasn't any other living thing to listen.

To the exalted memory of the Third Company, Fourth Provisional Regiment, of the Army of the glorious Republic of Mexico: these brave men did their duty at Colonia Federico in the face of hundreds of Apaches and Yaquis, and decisively defeated them despite the great disparity in numbers. Here are inscribed the names of the honored dead and the few living men of the Third Company, who under the command of Teniente Teodoro Abeyta wrote in heroic blood a page of Mexican history. Honor to them! Learn here a lesson, you who read this: Learn that only men who do their duty are entitled to be honored on such a monument as this. To the coward: Slink silently away! Your curse is that you will always wander, but you will never escape the memory of what you did here at Colonia Federico!

Jim slowly rolled a cigarette. The monument was unusual. The "heroic" dead and the "heroic" living had indeed been honored, although few would travel to this abandoned place to read the glorious words, and the memory of man is short even when he can read the wording on such monuments. What was unusual was that there was a thrusting reference to cowardice. The cowardice of a number of men, perhaps, but more likely of one. Jim lighted the cigarette and blew a reflective puff of smoke. He hadn't expected to learn much at Colonia Federico, but Augustin had said it was only a few miles out of the way on the route to Santo Tomas in the sierra to the west.

The moonlight was beginning to flood the desert. Far across the cold wastes came the faint howling of a coyote, greeting the pallid beauty of the new moon.

Jim sat there beside the eroding monument for a long time. Bits and pieces were fitting into the puzzle that had been the fatalistic Mexican known as Orlando Abeyta. A brave man who had died ingloriously with a drunkard and a frightened boy. *"He was such a gentle lad. Brave in his own way. Not a hero like his elder brother, of course, but then Orlando had never wanted to be a soldier. Had he been stronger in spirit he would have resisted all efforts to make him a soldier, except for being a soldier of God."* Jim whirled and was on his feet, fingertips brushing the worn butt of his Colt, before he realized the voice had been only in his mind. And yet it had seemed at the moment that someone, the old padre, had spoken to Jim as he had spoken to him that night in Chihuahua City, when they had talked about Orlando Abeyta, the boy who had wanted to be a priest.

The searching wind shifted, rattling bits of gravel against the monument. The moon shone upon the ruins of Colonia Federico in an eerie silvery light, etching sharp shadows from the few walls that still stood free from the harsh embrace of the desert that was again taking over the country.

Was it indeed Orlando Abeyta, the condemned and executed murderer, who had been the coward of Colonia Federico? But his brother had been the hero of Colonia Federico. Jim withdrew the fine presentation watch from his pocket. He opened the back cover and eyed the faint inscription in the clear light of the moon. His lips wordlessly shaped the inscription. "To Teniente Teodoro . . . For heroic services rendered at Colonia . . ." He closed the back of the case and pressed the repeater button. The soft, sweet chime struck six o'clock.

The dun had strayed. Jim could hardly blame him. It had been a long day's ride to Colonia Federico across rough, cold country. He stowed away the watch and walked past the dead *placeta*, heading for the ridge. There was nothing more to be learned from the place.

He slowly walked up the ridge, his thoughts miles away. A horse nickered. He turned toward the sound. A movement in the scant brush of a hollow drew him to it. He saw a horse, and his eyes narrowed. It wasn't the dun. It was a claybank, saddled and with pommel and cantle packs as well as filled saddlebags. He looked about. There would be no tracks on that hard ground. The horse nickered again, and when Jim turned to look at him he saw another horse further up the draw. A black, saddled and with cantle and pommel packs. Both horses had been tethered to the tough brush.

He whirled at another sound and saw the dun trotting up the slope toward the other horses. One of them whinnied. Jim met the dun and led him far down the slope into a deep arroyo, tethered him, and then unsheathed his Winchester, levering a .44/40 into the chamber. He removed his spurs and padded up the ridge again, falling belly flat on the near side of the crest, dropping his hat behind him as he wormed his way up to the top of the ridge and thrust his head between two clumps of growth to peer down the far side. The moonlight glinted from the calm surface of the water hole. A thread of smoke arose from the embers of a fire set in a ring of smoke-blackened rocks. Here and there lay packs and other gear. Three men stood there in the bright moonlight, two of them tall men, Americans, no doubt, with pistols in their hands, looking at Augustin Galeras, who stood there hatless, his white hair clear and sharp in the moonlight, and a trickle of blood glistening on his brown face as it crept from his scalp to his lined jaw.

The wind shifted and blew toward Jim from the trio of motionless men. "Where is he, greaser?" said one of the men.

"I do not know of whom you speak, senor," said Augustin.

"The big gringo! Murdock! You left Gran Morelos with him three days ago! Where is that scar-faced son of a bitch?"

Jim wet his lips. The voice was that of the man named Slim, and further, there was no mistaking his build and height, for the man was a good four inches taller than Jim's six feet even.

"Talk, damn you!" said the other man.

Jim knew him too. It was the man named Jules, another member of the lynching party.

"He has gone north," said Augustin at last. A hard hand slapped the Mexican's white head back and forth until he swayed on his feet.

"You talk, by God," said Slim, "or we'll toast your dirty feet over them coals! Where did he go? What's he aimin' to do?"

Jim stood up and Augustin saw him, but the Mexican's face did not betray what he had seen. Jim walked softly down the ridge, rifle at hip level, hammer back, fingertip pressing lightly against trigger, taking up the slack. If Slim

75

and Jules saw him or heard him, they could kill Augustin before Jim could open fire for fear of hitting the old man.

"He has gone to Temosachic," said Augustin in a quavering voice.

"Where is that?" demanded Slim.

Jim was fifty yards away now, still too far to open fire.

"In the Sierra Vallecillos, not far from Laguna de Bavicora. He goes there to talk about mining."

Slim's hard hand slashed across Augustin's face, and bright droplets of blood glistened in the moonlight as they flew from the Mexican's slack mouth. "You lie!" yelled Slim. "That bastard ain't no miner! He's looking for someone's kin, ain't he? Name of Orlando or somethin'! Ain't he?"

Jim was twenty-five feet away now. His left boot kicked a stone. "Drop!" yelled Jim to Augustin. As the old man hit the ground the two Americans whirled. Jim fired once into Jules' lean gut, and the two-hundred-grain slug doubled the man up and drove him back against Slim as though a mule had kicked him. Jim had jumped sideways as soon as he had fired, slamming the Winchester lever up and down and firing the instant the lever closed home. Slim cursed. He shoved the falling Jules aside and slapped out two rounds. Something plucked at Jim's left sleeve. He reloaded and charged directly toward the cursing man slamming out round after round. Slim went down on one knee, game, though wounded, and raised his six-shooter for his last shot. Echoes slammed back and forth between the ridges.

Augustin rolled to his feet like a cat, and something glittered in his hand as he closed in on Slim. Slim turned and struggled to his feet. The old man was in under the smoking six-shooter and the knife sank deep into Slim's hard-muscled gut, and then, with a terrible, wrenching pull across the belly and down into the soft groin, a figure seven stroke, Augustin finished the job.

Slim dropped the hot six-shooter, clutching his opened belly. He looked at Jim with terrible, staring eyes. Jim raised the rifle and fired once, right between the eyes, and Slim fell at Augustin's feet and lay still. Slowly the moon-whitened ground beneath him began to turn black from the soaking of the flood of blood.

The echoes died, fleeing off into the grim silence of the watching hills. The stench of acrid smoke hung in the draw between the moon-washed ridges.

Augustin bent on one knee and calmly wiped the bloody knife on Slim's coat. He stood up and looked at Jim. "I did not tell them," he said proudly.

"You did well, old one," said Jim quietly.

Augustin sheathed the blade. He spat on the two bodies. Jim wiped the cold sweat from his face. It had been a near thing.

"Why do they seek you, Jaime?" asked the old man. He studied Jim with narrowed eyes.

"I have done nothing to them," said Jim. "It seems to be something that they helped do to others that makes such men follow me." He looked about. "This is a bad thing. The killing of two Americanos here in your country."

Augustin picked up his sweat-stained old hat. He looked sideways at Jim. "Who is to know?" he said softly. He smiled. "As I said before: Only the bat and the owl, the lizard and the snake, live here."

"You said something else, old man," said Jim.

"Eh?"

Jim looked at him. "It is an accursed place. . . ."

"That is true." Augustin looked at the fire. "The meal is ready." He laughed. "They did not touch my beans or tortillas, Jaime."

"You would eat here?" asked Jim.

Augustin walked to the fire and pulled free the blackened clay pot of beans. He looked back at Jim, his great eyes peering beneath his wide, upturned hat brim. "Those two will not share our food," he said. "There is more than enough for two of us, but not enough for four. Come! Eat! We will get rid of them and hide them so not even God can find their bodies. So, then, what is to fear? *Los muertos no hablan.* . . ."

Jim nodded. The dead do not speak. It was enough. They would have killed Jim and the old man as well if they had had the chance.

There was moonlight aplenty for the ride west, after the bodies had been buried and the gear hidden. There were no brands on the two horses. Augustin picketed them lightly not far from the water hole. In time they would break free, but by then Jim and his guide would be many miles into the looming mountains.

They took the dim trail toward Santo Tomas in the last hours of the cold moonlight. Jim looked back at the dreary, godforsaken site of Colonia Federico. He had left three dead men behind him on his quest for the kin of the three men who had been hanged at Ute Crossing. Perhaps a poetic justice, for he was almost sure that there had been much more behind those lynchings than just the outraged feelings of the hard men of the valley of the Ute. Something dark and evil, so evil he did not want to think about it. Not yet, anyway; not that night, for a certainty.

As they entered the first gateway into the quiet hills a coyote broke voice far in the lonely distance.

Chapter Nine

The high peaks of the Sierra Madre were snow-clad, serene and distant, as though belonging to another world. Always they looked down impassively into the terribly deep barrancas and the timbered mesas, covered with spruce and pine and red-hued madronas. They seemed not to notice the antlike creatures that walked upon two legs or rode upon larger antlike creatures with four legs. These antlike beings came and went during the centuries on some meaningless business of their own, and although they changed over the years, they were always the same to the peaks of the Sierra Madre.

For days and then weeks Jim Murdock had waited in a tiny village in a valley far below those stupendous mountains, while old Augustin Galeras struggled with life and death. In the weeks that the old man and Jim had worked their way upward into the mountains, Jim had grown to like, then to respect, and then to love the old man. He would never return to Gran Morelos. Jim knew that and Augustin knew that. A bad fall from his mule had broken many of his ribs. He had broken ribs before, but then he had been a much younger man. Still, as he had always done, he fought, but this time he fought against the one enemy who could never be defeated by man.

The old year had slipped away with hardly a murmur into the past. The mountains didn't care. The simple mountain people seemed to care less. This was a world far removed from dates and places. How could one feel important with those mountains watching him with half-lidded eyes all day?

They buried old Augustin in a grave punched out of resisting earth on a shelf that overlooked the brawling stream, with a good view of the great peaks. Jim Murdock had wanted to leave then, but a great norther had swept across

he Sierra Vallecillos and carried with it a weight of snow
hat recapped the peaks, bringing the white mantles lower
han anyone living in the village could ever remember, even
ld Santiago Esquivel, of whom it was said that he had lived
n those mountains longer than the Devil himself. The snow
hoked the narrow passes and filled the canyons and bar-
ancas, until, Body of God, it seemed as though no one
vould ever again get in or out of the lonely, almost forgotten
alley.

Yet, no one really wanted to leave, and cared less about
nyone coming into the valley. Even the big gringo, the
aunt man with the scar upon his face, and the big brown
ands that carved such wonderful toys for the boys and
irls, seemed to care little. If there was anything broken in
he village he fixed it. If a horse, a goat, or a burro became
ll, he knew how to treat it, and he even could treat the
uman sick with the little store of medicines he carried with
im.

He kept his two well-oiled guns in their worn sheaths in
he little hut he had shared with the old man before the old
nan had died. The simple villagers would surreptitiously eye
hat disfiguring scar on the Americano's face, the stubborn
et of the strong jaw, and those steady, penetrating eyes, eyes
o light in color, to the villagers, at least, that they seemed al-
nost disfiguring. Those eyes could be as hard as granite, and
et when the Americano helped the sick or comforted a
hild, they would soften marvelously. They had seen him
se that heavy rifle to bring down deer and bear at in-
redible ranges.

In the third month of the new year the big Americano
ode from the village on the soft trails, guided by a silent
nozo, a tribeless Tarahumare who spoke no English and
ery little Spanish but who knew those mountains as few
ther men did. Yet, not even the mozo had heard of San
ederico, and not even old Santiago Esquivel himself had
eard of it.

The mozo parted company with Jim at the junction of the
io Yaqui and the Rio Moctezuma and faded away into the
nountains. In two weeks he had not spoken a word to Jim.

Jim had been away from Ute Crossing for many months
ow. He was on a long, long trail to which there seemed to
e no ending. He could not quit. *"There are those under a
urse who must wander on and on until the curse is lifted."*
hose had been the wise words of old Augustin Galeras to
im Murdock. Since the deaths of Slim and Jules, Jim had
eard nothing about Ute Crossing before the mountain trails

had been blocked, stopping even the hardy monthly mail runner. Nothing. It had been as though he had moved into another world once he and the old man had left Santo Tomas.

The days faded into weeks, and the mountain world grew warm as Jim patiently worked his way through the mountains as far west as La Colorado on the road to Hermosillo as far south as the Sierra Baroyeca, thence east into the Rio Mayo country, then back again to the Sierra Baroyeca, to Esperanza, and up the Rio Yaqui to Tecoripa and thence north to Nacozari and Bacoachi, thence south again and east to the wild Rio Escondido. There *was* no San Federico. There never *had* been a San Federico. Perhaps there never *would* be a San Federico, senor. *Quién sabe?* Who knows? The phrase echoed in his ears in the lonely camps and in the little *placitas* and mining camps, on the twisting trails and beside the calm waters of the *lagunas*. The spring had shifted into the early summer, and still he had progressed no further than he had been when he had entered those great mountains with old Augustin Galeras so many months ago and had paid the blood price for the passage with the life of the old man. Stranger than the unknown San Federico was the complete lack of knowledge of the name of Abeyta. It seemed as though that name had never been known in those wild and forbidding mountains.

With the coming of the summer came dark news. The Chiricahua Apaches had raided down as far as Casa Blanca. The notorious Streeter Gang of half-breeds, pure quill Apaches, and renegade whites had struck in the vicinity of Fronteras. Bandits haunted the roads between the border and Hermosillo and ranged as far east as the San Miguel. Hard times, hard times indeed, senor, had come to Sonora.

Not far from Magdalena was a good spring where Jim Murdock, the gringo with the curse upon him, would camp when he was in that vicinity, resting his horse and his pack burro, letting them get fat again, although no amount of food or resting would layer fat upon the tall Americano's muscular body, gaunt from too many months on the trail that had no ending.

He approached the spring one early summer evening, an unlit Mexican cigar stuck in the corner of his mouth, the dust of the trail thick upon his animals, his clothing, and his own tanned flesh. He had seen smoke rising from the spring area on his slow climb up toward the spring from the desertlike country below. He was within a quarter of a mile of the spring when he noticed that the smoke had

ickened, and the shifting breeze of the oncoming darkness
rought with it the smell of burning cloth and something
se he recognized, and as he recognized it, he dropped from
is horse, slapped it on the rump, and jerked his Winchester
om its saddle scabbard as he did so.

He drifted like a cloud shadow across the dry ground and
ito the shelter of rocks and scrub trees. The wind shifted
gain, and he was positive of the odor that came with it.
urning flesh. . . . There was only one possible source for *that*
lor. It was a favorite device of Apaches and Yaquis to use
·e on their victims.

The horse had led the docile pack burro into the shelter
' the trees down the slope, unseen if anyone looked down
om the spring area. Jim worked his way through the trees
ıd tumbled boulders until he could belly forward to over-
ok the spring. Years ago someone had built a rock house
ere, but now the roof had partially tumbled in and one
the walls had collapsed. The spring was beyond the
ɔuse in a great cup of sun-bleached rocks. The thickening
ıoke rose from a fire at the edge of the rocks where a man,
Mexican by his clothing, lay sprawled on his back across
e coals, his arms outflung and his face a red mask of
ood. Beyond him lay another man, more likely a big boy,
ɔubled up, with a dark stain on the back of his shirt. A
ule, tethered to a tree, was fighting the rope that tied him
the tree.

Jim wet his dry lips, studying the scene with slitted eyes.
ıere were others down there somewhere. He was sure of it.
e looked back over his shoulder to make sure he wasn't
:ing flanked. There was no one there.

Suddenly a woman screamed, and Jim's head snapped
ound. He raised his rifle. She had come staggering out
om the old house, holding rags of clothing about her almost
ıked body, running across the empty ground toward the
ring. A man stood up from among the rocks, his steeple-
·owned hat on the back of his head, a grin on his brown
.ce, and his arms outstretched to catch this ripe plum of
mininity. She darted sideways and ran down the slope.
wo more men appeared from the brush, grinning at her,
eir white teeth in sharp contrast to their dusty moustaches
ıd dark skins. One of them snatched at her rags, and as
ıe pulled away she stood there trembling, mother-naked,
·ying to cover her full breasts with her arms, while the
ree men roared with drunken laughter.

Jim slid down the slope. They were too busy to see him.
he woman turned again and ran in the direction of the rock

81

tangle just below Jim. He dropped into a cup thick wi
brush. Something buzzed dryly, and he smashed down tl
metal-shod butt of the rifle on the ugly, flat, triangular hea
of a rattlesnake. The thick, powerful body wound itse
about his left leg.

Another man came from the house, staggering a little
his drunkenness and eagerness as he ran toward the despera
woman. Her great dark eyes saw the face in the brush.

"Bandidos!" she screamed.

There was no time for Jim to deliberate now. He'd ha
to take her word for it. In any case they meant little go
toward the naked woman, and the two bodies mutely testifi
to their profession.

Jim fired once. The two men who stood together dash
back into the brush. The man at the spring raised a rifl
Jim fired twice. The Mexican was slammed back over tl
rocks and his rifle exploded as he fell, sending a whini
slug up into the blue. The rifle shot echoes thundered agair
the hill slopes and ran along the mountain face to die in tl
distance, but they were closely pursued by others.

Jim hurdled the rocks at his feet, pushing the screami
woman back into the brush. The writhing snake tripped hi
He fell headlong, thrusting forward his rifle as he did s
and the snake saved his life, for slashing lead cut the a
where Jim had been standing. He rolled over and fired in
the brush where the pair of bandits had vanished, aiming
the gun flashes and puffs of smoke. A man screamed ar
fell thrashing down the slope, rolling over and over until l
fell from a low cliff to crash into the thick brush below.

A bullet smashed into Jim's right boot heel, tearing it o
numbing his lower leg. Another plucked his hat from h
head. He fired into the brush again. The Mexican stood u
and fired at a fifty-foot range. Jim grunted as the sl
smashed into his left shoulder. He fired a round from tl
rifle with his right hand and then dropped the weapon. l
swayed up to his feet, pulling free his Colt. Three tim
the six-shooter slammed back into his hand, and the Mexic
fell backward in death, dropping his smoking rifle.

The big gringo swayed on his feet, his eyes wide wi
shock. The hot blood ran down inside his shirt and unde
shirt. He turned slowly to look at the remaining bandit. Tl
Colt fell from Jim's hand.

The Mexican stood there, head and shoulders bent fc
ward, looking at Jim with his one eye, for the other was
puckered hole in his seamed brown face. The Mexican slow
sheathed his nickel-plated pistol and swiftly drew his *sa*

82

ripas. This gringo would have to be gutted like a chicken for what he had done. No easy, swift death for him.

The woman screamed again, the echoes flying down the now strangely quiet hillside.

The Mexican tested the razor edge of his curved knife with his thumb. He walked slowly toward Jim, his one eye like an amber marble, unblinking as the stare of a basilisk. He faded in and out of Jim's sight like a chimera.

The Mexican was within ten feet of Jim when Jim went down, clawing at his belly with both hands in what seemed to be intense pain. The Mexican laughed. He closed in and thrust down with the knife.

The silver-mounted derringer in Jim's right hand spat flame and smoke. The soft-nosed .41 slug caught the Mexican low in the guts. As he fell he drove the knife at Jim's contorted face, and the razor edge ripped across Jim's right cheek to match the scar on the other side. Jim fired the second barrel of the stingy gun. The slug smashed into the bandit's mouth and up into his brain. He fell heavily across him.

Then it was very quiet. Jim lay with his blood-masked face against the harsh ground. His left arm and shoulder were completely numbed. The waves of excruciating pain would come after the shock of the impact died away. Slowly he raised his right hand to his slashed face, and he winced as he felt the torn lips of the wound.

The bandit's body was rolled off him. Jim turned his face upward to look at the woman. She was still naked. Her eyes were wide in fear and compassion for the big gringo who had come out of nowhere to save her from multiple rape and possible murder. She was not young, but not very old either, and her body was that of a much younger woman, firm-fleshed and luscious. Jim closed his eyes. Waves of faintness swept over him. He felt his face strike the ground once more.

The last thing he remembered was soft hands working on him, ripping away shirt and undershirt, stanching the big hole in his shoulder, washing the wound in his face and binding it, and all the time she worked on him he was acutely conscious that her warm, full breasts touched him constantly, and once his hand touched the velvet smoothness of a full thigh. After that there was nothing but limbo.

Chapter Ten

He came out of the fever very slowly. There were times
when he was aware of movements, voices, actions, and then
he would drift off into that vague, hazy land where nothing
was ever very clear, and where, at times, he was sure he was
dreaming. But gradually he grew aware of other things. Of
deft, sure hands bathing him and shaving him. Of soft flesh
pressing against him as he was moved about. Once he opened
his eyes to see a thick tress of dark hair just above his face,
and the faint fragrance of perfume mingled with that of
warm, feminine flesh came to him, and then he was gone
again.

He opened his eyes one day and did not move. Above him
was a corbeled, whitewashed ceiling. He moved only his
eyes. To his right were two deep-set windows, and through
them came sunlight, shifting as though it came through the
moving branches of trees. In one corner was a neat beehive
fireplace. A massive chest of drawers stood against a wall,
and a crucifix hung above it. There were several wall niches
with Indian-faced *santos* within them. The bed in which he
lay was massive also. He looked down at his arms lying
atop the neat spread, and at his hands. He was stunned as he
saw his hands. Once strong and brown, they were now white
and lifeless looking, and the hairs seemed to stand alone
like the charred trunks of trees left when fire has swept a
mesa.

Birds twittered beyond the windows. He heard the faint
braying of a burro. The wind shifted, and an unseen windmill began to hum its busy song. Then clearest of all came
the heady, pleasing laughter of children at play.

He closed his eyes. Weakness filled his limbs, and for a
moment he thought he was going to drift off into limbo
again, but by a conscious effort of his will he held himself
in the land of the living. Memories came slowly back to
him, piece by puzzling piece, and he fitted them together like
a child, by patient trial and error. There had been a day of
hazy sunshine. No, it had been late afternoon, closing swiftly

84

nto dusk. There had been the smoke of a campfire. No, a
ouse. No, the house had long been abandoned. Smoke. . . .
moke? It had been smoke, but not from a house, but from
fire where clothing, leather, and flesh had burned in an
crid, sweetish-smelling combination. For a long time he lay
hinking. There had been some shooting. He thought hard.
Men had died there in the hazy sunlight and the drifting
moke of the fire and the gun muzzles. Who had died, and
vhy?

He slowly dragged his right hand over to his left shoulder
vhere a dull, nagging ache persisted, like the beginning of an
bscessed tooth. His shoulder was neatly bandaged. He had
een wounded, then. He remembered that. Slowly, like a
nake uncoiling in its den after the sleep of winter, his right
and touched his chin and then passed up to his right cheek
here something lay on the taut skin like a thick-bodied
orm. His questing fingers touched the hard granulation of a
ewly healed wound.

Jim wet his dry lips. His mind drifted again. Again he
rove it back to its task. Then, with startling clarity, he saw
er, naked, screaming, wide-eyed with pain and sheer terror,
unning across the ground toward him. "Mother of the
evil!" he yelled in a hoarse, cracked voice. "The woman!
Vhat happened to the woman?"

Soft footfalls sounded outside the room, and the thick
oor swung back on gently creaking hinges. She stood there
ramed in the wide doorway, dark, thick hair plaited in a
eavy coil which crossed a smooth white shoulder exposed
y the low, wide neck of the white blouse she wore, and
ested high on a full breast, like a kitten asleep. Her full
kirt fell from her smoothly rounded hips, and beneath the
mbroidered edge of the skirt he saw the tiniest of feet, bare
xcept for huaraches. It was her eyes that held him fascinated.
ike those of a fawn, but full of a compassion and a life no
wn had ever exhibited.

She crossed herself. "Con el favor de Dios," she said in
soft, almost husky voice. "With the favor of God you are
ith us again, Senor Murdock."

She came beside the bed and placed a soft, smooth little
and on his forehead. She smiled. "Yes," she said with de-
ght. "Everyone will be so pleased."

He looked up at her, wincing a little as the muscles drew
his shoulder. "You know who I am," he said. "Who are
ou?"

"You do not remember?"

He narrowed his eyes. "The woman at the spring!" he said "Yes! I remember now."

She reddened and looked away. "I am Rafaela Velarde" she said.

"Your servant, Senorita Velarde," he said.

She straightened the spread. "Senora Velarde," she corrected him.

"I am sorry for that, senora," he said with a smile.

"You Americans," she said with a flirt of her lovely head

He looked about the room. "How long have I been here?"

She tilted her head to one side and counted on the tips of her slim fingers. "Five, no six!" she said.

He eyed her narrowly. "Days?"

"*Weeks*, Senor Murdock."

He closed his eyes again. It was impossible.

"The doctor said the bullet might have been poisoned."

"There was much fever, then?"

She placed her hand on his forehead again, and he looked up at her. "It was very close," she said quietly. "The doctor said you had the strength of a dozen men and the stubbornness of a mule."

Jim smiled. "I think he knows me pretty well."

"Would you like a mirror?"

"Yes, please."

She brought it to him and held it in front of his face. A stranger stared back at him with deep-set gray eyes. A gaunt death's-head of a face. A thin white scar traced a course down his hollow left cheek, and on the other cheek was a twisted reddish scar. He shook his head. "He did a neat job," he said.

She took away the mirror. "When you have strength you will feel and look better. I will get some soup." She placed the mirror on the wardrobe and walked to the door, gently swaying hips intriguing Jim. He *must* be recovering.

"Where am I?" he asked.

She turned and smiled. "San Federico," she said, and then she was gone, closing the door behind her.

The children laughed again. The mule brayed. The wind mill hummed on and on.

"San Federico?" said Jim. He shook his head. "*San Federico?*" He rested his head on the pillow. "Well, I'll be double dipped in a vat of fresh manure!"

He shifted in the bed, and slowly worked himself into a semi-sitting position. "Rafaela," he said softly. He remembered all too clearly now. He remembered that lush body, exposed to the hot, lusting eyes of those two-legged animals at the spring. He remembered, too, when she had come to him to help him, forgetting her nakedness in her efforts to stanch his wounds. He might very well have died except for her. "Six weeks," he whispered. He shook his head. With all his months of searching he had not found San Federico, only to find it by sheer luck. The hard way, he thought.

The sun had gone when she returned with a tray. She lighted candles as Jim watched her. Everything she did she did with an effortless grace. He ate slowly as she busied herself about the room. "I have been looking for San Federico for a long time," he said.

"It has been here a long time," she said.

He finished his soup and leaned back against a pillow. She rolled a cigarette for him and placed it between his lips, then lighted it, leaning close, so close that he did not dare look down, for he knew that her blouse would be hanging free from her body. She straightened up and rolled herself a cigarette. She lighted it and blew a puff of smoke.

"There was a Colonia Federico beyond the mountains," he said at last. "I was told the people who had lived there had left that place because of a curse and had come beyond the Sierra Vallecillos to make a new home, a place to be called San Federico. That was all I knew. Strange that I have spent so many weeks on the trail in Sonora, and yet no one knew of this place. Not a word from anyone. Not a trace, and then to find it this way, or rather, to have it find me."

She studied him closely. "Did you not think of looking elsewhere for San Federico?"

"No," he said. "Beyond the Sierra Vallecillos. That was what I was told. But no one knew for sure."

She took the cigarette from her full lips. "It is very simple," she said. "You are not in Sonora, Senor Murdock, but in Arizona Territory, in your United States of America." She laughed at the surprised look on his face. "The people of Colonia Federico did come west of the Sierra Vallecillos to find a new home. It was too wild, too dangerous, because of the Apaches and Yaquis. The people scattered. Some of them drifted west to Hermosillo and Guaymas, or into the mining country. My husband and I came to Arizona for better medical care because of his wounds, and because he had a cousin who was an American citizen. My husband died."

There was a flicker of interest in Jim's eyes.

She ground out the cigarette butt in a dish and looked sideways at him. "He was my first husband," she said quietly. "I married his cousin a year ago. Senor Velarde. The owner of Rancho San Federico. I think you must already know the name of my first husband."

He narrowed his brows and stared uncomprehendingly at her.

"He was Teniente Teodoro Abeyta," she said. "The hero of Colonia Federico."

"How did you know I knew about him?"

She shrugged. "We were on our way here when the bandits struck. I did not know who you were when I had you brought here, north of the border. It was necessary, you understand, to identify you. We looked through your things. I found a picture of myself taken some years ago with my two children. There was a watch, too. I knew it well. It had been presented to my husband for his heroism at Colonia Federico. I have not seen that watch for many years. Where did you get it?"

Jim rolled another cigarette and lighted it. He eyed her through the thin cloud of smoke that drifted toward the open window. How much did she know? Was it possible that she knew Orlando Abeyta had died a felon's death far north of Rancho San Federico?

"There was some question about you having the watch," she added. "But, for what you did at the spring, we forgave anything else."

"I did not steal it," he said.

"I never believed that you did," she said. She sat down on the edge of the bed and studied him closely with those lovely eyes of hers. Something else came back to Jim. Something the priest had said about Orlando Abeyta. *He once told me he would never marry. Orlando Abeyta was in love when he was very young, but it was an unrequited love.* A piece of the puzzle slipped suddenly into place. Rafaela was older than Orlando would have been, perhaps not by very much, but these Mexican women married very young. A coward, a boy who had wanted to be a priest, sensitive and proud, who had become a soldier, not by choice, perhaps because he had deeply loved the woman who had married his elder brother, an officer and a hero.

"Where is he?" she asked softly.

Jim looked at the tip of his cigarette.

"Is he dead?"

Jim nodded.

"He was a friend of yours? Is that why you came to find us?"

Jim looked at her. "He was not my friend," he said.

Could he tell her how Orlando had died?

She stood up and paced back and forth. "Something terrible happened to him," she said. "I know."

The wind had shifted. It blew in through the window. The candles guttered and flared, casting her shadow on the white-washed wall. She stopped pacing and looked directly at Jim. "How did he die? Why have you come here to tell us?"

Jim fingered his new face scar. "Who was the coward of Colonia Federico?" he countered.

"How did you know about that?"

He shrugged. "I know," he said quietly. He looked up at her. "It was Orlando, wasn't it?"

"It was not his fault! He was no coward. There are many kinds of cowards. In his own way he was a brave man. It was a label they placed on him."

"Why did they do it?" he asked.

She wet her full lips and looked away. "It was after the fight. There were many wounded. The ground was stained with blood. Men were screaming in their pain. There was no doctor at Colonia Federico." Her voice died away.

"Go on," he said gently.

She caught her breath. "There were only a few soldiers left standing on their feet. My husband was badly wounded. He was wounded, but he was an officer and a soldier of Mexico. He gave orders to kill the enemy wounded. It was the custom. There was never any quarter given or asked for in that type of warfare. You understand?"

Jim nodded. "I have experienced such warfare," he said.

"Orlando was thought to have been killed or wounded. It was not so. He had hidden himself away so that he would not kill. My husband found out about it. In front of the people of Colonia Federico and the few soldiers left alive he gave Orlando a direct order to kill the enemy wounded. Orlando must do it alone to redeem himself." She laughed bitterly.

"He did not do it?" asked Jim.

She shook her head. "It was not within that gentle boy to kill like that, or any other way. . . ."

"I can guess what happened to him," he said.

She nodded. "They shaved his head, stripped his buttons from him, and drummed him from the ranks."

"Because he could not kill."

"Yes," she said. She took the makings and rolled a cigarette. She looked at Jim over the flare of the match. "How did he die?"

"Bravely."

"But why?" she said.

He could at least tell a little lie. "There was a gunfight. A man was killed. It was thought that Orlando had killed this man. His friends shot down Orlando. Before he died he gave me those things you found."

She walked to the window and turned her back toward Jim. Her lovely shoulders shook a little. "Was there anything he said?" she asked.

The wind seemed to die away and it was very quiet, as though the oncoming night too wanted to hear what Jim Murdock had to say.

"Rafaela," said Jim. "That was what he said."

"There are many women named Rafaela," she said huskily.

"Perhaps. But that is what he said."

Her shoulders drooped a little. "It was I who gave him the watch," she said, without turning.

"A little cruelty, perhaps?"

She shook her head. "He wanted it."

"And the picture?"

"I did not know he had it."

Jim wet his dry lips. This was more painful than his healing wounds.

She turned slowly. "Would you like to see the children?" she said.

"Very much. Your husband as well."

She took the tray and walked to the door, looking back over her shoulder at him. "He is in Tucson on business," she said. "He will not be back for at least a week. Two days ago a package came from him for you. Medicines. Don Federico Velarde, my husband, is a fine man, and a good stepfather to my children."

"Federico again?" His eyes held hers. *He will be gone at least a week,* thought Jim.

She nodded. "There was a *cura* here at one time, many years ago, long before the Americans took Arizona from my people. This was a holy place, but it fell upon evil times. My husband's grandfather took it over and named this place after his patron saint, Saint Federico. After that, each eldest son has taken that name. You must rest now."

The door closed behind her. Jim slowly fashioned another cigarette. There was something in the woman that cried out to him, but why he did not know. She had been married twice, and surely both husbands had been good to her, and she had probably loved Teodoro. Jim wet the end of the paper and thumbed the paper together. He snapped a match on his thumbnail and lighted the cigarette. But she had been loved by the ill-fated Orlando and she had wanted to know his last words. Had she loved him too? What kind of woman was this? He closed his eyes. *"Don Federico Velarde, my husband, is a fine man, and a good stepfather to my children."* He opened his eyes and blew a smoke ring. "He will not be back for at least a week," he said aloud.

The wind shifted. A shutter banged. A draft of air swirled in through the open windows and played with the guttering candles.

Jim felt his wounded shoulder. It would be some time before he could ride. Until that time he would be a guest in the casa of Don Federico Velarde.

The door opened and Rafaela brought in her two children. There was Teodoro, a grave-faced faced boy of perhaps twelve, and little Teresa, perhaps seven or eight years of age. Teresa was formed from the same pattern as her mother, with mischievous eyes and a flirtatious look. Teodoro? Once, the boy looked quickly sideways at Jim, and for an instant, the blinking of an eye, perhaps, Jim thought he saw the face of Orlando Abeyta.

When they were gone, Jim lay there for a long time staring up at the dim ceiling. He had to leave this place. He had done what he had set out to do. He had told Orlando's kin of his death. He had found out what kind of man Orlando Abeyta had been. It had taken many months. It would soon be time for him to ride north, back to his own country, to find Three Forks and a girl named Jessica. Then it would all be over, and he'd be able to sleep well once again, and the dog would be off his back. So far it had not been an easy task, nor were his problems over. He dropped off to sleep, and as he did so the oval face of Rafaela appeared to him, and there were other things as well. Things that disturbed his sleep as it had not been disturbed for many months.

The sixth day after Jim's return to the world of the living he had spent outside in the bright sunshine of late summer, watching the children at play, looking at the purple haze over the hills, listening to the distant bawling of the cattle, and also to the voice of Rafaela as she gave orders to her servants. The doctor had visited Jim twice in that time. All Jim needed now was rest and good food. The doctor had done all he could do. The doctor, and Rafaela, thought Jim. *Rafaela.* She was rarely out of his mind.

That night they dined together in the huge, low-ceilinged dining room of the sprawling hacienda, after the children had gone to bed, and if Rafaela Velarde had not known she had made a conquest prior to that dinner, she must surely have known it then.

They sat together a long time in the moonlight of the patio, talking of Orlando and of Teodoro, of Colonia Federico, which was well remembered by Rafaela. She remembered, too, the old padre who had given Jim his first real lead in his search for the kin of Orlando Abeyta.

Later, in his room, with the dying moonlight silvering patches of the polished floor, Jim paced back and forth, smoking, his arm in a sling to ease his shoulder, thinking of Rafaela until he thought he must be going mad.

It took a long time for him to sleep. He did not know when he dropped off, but the scene that came before him in his sleep occurred some hours before the coming of the dawn. He saw those damned trees of hell standing on the cold, windswept ridge. He saw the bitter fruit of men's sudden madness swinging like grisly pendulums in the eerie grip of the whining wind, and he shouted aloud in his terror.

He opened his eyes to feel the icy sweat covering his naked flesh, and his body shook like aspen leaves. He closed his eyes and turned his head desperately from side to side to shake the awful dregs of the nightmare from his mind. The room was pitch-dark when he opened his eyes. Then the door swung open to reveal Rafaela standing there in her thin gown, a candle in her hand and fear upon her lovely face. Fear, not for herself, but for Jim Murdock. She came quickly to him and sat on the edge of the bed, holding the candle in her free hand as she stroked his wet brow. He slid his right arm about her slender waist and looked up at her face. For a long, long moment they looked into each other's eyes, forgetting why he had cried out and why she had come. She bent close to him. The candle fell to the floor and extinguished itself, and she was in his arms, lips pressing hotly against his mouth while his free hand roved her soft, warm body.

Now was the time. There was nothing, no one, to hold them back from each other, from what both of them had known in their own minds for days. They were on the very edge of complete surrender to each other. Then they seemed suspended, balanced in time, as though it were really non-existent, and a moment later her hot lips parted from his and she drew back her long dark hair from his face and naked chest. His right arm fell away from her. Slowly she sat up and pulled her filmy gown about her shoulders. Another moment or two drifted slowly past. A cold, searching wind crept in through the windows and chilled the two of them.

"Good night, Jaime," she whispered.

"Good night, Rafaela," he said huskily.

She walked slowly to the door, half expecting him to call her back and knowing she could not refuse him, while he wanted to call her back and knew in full conscience that he could not.

"I am leaving in the morning," he said at last.

She nodded her head and then closed the door behind her.

He lay there for a long time until the inner fires waned and then sank into a dim glow, leaving a thick layer of ashes on the deep-seated passion within him. There seemed no longer a great haste to leave the rancho and travel north on the last part of his self-imposed mission. As he had left a part of himself on the grim gallows hill back in Ute Crossing that cold morning when three men had been lynched, so he had also left a part of himself when old Augustin Galeras had died in the Sierra Vallecillos. The deaths of Lyss, Slim, Jules, and the four *bandidos* meant nothing to Jim, for he had killed in such fashion before, but the deaths of the others had affected him deeply.

Something was driving him on and on. Perhaps he was seeking himself. Loneliness had become part and parcel of his life. Perhaps he needed someone to share his thoughts and plans. It might be that this was assuming far more importance in his mind than it merited, but what else was there for a man to do in an effort to achieve wholeness?

He knew there was deadly danger for him up north. Lyss had died in a muddy alley in Las Cruces and Slim and Jules had died near Colonia Federico for some deep, dark reason that had something to do with the hanging of those three men in Ute Crossing. Someone wanted Jim Murdock permanently out of the way. Perhaps they had lost track of him, thought him dead in the Sierra Madre. It would be easy to stay in the south and avoid the prospect of sudden, violent death if he returned north.

He opened his eyes and stared at the dim ceiling. "Jessica," he said. He knew he had to go.

Chapter Eleven

The summer was dying as the tall, gaunt man, his set face marked for life with two scars, rode slowly north from the border country, gathering his strength as he rode, camping out at times in the lonely canyons beside chuckling streams, lingering there for days, only to saddle up and ride on again. Patagonia saw him, and Sonoita, and he lingered for days in brawling Tombstone, quietly walking the streets of the toughest town in the West. He bothered no one and no one bothered him. They knew the stamp and quality of his breed. Such men were better left alone. His drift took him north to Benson, and then by train to Lordsburg, in New Mexico Territory. He dallied for a time in Silver City, finding the food passable, the liquor good, his luck at the tables better than it had ever been, and the company of a little, dark-eyed Cajun girl gradually dulled the sharp edge of his memories of Rafaela Velarde.

In Albuquerque an ex-army surgeon he had known along the border inspected his shoulder and pronounced it well again. The hollows had filled out in his face and the sun, wind, rain, and good air had made him seem like the old Jim Murdock. The real wounds were invisible.

It was easy, far too easy, to try to avoid the inevitable. He turned away from the valley of the Rio Grande at Bernalillo and rode northwesterly at a steady pace for days through the lonely, windswept country until he reached the San Juan. It occurred to him only then that he was really heading for Meadows to see a little man in a derby hat who bought and sold anything and everything. Fella by the name of Sam. *"You will stop by on your way back, maybe? It was a pleasure doing business with you."* Jim grinned.

The leaves had turned when he reached Meadows. The country was a glory of scarlet, purple, and gold, with a haziness always in the distance. He could see the wolf-fanged mountains to the north that held Ute Crossing in their grasp, and the highest peak of them all, Warrior Peak, was just visible, tipped with a golden cap from the rays of the sinking sun. He was getting close to home, if one could still call it that.

Meadows dozed in the bright, clear sunlight. The air had a thin and brittle quality to it. The cottonwoods along the street were like yellow flames. A blacksmith's hammer beat a steady, metallic song that echoed against the low hills just beyond the town.

Jim dismounted and tethered the dun. He slapped the dust from his trail clothing. The building where Sam held forth in solitary splendor seemed to lean just a little more from the perpendicular. Jim opened the door. The bell tinkled rustily. He walked slowly between the piles of dusty boxes, a vast mausoleum of the unused and useless, waiting for someone who might, just *might*, mind you, have use for them. Their hope was as dead as the dusty air of the gloomy cavern in which they waited.

The bell stopped tinkling.

"You are wanting to buy or sell, maybe?" a soft voice asked out of nowhere, like a disembodied spirit trying to establish contact with the world of the living. A derby hat seemed to rise by itself from behind a rampart of dusty feed sacks.

"Hello, Sam," said Jim.

Sam studied Jim. "Mr. Murdock," he said quietly. "It has been a long time. You have changed."

Jim instinctively touched the scar on his right cheek.

Sam held up a hand. "No, it is not that. Not that alone, my friend. It is something else. I cannot put my hand on it."

Jim nodded. "I know what you mean," he said.

"The drinks are on you, stranger!" shrieked the parrot.

Jim grinned. He took out his cigar case and opened it, holding it out to Sam. "I know," said Jim. "You came west from Pittsburg because you had a cough. You should smoke? Crazy you'd be!"

Sam smiled. "It is good to see you in such a mood," he said. "It has not been easy for you. Tell me! You found, maybe, the woman Sarah?"

Jim nodded. "I left her the money you gave me, Sam."

"Good!" Sam tilted his head to one side. "You want to talk, maybe, about it?"

Jim shook his head.

"You found, maybe, the others you were looking for?"

"I didn't say I was looking for any others."

"You didn't have to, Jim."

"I found the kin of the Mexican who was hanged."

"But the kin of the boy, you did not find them?"

95

"That is why I came back, Sam." Jim bit the end from a cigar and held a match to the tip.

Sam rubbed his cheek. "Maybe you should have stayed down south."

"Why?"

"After you left for the south there was a man who came looking for you. A big man. Such a nose he had! A big, thick moustache. Eyebrows like raveled rope above his eyes. a mean-looking character, Jim. I was afraid from him. I told him you had gone to Albuquerque. But nothing more, Jim! I swear!"

Jim blew out the match. "He won't be coming back," he said quietly.

Sam shivered. "There were two more men some time after he was gone."

"One of them tall and slim with sandy hair? The other dark, very dark, broad-shouldered, and had a slight limp? Names of Jules and Slim?"

Sam smiled weakly. "They won't be back either?"

"No." Jim blew a smoke ring. "Were there any others?"

"None that I saw or talked to, Jim. But I heard there was two men here a month or so after the second two left. They hung around drinking and then went south."

"Any names?"

"One of them was called Barney. The other I do not know. Like I said, Jim, I didn't see them or talk to them, and I didn't want to. But there is something else, my friend. Something you should know. About your brother."

Jim took the cigar from his mouth. "Ben?"

"Yes. You did not know?"

"Know what?" asked Jim quietly.

Sam looked away. He took off his faded derby and turned the brim around and around in his thin hands. "It is a terrible thing to tell a friend," said Sam softly.

"Tell me, Sam," said Jim in a harsh voice.

Sam looked directly at Jim. "He is dead, my friend."

"How did he die?"

"It was not long after you left. We heard the story here in little bits and pieces. It was said he drove his buggy very fast."

"He did," agreed Jim.

"They found the team still drawing the front wheels. They searched back along the road. The rest of the buggy they found in the creek near his house." Sam stopped and wet his dry lips. He swallowed. "Your brother was a cripple? No?"

Jim nodded. He could plainly see Warrior Creek and the

black water against the newly fallen snow as he had last seen it. The creek wasn't deep but it ran very fast, and the water would be icy cold.

Sam rubbed his thin throat. "They found him in the spring. Very strange, too, for his body was found on the bank on the ranch that used to belong to your family, Jim. Like maybe he had come home. No one knew where you were."

It was very quiet in the big store. Even the parrot had stopped rustling, preening, and squawking in his cage.

Jim shook his head. "He was a man of principle, Sam. A man who fought for justice. It was almost an obsession with him."

"Such things are not obsessions," said the little man. "If they are, then more of us should maybe be obsessed." He eyed Jim. "He was, maybe, the only one of your family left?"

"Yes."

"It is a lonely thing for a man to have no family. I know."

Jim relighted his cigar. It wasn't in him to accept sympathy. Much as he might want it, he always avoided it. To him it was a mark of weakness, and yet he knew not why he felt that way. He was like a lobo or a wild dog who would crawl away to lick his own wounds without benefit of sympathy. Would it be that way the rest of his life?

"You are going north again?" asked Sam.

"Yes."

Sam shrugged. "You are like a man who courts death."

"There are things a man has to do."

"He does not have to seek his own self-destruction."

"You talk like a preacher."

Sam smiled. "A rabbi! You will stay a few days? There is room here for you."

"Here?"

"Come and see."

Sam led the way into the back of the immensely long store. He opened a door and ushered Jim into a surprising room. Books lined two of the walls. A polished piano stood against one wall. Pictures graced the walls here and there. A fine Navajo rug was on the floor.

"You surprise me, Sam," said Jim.

"This is my hideout, Jim. Days I spend in the front. Nights and Sundays here, reading my good friends the books."

"You have no real friends here, Sam?"

Sam shook his head. He glanced sideways at Jim. "I have been waiting. Maybe I have found such a friend."

Jim blew a ring of smoke and punched a lean finger

97

through it. "A gunman? A killer? Me? Not me, Sam. I'm not your style."

Sam busied himself with a dusty wine bottle. "Not the guns and the killings, Jim. It is something else. We make a strange pair, but we are friends, and you know it."

Jim nodded.

Sam filled two glasses and handed one to Jim. "While you are here, stay with me, Jim. I know you have to go. Maybe if I was in your boots I would do the same thing. Who is to say?"

They touched the glasses together. The wine was delicious. In a little while the two of them began to talk of many things, far removed from violent death and dusty merchandise, and when the dusk came, and Sam locked up the store and turned to the big range in his kitchen to fashion a meal, Jim knew that the little man was right. Sam had found a friend.

When Jim left his new friend, Sam came to the door of the store with him. "You will maybe let me know how you make out?" he asked.

Jim checked his saddle girth. "If I can't, someone else will," he said dryly.

"Do not talk like that, my friend. Find this Jessica. Tell her of her brother."

"She likely already knows the story, Sam."

"Even so, she would like to hear it, maybe, from a man who has spent so many months of his time to tell the kin of those three unfortunate men."

Jim turned and stuck out a big hand. Sam gripped it. "When this is all over and you are at peace," said Sam, "what do you plan to do?"

"Get a little ranch. Hunt and fish. Read a few books."

"You will do this alone?"

"Probably."

Sam hesitated. "When I first met you I said a partner I didn't need. Maybe, when you look for this ranch, you could use some cash. A partner, maybe?"

"You, Sam?"

Sam nodded. He looked back at the leaning building. "Of this place I am sick."

"I'll consider the offer, Sam."

Sam turned. "Maybe I could be a Yiddisher cowboy, hey?"

Jim grinned as he mounted. "Adios, Sam." He rode west along the wide street, then turned in his saddle. "Hey, Sam!" he called out. "If we have a Yiddisher cowboy we'd have to have kosher cows!"

The little man was still laughing when Jim turned off from the street and took the road north out of Meadows. The smile vanished from Sam's face. He opened the door and walked inside. The bell tinkled. "Shut up!" snapped Sam at the bell.

"The drinks are on you, stranger!" squawked the parrot.

"You too!" shouted Sam. He vanished into his hideout.

For a man carrying a message of death, and wondering in the back of his mind what further violence lay in store for him, there was deep enjoyment in Jim Murdock as he worked his way through the mountain approaches that bright morning. He was going home, for better or for worse. It had been a long time. A long, dusty, deadly trail from Ute Crossing to Las Cruces, Chihuahua City, Colonia Federico, and Rancho San Federico, and now he was nearing the end.

A fine, needlelike drizzle was falling on the valley, slanting down from the great range of mountains to the east, drifting across the thick timber at the bases of the heights, and stippling the leaden surface of the river. The rain had darkened the false-fronted wooden buildings of the town and was puddling in the hollows and ruts of the road. Hip-shot horses stood patiently at the racks in front of the stores and the saloons, mostly the saloons. The harder rains, the gully washers and fence lifters, would come later, forecasting the bitter winter. It was getting along toward that time.

A chain of sheet lightning zigzagged across the streaming sky and forked into a bluff. A low rumble of drums came from the thunder gods. The rain came down harder and harder until the bluffs were hidden from sight.

A lone horseman crossed the wooden bridge that spanned the rushing river, hunched into his slicker collar, hat pulled low over his eyes, a tiny spark of flame showing from the cigarette he cupped in his hand. He looked at the high, warped front of a store. "Three Forks General Mercantile Company," he read. Jim kneed the horse toward the nearest rack and swung down into the thick mud. He unstrapped a poncho from the cantle and hung it over the horse. He stepped up onto the sagging wooden sidewalk and found himself looking directly at a dirty-windowed saloon. "Well, fancy that," he said with a tired smile. It had been a three-day ride through the mountains.

He walked into the saloon and rested an elbow on the end of the bar. The bar was pretty well lined. Four men played poker at a rear table. A swamper was listlessly mopping up the water from a leak in the roof. There wasn't much talking. It wasn't talking weather. Just drinking weather.

"Rye," said Jim to the bartender.

Bottle and glass were placed in front of Jim. The bartender was a melancholy-looking soul with an uneasy Adam's apple. One of his eyes, slightly larger than the other, seemed to wander off on a mission of its own now and then, to be brought back only by a conscious effort. "Long ride?" said the bar critter.

"Passable," said Jim. He filled the glass.

"From the north?"

"South."

No one looked at Jim. Saddle tramps were a dime a dozen in the Three Forks country.

"Looking for work?" said the bar critter.

Jim tossed down the drink. "Not exactly," he said.

The man wiped the zinc-topped bar. "Well, you are or you ain't," he said. "Temple Smeed is looking for teamsters."

"Out of my line," said Jim. He felt the rye hit his cold guts and explode. His face suddenly felt warm.

"Buck Witty is looking for riders."

Jim eyed the man. "You run the employment agency here?" he asked with a smile.

"No. Sort of a hobby of mine, mister." The sad eyes studied Jim and the two scars, the hard set of the jaw, the gray eyes that seemed to make a man a little too uncomfortable to stare at very long. He had known all along that this wasn't any teamster or line rider. No, and not a livery hand, and certainly not a townsman. Gambler? No. Gunfighter. . . .

Jim refilled the glass. "I'm looking for a girl named Jessica," he said quietly.

A broad-shouldered, bearded man laughed. "Hell!" he said explosively. "Who ain't?"

Jim looked at him. "You know her?" he asked.

"No."

"I wasn't talking to you, mister," said Jim evenly.

Hard dark eyes peered into Jim's eyes, and what the bearded man saw he did not like. "Sorry," he said. "I thought it was funny at the time. No offense, mister."

"Forget it," said Jim. "Pour yourself a drink."

The man nodded. He wanted no part of this lobo.

The bartender leaned on the bar. "Girl by the name of Jessica lives up the North Fork," he said. "Jessica Lyle. Lives

100

by herself except for one hand." He grinned. "She shoots as good as any man too, mister."

"Lives alone? No people?"

The bartender shrugged. "She had a brother named Jesse. They was twins. No, there ain't no one out there but her and old Jonas."

Jim downed his second drink. The cold was leaving his body. "What happened to her brother?"

The bartender rubbed industriously at an imaginary spot on the zinc while his wandering eye moved back and forth. "What do you want to know for?" he asked quietly.

A gray-faced man halfway up the bar looked at Jim. "Tell him, Les," he said. "Go on. Tell him. I'd like to see the look on his face."

The saloon was suddenly very quiet. The poker players were watching Jim. The swamper was leaning on his mop handle doing the same thing. Every man at the bar except a drunken fool at the end was looking at Jim. The drunk was looking into his empty whiskey glass. It was all that really seemed to interest him.

Les took a final swipe at the imaginary spot. He looked directly at Jim, and for once his loose eye was steady. "The kid was lynched over to Ute Crossing a little less than a year ago," he said. "Lynched for murder."

There was no expression on Jim's face. "I know," he said.

The gray-faced man's hand tightened about his shot glass. "No one bothered to tell the girl," he said bitterly. "No one told her until the whole damned town knew about it from the Denver newspapers. It was too late then to remember she got delivery of the same newspaper. Someone should have broken the news to her before that."

"Take it easy, Kyle," said the bartender.

"The sons of bitches," said Kyle. "That kid never killed no one. His sister has more guts in her little finger than he had in his whole body. There was only the two of them, and some of the bastards around here used to chase after Jessica, and the kid couldn't do anything about it. They drove that boy outa here."

Les rubbed his thin throat. "Well, anyways, there ain't no one bothers her now," he said.

A short, red-faced man nodded. "Beats the hell outa me how she keeps that place a-goin'," he said. "My missus told me to go over and give her a hand. She says to me: 'No thanks, *Mr.* Watts, I kin take care of myself and my property.' I felt like a damned jackass about it. She don't want nothin' to do with nobody, I tell you."

"Cute trick, too," said a grinning cowpoke. "One time I was hunting strays over on the North Fork. I stops to pass the time of day. Well, maybe I did get too fresh. I crossed the North Fork two jumps and a holler ahead of a .44/40 slug."

The gray-faced man looked at him. "You let her alone, Kelly," he said thinly.

Kelly shoved back his glass. "What for, Kyle? You got a brand on her? She turned you down half a dozen times, from what I hear."

Kyle turned and looked at him. "You got a big mouth, Kelly," he said softly.

Les walked to the middle of the bar. "Drinks on the house," he said. "Sam! Get to leaning on that mop handle! Jerry! Stick some nickels in the piano! You boys at the table want fresh drinks!"

The man named Kyle emptied his glass, wiped his mouth with the back of a hand, and looked at Jim. "What business you got with Jessica Lyle?" he demanded.

"That's my business," said Jim.

Kelly whistled softly. "Now it's you with the big mouth, Kyle," he said.

"Something about her brother?" said Kyle.

Jim emptied his glass and shoved it back. He paid for the drinks. He felt inside his coat for his cigar case, withdrew a long nine, lighted it, and fanned out the match.

"Well?" said Kyle. He stood a little way back from the bar.

Les leaned forward. "One more remark out of you, Kyle," he said quietly, "and I'll cut you off. You know Marshal Craig will back me up. He's had a bellyful of your trouble-making lately."

Kyle wet his lips. He turned back to the bar. He wasn't so damned sure at that that he wanted trouble with the tall, scar-faced man at the end of the bar. There was plenty of time to find out what business he had with Jessica Lyle.

Les looked at Jim. "Cross back over the bridge," he said. "Take the first road to the right. Follow it about five miles to the North Fork. You can't miss it. There's a plank bridge there. The other side of the bridge is Jessica Lyle's property."

"Watch out she don't come a-shootin'!" said Kelly. "Hawwww!"

Jim walked to the door, feeling the eyes of every man in the place, except likely the drunk at the end of the bar, boring a hole into his back.

"You never did tell us your name," said Les.

102

Jim turned a little. "Murdock," he said. "Jim Murdock." He closed the door behind him.

The drunk slowly raised his head. Just as slowly he looked toward the door. Suddenly it seemed as though he wasn't drunk at all. He paid his tab and put on his slicker. "What time does the company telegraph office close, Les?" he asked.

"Half an hour, Monk."

Monk walked slowly to the door, peered out into the dimness, and saw Jim riding toward the bridge. Monk stepped out onto the boardwalk and hurried up the street toward the telegraph office. It had been a long, long time ago that he had been told to keep an eye out for a tall, scar-faced man named Murdock. Jim Murdock. . . .

Chapter Twelve

The fall rain had thinned out to a misty drizzle when Jim Murdock reached the sagging bridge across the North Fork. Now and then eerie lightning flashes illuminated the dusk and silvered the falling rain. The North Fork was bank-full and already beginning to lap over the rotten planking of the bridge. The structure creaked and groaned in the current. The bloated body of a drowned calf swirled lazily in an eddy on the far side of the stream. There was nothing to be seen beyond the bridge except the dripping woods, dark and secretive, parted by the narrow road, just wide enough for a wagon, which vanished into the dimness. No sign of a house, a cabin, or a shed. Not a sight of an animal or a fence. Nothing but the dark, dripping woods, a rusted mailbox on a tilted post, and the leaden-colored waters of the stream.

Jim rolled a quirly and lighted it, flipping the match into the water. Words came back to him: *"She shoots as good as any man too, mister. . . . That kid never killed no one. His sister has more guts in her little finger than he had in his whole body. . . . She don't want nothin' to do with nobody, I tell you. . . . I crossed the North Fork two jumps and a holler ahead of a .44/40 slug. . . . Watch out she don't come a-shootin'!"*

Jim tapped his side pocket. He could feel the hard lump of the bluish-looking stone within it. It was all he had brought those hundreds of miles and after so many months to give to a girl who had lost her twin brother; likely, according to the barflies in the local saloon, the only near kin she had had around Three Forks.

"By God," said Jim. "What the hell is the matter with me? I didn't come all this distance to be scared of a female gun toter!" He grinned, his saturnine face lighted momentarily by the flare of the cigarette tip as he took a drag. "All the same, I'd rather face a bee-stung she-bear with cubs than a gal wearin' pants and making Winchester music around my ears. You can't shoot back. All you can do is cut stick for the *rio* and hope you reach the brush on the far side ahead of a .44/40 slug, like the man in the saloon said. He was laughing then. He wasn't laughing when she was helping him make up his mind he ought to leave."

He touched the horse with his heels and rode slowly out on the creaking bridge, nervously eyeing that swirling water which had risen higher even as he had watched it. He reached the far side and looked back. "By God," he said. "I won't try that bridge until the North Fork goes down, gun-totin' woman and all!"

The way through the woods was an uneasy way for Jim. Wasn't likely she'd be squatting there in the brush cuddling that damned Winchester of hers, looking for fair game. Not with the rain and the darkness coming on. Still . . .

He had ridden almost a mile and half through the woods when at last he saw them thinning out as the lightning lanced across the sky and struck into a towering, naked butte that dominated the landscape like a brooding giant. He drew rein at the edge of the woods and waited for the next eerie flash. When it came he saw a wide meadowland area stretching beyond the woods, bisected by the road. To the right he thought he caught a glimpse of some cattle bedded down in the edge of the woods. Here and there on the meadowland were outcroppings of lichened rocks, like dislocated bones thrust up against the surface flesh of the earth. The ground at the far end of the open area sloped upward, and the road climbed it and vanished on the far side. There was nothing else to do but traverse that open area, hoping that Jessica Lyle wasn't out prowling with her trusty Winchester.

It was fully dark when he reached the far side. A dilapidated barbed-wire fence stretched on either side of the road, and the remains of a Texas gate had been hauled to one side to clear the road. He rode down the far side of the rise, and then suddenly, when he least expected it, he saw a faint yellowish glow of light beyond a motte of wind-swaying trees. He halted the tired horse and began to roll a cigarette, then thought better of it. A lighted match or the glow of a cigarette could be seen etched against the darkness, giving just enough target and time to slam out a round or two.

He rode slowly forward, then dismounted, and led the dun on. A man on a horse is too big a target. He tethered the dun to a shattered tree, and for a moment his hand lingered on the wet buttstock of his saddle gun, and then he shook his head. A flash of lingering lightning revealed a well-built house of peeled logs, set on a knoll. Light showed from two windows at the side of the house and from one in front. There were other buildings beyond the house. Sheds and a big barn, slightly the worse for wear, a fallen-in log building and a dark-looking structure, likely a bunkhouse. Jim whistled softly. This had been a nice spread at one time.

A dog barked suddenly from an outbuilding. Jim watched the house. The dog barked again and again. Likely he was penned in or chained. The wind shifted and brought the bittersweet odor of woodsmoke to Jim. It brought something else as well, the lovely odor of cooking food. He could have sworn there were fresh-baked rolls or bread, and maybe even a pie or two. He remembered then that he had not eaten all day, except for a few scraps of trail rations around noon.

A dark shape moved near one of the outbuildings. Too low for a man or woman. The dog barked, and Jim knew what the shape was, but it didn't move any closer. He had been right about the animal being chained. Something moved between the light and the window in one of the lighted rooms. The wind brought the sound of a closing door to him. Then he saw someone standing on the edge of the rear porch.

"Hello, the house!" yelled Jim.

The dog slammed against his chain, barking and growling in turns.

Jim walked slowly forward, hands at shoulder level. "You there!" he called out. "I've come to see Miss Lyle on business! Are you Miss Lyle?"

The figure moved. "Not likely," said a man.

"You must be Jonas, then."

"You know a lot about this place, don't you?"

"Damn it! All I know is that Miss Lyle lives here and that

my slicker is leaking in this rain! Water running down my sleeves!"

The man laughed. "Then put your hands down, mister! Who are you? What do you want?"

"The name is Murdock! Jim Murdock! I've come to see Miss Lyle." Jim lowered his hands, cursing softly as he felt the water soak the sleeves of his shirt and coat.

Jim waited. He narrowed his eyes. He had the damnedest feeling that someone else was watching him. He saw the man turn his head a little as though someone had spoken to him, and then he nodded. "Bring on your cayuse," said Jonas. "Put him in the barn there. I'll get a lantern."

By the time Jim reached the barn the man was coming from the house with the lantern. He was a short bench-legged man who walked with a slight limp. He grinned at Jim from as homely a face as Jim had ever experienced, but his eyes were squirrel-bright and seemingly friendly. He didn't have on a slicker or a coat, and there was no belt gun at his narrow waist. His face was wrinkled like a dried apple, and it was difficult to tell how old he was, perhaps fifty-five or sixty years of age. His eyes, at least, were still young.

Jim led the dun into the barn. He looked at Jonas. "All right to unsaddle?"

"Why not?"

Jim grinned. "I didn't know what kind of reception I'd get around here."

"Sho! Well, you can't expect a man to go all the way back from where he come from on a night like this."

Jim unsaddled the dun and rubbed him down, covered him with a worn blanket he found in a stall, and fed him. "Times a little hard around here?" he said conversationally as he picked up his saddlebags and cantle roll.

"Not so's you'd notice it. Nice country around here. Good stock. Plenty of water and grazing."

"I noticed that." Jim looked about the cavernous barn. Half a dozen streams of water came down from the roof at the rear of the structure. "Plenty of water. . . ."

"Well, we ain't exactly in business right now."

Jim looked at him. "I heard Miss Lyle would run off any-one in pants."

"She never run me off. 'Course, I'm too damned old to bother much with fillies now. Been a confirmed bachelor all my life, anyways. I never give the name Barlow to no filly. Saves time, money, and trouble, with the accent on trouble." Jonas lifted the lantern from a box. "I sleep in the bunkhouse. Kinda lonely with all them bunks empty there,

106

but I use the foreman's room. There are two bunks in there."

Jim followed the short man through the wet darkness to the sagging bunkhouse. Jonas hung the lantern on a hook in the room. "You can clean up if you like. Supper will be ready in an hour."

Jim nodded. "Does she know I'm here?"

"You joshing? Mister, that gal don't miss a thing." Jonas felt for the makings and rolled a cigarette. He tossed the makings to Jim. "You can start a fire in the stove there and dry out." He lighted the cigarette and fanned out the match. "Where you from, Murdock?"

Jim smiled as he peeled off his slicker, coat, and shirt. "Anywhere and everywhere." He rolled a cigarette and lighted it.

"Colorado man?"

"Originally."

Jonas walked to the door. He looked back. "Ute Crossing, maybe?" he asked quietly.

"I was born in the valley of the Ute."

"Been there lately?"

"Almost a year ago."

The wind shifted and rattled the windowpanes. A cold draft crept through a broken pane and swirled the cigarette smoke about the room.

"Maybe last November, mister?"

Jim looked at the little man. "You're asking a helluva lot of questions, aren't you, mister?"

For a second the bright eyes hardened. "Sorry, Murdock. It really ain't none of my business, is it?"

"You're getting the general idea, Barlow."

Jonas nodded. He closed the door behind him. Jim heard his boots squelch in the mud, and then the sound died away. He heard a door slam.

Jim started a fire and hung his clothing near it. He examined the puckered bullet hole in his shoulder. The cold had made his shoulder a little stiff. He heated water and then washed and shaved. He studied himself in the cracked, gold-flecked mirror. "My God," he breathed. "I look like the devil's twin brother."

He dressed in dry, clean clothing and tied a string tie about his corded neck. He reached for his gun belt and then stopped. He rubbed his jaw. Wasn't exactly polite to walk into a house and sit down to supper carrying a six-gun at your hip. On the other hand, he remembered too well the reputation the young woman had for dealing with men. He satisfied himself with placing his double-barreled derringer in his coat pocket. Maybe the characters in the saloon had been building up a stack about Jessica Lyle, the sharpshooting gal of Three Forks. He grinned. He must have walked into a real setup on that rainy afternoon. He'd be willing to bet they were still laughing into their tanglefoot.

Still, Jessica must know who he was, as Jonas had. Maybe the story of his mission to find the kinfolk of the three dead men had passed through that country. Maybe she was just wondering why it had taken the most part of a year for him to reach Three Forks. He'd have to explain that one. He was sorry for her without even meeting her. He had been sorry for her ever since he had seen the kid die with a hemp necktie cutting off his young life. He was sorrier still that she had learned about his death in clear, cold print in a three-day-old newspaper deposited in that rusty mailbox on the banks of the North Fork.

Jim turned out the lantern and opened the door. The rain was hardly more than a thick mist now. He walked toward the house, the lights warm and cheery through the darkness and mistiness. He stepped up onto the rear porch and flipped away his cigarette. He rapped on the door.

Jonas opened the door. "Almost in time," he said. "Go on in, Murdock. Miss Lyle is waiting for you in the living room." He glanced over his shoulder, then came closer to Jim. "Take it easy on her. She ain't forgot a thing about the kid's death."

Jim wiped his feet and took off his hat. He crossed the brightly lighted kitchen, eyeing a row of fresh-built pies as he did so. The little man, or Jessica, was a prime cook.

He entered the big living room. A fire crackled in the cavernous fieldstone fireplace. A woman, slim as a birch, stood beside the fire, looking down into it. Jim cleared his throat. For a moment she stood there, and then she turned and looked directly at him, and it was like a shade from the other world for the brief span of a second or two, for she was an identical twin, as much as a woman can be twin to a man and not show masculinity, and yet in a way the kid had been more feminine in his appearance. He remembered all too well the sick, ghastly look on the boy's face before he had died. He remembered as well the set blue face of the boy when Jim had cut him down.

"Mr. Murdock," she said quietly. Her voice was much like her brother's had been, as Jim could recall, but there was a firmness in it, a resolution, that the kid had lacked. But then, maybe most any man would have lacked resolution and firmness if he knew he had only minutes before he was to be lynched.

"Miss Lyle," said Jim. He bent his head.

"Jonas said you came from Ute Crossing."

She knew where Jim came from, and it hadn't been Jonas who had told her. This much Jim knew. "I was born in the valley of the Ute," he said quietly. "I returned there almost a year ago after an absence of seven years. I spent only a short time there before leaving for New Mexico and Mexico."

There was a long pause. Jim narrowed his eyes. His impression of her was quite different from that which he had expected, even before the jokesters had ribbed him in the saloon in Three Forks.

"Jonas said you told him you had business with me," she said."

"It can wait until after supper, if you like."

"No," she said. She looked directly at him, and pretty as she was, all blue eyes, fine blonde hair and smooth skin, soft, full mouth, he had the uncanny feeling she was indeed the expert markswoman she was said to be.

How does one tell a lovely young woman that one was an unwilling witness to the lynching of her brother?

"Well, Mr. Murdock?"

"I think you know why I am here," he said quietly. "I think you know who I am, and that I witnessed the death of your brother Jesse. The story about that terrible day must have spread clear through this country not long after it happened."

"It came to me by newspaper," she said. "It was the first knowledge I had of his death. In later editions of the paper I learned of a man named Murdock who left Ute Crossing shortly after the lynchings. It was said that he knew a great deal more about those lynchings than he had let on."

It was suddenly too quiet in that big room. Jim had the uneasy knowledge too that Jonas was not rattling around in the kitchen, and that he was not far behind Jim, maybe with a scatter-gun in his hands, or a cocked six-gun. He dropped his left hand into his coat pocket.

"Don't move, mister," said a dry voice a few feet behind him.

"I wasn't reaching for a hideout gun," said Jim. "Can I draw out my hand?"

Jessica nodded to Jonas.

Jim breathed easier as he withdrew his hand. He held out the Ridgewood tobacco sack with the stone in it. "This was about all I found of value in his clothing," he said.

She came to him and took the sack, her cool fingers touching his calloused hand. She opened the sack and emptied the stone into her left palm. For a moment she stared at the stone, and then she quickly turned away. Her shoulders shook a little.

"I'm sorry, ma'am," said Jim.

"You damned fool," hissed Jonas.

"It took you a long time," said Jessica at last.

Jim smiled. "It wasn't intentional," he said dryly.

She turned slowly. "You must be mad to come here."

Jim's eyes narrowed. "Why? Someone had to come and tell you. I am sorry you learned by other means. They told me about it in town."

"Who told you?"

"Man by the name of Kyle."

Her face tightened. "Chris Kyle," she said. She looked past Jim at Jonas. "Did Mr. Kyle, or any of the other *men* of Three Forks, tell you about me?"

Jim grinned. "They said you were right handy with a Winchester."

"You can copper that bet," said Jonas.

"I've had to build up that reputation," she said. "I'm not sorry for it."

"Can you have the little man take that gun out of my back?" said Jim. "What crime have I committed?"

She walked to the fireplace and held the stone up between her and the firelight, which caught and reflected the hidden glow of the semiprecious gem. "You were one of the men who murdered my brother," she said.

"That's a damned lie!" Jim said harshly.

"Take it easy!" snapped Jonas.

"Would I have come here into this damned trap if I had been one of those murderers?" said Jim. "What kind of fool do you take me for?"

"He might have a point there," said Jonas.

"You don't know everything I know, Jonas," said Jessica. "There was a man here last spring looking for you, Mr. Murdock. He came to this ranch. He was a deputy sheriff from Ute Crossing. He had a warrant for your arrest."

"On what charge?"

"Being part of that gang of lynchers. Stealing from the bodies of the dead."

"Well, I'll be double-damned," said Jim. "Begging your pardon, ma'am." He studied her. "Did he give his name?"

She nodded. "Meigs. Harlan Meigs."

"The man who was dead drunk the morning they took your brother and those other two men from the Ute Crossing jail."

"By God," said Jonas. "We never heard that one before!"

"Did he say that any of the others had been apprehended?" asked Jim.

"Most of them were unknowns."

"That's the biggest lie yet," said Jim angrily. "Every one of those men was well known in Ute Crossing!"

"None of their names were in the papers."

"No one would state that they had been in on it, that's why!" said Jim. "You don't know that town!"

"I know it well enough," she said bitterly.

"I'm beginning to see a little light coming through my thick skull. For some reason I'm not wanted back in Ute Crossing. It seems to me that someone tried to lay a trap for me here. A young woman whose brother was lynched, an expert riflewoman who supposedly had a habit of shooting first and asking questions afterward. Very neat. Perhaps if I hadn't managed to reach this place under cover of bad weather I'd have been shot when I put foot on your land."

"I wish I knew what you were talking about," said Jessica.

"Look," he said patiently. "Would it make sense for me to come here if I felt guilty for your brother's death? What logical reason would I have for coming here at all?"

"I have been wondering about that," she admitted. "A few months ago I might have shot you on sight. Now I don't know what to think."

"I have a suggestion," said Jim.

"Yes?"

"If you're as hungry as I am, I give my word I won't give you any trouble. There's a derringer in my right coat pocket, Jonas, but I won't reach for it. Take it out. Good! Now you can both sit at the other end of the table with six-guns beside your plates. The only weapons I want are a knife and a fork."

Jonas began to laugh. Even Jessica had a faint smile on her lovely face. "I guess we can afford to give a condemned man a good meal," she said.

"Ma'am," said Jim seriously, "I'm almost as good a talker as I am an eater. Let me tell you why I came here, and why it took me so long. About the time we ruin one of those pies out there you'll either believe me, or you can give me five minutes' start for the North Fork."

She nodded. Then she reached inside the bodice of her dress and withdrew a slender chain. She held it away from her breasts, and Jim saw a twin stone to the one he had brought from Ute Crossing, taken from the pocket of a dead boy to give to his twin sister. "We found these stones together when we were very young," she said softly. "Jesse always said they'd be good luck for us. He was wrong about that."

"Maybe he meant as long as you stayed together," said Jim.

She held the two stones side by side. "I never quite thought of it that way, Mr. Murdock," she said.

Chapter Thirteen

Jim Murdock led his horse up the narrow, twisting trail, following Jessica Lyle as she guided him up atop the great butte that seemed almost to hang over the North Fork far, far below, a glinting, sparkling stream that dashed across the stones in its shallow bed. The heavy rains of the past week had stopped at last, and the runoff was almost gone, although the ground was still soft with the soaking it had received. It was nice country, as Jonas had said. Plenty of water and grazing, but hardly any stock.

She rounded a turn in the trail and vanished. Jim slowly led the dun around the outthrust shoulder of the butte into a tangled jungle of scrub trees and brush that choked a great gash in the living rock, affording a shallow layer of earth for the tenacious roots of the growths. He climbed up a steep slope and then suddenly, as though someone had dropped the walls of the room, he found himself standing in the open, on naked, lichened rock, with a cool breeze sweeping about him, drying the sweat on his face. He looked about and whistled softly.

She turned and smiled. "It's worth the climb, isn't it, Jim?" she said. She pushed back her hat and let it drop to her back, hanging from the barbiquejo strap. The vagrant breeze toyed coyly with her fine hair. "You can smoke if you like."

He shoved back his own hat, watching her instead of the

magnificent western view that seemed to extend all the way into Utah. He rolled a cigarette and lighted it. She was right. The view alone was worth the whole ranch that lay below the butte, neatly encompassed by the North Fork, but the view wouldn't bring in the beans and bacon.

The sky was dotted with white cloud puffs that drifted, one after the other, like leaves on a stream, toward the west, while their fleeting shadows raced along the terrain below, up heights and down deep into the canyons, in a race that could never be lost or won. The air had a lift to it that hit a man's lungs and made him feel ten feet high.

He looked down at the ranch. A wraith of smoke drifted up from the big log house. The sun glinted from the windows. It was a good spread. There was timber to spare. A man could set up a sawmill and do some business. There was plenty of land for cattle. Water in plenty. Jim eyed the stream. Probably alive with trout. He smiled at the thought.

She sat down on a rock and wrapped her arms about her knees, tilting her head to one side to study him. "What's tickling you?" she asked.

"Nothing much. I was thinking there might be trout in that stream."

"There are. My father fished quite a bit. My mother sometimes said he fished too much, but then she never attempted to stop him. He was English and talked a lot at times about the fine fishing in Scotland."

"An educated man, no doubt."

"Yes. He had taught school in England, and later here in America. He was a college professor when he came west for his health, met my mother, and bought this place."

Jim blew a smoke ring. "A good rancher?"

She shrugged. "He got by. He liked his books. Mother was the real ramrod around here, but the two of them were happy." She smiled. "I'm more like her, I suppose."

"And Jesse?"

She looked away. "He was a great deal like Father. Sensitive, moody, more interested in books than in ranching. Father always said I should have been the male."

Jim shook his head. "What a terrible waste that would have been."

She flushed prettily. "I never wanted to be a man."

"Thank God for that," he said fervently.

"Mother didn't live long after Father passed on. As different as they were in many ways, they still seemed to have a great deal in common. Jesse had been planning to go to college, but when they were gone we found we had just enough money to hold onto the place. This is a hard country. A woman can't very well run a ranch, although my mother seemed to do rather well at it, but then she had Father there to back her up. As refined and educated as he was, he was no coward. It didn't take the local men long to find that out. After the two of them passed away there was no choice for Jesse. He had to stay here and try to run the place." Her voice died away.

Jim remembered the bitter voice of Chris Kyle. "*There was only the two of them, and some of the bastards around here used to chase after Jessica, and the kid couldn't do anything about it. They drove that boy outa here.*"

She looked out across the great span of country to the west. "Jesse said he had to leave. To find himself. I knew he never would. That is, he wouldn't find himself like the others. If Jesse had been raised in a city he would have risen to be a success. He couldn't adapt himself to this kind of life. Oh, I know what you're thinking! Why couldn't he adapt himself? You'd like this country and this ranch and everything about it if you had been raised here. Jesse was a loner. His only fault was that he was different. *So different. . . .*"

"And he never carried a gun?"

She shook her head. "I had to learn to shoot for the two of us. My father was an excellent shot, and my mother handled a gun as well as most ranch women. Jesse would have nothing to do with them." She looked at Jim. "He never shot anything in his life. The other boys used to haze him because he watched birds and animals rather than shoot them."

There was a long silence during which both of them were occupied with their own thoughts. Jim rolled another cigarette. "I'll be leaving in a day or two," he said quietly.

"To go back to Ute Crossing?"

"Yes."

"You can't bring Jesse back," she said.

"There's more to it than that, Jessica."

"The principle of the thing? You sound like my father now."

"Don't you agree with him?"

She looked away. "Someone is trying to kill you, Jim. Don't go back."

"I have to," he said. "I don't know whether Gil Drinkwater, Orlando Abeyta, and Jesse Lyle actually murdered Cass Crowley, and I know I can't bring the three of them back, but from what I have learned I find it difficult to believe

114

those three men did it. I nearly lost my own life on that same gallows hill because of circumstantial evidence, and I am beginning to believe that the circumstantial evidence against them was fixed. Jessica, those three men were lynched to cover up the real murderer or murderers. I mean to find out who actually did it, and to clear the names of Gil, Orlando, and Jesse."

"Does it really matter now?"

"It does to me." He smiled thinly. "I never got along too well with my own brother. I respected him, but I couldn't ever think like he could. I was the wild one."

She stood up. "So? A man who takes a full year out of his own life, rides hundreds of miles, and is trailed by men who would kill him if they could. A man who *had* to tell the kinfolk of those three lynched men their last words and actions. You are more like your brother than you'll admit."

She led the way down the steep, twisting trail, and there was no time to talk or look at the view. It took them the better part of an hour to reach the talus slope at the foot of the gaunt butte and then cross that into the cool shade of the trees. It was unseasonably warm weather, but the snow would be flying before too long, perhaps to block the passes to the east. Jim would have to leave before that time.

The North Fork rushed through the thick timber, drowning out all other sound. Jim led the horses to water. He turned to look at Jessica. The flat, whiplike crack of a rifle sounded above the rushing of the stream. Just as the rifle was fired Jim's dun tossed its head between Jim and the oncoming bullet. The dun died on its feet and fell heavily against Jim. He leaped clear of the horse and drove a shoulder against Jessica, felling her across a mossy log that lay on the damp ground. An instant later the rifle flatted off again, raising canyon echoes. The slug whipped within inches of Jim's head. He dived for cover as the slug slapped into a tree.

Then it was peaceful again. The stream rushed on. The clear waters were stained pink from the blood of the dun. Jessica's bay had taken off through the woods like the Devil beating tanbark. Jim studied the woods across the stream. Shafts of sunlight came slantingly through the timber and made spotlights on the ground. The rest of the woods were in shadow. There was neither sight nor sound of anyone. Whoever the ambusher was, he had either pulled leather out of there, or was waiting for another shot. Only by the grace of God had the dun raised his head to intercept that deadly slug.

Jessica lay flat, her soft cheek pressed against the grass. "Why?" she whispered.

"*Quién sabe?*" he said. His rifle was under the horse, pressed into the bottom of the shallow stream. It was too far for pistol range, and Jessica's bay had carried off her rifle.

Jim lay flat, peering across the stream from under the brim of his hat. He knew the slug had been meant for him. Jessica had been beyond a thick-boled tree. Besides, who would want to kill her? This was a question that was easier to answer in reference to Jim Murdock, but even so, it gave him an eerie feeling to know that they, whoever *they* were, had not given up on him. There was no one in Three Forks who would want to kill him. No, whoever it was had come from Ute Crossing. Who had notified them that Jim Murdock had returned from the dead to finish his self-imposed mission?

Jim bellied along the ground until he was in thick brush beyond a bend in the stream. He waded quickly across the stream and lay flat in brush on the far side. He drew his Colt and cocked it, inching his way across the ground until he could see the area where the ambusher should be if he had not left. There was no one in sight, no movement, no thickened shadow. Then he felt earth tremors beneath him, and he knew that a horse was being ridden swiftly away from the stream area. He stood up behind a tree and studied the area for five minutes until he was sure there was no one there.

Jim walked toward the place where the rifleman had waited. He looked across the stream and saw a thick tree trunk which had fallen long ago. Behind it he saw half a dozen cigarette butts, and twin depressions in the ground where boot toes had dug in. Jim knelt and then lay flat behind the log. Whoever had waited there must have known there was but one trail from the talus slope through the woods to the stream. He had known something else, that Jessica and Jim had been up on the butte. It had been a close thing; too damned close.

There was no other evidence except the crushed cigarette butts and the marks left by the ambusher. That and the dead dun staining the clear waters with his life's blood. It had been a good saddle horse, one of the best he had ridden since he had left Ute Crossing seemingly so long ago.

He waded across the stream and beckoned to Jessica. "Who knew we were going up on the butte?" he asked.

"Only Jonas."

116

He rubbed his scarred face. "Yeh," he said. He looked back across that peaceful-looking stream. "How well can you trust him?" he asked.

"It wasn't him," she said quickly.

"He might have told someone we were up there."

"No, Jim," she said firmly.

He looked at her and knew she was right.

"Now maybe you'll reconsider about going back to Ute Crossing," she said.

He did not answer. He caught Jessica's bay and then roped the dead dun, pulling it with the bay until he could get saddle and rifle from the dead animal. They rode double back to the ranch as the late afternoon sun slanted down into the huge canyon. The sun was gone when they reached the ranch, and a cold breeze drifted down the canyon.

"Goin' to be a hard winter," said Jonas from the porch. "Got lots of work to do before then. Sure could use a hand or two around here, Miss Jessica."

"No," she said.

"We can't keep on tryin' to keep this place up." Jonas glanced casually at Jim as Jim led the horse to the barn. "Where's the dun?"

Jessica told the little man. His face grew dark. "Drygulching! Bad enough they run off the stock and pester you without that going on."

"It wasn't meant for me," she said. "Whoever it was, he meant to kill Jim, Jonas."

"If he goes back to Ute Crossing he oughta have his head examined before it gets a bullet in it and spoils it."

"He's going," she said simply. "I can't stop him."

Jonas looked at the lovely young woman. "All the more reason he oughta have that head of his examined."

She flushed as she walked into the kitchen. "He must go," she said. She walked to the inner door and looked back. "Oh, Jonas! It isn't important anymore! Can't he understand that?"

Jonas shook his head. "You can't turn a man like him away from what he thinks he has to do."

"They'll kill him, Jonas!"

Jonas poked up the stove. He looked at her. "It takes a heap of killin' to get a man like Jim Murdock, and from the looks of him, he can do a mess of killin' himself if he has to."

The darkness had filled the canyon when Jim returned from the barn. He eyed the lighted windows. It reminded him of the time he had been fired upon when he had been sitting in Ben's little house outside of Ute Crossing. He

117

had never learned who had fired on him then either. He could hear Jonas singing "The Sago Lily" in the kitchen and got a scent of the evening meal. Something held him back. He stopped in the thick shadows beside an outbuilding, watching Jonas pass back and forth in front of the windows, a fair target for even a middling rifle shot.

He narrowed his eyes, probing into the darkness. The wind was seeping down the canyon, carrying man scent away from the dog Jonas kept chained at night in one of the outbuildings.

Something held him back from walking to the house. If he opened that kitchen door he'd be sharply silhouetted in light. There was the wariness of the wild animal in Jim Murdock. Ben had hit it on the head when he had said that Jim still had much of the lobo in him. Jim drifted through the darkness, a lean, scar-faced ghost of a man. He crouched and crossed to the front porch of the house. Jessica was in her room. There was no light in the living room. He crawled to the front door and softly opened it, wriggling inside. The door to the kitchen was closed, and no light showed except a thin crack at the bottom of the door. He walked softly to the door and tapped on it, stepping aside when Jonas opened it. "What the hell!" said the little man.

Jim drew him into the dark living room. "I smell something out there in the darkness," said Jim.

"Like what?"

"Like the son of a bitch who tried to kill me this afternoon."

"You see him? Hear him?"

"No."

"Then how the hell do you know he's there?"

Jim drew the little man close and looked into his wizened face, and the sight of that scarred mask Jim wore for a face shook Jonas more than he'd care to admit. "I *know!*" said Jim softly. He released the little man. "Tell Jessica to act like nothing is going on. You keep up your usual work. Is there a rifle in the house?"

"Mine. I'll get it. Best damned saddle gun I ever had."

Jim drifted out into the thick, pre-moon darkness, working his way into the timber a hundred yards in front of the brightly lighted house. He took to the ground and inched along until he was well into the timber. Now and then he would stop and raise his head, testing the windy darkness with his senses. The wind shifted and brought the bittersweet odor of woodsmoke to him, mingled with the good aroma of food.

Half an hour drifted past on the moaning wind.

Jim lay behind a rock outcropping. Maybe he was a fool.

There was a sudden flare of light not thirty feet away from Jim. A hand cupped a match to a cigarette, softly illuminating a hard-looking face. Then the match went out, and all Jim could see was the alternate lighting and darkening of the face as the man drew in on the cigarette. Damned fool! He was so sure of himself. Jim recognized him from somewhere, but he wasn't sure where. Ute Crossing? No. Meadows? No. He lay flat and cudgeled his memory. Then it came to him. This was the drunk he had seen in the saloon the day he had arrived at Three Forks!

Jim rubbed his scarred face. The rifle was at his side, half-cocked, and he could drive a .44/40 slug into the man before he'd hear the shot. He heard the man move. The cigarette was ground out. Softly, ever so softly, like a hunting cat, the man moved through the motte toward the house, until he was fifty yards from it. He held a rifle in his hands. He was so interested in the house that he never saw the man standing behind the tree fifty feet behind him, watching his every move, nor did he realize his shoulders and head were etched against the darkness by the light from the windows.

Jim looked beyond the man. Jonas was still moving back and forth. He saw Jessica come into the room. She was still wearing her hat. It was difficult to see that she was a woman from that distance. Suddenly the dog barked. The man raised his rifle, moved it a little, and tilted his head to get a sight.

"Drop that rifle!" snapped Jim.

The man swung and the rifle spat flame and smoke toward Jim. The bullet almost touched Jim's right cheek. He fired from the hip. The big slug smashed into the man's chest. He grunted, spun about, dropped the rifle, and fell heavily. The twin rifle reports slammed back and forth in the canyon and then fled muttering to die away. The wind whipped a tendril of acrid-smelling smoke across Jim's face.

The lights blinked out in the house. The dog went wild.

Jim walked forward, then knelt beside the man. He snapped a match on his thumbnail and held it over the man's face. A pair of staring, sightless eyes looked up into his. Jim fanned out the match. A door slammed up at the house. Someone ran across the porch and toward Jim.

"Jim! Jim!" cried Jessica. *"Jim!"*

"It's all right," he called out.

119

She was in his arms with such a force that she staggered him. He dropped the rifle and held her close.

Jonas trotted through the darkness with a six-gun in his hand. "You all right, Jim?" he called.

"Yes, Jonas."

Jonas knelt beside the dead man and lighted a match. He whistled softly. "Monk!" he said.

"You know him?" asked Jim.

Jonas shrugged. "I've seen him around. He's a drifter. No one knows where he came from. He always seemed to have a dollar in his pocket. He'd come and go for long periods of time. Why would he want to kill you?"

Jim looked down at the dead man. "Someone hired him to do it. The only time I ever saw him was in the saloon in Three Forks. The one where Les is the barkeeper."

Jonas stood up. "He got his orders from somewhere. Ute Crossing, likely."

"But from who?"

"There's the question," said Jonas.

Jim nodded. "He didn't have time to go back there. Maybe someone came here to tell him what to do."

Jonas looked at Jim. "There's a company telegraph line between here and Ute Crossing."

"That might be the answer."

Jonas nodded. "Ben Cole is the operator. He'd have a record of any messages sent."

"Can we get a look at those records?"

Jonas grinned. "I can. Ben and I served together in the war. First Colorado Volunteers. Ben would do anything for me." Jonas looked down at Monk. "What about him?"

An idea had drifted into Jim's mind. Monk was about his size, build, and coloring. "A dead man can move around for a time without being expected," he said.

Jonas stared at him. "You gone loco?"

"Not yet. I have hopes. You go into Three Forks in the morning and find out what, if any, message Monk sent out. Keep your mouth shut about this. Find out where Monk is supposed to be. When you get back I'll tell you what I plan to do."

They carried Monk to an outbuilding and covered his stiffening body. Jessica was waiting for them in the house. "Jim," she said pleadingly. "Must you go back to Ute Crossing?"

"Yes."

"I won't let you go."

The look in his eyes silenced her even before his words. "I'm going, Jessica," he said flatly.

"We never did get to eat," said Jonas.

"After a killing?" said Jessica.

"Far's I'm concerned, Miss Jessica," said Jonas, "it's like a celebration when you kill a dry-gulcher."

"Amen," said Jim.

Chapter Fourteen

Jonas was back by noon of the next day with a wagon-load of supplies and a nose full of news. Jim helped him unload the wagon. "Monk sent a telegram the day you got to Three Forks," said the little man. "Got there just when Ben was closing the office. Message was sent to Ute Crossing. *'Consignment arrived,'* it read, *'please advise disposition.'* The next day there was a reply from Ute Crossing. *'Dispose of merchandise as previously directed,'* it read."

Jim slid a box of canned goods onto a storeroom shelf and wiped the sweat from his face. "Who had signed it?" he asked.

"It was from a Ute Valley Mercantile Company. Signed by a man named Alfred Hitchins."

Jim turned slowly, and his eyes were like twin lances boring into Jonas' eyes. "Alfred Hitchins?" he said softly.

"That was the name. You know him?"

Jim nodded. "I know him," he said. He seemed to see the round, smooth face of the man in the reflection of a can of peaches. Peaches thick in syrup. Alfred Hitchins, for all his good works, had always been a little too syrupy to suit Jim. The Reverend Matthew Jarvis was next to God in Ute Crossing, and Alfred Hitchins was next to the reverend.

"What do you aim to do?"

Jim lifted a sack of flour and placed it on a shelf. "Saddle a horse, Jonas," he said over his shoulder.

"For you?"

"For you, amigo. Go back to town. Send this wire to

121

Alfred Hitchins, Ute Valley Mercantile Company: '*Merchandise disposed of as ordered.*' Sign it '*Monk.*'"

They finished unloading the supplies, rolled cigarettes, and lighted them. Jonas eyed Jim. "You're taking a hell of a risk," he said.

"No worse than if I had gone back there without doing it."

Jonas grinned. "It's a prime idea," he said. "If you're right in your hunch they'll think you're dead."

Jim nodded. "That's why I wanted to save Monk. What did you find out about him?"

"Les told me he had left for Utah some days ago, and said he wouldn't likely be back until spring, if he came back at all."

"*Bueno!* We'll dress him in some of my old clothes and plant him."

"You mean bury him?"

Jim shook his head. "Put him where he'll be sure to be found. On the other side of town."

"Hell! That ain't so bright! They can see he ain't you."

Jim blew a smoke ring. "Dead body lying out in the woods gets the face eaten away first, doesn't it?"

"We can't take a chance they will eat it."

Jim looked at him. "A man could fake it, couldn't he?"

Jonas swallowed. "Yeh. A dirty job, Jim."

Jim spat. "It would have been a helluva lot dirtier job if he had killed me that day at the river, or if he had killed Jessica by mistake last night."

"I get your point. Leave it to me. There's only one thing, Jim. People in town know you came out here."

"They don't know I stayed here."

"Still looks bad for us."

Jim shrugged. "Shoot one round out of a pistol. Here, take mine and I'll take Monk's. It's a good one. Better than mine. Put the pistol in his hand, or near it."

"Suicide, eh?"

"You're getting brighter every minute, Jonas."

"What happens when you come back? If you do come back?"

"They made a mistake in identifying the body, is all."

Jonas flipped away his cigarette. "It might work at that, Jim."

Jim grinned like a lobo. "It will work long enough for me to do my job in Ute Crossing." He rubbed his scarred face. "By God," he added. "Alfred Hitchins! Who would have believed it?"

He said good-bye to Jessica at dusk that same day. Jonas had told him of a trail over the butte that would take him to the foot of the pass which he could cross that night. There would be a moon. The weather was making up, hinting at more rain. He could be across the pass by dawn with a bit of luck, hole up on the other side during daylight hours, then move on during the night. In three to four days he could be in Ute Crossing.

He kissed Jessica and drew her close.

"You'll come back?" she asked.

"Yes."

She looked up at him. "Maybe you'll want to stay in Ute Crossing," she said quietly.

Jim shook his head. "Never. There's nothing there for me now. My brother is gone. When my job is done I'll be back."

He kissed her again and swung up on the chunky roan Jonas had selected for him. "Adios," he said. He touched the horse with his spurs and rode off into the windy darkness.

"*Vaya con Dios,*" she said.

The wind shifted, moaning down the valley, and bringing with it a hint of the cold rain to follow before the dawn.

"He'll be back," said Jonas.

She did not answer. She walked to the house and entered it. Jonas rolled a cigarette. He lighted it. "He has to come back, God," he said softly. "For her. . . ."

The rain had started the dawn of the day Jim reached the eastern entrance of the pass. Warrior Peak, towering high to his left, had a skullcap of snow on it. In a matter of weeks, perhaps, the first snows of the season would fall. He rode through the dark, wet nights, holing up in the daytime under the tarp Jonas had given him, drinking coffee and smoking, trying to fit together the pieces of the puzzle he had blundered into by becoming an unwilling witness to a triple lynching. The enigma was Alfred Hitchins. "Deacon" Hitchins . . . the man who had helped Ben Murdock get his education after he had been crippled in his fight to clear Jim of murder charges. The man who had fought against public opinion to get Ben his job as schoolteacher in Ute Crossing, and who had won his fight. A man respected by one and all for his business ability, his civic pride, and his support of the local church. A man said to be as close to God as a man could be within reason. "Jesus wept," he had said when he had seen the lynchers take those three men up the gallows hill.

123

The rain was a fine, misty drizzle when Jim Murdock passed his brother's house on the banks of roaring Warrior Creek. The place was nothing but a blackened shell dimly seen through the mist. Warrior Creek swirled blackly beneath the creaking bridge. It was here that Ben had gone to his death over the low rail into the dark, cold waters, not to be found until the spring, on land that had once belonged to the Murdocks.

There was only one man he could go to in Ute Crossing and be sure of secrecy. Meany Gillis. It was well after midnight when he entered the town. Here and there along the main street he could see watery-looking yellow light as a saloon or two remained in business. One of them was the Grape Arbor.

There was a light in one of the rear windows of the Ute Valley Mercantile Company. Jim looked at it thoughtfully as he kneed the tired roan into an alleyway and then led him toward the rear of Slade's Livery Stable, where Meanwell Gillis held sway. Meany lived in a set of rooms built into the livery stable, a little strong-smelling, but comfortable and cozy, and besides, as Meany had always said, he preferred the company of horses and dogs to that of many people.

The alleyway was empty and dark. Jim walked around the side of the big frame building and tapped on the window of Meany's bedroom. The window was up a few inches. "Meany!" called Jim.

Bedsprings squeaked. "Who's that?" said Meany in a frightened voice.

"Jim. Jim Murdock."

"Oh, my God! You've come back from the dead! You always was a restless sort. I didn't think you was that restless."

Jim grinned. "Meany," he said softly. "It was a dodge. A trick to throw them off the trail."

Feet padded on the floor, and Meany's familiar, homely face appeared, white as a sheet. "Lemme touch you, Jim," he said. "Just to make sure." A thin hand felt Jim's arm. "Keno!"

"Open up the back door and let me get my horse inside."

Meany opened the back door. He peered up and down the alleyway. "Anyone see you?"

"No."

The door swung shut and was barred. "You hungry, Jim?"

"No. But cold as ice."

"I got something to take care of that. Take care of your hoss."

Jim came into Meany's little combination kitchen and sitting room after he had unsaddled and rubbed down the roan. The liveryman had drawn the curtains and pulled down the shade. He handed Jim a tumbler full of spirits. "You got guts comin' back here," he said.

Jim sipped the whiskey. "How'd you find out I was dead?"

"The story was all over town a few days ago. I don't know where it started. That's the second time it came around."

"When was the first time?"

Meany shrugged. "Damned near a year ago. They said you was killed down in Mexico somewheres."

Jim touched the scar on his right cheek. "I damned near was. Anyone miss Lyss, Slim, and Jules around here?"

Meany stared at Jim. His jaw dropped. "You!" he said.

Jim smiled thinly. "It was them or me, Meany."

"Wasn't nothing said about them. They was just supposed to have left. Rumor come that Lyss was murdered by bandits in Las Cruces, and Slim and Jules disappeared in Chihuahua or somewheres. They meant to kill you then?"

Jim nodded. "Why did they come after me? Who sent them, Meany?"

Meany poured a drink. He was pale again. "Jesus God," he mumbled. "Three hardcases if there ever was any. You took care of all *three* of them?"

"Two of them. I had a little help with the third."

Meany sat down heavily. He drained his glass. "Thank God you was always a friend of mine, James."

Jim leaned forward. "A man was ordered to kill me at Three Forks a few days ago, Meany. The order came from Ute Crossing."

Meany wiped his mouth. "Who sent it?"

"I think it was sent by Alfred Hitchins."

Meany was less surprised than Jim thought he should be. "I never liked that sanctimonious son of a bitch," he said. "Never could stand a man who's always telling you how honest he is. You sure about that?"

Jim told him of the cryptic telegraph messages.

"Sounds logical," said Meany.

"But why?" said Jim.

Meany swirled the liquor in his glass. "Beats the hell out of me," he said. "There is one thing I do know. 'Bout a year or so ago before you came back, he was having financial trouble. Rumor had it he was in hock for quite a bit. Someone had a big note on him and was hounding him for the money."

"Like who?" said Jim.

Meany looked into his glass. "Cass Crowley," he said. He

125

looked up at Jim. "After them three drifters killed Cass, Hitchins seemed to be doing all right again."

"The note would have been found in Crowley's papers," said Jim. "Hitchins would have been forced to pay the estate."

"If they found the note," said Meany. "Far's I know, it never was found. Hitchins denied there ever had been a loan."

"Seems to me it would have been a big break for him if Cass Crowley had died."

Meany looked up again. "*Murdered*," he said.

"By three drifters. One of them a drunk who wouldn't carry a six-gun and was supposedly unarmed when he came to the valley of the Ute. A Mexican who had wanted to be a priest and was afraid of firearms. A frightened, sensitive kid who likely fell in with the other two because they thought the same way he did."

"What are you driving at? You mean them three who was hung?"

Jim nodded. "It has taken me a year to find out about them, Meany. If those three men killed Crowley, it was certainly out of character."

"Then who done it if they didn't?"

Jim stood up and drained his glass. "That's exactly why I came back to Ute Crossing," he said.

Meany shivered. "I don't envy you."

Jim picked up his hat. "Keep your mouth shut about me," he said. "Can you put me up here at night?"

"Sure thing! Where you goin' now?"

Jim smiled. "Looks like Al Hitchins is working late."

Meany spat into the garboon. "He always is. Got a Bible in one hand and his cashbox in the other."

"Is Van Lassen still around town?"

Meany nodded. "Don't ever seem to work, but always has dinero. Beats me how he does it."

Jim flipped his cigarette butt into the garboon. "I wonder," he said quietly. He left the room, followed by Meany. He passed a dusty buggy and stopped suddenly to look at it.

"Yes," said Meany from behind Jim. "It's Ben's." He placed a hand on the dashboard. "I had it hauled here. Kept it for you, Jim, in case you wanted it."

Jim looked back at him. "Thanks. You keep it, Meany. I have no use for it."

"When you get back, providing someone don't put a slug into you, I'll tell you something about that buggy."

Jim nodded. He let himself out into the drizzle and heard

Meany close the door behind him and drop the bar. He padded through the pasty mud, cutting swiftly across the cross streets. Ute Crossing was quiet beneath the cold drizzle. The faint thudding of a mechanical piano came from the Grape Arbor as Jim passed behind it. He reached the rear of the Ute Valley Mercantile Company. The light was still on in the rear office. Jim peered into the rain-streaked window. A man was seated at a rolltop desk, hard at work on some papers. There was no mistaking the plump back of the merchant and the bald spot at the back of his head.

Jim gently tried the back door, but it was locked. He walked along the other side of the building until he found a warped window. He forced a piece of wood under the sash and pried upward. The lock snapped. He eased up the window and stepped inside. He could see a faint streak of light from the rear of the long building. Cautiously he worked his way past piles of sacks and ranks of boxed goods until he found himself in the aisle that led to the offices in the rear of the establishment. He paused, listening to the rain drumming on the tin roof. There was neither sound nor sign of anyone else in the place besides Hitchins.

Jim walked softly to the rear hall that opened to offices on either side. Hitchins did a big business. It was the same type of business Jim's father had successfully run until Jim's trouble with the law. An odd thought came to Jim. Al Hitchins had been small potatoes in this line of work until Jim's father's business had failed because of people talking. It was only after his father had failed that Hitchins had gained prominence in the business. He had taken over the lucrative Crowley account, one of the mainstays of the Murdock business. Maybe it had been Hitchins himself who had started the talk against Jim's father. People listened to Alfred Hitchins.

Jim walked softly into the hallway and stood in the open door of Hitchins' private office. The merchant's pen scratched on. Jim studied him. It wasn't going to be easy to beard Al Hitchins in his own den. It seemed ridiculous to suspect this godly man of having anything to do with ordering a killer to get rid of a man who stood in the way. It was loco, and yet. . .

Hitchins stopped writing. He raised his head. He sat still for a moment or two, then shook his head and started writing again. Jim stood there, boring a hole in the bald spot at the back of Hitchins' head with his cold eyes. Hitchins stopped writing again. He sat there for another moment, and then he slowly turned his head, to see an apparition standing in the

127

doorway. A tall, gaunt man, scarred on both lean cheeks, with granite-hard eyes looking at him with an unblinking stare. Hitchins sharply drew in his breath. His face went fish belly white. Slowly he extended a hand toward Jim and shook his eyes. "For the love of God," he husked. "Go away! I didn't want to do it! Go away! I'll forswear my God if you'll go away!"

Jim did not move. He tried not to blink.

Hitchins began to tremble. His mouth opened and closed. "They made me do it! They told me I was in it as deep as they were! I had to do it! Don't you understand! All I wanted was that note from Cass Crowley. That was all! I didn't want to put a bullet into his head!" He stood up and held out both hands, as though to ward off the cold, basilisk stare of the man he was sure had come back from the dead. Then he shook spasmodically. He fell to his knees. His head jerked and he cried out in savage pain, gripping his left side. He fell heavily and stared at Jim with unblinking eyes. Spittle drooled from his slack mouth.

Jim walked toward him. "Who made you do it?" he asked.

The man tried to speak. His breathing was sharp and erratic.

"Talk, damn you!" said Jim.

"They said I *had* to put a bullet into his head! All three of us did it! It was a pact with the Devil!"

"Who were the other two?" demanded Jim.

Hitchins' eyes widened. "You're alive," he whispered.

Jim nodded. "Tell me," he said.

Hitchins raised his head and suddenly it fell again. He stiffened, then relaxed, and his eyes still looked at Jim, but they did not see him. They would never see anything on earth again.

Jim stood up. "Score one," he said quietly. All he knew now was that the three men who had been lynched had not killed Cass Crowley, but who had been the other two men who had put bullets into the rancher's head? He rubbed his newest scar and looked down at Hitchins. God had dealt out his own kind of justice to this man. It was just as well. Jim wanted no more blood on his own hands. Justice, yes, but not blood. . . . . No one would know Jim had been there. They would find Hitchins in the morning, dead of a heart attack. The whole town would mourn. Likely his two partners in murder would breathe more freely. Hitchins had probably been the weak link in the chain. They would breathe more freely, but they did not know that retribution was stalking the wet streets of Ute Crossing in the guise of a man who was thought to be dead of a dry-gulcher's bullet.

Jim left the same way he had come, lowering the window against the rain. He padded into the alleyway. His work was done for this night, at least. He heard the thudding of the mechanical piano in the Grape Arbor as he neared it, and then the sound stopped. Jim stopped beside a rear window. A man was walking toward the mechanical piano, flipping a coin into the air and catching it again. Beyond him were the hunched backs of other men at the long bar. The man reached out with the coin to insert it in the piano slot. He stared at the rain-streaked window and saw a lean, scarred face staring at him, and then it was gone. Barney Kessler's eyes widened. The coin fell to the floor from nerveless fingers and rolled under the piano. Barney turned on his heel and ran to the bar and filled a glass, which he downed in one gulp.

Van Lassen looked at Barney. "What the hell is the matter with you?" he said sarcastically. "You see a ghost?"

Barney slowly wiped his mouth. His eyes were glassy with tanglefoot and fear. "I don't know," he said slowly. "*I don't know....*"

Baldy Victor grinned. "Oughta cut you off, Barney," he said.

Buck Grant spat into the filthy garboon. "Who was it you seen, Barney?" he asked.

Barney refilled the glass. "I'll swear to Christ it was Jim Murdock! Them eyes! The scars!"

Van grinned. "Jim Murdock had only one scar," he said. He drew a thick finger down the left side of his face. "There!"

Buck laughed. "Maybe Monk give him another one," he said. "Afore he died, that is."

Baldy studied Barney. "Maybe he did see something," he said curiously. He walked around the end of the bar and peered through the window. He unbarred and opened the back door and peered up and down the muddy alleyway, with the rain sleeting down, cold and penetrating. He grinned, and then the grin faded. He felt something in the atmosphere, something that sent a crawling chill through him. He closed and barred the door, picked up Barney's coin, and dropped it into the piano slot. The piano began to thud out a tune. Baldy walked back to the bar.

"Well?" said Lassen.

"Nothing," said Baldy. But for the rest of the night he kept shifting his eyes toward that back door when he was sure no one was watching him.

Chapter Fifteen

Jim Murdock knelt in the damp straw that covered the livery stable floor, holding a lantern while Meany Gillis, underneath Ben Murdock's buggy, pointed out something to Jim. "The team was found at the edge of town still pulling the front wheels, Jim," said Meany. "The rest of the buggy was found in the creek. The rail had been busted as it went through. I pulled out the buggy body and rear wheels and had it hauled here. I already had the team and the front wheels. I had a little free time one day, so I started work on it. I noticed marks on the wood around where the kingbolt goes through. Like someone had been sawing or filing. Then I finds the upper part of the kingbolt still in its socket. It was a good sound bolt, Jim, but it was in two pieces, and all I had was the upper piece."

"It broke, and caused the accident?"

Meany shook his head. He reached up inside the buggy and handed Jim the upper part of a kingbolt. "Take a good look at it," he said.

Jim held it close to the lantern. A cold feeling came over him as he saw file marks on the bolt.

Meany crawled out. "I went back to the bridge and found this." He handed Jim the rest of the bolt. Jim studied it. It had file marks on it, and at one edge was a slightly raised lip of metal as though the bolt had been filed almost through, leaving just enough so that the strain on it would eventually snap it off.

Meany wiped his hands. "You know how fast Ben drove. Likely he come out of his gate and turned hard, hit the bridge at a good clip, and the bolt busted right there. Talk about timing!"

Jim looked up. "But why, Meany?"

Meany held out his hands, palms upward. "After you left Ben did a lot of talking about those three men that got lynched. He was talking about justice before they got lynched. Looks like you put a head on his suspicions, or whatever they were. Ben might have been on to something at that.

130

Anyways, he was drowned before he could do anything about it. A week or so later his house goes up in flames. People said drifters had been bunking there and accidentally set it afire."

"Maybe there was something in there that might have pinned the guilt on whoever killed Cass Crowley."

"Mebbe," said the liveryman. "Whatever *might* have been here is gone now. No one will ever know now."

Jim rolled a cigarette and lighted it. He fanned out the match. "You're wrong there," he said. "I told you Hitchins was in on it. He implied there were two others. They're likely still around here, Meany. I won't stop until I find out who they were. This is a personal thing now. They murdered Cass Crowley and they murdered my brother. That type never stops killing to cover up, and the first killing is the hardest. After that they get easier and easier."

"Hard to figure out why they killed Cass," said Meany.

"We know why Hitchins was in on it. Money was his real god. Cass could have ruined Hitchins. Maybe money had something to do with the others as well."

Meany led the way to his rooms and poured two glasses of whiskey. "Maybe not," he said quietly. "Cass was in a lot of things. Finance, politics, and anything else he had a mind to get into. Cass liked power of any kind. You know damned well there never was an appointment in this county he wasn't behind, one way or another."

"You can say that about the whole state," said Jim dryly.

Meany sipped his drink. "If Cass stood in Al Hitchins' way, maybe the other two hombres what killed him felt the same way he did. Cass was as tough as whang leather when you crossed him. Many a coming man run into old Cass when he wasn't feelin' too well, said the wrong thing, and ruined his whole career. Just like that!"

"Just like that," repeated Jim. "Like who?" he added.

Meany laughed. "Well, they can be numbered by the dozens. I run into trouble with him once and was lucky enough to get off the hook." He grinned. "One time I took a repaired surrey out to Brady Short's place. I went up to the house to get paid and heard Brady sounding off to his wife. He was cutting ol' Cass to ribbons, being as how ol' Cass wasn't there. Seems like Brady had been counting on Cass to back him up politically. Brady could hardly get anywheres without Cass backing his play. You know the old story. The 'boy wonder' of the Ute Valley. Marries old Whitcomb's daughter, getting a nice piece of change in the process, plus that cliff dwelling of a house. By God, he's ambitious, and his wife is worse, or so they say."

"Take it easy, Meany," said Jim quietly. He swirled the liquor in his glass and then looked up at the liveryman. "When did all this take place, Meany?"

Meany looked at the ceiling and closed one eye. "About a year and a half ago. No! It was less than that. It was late summer of last year."

"Just before those three men were arrested for the killing of Cass Crowley."

"Yeh." Meany stared at Jim. "You mean?"

Jim finished his drink. "I don't know," he said. "Who would have suspected Alfred Hitchins?"

"Who indeed?" echoed Meany.

Something came back to Jim. The night he had gone out to Brady Short's house at the lawyer's request, only to find that the man was gone, Ann was in her cups and willing to play games with Jim. She had practically thrown herself at him. An icy, evil feeling crept through him. She was ambitious. Meany himself had just said that. She'd get behind a man and drive him on. Supposing she had been grooming Brady for big things and the fool had antagonized the one man in the county he had to have behind him to win political success. She had warned Jim to leave the country. Brady Short had never intended to be at the house when Jim arrived, or perhaps he had been in the house, keeping out of the way while he let his lovely wife bargain with Jim, using her lush body as bait. If a man was making love to Ann Short he'd damned well forget anything else he had in mind at the time.

Meany filled the glasses. He looked at Jim. "You're sure talkative tonight, James."

Jim took the refilled glass. The whiskey had no effect on him. Ann's last cast of the dice had been the blunt invitation to Jim to visit her in Denver. "Did Mrs. Short go to Denver last fall, Meany?" he asked. Meany would know. Nothing much went on in the valley of the Ute without Meany knowing about it.

Meany laughed. "Hell, no! She's hardly been outa that house. They say she's always on a high lonesome up there while Brady's chasin' around doing his political maneuvers. Sits up most of the night, they say, dozing in a chair, with a wine decanter next to her. When it's empty she gets another, and another. . . ."

"Every night?" asked Jim.

"Just about."

Jim emptied his glass. "Let me have a horse," he said.

"This late?"

Jim stood up. "I haven't much time," he said.

"You've done enough tonight."

Jim shook his head. "If I'm not back by daylight I'll hide out in the hills. I don't want to be seen. Not yet. . . ."

The streets of Ute Crossing were empty as Jim Murdock rode north out of town, heading into the slanting rain. The last time he had passed that way the road had been iron hard in the grip of the winter's first freeze. That time was close again.

This time he did not see lights in the huge house until he was close to it. The shades had been drawn in the sitting room that opened off the huge parlor where he had last talked to Ann Short, but he saw thin lines of light about the edges of the shades. There were no other lights on in the house. He tethered the horse to the picket fence and softly opened the gate. He walked to the front steps and softly padded to the side window of the sitting room. Through the narrow slit at the side of the shade he could see into the room. A woman sat in an armchair, facing a dying fire in the grate. A decanter stood on the little table beside her, and even as he looked he saw her fill a glass with wine.

He walked to the parlor windows. One of them was open a few inches. He eased it up and stepped inside, careless of the mud that stained the thick carpeting. He walked into the wide hallway and looked up the stairway. The house was dark and quiet. Jim crossed the parlor and softly slid back the sliding door that separated parlor from sitting room. The woman did not move.

Jim walked forward a little. "Ann," he said softly.

For a moment she did not move, and then slowly she turned to look at him. Shock fled across her flushed face, and then she smiled, although there was no mirth in her great eyes. "I knew they'd never kill you," she said.

"You're not surprised to see me, then?"

She shrugged. "Why should I be?" She glanced at the wine decanter. "I don't get surprised at anything anymore, Jim."

She had changed, even in the space of one year. Her face was flushed looking, and not from the bloom of health. Her once clear eyes had a slightly glassy look to them, and her hands trembled a little until she clasped them firmly in her lap.

"Where's Brady?" he said.

She laughed. "Out on his political maneuvers. Likely in one of the back rooms of the Ute House with one of the high-class doxys who ply their business there."

"Not Brady," he said dryly.

She sipped her wine. "Brady likes his women from the gutter," she said. "They give him what he wants. I won't."

She was almost stinking drunk. She wouldn't care what she said. "Did you ever go to Denver?" he asked.

She shook her lovely head. "I had no reason to go after you left," she said.

"You really wanted me to meet you there?"

A log snapped in the fireplace, and a little cloud of ashes drifted out onto the carpet. She laughed softly. "No," she said. "Does that sting your ego, Jim? Your man's ego?"

"Not really," he said. "Whose idea was it?"

She emptied her glass and refilled it. "I think you already know," she said.

"I want to be sure."

She nodded. "It was him. He was scared to death of you. I told him to kill you or have you killed. He's yellow."

"You would have done what you told him to do if you were in his position?"

She looked at him with thoughtful eyes. "Why not?" she said coldly. "He should have known he'd never sidetrack you. If you had that man's legal mind and his appearance, with your guts and me to back you up you'd have been governor someday. He lost his nerve. He could have gone a long way. I agreed to ask you to meet me in Denver just to help him." She wrinkled her nose and shook her head. "Making a whore out of myself to help him. Putting myself at your feet after you walked out on me." She hiccupped.

"That's a switch," he murmured. "You never intended to marry me, Ann. You had bigger game in mind."

"Go to hell," she said.

"Was Brady mixed up in the killing of Cass Crowley?"

"Ask him," she said shortly. "He's standing right behind you."

Jim turned slowly. Brady Short stood in the doorway wearing a wet slicker, his hat dark with rainwater. His face was pasty white beneath its tan. A nickel-plated, short-barreled Colt was in his right hand, pointing at Jim's guts. His handsome face was set, and there was haunting fear in his dark eyes. "What are you doing here?" he said in a low voice.

"Just a social call, Brady."

"At two o'clock in the morning?"

Jim smiled. "My, my! Is it that late?"

"Why didn't you stay away?" asked the lawyer. "Why did you have to come back, grinning like a death's-head at the feast?"

134

"You did your best to keep me away," said Jim. He glanced at Ann. "In more ways than one. The game is up, Brady."

"What do you know? What can you prove?"

Jim smiled. "Al Hitchins told me the whole story," he said. The shot struck home. Brady stared at Jim. "He doesn't know anything," he said.

"He said you forced him into the deal. That he was in it as deep as you were. That Cass Crowley had turned against you, and that you knew damned well you'd never get anywhere in this state politically without Cass backing up your play. You had to kill him, Brady, or your career was shot, just as Al Hitchins had to be in on the deal to keep from being ruined financially."

"For God's sake!" said Brady. "You devil! No one outside of the three of us knew that!"

Ann stood up and began to fill her glass. "You'd better kill him, Brady," she said. "It's your only chance."

The lawyer's finger tightened on the trigger. Jim wet his dry lips. Did he have a chance to draw and shoot before Brady got up his nerve?

"Go on, Brady," taunted Ann. "Show us you're a man! He's all that stands in your way. You helped kill Cass Crowley. The first one is the easiest one. Go on!"

"Shut your drunken mouth," said her husband.

She laughed. "One little press of that trigger and you're on your way again. Who can prove otherwise? You're a lawyer. You know I can't testify against you. I'll even help you, Brady. I'll say he came in here drunk and tried to rape me. This is your last chance, you fool!"

He drew in a deep breath and raised the pistol. For a moment he looked into Jim's eyes, and then his gaze wavered. He raised the pistol again. The empty wine decanter was hurled past Jim, and it struck Brady's gun arm. The pistol exploded, driving a slug into the floor at Jim's feet. He ran forward through the swirling smoke to grapple with Brady. Brady swung the smoking pistol up and down, cutting viciously at Jim's head. Jim deflected the blow with his forearm, but the gun still struck his face, staggering him. Brady whirled and ran. The front door was opened and then slammed. Feet thudded on the gravel walk, and a moment later the thudding of hoofs came back to the two people in the sitting room.

Jim wiped the blood from his face. He turned to look at her. "Why?" he said.

She shrugged. "I couldn't live with him any longer, Jim," she said. "I wanted to see if he had the guts to kill you."

"Thanks," he said dryly.

"How far can he get?"

Jim held out his hands, palms upward. "Brady Short is too well known to get very far. He'll run and keep on running, but someday they'll find him. He'll live a hell on earth until they do find him. Who is the third man, Ann?"

She walked to a side table and picked up a full wine decanter. "I saved your life tonight," she said over her shoulder. "Isn't that enough?"

"No."

She turned. "If I told you I didn't know would you believe me?"

He studied her. "Yes."

"You're walking a thin line, Jim. There are men in Ute Crossing who have sworn to kill you. You were nearly killed tonight. Get out of town and keep going, Jim."

"I can't do that."

She filled her wineglass and studied the ruby contents. "I didn't think you would. Good luck, Jim."

"I'm sorry about Brady," he said.

"I'm not."

He turned on a heel and walked from that house and he knew he'd never enter it again or see her again. He closed the front door and walked to his horse through the cold, drifting rain. He mounted and rode south toward Ute Crossing. "Score two," he said to the night.

She had parted the curtains to see him ride off. *"If you had had that man's legal mind and his appearance, with your guts and me to back you up you'd have been governor someday."* She drew the curtains and walked back to her chair, moved the wine decanter a little closer, and stared unseeingly into the dying fire.

Chapter Sixteen

The wind shifted just before dawn and carried the rain off with it. With the coming of daylight the wind died away altogether, and left a drifting mist in the bottoms of the Ute that seeped through the streets of Ute Crossing.

Jim awoke to Meany's shaking hand and low voice. "Rise

and shine," said the liveryman. "It's nigh nine o'clock. Murray Cullin just came into town and is at the jail."

Jim rolled over on the cot and looked up at Meany. "How's the weather?"

Meany rubbed a hand over the fogged panes of window glass. "Never seen the like of it in many a year. You can hardly see across the street."

"Suits me," said Jim. He sat up and accepted a cup of Arbuckle's from Meany.

"This fog won't stop a bullet, James."

"They have to see me to shoot at me."

"You sure no one else outside of Al Hitchins, Brady and Ann Short has seen you?"

Jim grinned. "Barney Kessler saw me, or thinks he saw me."

Meany spat. "Him? He's usually so full of booze he ain't never quite sure of what he does see, less'n it's another drink. Now, if that had been Van Lassen, he would have come right through that window glass after you."

"Have you seen him in town?"

"Every day, just about. Beats me how he can loaf and drink most all day without working."

"I wonder," said Jim. He drained his cup.

"Usually shows up at the Grape Arbor as soon as Baldy Victor opens up at ten o'clock. Him, Barney Kessler, and Buck Grant."

Jim pulled on his pants and then his boots. "Al Hitchins saw me, but he's dead. Brady Short is still running."

"What about his missus?"

"She could have let him kill me. She doesn't care anything anymore about Brady. Right now she's playing the wine jug. She doesn't care about *anything*."

"All the same, you'd better stop playin' a lone hand. You ain't killed anyone yet, but you keep foolin' around and you will. Murray Cullin never accepted the fact you was cleared of killin' young Crowley. Best thing for you to do is go see him, explain everything, and let him settle this business. Cass Crowley was like a brother to him. Besides, Murray Cullin is the law in this county, and you know damned well he is. He won't sleep or eat until he rounds up Brady Short. He never had much use for Brady Short, anyways."

Jim nodded. He was tired. Mentally and physically he felt the great strain that had been on him this past year. Murray Cullin really had nothing on Jim except the fact that he still believed Jim was guilty of the killing of Curt Crowley, but he was still lawman enough to know he had to have definite proof, not just suspicions.

Jim washed out in the stable, shivering in the damp cold. Winter was closing in. He dressed slowly, fortified himself with another cup of coffee and then peered through the fogged window. The drifting mist was almost opaque, swirling slowly through the seemingly deserted streets. Now and then the sound of voices came to him, magnified by the fog. He left the stable by the rear door and walked softly to the street, right about where he had stood almost a year ago to witness the mob breaking into the jail. It was almost nine-thirty. He looked quickly up and down the street and then crossed it swiftly, angling toward the ugly, slab-sided two-story building where Murray Cullin held forth when he wasn't out on other business.

Jim stepped into the deep-set doorway and opened one of the two double doors, letting himself into the hallway that led past the sheriff's office to the bullpen and the cells. The place seemed empty of life. The narrow staircase that led up to the county offices was to his left. He peered up the staircase. There were no lights up there, and then he remembered that county employees worked only part time and never on Saturdays.

He looked back over his shoulder and then opened the door of the sheriff's office. The tall, broad-shouldered lawman was seated in front of the big stove, warming his hands. A coffeepot sat atop the stove with a wisp of steam coming from the spout. Murray Cullin turned his swivel chair slowly as Jim walked toward the desk. "Murdock," he said coldly. "Come to give yourself up?"

Jim shook his head. "I have information as to who actually killed Cass Crowley," he said.

"A likely story. Those three men who were lynched here last year did the job and you know it, Murdock."

"Not me. Will you listen to me, Cullin?"

"Why not? Sit down. When you're done we'll do a little more talking about *you*."

Jim sat down across the desk from the lawman. "Three men were responsible for the murder of Crowley."

"I know that! The three that were strung up."

"No! None of those three men could possibly have murdered him. It's taken me almost a year to track down their kin. Cullin, you've got to believe me on that score."

"All right," said Cullen patiently. He dropped his hands from the desk and leaned back in his chair. "Shoot! What three men were responsible for killing Crowley?"

"I know of only two of them, Sheriff. Alfred Hitchins and Brady Short are two of them."

Cullin narrowed his eyes. "By God!" he said. "Have you been drinking? Are you out of your mind?"

"No. I can prove what I say."

"Al Hitchins was found dead of a heart attack in his office early this morning when his chief clerk came to work. Accusing a dead man of murder is an old dodge, Murdock. In any case, slandering the name of a godly man like Hitchins will get you nowhere. What's your game, Murdock?"

"I said I knew two of them," said Jim quietly. "The second man is Brady Short, and he's not dead, Cullin. He's running like a coyote."

Cullin smiled faintly. "Great," he said. "You come in here and tell me you know two of the three murderers of Cass Crowley. Then you name a man who is dead and can't answer for himself, and accuse another who doesn't happen to be around."

"The fact that Short is on the run should make you suspicious."

Cullin waved a hand. "Brady Short is on the move quite a bit."

"His wife can tell you that he admitted killing Crowley."

"A wife's testimony has no weight against her husband."

Jim began to feel uncomfortable. He should have known better. Cullin wouldn't give Jim an inch.

Cullin eyed Jim speculatively. "Just for a laugh," he said. "Tell me why men like Short and Hitchins would want to kill Cass Crowley?"

"Hitchins was into Cass for a large sum of money. Payment of that debt would have ruined Hitchins."

"Go on," said the sheriff. "What about Brady Short?"

Jim felt for the makings and began to roll a cigarette. He lighted it and eyed Cullin through the wreathing smoke. "Cass had turned against Short. Short knew he'd never get anywhere politically without the support of Crowley. It is as simple as that."

"You've given me two good reasons, in your opinion, why Hitchins and Short wanted to get rid of Cass Crowley. That leaves the third man. Who is he? Why should he want to kill Crowley?"

"He must have been the ringleader. Neither of those two men had the guts to think up a plan like that and carry it through. They must have been sure of their hand. So sure. . . . By God! Brady Short tried his damnedest to stop that lynching and he knew all along he'd never stop them,

139

nor did he want them to stop. Al Hitchins did the same thing."

"And the third man?"

It was very quiet in the office. Not a sound came from the fog-shrouded streets or from anywhere in the big building. Jim looked into the cold, hard eyes of Murray Cullin. *Then he knew.* Where had Cullin been when he should have been protecting those three innocent men? Off on a wild chase to get a change of venue from the governor, while his deputy was dead drunk and unable to stop the mob.

"Well, Murdock?" said the sheriff softly, very softly.

"You!" said Jim. He took the cigarette from his lips.

Something double-clicked beneath the big desk. "I've got a six-gun pointed at the pit of your belly," said Cullin. "*Don't you move!*"

"I wasn't thinking of it," said Jim quietly. "But why you, Cullin? By God, you had me completely fooled!"

The lawman's eyes narrowed. "I've hated Cass Crowley's guts for years," he said thinly. "He married the girl I loved. He got me over a barrel years ago and I lost my ranch to him. He tried to compensate by getting me the sheriff's job in this county, and I did the best I could with it. You'll have to admit that, Murdock."

"Granted," said Jim.

Cullin leaned forward. "He began to needle me about the death of his son. He wanted the killer brought to justice. He wouldn't let up on me, Murdock! I was sure it was you. A lot of people were positive it was you until that damned brother of yours got you cleared. I began to hate Crowley as I never hated anyone before, and he knew it! It was only a matter of time before he changed from backing me at elections to someone else. He could make or break anyone in this county, and a lot of men in this state as well. I had to get rid of him!"

"So you rigged an arrest of those three drifters and brought them in. Why didn't you kill them then, Cullin? *Los muertos no hablan.*"

"They didn't have a chance. I wasn't sure that I would be unsuspected. It was Brady Short who thought up the lynching deal. It was Al Hitchins who agreed to pay off Van Lassen and the boys. You've got to admit it worked."

"Almost," said Jim quietly.

Cullin laughed softly. "Almost? I can kill you here and now and cover up. Al Hitchins can't talk. I can find Brady Short and shut his mouth as well, one way or another, Murdock. One way or another. You see, I hold all the aces."

The coal fell in the stove. A wagon rattled by in the street. A dog barked in the distance.

Jim dropped his cigarette into the garboon and slowly rolled another. "I left a letter with a friend of mine," he said quietly. "In it I have written everything I know. There's enough evidence in that letter to fully incriminate Hitchins and Short, but not you, Cullin. However, by piecing things together, and making an official inquiry, I think the governor may soon learn who the third man was who was in on the deal."

"You're lying!"

"Am I? Did you think I was a big enough fool to come back to Ute Crossing with a price on my head? I knew the odds, Cullin."

Cullin sat there for a long time, and then slowly he raised his right hand and placed the cocked pistol on the desk. "I might have known," he said huskily.

Jim lighted the cigarette and eyed Cullin over the flare of the match. "Who rigged my brother's buggy for that last ride, Cullin?" he asked.

"I don't know."

Jim fanned out the match. "It would be the sort of dirty work Barney Kessler would do."

Cullin wet his dry lips. "It was him and Van Lassen. Barney filed the kingbolt. Van waited on this side of the bridge until he saw Ben come out of the drive and head for the bridge. Van timed it to ride onto the bridge at the same time Ben rode out on it. Van slammed his horse against the side of the buggy. I guess you know the rest."

Jim stood up and waited. Cullin stared at the cocked pistol on his desk. "Get out of here," he said, without raising his head. "I've got work to do."

Jim closed the door behind him. He was in the street when he heard the muffled sound of the shot from the sheriff's office. "Score three," he said.

He looked through the wreathing mist toward the Grape Arbor. Down the street the clock atop Al Hitchins' Ute Valley Mercantile Company began to strike the hour. "Next time I ever get in a mess like this," said Jim to himself, "I'll be damned sure I do write such a letter." The clock rang for the tenth time.

Jim unbuttoned his coat. He walked slowly across the street. A man was walking toward the Grape Arbor. The man stopped to light a cigar, and when he looked up he saw the lean, scarred face of a man he knew well. Too well. . . .

141

"Buck Grant," said Jim softly. "Where are your drinking amigos?"

"I don't know, Murdock."

"You're lying. Don't try to call out to them."

Buck slowly took the cigar from his mouth. "I had nothing to do with killing your brother," he said. He glanced sideways at the saloon and opened his mouth to yell a warning. The heavy barrel of a Colt slammed alongside his skull and dropped him on the boardwalk. Jim stepped over him, looked up and down the street, then sheathed the Colt. He pushed through the swinging door.

A man leaned on the bar watching Baldy Victor removing the cork from a fresh bottle of rye. Another man stood in front of the mechanical piano idly flipping a coin in the air as he eyed the selections. Baldy looked toward the door and his jaw sagged. Van Lassen turned slowly. "Barney!" he said over his shoulder. Barney turned as Jim walked toward Van Lassen. His eyes widened.

Baldy stepped back against the backbar and glanced nervously from side to side. "Oh, my God," he husked.

"Have you been drinking, Lassen?" asked Jim quietly.

"What the hell is it to you?"

"I want no advantages."

"I haven't had a drink yet, Murdock. I will when I'm through with you."

"You know why I'm here?"

"You don't have to write it out, Murdock."

Barney wet his loose lips. His face seemed to go in and out of focus. "I ain't done nothing, Jim," he said.

"Nothing but a little filing, eh, Barney?"

Van Lassen smiled thinly. "It was him that done it," he said.

"Who drove his horse against the side of the buggy?"

Van jumped sideways from the bar, clawing for his Colt. Jim gripped the brim of his hat with his left hand and scaled it at Van's flushed face. The gunman flinched. Jim jumped to one side and fired at Barney Kessler as the man fumbled for his Colt. The first slug caught Barney in the guts, dumping him forward. The second slug caught him in the top of the skull, and the third smashed into the piano. It tinkled erratically into life.

Van Lassen fired. The slug whipped past Jim's face and shattered the backbar mirror, cascading shards of glass down on Baldy Victor, flat on his face on the duckboards. Jim fired once, jumped to one side, and fired again. Van opened his mouth in squared fashion like a Greek tragic mask as the two slugs thudded into his chest. He fell heavily and lay still beneath the wreathing gun smoke while the piano ground steadily away.

Jim picked up his hat and placed it on his head. Slowly and mechanically he opened the loading gate of his Colt and began to load the hot cylinder. He could hear men shouting and calling out in the foggy street.

Baldy's head showed above the bar. "My God," he said. "No more than three minutes by the clock!"

Jim looked at him. "Was it self-defense, Baldy?"

"Absolutely! I'll swear to that!"

"They were your friends, Baldy."

Baldy brushed broken glass from the bar. "Hellsfire," he said. "They drove away more business than they brought."

Jim walked to the door and out into the foggy street. No one stopped him. He walked to the livery stable. He asked Meany Gillis to go to the general store on an errand for him. When Meany got back with the purchases, Jim had saddled the roan. He shook hands with Meany. "If the law wants me," he said, "you can tell them where to find me."

He mounted and rode east on the wide street. The wind was rising and the fog was being driven away. In a matter of minutes the wind had begun to hone a bitter edge to itself. It drove up the valley of the Ute, thrashing the trees and whipping the fog to tatters and then into nothingness.

Jim rode up the gallows hill. He dismounted and took a spade from the cantle. Slowly and deliberately he dug a hole at the base of the first of the three great trees that stood there. By the time he had dug a hole at the base of each of the trees the wind had cleared the valley of fog. People down in the streets of Ute Crossing could see him moving about on the gaunt hill.

He placed a can of Kepauno Giant Blasting Powder in each of the holes and carefully fused each one of them, then tamped in the earth. He lighted a short six, sucked it into life, and touched its end to each of the fuses. Then he mounted the dun. He was almost at the bottom of the hill when the first explosion came, followed rapidly by the others. Clods and dirt flew through the air, and the harsh echoes slammed back and forth between the valley walls and were lost in the windy distance. The trees thudded heavily to the wet ground.

He had a long ride to the west through bitter weather, but he'd make Three Forks before the passes were closed. He would be there in the spring if the law came looking for him.

He had a feeling it never would. As far as Jim Murdock was concerned he'd never ride east of Warrior Peak again.

It was almost time for the first snow of the year. There was a different feeling in the wind. A driving gust of it struck Jim's face like stinging, sharp-edged grit, and it wasn't until he reached the bottom of the slope that he realized that it wasn't grit at all, but the harsh reality of the first snowfall of the year.

GORDON D. SHIRREFFS

**Two Classic Westerns
In One Rip-roaring Volume!
A $7.00 Value For Only 4.50!**

"These Westerns are written by the hand of a master!"
—New York *Times*

**LAST TRAIN FROM GUN HILL/THE BORDER
    GUIDON**
__3361-5 $4.50

BARRANCA/JACK OF SPADES
__3384-4 $4.50

BRASADA/BLOOD JUSTICE
__3410-7 $4.50

**LEISURE BOOKS
ATTN: Order Department
276 5th Avenue, New York, NY 10001**

Please add $1.50 for shipping and handling for the first book and
$.35 for each book thereafter. PA., N.Y.S. and N.Y.C. residents,
please add appropriate sales tax. No cash, stamps, or C.O.D.s. All
orders shipped within 6 weeks via postal service book rate.
Canadian orders require $2.00 extra postage and must be paid in
U.S. dollars through a U.S. banking facility.

Name _____

Address _____

City _____ State _____ Zip _____

I have enclosed $_____ in payment for the checked book(s).
Payment <u>must</u> accompany all orders. ☐ Please send a free catalog.

WILDERNESS

By David Thompson

Tough mountain men, proud Indians, and an America that was wild and free—authentic frontier adventure set in America's black powder days.